Praise for Ursula DeYoung's
Shorecliff

"Appealing....*Shorecliff* is not a family saga so much as it is a family portrait of a pivotal time, one that exposes secrets of the older generation and reshapes relationships among the younger one....The revelations are poignant and avoid cliché. This is primarily due to DeYoung's talent at so fittingly connecting everyone's actions and choices to the cultural mores of the era.... Written with grace and compassion of what it feels like to yearn and stumble, and grow, finally, past thirteen."

—Carol Iaciofano, NPR

"Everything about Ursula DeYoung's debut novel *Shorecliff* evokes the 1920s.... *Shorecliff* is a curious book, a deliberately and surprisingly innocent story about the loss of innocence....It's true to itself, this novel, and to the experience of the young protagonist. DeYoung succeeds in reminding us of how it felt to be young, when the realization that adults had pasts and lives independent of their role as masters and caregivers came as a shock, and overheard conversations among teenage cousins were a gateway to wisdom."

—Julie Wittes Schlack, *Boston Globe*

"*Shorecliff* is a classic coming-of-age story told through the eyes of a naive young boy who doesn't fully grasp half of what was unfolding around him until many years later. Part *A Separate Peace*, part *I Capture the Castle,* it's the story of a momentous summer when illusions are dashed, family ties are tested, and secrets come spilling out. DeYoung effectively demonstrates how certain events, no matter how big or small, can imprint the rest of our lives forever."

—Bronwyn Miller, *Bookreporter*

"Ursula DeYoung's divine first novel, *Shorecliff,* gives readers a vivid picture of what happens when a sprawling family spends time in close quarters. Although set nearly a century ago on a picturesque Maine estate, DeYoung's novel is immediate and familiar, and her character development is nothing short of brilliant. A delicious summer read."   —Elin Hilderbrand, author of *The Matchmaker*

"A gripping and magical read....This excellent novel about cousins interacting continues a genre that has New England antecedents, the earliest perhaps being Louisa May Alcott's high-minded 1875 *Eight Cousins*....DeYoung writes with an easy grace."   —Kay Bourne, EDGEBoston.com

"*Shorecliff* reads like the work of a seasoned veteran of the form, not a debut novelist. DeYoung's vivid evocation of a summer home in Maine along with the enthralling, flawed members of the extended Hatfield clan held me captive from the very first page to the electrifying conclusion." —Meg Mitchell Moore, author of *So Far Away*

"Scintillates with excitement as the scandalous secrets start spilling out. DeYoung keeps readers hanging, wondering which family member's shocking revelation will be unveiled next. An explosive debut."   —Anna Redman, *Chatelaine*

"I was swept away by *Shorecliff* from its very first page, captivated by the Hatfields as they teeter between beauty and loss of innocence in one dreamlike summer. DeYoung is a master of character in this affecting novel, and her writing glitters with clarity, confidence, and depth, all the way to the book's stunning ending. A debut of a wonderful new literary voice." —Rae Meadows, author of *Mercy Train*

"Engrossing and exquisite....Thirteen-year-old Richard's retrospective account of a family gathering at Shorecliff, his mother's old family home, is filled with longing, love, and regret."   —*Kirkus Reviews*

Shorecliff

Shorecliff

A NOVEL

Ursula DeYoung

BACK BAY BOOKS
LITTLE, BROWN AND COMPANY
New York Boston London

Copyright © 2013 by Ursula DeYoung
Reading group guide copyright © 2014 by Ursula DeYoung and Little, Brown and Company

Back Bay Books / Little, Brown and Company
Hachette Book Group
237 Park Avenue, New York, NY 10017
littlebrown.com

Originally published in hardcover by Little, Brown and Company, July 2013
First Back Bay paperback edition, June 2014

Back Bay Books is an imprint of Little, Brown and Company. The Back Bay Books name and logo are trademarks of Hachette Book Group, Inc.

The publisher is not responsible for websites (or their content) that are not owned by the publisher.

The Hachette Speakers Bureau provides a wide range of authors for speaking events. To find out more, go to hachettespeakersbureau.com or call (866) 376-6591.

Library of Congress Cataloging-in-Publication Data

DeYoung, Ursula.
    Shorecliff : a novel / Ursula DeYoung.—1st ed.
        p. cm.
    ISBN 978-0-316-21339-4 (hc) / 978-0-316-21338-7 (pb)
    1. Family secrets—Fiction. 2. Families—Maine—Fiction. I. Title.
    PS3604.E935S56 2013
    813'.6—dc23   2012034605

10 9 8 7 6 5 4 3 2 1

RRD-C

Printed in the United States of America

Contents

The Hatfield Family in 1928

Jane Ladislaw (d.) m. Tom Hatfield (d.) — Eberhardt Hatfield (76)

Harold (d.)

Edie (46)

Loretta (44) m. Rodrigo Ybarra (d.)

Margery (40) m. Frank Wight (42) — Kurt (34)

Richard Killing (40) m. Caroline (33)

Rose (49) m. Cedric Robierre (54)

Tom (18) Isabella (17) Delia (15)

Francesca (21) Philip (18) Cordelia (15)

Charlie (20) Yvette (18) Fisher (16) Pamela (13)

Richard (13)

THE ROBIERRE FAMILY

THE YBARRA FAMILY

THE WIGHT FAMILY

THE KILLING FAMILY

Shorecliff

1

Arrival

The summer when I was thirteen years old changed everything for me. Looking back on it now, I can fill in the gaps with what I learned later, but at the time it seemed like a story unto itself, and that is the way I want to tell it. When I got back to school in September, I thought to myself, "I've been through hell this past month, and not one of you knows a goddamn thing about it." I'd picked up swearing that summer, but it wasn't the worst thing I had picked up, and it wasn't the most lasting. What I like to remember best are the mornings in Uncle Kurt's room when he would regale me with tales of the war. But what I remember most vividly is a bright patch of flames surrounding something so horrible I couldn't bear to look at it. That comes at the end. I will take my time getting there.

It began on a train. My mother and I were traveling up to Maine from New York at the beginning of June, riding a series of day trains. I always hoped uselessly for one long ride on a sleeper, but the view through the windows still offered plenty of fodder for my imagination. At thirteen I was short, stocky, and brown-haired. My round face refused to lengthen into manliness, though my mother claimed she could see cheekbones; to me it seemed unpleasantly chubby. My limbs were only just beginning to replace baby fat with muscle. The combination made me appear bulky but tough, and I had withstood much friendly roughhousing from bigger boys at school. My eyes were too small, and one limp frond of hair drooped over them and tickled my nose. My aunts told me I had a cherubic smile.

I spent nearly the entire trip from New York to Maine in a state of euphoria. My mother and I were traveling alone. My father was staying in New York and planned to remain there for the rest of the summer, a situation that only my mother pretended to object to. He was a stern, humorless lawyer; I was frightened of him and didn't like being near him. Now, years later, I feel the same way, though for different reasons. At the time his death-grip on life unnerved me, and now that death is coming to grip him instead, I prefer not to stand in its way. My mother, however, was an angel. She let me sit on my own, stationing herself several rows behind me, and as I looked out the window I imagined myself an explorer heading into the unknown, either on the back of an elephant or at the bow of a steamship as the mood struck me. For some reason being on a train, exciting as these vehicles were whenever I wasn't riding in one, never seemed thrilling enough from the inside.

We were headed up to Shorecliff. It was the old family place; not the Killing family—that murderous surname had been given to me by my father—but the Hatfield family, my mother's clan. My mother had four sisters and, originally, two brothers. All but one of the sisters had children, and all of the families were coming for the summer. It was the first time we had all gathered in one place for an extended period. My Aunt Rose had put her foot down some months before and said that the fact that we had never before spent time at Shorecliff as a complete, united family was a crime. This summer, she announced, was the perfect opportunity to remedy the situation. Her sisters agreed. With varying amounts of difficulty, they convinced the men involved that fighting the combined forces of the Hatfield women would be futile once they had decided on a course of action. As a result, here we were.

I had traveled to Shorecliff many times before—my mother took me up for a week or two every summer—but we were often the only visitors, and I had never encountered more than a few family members at a time there. Now the thought of months with all of my cousins and aunts and uncles made bursts of pleasure explode in my stomach. I, Richard Killing II, had no brothers or sisters. My father approved of one son and heir, no more and no less. But I had inherited my mother's love of large families, and since I had no other option, I adopted my cousins as members of my immediate family. The fact that I rarely saw them, and that they were all older than I was, didn't stop me. Depending on my mood, I was either the hero or the chronicler of my family. Their exploits, created by my own fancy for the most part, filled my imagination year in and year out, at school, at home, and most of all when I was trapped in my father's study.

The personages of the sprawling Hatfield family will drift into the story as they please, but I must mention Uncle Kurt now, before the others appear. Uncle Kurt was my mother's only surviving brother. Harold had been killed in the Great War, but Kurt had returned home swathed in laurels. He had been a private, a sailor, an ambulance driver, a pilot...It was a mystery to me how he managed to cover so many branches of the U.S. military, but I could not believe that he made up all the stories for my benefit. Some of them, maybe, but surely not all of the hundreds he spun for me that summer.

Uncle Kurt was tall and handsome, with brown hair slicked back in the soldier's fashion and an upright posture that put my stubby figure to shame. I remember him in khaki; whether or not he really wore it I can't say, since my youthful imagination surrounded him with the splendor of war. What is certain, however, is that he was exciting and lighthearted and unfailingly kind to me. He was by far the friendliest male I had ever encountered. I adored him without reservation, and on the rare occasions when I saw him, I followed him around like a puppy. My mother claimed that Uncle Kurt lived like a mallard duck, gliding through life and letting all its miseries slide off his back. Before that summer at Shorecliff, I thought so too.

The train ride was long, so long that after we changed in Boston my excitement wore off, leaving a dull residue that threatened to turn into disappointment before we had even arrived. I tried to keep my anticipation alive, but eventually I moved back to sit next to my mother and went to sleep, soaking up her reassurance without speaking. We arrived at last in the evening, after a final change in Portland onto a tiny local train, and I woke up to my mother pointing out the window.

"There's Aunt Margery with the car," she said.

Margery Wight was one of her many sisters, and the most important thing about her, as far as I was concerned, was that she had a daughter, Pamela. Pamela and I felt an automatic affinity because we were the closest to each other in age. She was thirteen that summer too, due to turn fourteen in September. I had turned thirteen in May, and therefore, though I thought of her as being my own age, she thought of me as being nearly a year younger than she was. Usually she didn't let the gap interfere with our friendship, however. I was grateful to her for being the one person in the family I could justifiably call a playmate. She had two older brothers, both objects of fascination for me, and an older sister, Yvette, with whom she shared a bedroom at Shorecliff.

Pamela had come with Aunt Margery to pick us up in the old black rattletrap that was the only means to get to Shorecliff. Pensbottom, the nearest town with a railway station, was a shabby, boring, colorless place, miles inland from the coast. I remember almost nothing about it. Uncle Harold had once said that the town was as obscene as its name, and since the statement had quickly become a family legend, we tried to spend as little time as possible within the town's boundaries. Shorecliff was a half-hour drive from the station, well away from Pensbottom's obscenity and cleansed by the sharp air that blew in off the ocean.

My mother and I stepped off the train, and Margery, a heavy, full-figured woman, thudded forward to embrace my mother with a cry of "Caroline!" that made the other people on the platform turn their heads. Margery had been blessed with an enormous bust, and the men in the family joked that she had kept it all to herself. The other sisters were thin and agile, built like fine china and so flat-chested that the low-slung dresses of the era made them look like boys. My mother, I had always been proud to note, either possessed a more womanly figure or else dressed well enough to seem more feminine than most of her sisters did. However she did it, she looked like a proper woman. Aunt Margery, in contrast, needed no help at all. She crowded the rest of her sisters out. Each year I looked expectantly at Pamela's upper body, waiting for her to follow suit, but she remained as obstinately flat as all the other women in the family.

She was standing by the car. While Aunt Margery smothered me with her bosom, I craned my neck to see the slim figure leaning against the rattletrap's door. Pamela was wearing a blue dress, reminiscent of a sailor suit, and her blond hair was pulled back with a ribbon on top and flowed halfway down her back. She claimed it was boring, but in the sunlight aureoles of gold would form around the ribbon. I loved to walk behind her and marvel at how round and luminous her head was. The day we arrived was cloudy, but I could see even from within Aunt Margery's embrace that Pamela's hair was glinting with light from somewhere.

Her greeting was notably less effusive than her mother's had been. "Hello," she said, moving away from the door.

"Hello," I said.

Aunt Margery opened the back door for us—the front seat was taken up with Shorecliff's weekly food supply—and we got in, Mother first, then me, then Pamela. Pamela looked out the window for most of the trip. Her habit of remaining silent and keeping her gray eyes averted always puzzled me—I could never decide whether the silence masked deep thought or mere serenity. Sometimes I suspected awkwardness, but if that was the case she veiled it masterfully. Whatever its cause, her reserve made her a perfect listener. I could talk at her for hours, and she would sit quietly, nodding at times and wandering over my face with her big, solemn eyes. When I finished she would decline to give me a single word of advice. If I was lucky, I might get an opinion. Needless to say, she sometimes exasperated me, but for the most part her quietness was well suited to fascinating an impetuous, imaginative boy like me, who rarely had anyone with whom I could share my innumerable ideas.

Pamela said nothing on the car ride, but Aunt Margery talked incessantly from the driver's seat. "Everyone else is already here. You two are the last to arrive except for Tom, who's still down at Harvard. He's going to join us after the seventh. I heard, you know"—here she turned around and attempted to speak over the seat, the car swerving—"that he barely made it through his first year. Naturally Rose is keeping quiet. She always was close-mouthed about her children, which I think is unnatural when you're talking to your own sister. But that's what Isabella said, and if she doesn't know the truth about her brother, who will? The other children are here, and the men have already gone off on a hunting trip. Thank the Lord we women get at least part of the summer to ourselves! If you can say 'ourselves' when we're stuck with all the children in a lunatic house—that's what Edie calls it. Just imagine, we counted it all up last night: with you here now, we'll have nineteen people in the house! When Tom comes it'll be twenty. It's beyond me how Charlie has no trouble being where his father and I want him to be, while Tom is always causing a fuss. He's inherited Rose's stubbornness if you ask me."

Aunt Margery had a knack for talking rubbish that only avoided being intolerably boring by referring constantly to people we knew. Any news of the cousins was nectar to me, and Tom's exploits at college rose before me full of potential, though in fact I never heard anything about them. On she talked, on we drove, and within half an hour we were approaching the towering white front of Shorecliff.

The house itself was a massive clapboarded box, with a little box built off of one side that contained the kitchen, a morning room, and some closets. The big box contained everything else—bedroom after bedroom, parlor after parlor, a library, a study, a dining room. It was a gargantuan mansion that had ceased moving forward in time at some point before the turn of the century, and I loved every inch of it. My favorite places were the telephone booth in the front hall and my little bedroom in the attic. We had no servants, the Hatfield money having been lost long before I was born. But the advantage of this was an array of bedrooms in the attic that had been fobbed off on us children. I had the last one, the original nesting place of the under-kitchen maid, no doubt. It was small, dark, musty, and cramped, but I had it all to myself, which was more than most of the other cousins could say.

Outside Shorecliff, at its front and sides, was a large, open expanse of grass. We all pretended it was a rolling lawn, but since the cliff for which the house was named dropped to the ocean only forty yards north of the building, the grass on the supposed lawn was salty and sea bitten, more dune grass than lawn grass. It cut our feet raw when we first came, but by the end of the summer those of us who had persevered in running barefoot had developed calluses able to withstand, for a few moments at least, the heat of a campfire.

There was nothing else around Shorecliff. The road stopped twenty feet from the front door, and a stretch of split-rail fence marked its end. I never understood that fence. It had perhaps five or six posts in all, and it kept nothing out and nothing in. There was no conceivable purpose to it, but it served as an excellent lookout post and climbing site. Away to the west, following the meandering line of the coast, was a stretch of woods, and if you walked through it for twenty minutes, you would pass first a little cottage and then the boundary of our property. Beyond the woods came civilization in the form of hayfields and cow barns. To the east of Shorecliff, after ten minutes' walk through brambles and blueberries, came the shore again—more inviting, though still rocky and wave-battered, and the place where we did all our swimming. Shorecliff was truly a desolate place, a long way from any policeman, any doctor, any prying eye or gossiping mouth.

I saw the house first, over Pamela's shoulder, and shouted with joy. All the enthusiasm in me that had expired on the train rose to life again. "There it is!" I cried. "I see it! We're here, Mother, we're really here!"

"Isn't it wonderful," sighed my mother.

"I saw it before you, didn't I, Pamela? You weren't watching for it, were you?"

"But I'd seen it before, Richard."

"Before me right now?"

Pamela did not respond.

That was a typical conversation between us. I was an irritating little boy—at least my father often said so. On the other hand, Pamela was infernally silent. She had no sense of debate.

Because my grandfather's funds had run out before a carriage house for Shorecliff could be built, the rattletrap lived in a cleared patch of dirt at the end of the road. Rain pelted it, snow covered it, heat warmed it, cold cracked it. It was miraculous that it hadn't fallen apart completely, that it still chugged its way successfully down the long, lonely road to Pensbottom and came back loaded with the week's supplies every Monday afternoon, year after year. My mother told me that she remembered her father buying the car when she was a girl, as a last extravagance after the family fortune had been lost. Despite endless questions on my part, she remained vague on the details of this catastrophe, but she loved telling me about the sunnier aspects of her youth. She said that when her father had bought the rattletrap in 1908, it had been a gleaming new automobile, the first Model T in Maine, a marvel in its time. The only reason no one had sold it later to pay the family's debts was that her father had put his foot down. "I won't let any of you touch it," he said. "It's for the girls to ride in and the boys to drive. We can't afford a horse and carriage now to replace it—it's all we have. And God knows anyone who arrives at Shorecliff wants to be sure there's a way to escape."

The walk from the car to the house was heaven. I was carrying all my own luggage—a suitcase, a valise full of adventure stories, and a telescope. Pamela and Aunt Margery helped Mother with the other things. I ran ahead. Shorecliff soared above me, the white walls like the stones girding a castle. The paint on the clapboards was peeling, and I indulged the urge many a time to chip away at it with my fingernails. Beneath it the wood was hard and knotty. I often contemplated it, thinking how many storms it had survived. The door opened, and that achingly familiar smell wafted out at me. For a moment my excitement blossomed into a delightful pain. Here I was...

The hall was dark because umbrella stands and heaped coats always obscured the strips of windows on either side of the door. I flung down my suitcase, books, and telescope and ran through the archway to the left into the main parlor—another dark, little-used room. Considering our numbers, it was strange that we lived so determinedly in the back of the house where the kitchen was. I jogged through the parlor without a glance; the furniture might as well have been shrouded in dustsheets. Onward to the addition, airy and light when the rest of the house was swamped in darkness.

Crossing the morning room (majestic in name only—it was an empty anteroom signaling the beginning of the lived-in portion of the house), I heard raised voices from the kitchen. A second later came a cry of impatience, unmistakably issuing from the lungs of Francesca Ybarra. We had arrived in time for an argument.

In fact, as my mother said later, battle royal was raging in the kitchen. The aunts sat at the table, and lined on either side of them, leaning on the stove, kicking the chairs, were my illustrious cousins. They had been separated by sex—I didn't know why. Three boys glowered by the left wall; five girls fumed by the right. It was an overwhelming array, and I realized that it had been well over a year since I had seen most of them. Even the ones I most often encountered, the Wights, had grown older and more distant, and the mysterious Ybarras and Robierres were so different from the way I had remembered them as to be almost unrecognizable.

Pamela, when she came in a few minutes later, hovered in the doorway as I did. We were too young to be in on the feud, but we were old enough to listen to it with our hearts thumping and our eyes shining. With a beginning so dramatic, the summer could not fail to be as thrilling as I had imagined.

"It's too much!" Francesca was saying. Francesca was the daughter of Aunt Loretta, the wild one of my mother's generation who had married a Spanish fugitive named Rodrigo Ybarra. We never learned how he had earned the title of fugitive, only that he had been running from the Spanish law. He and Loretta were married in Paris and lived there until Rodrigo died in a train accident during the war. Their youngest child, Cordelia, had been only five years old at the time. Loretta had moved back to America when the war ended, the wildness apparently crushed out of her. She brought three dark-haired, fiery children with her. It was impossible not to place them highest in my ranks of fascination, and Francesca, twenty-one years old, with cascades of nearly black hair and dark, glowing eyes, had the power to fell me with a single glance. When I entered the room she was stamping her foot, her hands clenched and her fine eyebrows drawn low over her eyes. Francesca in a rage was a sight to see.

"It's too much!" she was saying. "We're stuck in this godforsaken dump all summer like sardines in a can. There's no one to see and no place to go. And now we're not even allowed to drive into town. How do you expect us to live?"

The argument, I quickly divined, was about driving rights and the rattletrap. Thus far the adults had had sole use of the automobile. My grandfather's decree that the women would ride and the men would drive had been broken the day after he died, but I'm sure he would have been pleased at the strictness with which the next generation was kept from the steering wheel.

"Even if Francesca can't drive it," my cousin Charlie said, "there's no reason why I can't, and Tom too when he gets here."

Charlie was the oldest of the Wight children. A more different family from the Ybarra clan could not be imagined. Aunt Margery had married Frank Wight, a carpenter from upstate New York, and their four children were all blond and blue-eyed. Their two sons, Charlie and Fisher, had been raised in their father's workshop, and each was handy with an ax and ingenious with a chisel. Charlie was twenty and muscular and exhibited his father's red-faced shortness of breath, though in all other respects he was handsome. After two years at Cornell he had earned his stripes on the college football team, but what interested me far more was that some months earlier I had overheard his mother telling mine that Charlie "could never turn down a dare." This, I thought, heralded great things for the summer.

Charlie's three siblings were all slender and graceful—mysterious attributes when one looked at their parents, though the Hatfields traditionally run thin. Eighteen-year-old Yvette, a pale and lofty girl I rarely had the courage to speak to, came after Charlie. Fisher, at sixteen, was equally skinny and sprite-like. He liked his father's workshop, but he preferred to carve intricate scenes in blocks of wood while Uncle Frank taught Charlie the rudiments of furniture-building. Fisher went around perpetually in a dream, but the dream did not prevent him from picking up details with his misty blue eyes. Like Pamela, the youngest of the four, he soaked up information with quiet astuteness.

"None of you will be driving anywhere," Aunt Rose declared. She was the oldest aunt, with the voice of a general and a demeanor to match.

Aunt Margery added, "Don't you understand it's not safe? Uncle Kurt has had years of practice, and I learned from him."

"Safety be damned," Aunt Loretta growled. The one trace of wildness that remained in her was a tendency to swear, and her deep, sultry voice slid into a sailor's bark when she was angry.

"It's not a matter of whether they're able to drive the thing—it's whether they're allowed. And they're not. Francesca, you can stamp all you like, but rules are rules. You're here for the summer, and you might as well enjoy it."

"You realize we've got nothing to do," said Francesca. She pressed herself against the wall, drawing herself up to her full, glorious height. Masses of dark hair curled out around her head. "We're stuck here on top of each other. You all think of it as a fine holiday. You can chatter with each other all day, and the little ones, well"—she tossed us a look of contempt—"they'll be satisfied with anything. But we older ones, what are we supposed to do? We're a million miles from civilization. All we have is each other. Do you expect us to stand here for the next three months staring each other down?"

There was a moment of silence, during which Francesca fixed her gaze on the aunts and the rest of the cousins followed her lead.

Then my Aunt Edie entered the fray. Edie was the maiden aunt of the family, and she lived the part with a vengeance. She was angular, bony, and long-nosed. Her black hair, parted down the middle, was always knotted at the back of her head. None of us had any difficulty understanding why she had never married—no man in his right mind would come within ten yards of her. She had no mercy, her morals were lifted from Victorian guides to proper etiquette, and she saw the worst in everybody and everything. But the sheer force of her will made her remarks carry weight in family discussions.

Now she looked down her nose at the three boys—Charlie, Fisher, and Francesca's brother, Philip, who was eighteen, black-haired, and invariably aloof. Then she examined the five girls—Francesca, Yvette, Tom's sister Isabella, and the two Delias, whose story must be saved for later. Even Pamela and I were not exempt from Aunt Edie's scathing glance; for an instant her nose pointed at us, and we felt the impact of an unknown accusation. Then she made her proclamation. "This house," she said, "is primed for incest."

Incest. What did it mean? I had never heard the word before. Even in my ignorance, though, I sensed a scandalous undertone. The rest of the family—with the exception of Pamela, who also didn't know what it meant—dissolved into laughter. Without meaning to, Aunt Edie had ended the fight. There were a few minutes of hilarity, in which I saw Francesca raise her eyebrows at Charlie with an expression that combined humor, disdain, and mocking salaciousness. Aunt Edie caught the last of it and shouted, "Heathens!" which redoubled my cousins' laughter.

My mother, who had come in for the last of the argument, laughed with the rest of them and then sent me up to my room with my luggage. The other mothers shooed their children off too. They wanted a chance to discuss the situation among themselves before dinner. I went upstairs with my bags, lagging behind the others. We passed straight through the second floor, the forbidden kingdom of adult sleeping quarters. Each of the seven bedrooms there housed an adult or two. As the oldest cousin, Francesca had demanded a room on the second floor. It alarmed me to think that she could now be counted as an adult—it made her seem capable of anything.

Philip lived in the room next to mine on the third floor. For the moment he was alone, since his roommate, Tom, had yet to arrive. Though they were both eighteen, Philip had not yet started college. I didn't understand why, and no one ever bothered to explain it to me. When I passed his room he called to me from inside, and obediently I barged in, my valise of books banging against the doorframe.

"How are you, midget?" he said, looking me over.

Philip seemed the most Spanish of the Ybarras, and I imagined

Rodrigo as an older version of him. He wore his black hair slicked back from his forehead, and he had low eyebrows and dark, glowing eyes like Francesca's. He read constantly, but whereas I devoured boys' adventure novels, he read philosophy and incendiary texts. There was a hint of secrecy in all his actions that I admired and appreciated—he once told me that he thought of himself as an anarchist. This meant he had little time for humor, but if you caught him in an off moment, he could be friendly in a biting sort of way.

"What does 'incest' mean?" I asked him.

Philip let out a burst of laughter. "You want to join the fun, do you?"

"I just want to know what it means."

"Well, it means a lot of old busybodies clucking over other people's business. That's what it ends up meaning anyway."

I dropped my bags on the floor and dug through the valise for my dictionary. In a way this was my most precious book, since without it I wouldn't have been able to understand half of what my family members said. It was an ancient, beat-up volume that my mother had given to me long ago. When I looked up "incest," I found "indecent relations between blood-relatives."

"My God, how old is that thing?" Philip said. "It's a lie anyway. Sisters and brothers, my friend. That's the only thing that counts. All of us cousins—we're safe. So you don't have to worry."

"Don't have to worry about what?"

"Indecent relations," he said, grinning.

"Which doesn't he have to worry about?" said another voice at the door. It was Yvette Wight. She reminded me of a ghost: her hair was much whiter than her siblings', more of an ash-blond than a gold, and her lips and eyes were equally washed out. She moved to fit her appearance, gliding from room to room without any noise. One of her favorite occupations was interrupting conversations in this fashion. "Should he not worry about the indecency, or the relations?" she asked.

"Why, Yvette, what are you suggesting?" Philip said. He lay back on his bed and lounged, and there was something challenging in his attitude.

"I'm not suggesting anything. I was just wondering which you meant."

"Well, which would you have meant?"

"Neither," she sniffed. "I've read *Mansfield Park*. Besides, we didn't grow up with each other. I don't see anything wrong with it."

Philip sat upright. "Yvette!" he exclaimed. He was still joking, but I heard a note of surprise in his voice. "That's practically a proposition!"

"Don't be stupid, Philip," she said. She glided away, and I retired to my own bedroom. It had been a typical conversation between cousins, a tossing sea on which I strove to keep afloat. I had no idea what they were talking about, and probably they didn't either. All of them enjoyed throwing the ball of innuendo around their circle, keeping it aloft for as long as possible. I stood outside the group, watching and listening. The first thing I did in my room was look up "proposition." The dictionary defined it as "a suggestion or proposal," which didn't help at all.

The idea of a web of attractions between relatives was less shocking than it might have been to my Hatfield cousins because, as Yvette had pointed out, we hadn't grown up together. I saw Pamela regularly because my mother was closest with Aunt Margery, and she believed that Pamela was a good playmate for me. But even so we spent time with each other only two or three times a year, when our two families visited Shorecliff or when the Wights came down to New York City. Most of the year they lived in upstate New York, in Uncle Frank's hometown. The Ybarras lived near us in Manhattan, the original home of the vast Hatfield tribe, but we never visited them, and my mother once unwisely let slip that this was because my father disliked them, thereby confirming my theory that he had not a scrap of human feeling in him. Tom's family, the Robierre clan, lived in Boston so that his father, Cedric, a professor of paleontology, could be close to Harvard. Uncle Kurt moved around the country at will—at least that's how it seemed to me. Aunt Edie lived in Saratoga Springs, plaguing the nearby Wights. I never knew where my Great-Uncle Eberhardt resided when he wasn't stalking around Shorecliff like an enormous predatory bat. I suspect New York. At any rate, the various branches of the family rarely saw each other, and for the older cousins it must have seemed as if they had been locked for the summer in a cage of strangers—the kind of long-known stranger one can rely on as a lifetime fixture without really understanding at all.

There came now an inevitable letdown. I sat on my bed and thought, "What now?" There was still half an hour before dinner. My clothes were unpacked, my books lined up on the desk tucked into the gabled window. My telescope lay on the table next to my bed. I had made all conceivable preparations, and now I had to find something to have prepared for. From down the hall I heard the rise and fall of cousinly voices. That sound, as steady as the ocean crashing against the cliff, formed the background of my summer at Shorecliff. Always around the corner, up the stairs, in the distance, those voices sparred and tangled, speaking of things I half understood and yearned to know more of. It took excruciating courage to approach them, to appear in the doorway of whichever bedroom or alcove the group had chosen as a headquarters.

This time they were in the room occupied by Isabella Robierre. All of them were there except Yvette, Pamela, and Philip—the Wight girls had a way of making themselves scarce, and Philip generally disliked group discussions. The others had piled onto the two beds—Isabella, like me, had a room to herself, but hers had been furnished to house two people, and the spare bed served as a useful lounging place. Together the cousins formed a physical barrier as intimidating as their conversation. When I appeared before them, the talk died and they all looked at me. The pressure from those six pairs of eyes! They seemed twice as many. Then Isabella extricated herself from the pile and swooped down on me.

Isabella. She was the one cousin to whom no description of mine could do justice. All the others could be categorized in one way or another: Philip the revolutionary, Charlie the athlete, Francesca the blazing beauty, Tom the student, Fisher the dreamer, the two Delias identifiable in tandem. Isabella was not like the others. She was not as beautiful as Francesca nor as graceful as Yvette. She could be awkward and blunt. Sometimes she didn't know what to say. But there was an energy in her that surpassed all the others, an openness, an abandon. She was the only cousin who had ever hugged me and tousled me and tossed me around, and I had loved every minute of it—which made it all the more crushing this summer when she flung herself toward me, took in at a glance how much older I had grown since our last meeting, and stumbled to a halt with her hands still open, trying too late to pretend that there was no awkwardness in her movements. She felt, I suppose, that I was too old now to be cuddled, that I was no longer a child—though I wouldn't have minded. I would have relished the contact.

That summer, at seventeen, Isabella was recovering from a recent growth spurt and moved like a baby giraffe, all long legs and spindly arms. She was not as tall as Francesca, but she was taller than most of us, and her body was especially noticeable because it was so gangly. She had light brown hair, as all the Robierres did. It was straight and uninteresting, and she tied it back at the nape of her neck, letting a few wisps frame her face. Her hands and feet often gestured in unexpected directions, demanding to be noticed. Whenever the cousins were in a group, the two who stood out irresistibly were Isabella and Francesca.

Isabella stood in front of me now, not touching me but grinning her goofy, all-consuming grin. "Look at our Richard!" she cried.

I stared back at her, smiling like an imbecile.

"Don't make such a song and dance." Charlie yawned. "He won't know how we should entertain ourselves any more than we do."

Isabella laughed and beckoned me to the foot of her bed. I sat next to her and remembered how she used to hold me in her lap, even when I weighed nearly as much as she did. Now it seemed that not only her lap but all parts of her body were forbidden territory. I pondered this change, trying to ignore the snooty looks I kept receiving from the two Delias, who were seated on the other bed and clearly thought I should be kept from the room.

The two Delias' story shows the Hatfield tendency to create feuds out of thin air. When Aunt Rose and Aunt Loretta were pregnant with their last children, they got into a discussion of baby names. Rose had gone over to Paris to visit Loretta, who was still living there with Rodrigo. The two sisters' relationship was uneasy at best. Rose had raised the loudest cry against Rodrigo, and Loretta had always objected vociferously to Rose's high-handed control over the Hatfield family. Yet in many ways they were the most similar of the Hatfield sisters. They didn't like to admit it, but when they were together and managed to avoid fighting, they often laughed louder and harder than with anyone else.

The question of baby names was a serious one with the Hatfields. A host of preferences and responsibilities had to be taken into account, and it was only with these two last children that Rose and Loretta finally felt they had free rein. Loretta had taken care of

Rodrigo's requirements with Francesca and Philip. For Rose, Tom had been my grandfather's name, and Isabella was the name of Cedric's favorite sister. Now a clear horizon lay before them. The two women drank their tea, ate their croissants, patted their stomachs, and tossed names back and forth. Loretta suggested Delia. Rose glommed onto it like a snake snatching its prey—at least that is Loretta's version of the story. Rose herself claims she thought of it first, but none of us has ever believed her.

"I love it," she said. "I want that one. It's mine."

"I came up with it!" Loretta protested.

But Rose refused to back down. The talk developed into an argument and then an out-and-out fight. At last Rose flounced off and soon after returned to America, swearing that she would send the government a birth certificate first. That was exactly how it came about. Alas for Loretta, though she was due first, Rose gave birth prematurely (deliberately, Loretta claimed) and chose the name Delia while crowing in triumph. Two weeks later Loretta gave birth to her own baby and lay there in the Paris hospital bed, arguing with Rodrigo over the morals of also naming their daughter Delia. Rodrigo disapproved of sibling rivalry. At last Loretta said, "*Cor*delia then," and lay back exhausted on the pillows. From that point on the second Delia's name was always pronounced in that strange way, with the emphasis on the first syllable, for no one ever used her full first name except to distinguish her from the other Delia. Loretta rejected Cordie as a nickname, and so, despite Rose's exaggerated shock, the Hatfield family contained two Delias.

At fifteen, the Delias were inseparable. They had clung to each other from the first moment they met, and different though they were, we thought of them as a pair. Delia Robierre had light brown hair cut in a bob. She was stocky and freckly—more so than either Tom or Isabella—and easily pleased, with an infectious giggle that rang through the house. Delia Ybarra was destined to be nearly as great a beauty as Francesca. She had black curly hair as short as a boy's, a swanlike neck, snapping black eyes, tiny feet. There was more mischief in her than in Delia Robierre, though she presented a more serious front. Combined, they were a dangerous formula, not least because, as nearly the youngest cousins, they were constantly trying to prove themselves. I thought the two Delias owed Pamela and me a debt of gratitude—it was only because we were there to be excluded that they were allowed in on the colloquies of the older cousins. They knew this, but for them it required resentment rather than gratitude, so I avoided them as much as possible. In any case, they were small fry. Neither of them counted in comparison with the glorious older cousins.

I don't remember what they were all saying at that first meeting. Francesca was probably leading them in declarations of discontent. Coming from Manhattan where, according to Philip, young men often lined up outside the Ybarra residence to see her and where Aunt Loretta—despite raised eyebrows from the more cautious mothers in their set—let her gallivant through the streets with these eager escorts until after midnight, Francesca undoubtedly thought of Shorecliff as a desert wasteland. Her aunts said she was spoiled and, believing in education for girls as well as boys, frequently asked why she had not gone to college. But Loretta was skeptical of the value of a formal education, and she was proud, besides, of her own adventurous past. The lessons of real life, she was fond of saying, taught more than any college professor could imagine. When Francesca refused flat-out to consider Barnard or any other college, Loretta accepted her refusal without a murmur, and she stood by that decision in spite of the fact that Yvette was bound for Bryn Mawr in the fall and Isabella had been looking forward to Radcliffe since she was ten years old. Francesca defiantly took the route of the debutante, and though Loretta could barely afford her evening gowns, let alone the expense of hosting parties, she helped Francesca hide the difference between our Hatfield shabbiness and the fortunes of the New York elite. When her sisters remonstrated with her, Loretta said that she refused to deprive Francesca of the thrill of youth simply because of a lack of money.

Given the dazzling whirl she had been forced to abandon for the summer, it was hardly surprising that from the beginning, at Shorecliff, Francesca was determined not to enjoy herself except by means of rebellion. But that did not mean that she sulked or snapped or made life miserable. On the contrary, though she painted the summerhouse as a prison, she made it come to life for all of us.

Eventually, that first evening, she indicated that the audience was over, and we all filed out, in spite of the fact that the meeting had taken place in Isabella's room—Francesca instantly became queen of any room she entered. We were bunched up at the door, and I looked back to find Francesca nodding knowingly on Isabella's bed. "Wait until Tom comes," she said, half closing her eyes. "Then you'll see. Wait for Tom."

———

Wait for Tom was exactly what we did. He didn't come for a week, and during that week two events of importance occurred. The first was that Aunt Loretta left. The announcement was made on the second night, when we were all crowded around the long table in the dining room, a room used only once a day for our immense dinners. When Loretta said, "I'm going to return to New York tomorrow," I was baffled. She was prone to these sudden moves—apparently it was one such move that had taken her to Europe in the first place. Even so, the adults were clearly as mystified as we were. There was some talk about business needing to be taken care of, a financial situation gone awry, but that seemed insufficient reason for her to abandon our precious summer vacation.

Only her own children were unaffected by the news. Francesca gave her mother a look I found hard to identify; it was a strange, stony glance that seemed to combine resentment with empathy. Of course, I was always on the alert where my older cousins were concerned, and I was particularly alive to Francesca's expressions. To me she was a prophetess for nearly all of that summer, and I might have endowed her face with more subtlety than it really expressed. While she glowered, Philip continued to eat without any change whatsoever. Neither asked Loretta why she was going, which seemed to me to be filial negligence on a criminal level, excusable only because of Philip's secret mental life as a revolutionary. As for Cordelia, she was wrapped up in something Delia Robierre was saying. She looked up for half a second and said, "Oh, don't go, Mommy!" and then turned back to Delia. This was more negligence, and I wondered what the children's relationship with Aunt Loretta could possibly be like.

Certainly it was nothing like the relationship I had with my own mother. She, as the flipside of my father, had always been a warm and sheltering haven. She was not an assertive person—any loudness she might have had had been drained out of her long ago by the browbeating of six strong-minded older siblings—but she possessed a wordless determination that filled me with relief and admiration. When my father snapped at me or shooed me away, she would hold open her arms and with that gesture express not only her love for me but her disapproval of my father's behavior. Even when I was little, I understood her meaning and prayed that he did too. Now that I'm older, I know he did understand it. Sometimes I can find it in my heart to pity him—not often, though. My mother did not play a large role in that summer at Shorecliff, at least not an ostentatious one. Nevertheless, she was there, acting as my subterranean rock of security. Had she been absent, I could not have done half the daring things I carried out in the company of my wild cousins.

The second important event was the return of the uncles—Frank, Cedric, and Kurt—from their first hunting trip to the woodlands northwest of Shorecliff. Great-Uncle Eberhardt had not been on this trip. He did not approve of guns, nor of killing animals for sport, nor of conversing with other humans unless it was with Condor, the groundskeeper at Shorecliff. Condor was Uncle Eberhardt's constant companion, and Eberhardt spent many long days at Condor's cottage in the strip of woods separating Shorecliff from the surrounding farmland. When the other men were away on their hunting expeditions, Eberhardt moved to the cottage entirely, appearing at the house only occasionally for meals. He said that the company of women and children without respite was too much for any man and a death recipe for an old man like himself. As a result, he appeared to return when the rest of the men did, though in fact he had been within reach all the time.

Fantastical though it may be, I remember Uncle Eberhardt wearing a black cape. It seems impossible now that he actually wore one in that day and age, in the middle of the summer, but that is my memory of him. Thus Uncle Eberhardt stalked through the back door into the kitchen with the rest of the men, his back bent so that the cape swung over his shoulders and cast a shadow around his feet. He had a rough, hair-dotted face that never failed to scare me, beetled brows and squinting eyes, the remains of a white head of hair, and gnarled, bony hands. He was a gruesome creature from a child's fevered dream, but for all that, he was our uncle, and in our way we appreciated him. He tolerated nothing and approved of nothing; he was Aunt Edie times ten. They did not get on well together.

"How was Condor, Uncle Eberhardt?" Rose asked. It gave me great pleasure to see her, the tallest and most imposing of my aunts, quelled by Eberhardt's lightning gaze.

"Condor's well enough, girl," Eberhardt growled.

Aunt Margery and my mother smiled behind Rose's back. As with most of my family members, Eberhardt for them was simultaneously a terror and a joke. He knew it as well as anyone and chuckled as he made his way out of the room.

Then Uncle Frank and Uncle Cedric filed in, shuffling like delinquent schoolboys. Frank Wight was the carpenter who had married Margery, and he looked the part. A bigger but more subdued version of Charlie, he was brawny and blond, the sort of man who both pleased children and annoyed them. He was forever swinging me around, ruffling my hair, slapping my shoulder in what was meant to be a friendly pat. It was irritating to be manhandled, but at the same time he never talked down to me. He treated me as a miniature human rather than as a member of a different species, and I appreciated his matter-of-fact tone. That day he even let me look at the rabbit carcasses, which I had an extreme urge to do until the moment before he took them out of the bag, at which point I felt an anticipatory nausea and fled.

Cedric Robierre, the paleontologist from Boston, was utterly different from Frank. He was not an absentminded professor but rather a tall, businesslike man with an air of competence. He gave the impression of wearing a suit, though naturally during the summer he preferred linen trousers and an open-collared shirt, and on hunting trips he invariably wore a red plaid jacket. It was clear that his true home was in the esoteric chambers of Harvard. I liked Uncle Cedric much more than Uncle Frank because with Cedric, as with Philip Ybarra, I could sense a mighty brain pulsating behind his forehead. I loved the feeling that the minds of the people around me were working all the time, thinking new thoughts, turning over old ideas, pushing unknown boundaries.

Behind Frank and Cedric strode Uncle Kurt, the best uncle of all. When he came in he spied me before anyone else, even though I was the shortest, and said, "How's my youngest soldier!" Then he hugged me. How well I remember the feel of that crisp khaki against my skin! When he let me go I stared at him, breathless, while he leaned against the doorframe—a figure bathed in light, my personal war hero.

Three days later the day came. Tom Robierre, a celebrity by default because he was the last to arrive, the last unknown who might catapult excitement into our lives, was arriving by the 6:30 train into Pensbottom. The town was so small that it merited only two trains a day from Portland, one early and one late. All of our arrivals thus took place in the evening, necessitating a late dinner. The plan was that while my mother stayed behind to cook, Aunt Margery would drive the rattletrap to the station with Aunt Rose, Tom's mother, in the front seat and his sisters Isabella and Delia in the back. There was a momentary upset, however, when Delia announced that she had no interest in meeting the train.

"Don't you want to see your own brother?" Aunt Rose asked.

"I'll see him when he gets here," Delia said, shrugging. "Besides, Delia and I are going to the shore—can we?"

"Alone?"

"We'll be with each other." That was the Delian answer for everything. Behind her, Delia Ybarra erupted into giggles. "Seriously," Delia Robierre went on, adopting the solemn voice she found effective when negotiating with her parents, "of course I want to see Tom, but I know Philip is much more interested in meeting him at the station."

This was true. Philip and Tom had a bond that I envied and admired. I tried to emulate their offhand interactions, and for years afterward I would catch myself thinking, "What would Tom do?" or "What would Philip think?" It was unusual for Philip to come out of his lair, mental and physical, with enough vigor to state that he wanted something, but in this case he did step forward and say, "I want to meet him."

The aunts were suitably impressed. Now that Loretta was gone, the Ybarra children had become hopelessly mysterious to the other aunts. My mother, of course, was intimidated by nothing and no one, but she rarely intervened in situations like this one. As far as I was concerned, she was a Buddha, sitting quietly in her chair with a calm smile on her lips, hoarding all the answers. Aunt Rose was the one who dealt out decrees. She often reminded me of an admiral inspecting a ship, shouting orders, pacing the decks, directing her crew with unerring confidence. Aunt Margery, the family fussbudget, was more hotheaded and impulsive, though she also did most of the work in the house. She talked nonstop and often worked herself into states of half-hysterical emotion—I don't know how Yvette and Fisher and Pamela, with all their unflappable poise, could have come from her and Frank. As for Aunt Edie, her antiquated ideas of proper behavior made her as alien to us as we were to her. They were a disparate family, the Hatfield girls.

Aunt Margery, Aunt Rose, Isabella, and Philip rattled off to meet Tom. From my vantage point on the furthest fencepost, I could see Isabella turning to say something to Philip, then his elusive gleam of teeth, then her fit of laughter. I hadn't wanted to go meet Tom before, but now that Isabella and Philip were enjoying a private party in the backseat of the rattletrap, I was filled with jealousy. There were so many of us that moments with only one or two others were precious, no matter who those oth-

ers were, and Isabella and Philip were the *crème de la crème.*
I spent the hour until they returned daydreaming on the fencepost about what they were saying, deaf to Pamela's remark that
I would get splinters on my behind. She departed with the others, and I was thus the first to see the little cloud of dust that
signaled the approach of the old black car. In my excitement I
tried to stand on the post. A shriek came from behind me—Aunt
Edie had witnessed my antics. The whole crew came tumbling out
the front door, and I was deprived of my sentinel's prize. But it
didn't matter, for the rattletrap was chugging toward us with three
young heads in the back now, Tom sandwiched between Philip
and Isabella. We waved and shouted. Uncle Kurt stood next to
me and held me steady on the post, laughing his contagious, gunfire laugh. Tom was getting a Hatfield Special.

The rattletrap pulled to a halt, and the rear door closest to us
flew open, creaking on its hinges. There was a moment when all
we could see were Isabella's endless arms and legs, flailing like a
trapped octopus as she tried to get out before her brother. In the
end she scrambled almost into the dust before finding her foot-
ing and scooting to one side. Her mouth was stretched in a grin
that seemed to cut her face in half—she didn't mind making a fool
of herself as long as she knew why people were laughing. Philip,
meanwhile, had emerged on the far side with his usual serpentine
dignity. We ignored him.

Tom was luxuriating in this imperial arrival. He had enough dramatic sense to wait a second or two before following Isabella. Then
he slithered out feet first. He was still wearing his student's outfit
of white shirt and tweed suit. We fell silent. I was leaning against
Uncle Kurt's shoulder. Tom stood next to the car, squinting from
the sun. Like Isabella and Delia, he had light brown hair that sat
atop a comfortable, snub-nosed face. But he, much more than his
sisters, had inherited his father's handsomeness. He was magneti-

cally attractive, and now he stood before us, allowing us to drink in the sight of him.

"Hi, everyone," he said, waving a sheepish hand.

Such casual words—and yet, to me, they were the beginning of everything.

2

Croquet

The morning after he arrived, Tom proved our theories about his talent for action by suggesting a family tournament of croquet. We were all in the kitchen, eating breakfast in the Hatfield fashion, which was to come at will and linger for as long as the food held out. My mother and Margery usually prepared the meals, Rose being too lazy and Edie too pernickety to do well in the culinary realm.

"Is there a croquet set here?" Charlie asked. "I've never seen one."

"You've never looked," said Aunt Margery. "Of course there's one. We played croquet all the time when we were young, didn't we, Caroline?"

"I remember perhaps one or two games," my mother replied, smiling.

We found the set in one of the closets by the kitchen, a forgotten hideaway filled with antique sports equipment. Charlie crowed over an ancient baseball bat, and I located a bag of heavy balls that no one could identify. A few days later I asked Uncle Kurt about them, and he said they were bocce balls. He offered to teach me how to play but never did, so they remained a mystery until much later in the summer. Tom, of course, found the croquet bag, a big, unwieldy, canvas sack full of sharp wickets and clattering mallets. In uncovering the bag he threw a pile of litter into the room behind him, and Delia Robierre picked up an ancient kerosene lantern, stained with age. "What's this?" she asked, amused to find a reminder of the age of gas lighting—which, in those days, was not so many years in the past. But Tom had no time for distractions, and the lantern was returned to the closet with all the other paraphernalia.

"Outside, everyone!" he ordered. He had a way of taking command that made us forget how short he was, how slender and insignificant his boy's figure appeared as he strode onto the lawn. Only next to Uncle Kurt, who was so obviously a man, did his leadership falter. Kurt would have played, I was sure, but he was still in bed, recovering from the hunting expedition, which, according to Uncle Cedric, had been tiring for all concerned. That hadn't stopped either Cedric or Frank from being present at the opening of the grand tournament, but, in typical fashion, they said they would sit by the sidelines and produced lawn chairs to carry out this plan.

"Lemonade for our parched throats, sun hats for our balding heads, lawn chairs for our tired legs—it's all we need," Uncle Frank declared.

"Anyone would think you were two twittering old aunties," Francesca said.

"I don't believe any child coming from the Hatfield family should describe an aunt as a twitterer," Cedric replied. He had a dry monotone that perfectly set off his careful jokes.

Francesca laughed and turned around to demand the first mallet.

"There are only six," Tom said.

"Play in pairs," my mother suggested. "We often did that."

"We don't want to play," the Delias said. They spoke in unison with uncanny frequency, standing next to each other, pale and dark, stocky and skinny, straight-haired and curly-haired, and each grinning the same Cheshire-cat grin, as if between the two of them they were hiding a raft of secrets.

"That's fine. Caroline and I will play," Aunt Rose announced.

"And me?" Aunt Margery asked. "What will I do?"

"Sit with the uncles," Rose said, nodding over at them.

"That's all right. Margery can play for me," my mother said.

"But you're much better than Margery," Rose objected, frowning.

"We'll switch off," said my mother. "There's nothing wrong with three to a mallet."

Aunt Edie appeared at the door, and Isabella said at once, a smile twitching her lips, "Here comes Aunt Edie. She's a mean hand at croquet, you know. Back in her glory days, she would play in the nationals. They used to call her Edie the Invincible. But sometimes they called her Edie the Skunk."

"Be careful," Aunt Margery said. "You're closer to the truth than you know. Edie used to beat us every time we played. Even Kurt—he used to be absolutely furious when she skunked him across the lawn. He would dedicate the game to getting his revenge, and so, of course, he always lost."

"Croquet, is it?" Edie asked, sweeping over the lawn. She wore a blue skirt and a strange green jacket, short and old-fashioned. Her nose traveled well before the rest of her body. "Is there a free mallet?"

"The older generation can battle it out over the blue mallet," Tom said. "But the rest go to us. Who wants green?"

We paired off: Francesca with Charlie, Tom with Isabella,

Philip with Fisher. Yvette was given a mallet to herself, which indicated not so much that the other cousins were being generous
as that no one wanted to put up with her acerbic comments.
Pamela and I got stuck with the crooked yellow mallet, identified
by Tom as the runt of the litter. The wood of its handle had
warped, and whenever you hit a stroke with it, the ball inevitably
curved left.

"But we'll lose!" I protested.

"Just take the warp into account," said Tom, dismissing me.

"What does it matter?" said Pamela. "We would have lost anyway. This way we have an excuse."

Just as we were beginning to play, Uncle Frank asked,
"Shouldn't Kurt have made an appearance by now? It's unlike him
to miss something like this." From that point on, though Isabella
had only just made the first stroke, my interest in the game was
overshadowed by a stronger interest in Uncle Kurt's whereabouts.
When would he come? I played with one eye on the door leading into the kitchen and flubbed my shots even more than I would
have because of the warp.

"We'll never get anywhere if you play like that," Pamela pointed
out, her serenity undiminished. "Would you like me to play it all
the way through?"

"No, I want to play." I was determined to be visibly part of the
game when Uncle Kurt appeared.

Tom and Isabella, the only sibling pair, soon took the lead. Isabella told me later that all the members of their family were
fanatical players down in Boston and that she and Tom had devoted hours to improving the accuracy of their shots. They didn't
mention this at the time, though—they gave the credit to natural
talent. "Never picked up a mallet before in my life," Isabella said,
flexing her thin arms. Neither Aunt Rose nor Uncle Cedric saw fit
to contradict her.

Charlie swooped up from behind and hit their ball with his. "Watch out—you're going to be skunked," he warned.

"Let me do it," said Francesca. "You hit her. I get to skunk her."

"You don't know how."

"Of course I do! I've played before. My mother taught us, and she's better than any of you." Francesca put one dainty foot on her own ball and raised the mallet.

"You'll knock your foot off," said Charlie. "Let me help you." He wrapped his arms around her and put his hands over hers on the mallet. With one massive toe he nudged her foot off the ball.

Francesca's laugh rang out from within his embrace. "Charlie, we're in public!" she exclaimed, and the aunts' eyebrows rose. Then she said, "Get off me, you big bear," and all the cousins began to laugh. A few glanced toward Aunt Edie. It was the undying joke of the summer, with just enough flavor of reality to give it punch.

Aunt Edie was trying to dominate the blue mallet and finding strong opposition in Aunt Rose. My mother and Aunt Margery had dropped out after the first round. "What's the use?" Margery said, near to fuming. "They'll just shove us to one side when they think they can make a better shot."

Yvette, who could play a game with complete indifference or with competitive zeal but never with anything in between, had set her eyes on victory. It took her at least five minutes to prepare for every shot, and she ignored the shouts and groans of the other players. She would bend over her mallet, her blond hair falling in a curtain beside her face, her concentration like a fish cutting a line through a stream. Most of the time her shots were accurate, but she was still no match for Tom and Isabella.

The kitchen door remained obstinately shut, and Uncle Kurt did not appear. At last I asked my mother about him. "Why won't he come out? Doesn't he want to play with us? I thought he loved croquet."

"Well, you know, dear," she replied, "he's working on writing something this summer. I think he finds it hard to concentrate with all of us here, and that's why he has to lock himself in his room during the mornings. You mustn't bother him when he's working, but he'll find time to play with the rest of us, don't you worry."

"What is he working on?" I asked, intrigued.

"Oh, he's just writing something up. About the war, I think." My mother waved her hand vaguely. She didn't like to think about the war because it reminded her of Uncle Harold. The two of them had been very close, and when he died in the war, she had been so upset that she left my father and me for a time. At three years old, I felt her absence vividly, but I couldn't miss Uncle Harold because I had never met him. He is another famous Hatfield figure, one whose legendary status can never be dimmed by the mundanity of a long life.

Uncle Kurt, then, was consigned to his room. The croquet game suddenly held less interest for me, and I spent most of my time trying to figure out which window was his.

Though he never appeared, there was still a late entrant to the match. Our surprise was doubled because the latecomer was a stranger, and her arrival cost Tom and Isabella the game. Tom had just lined up their ball for the last shot before a certain victory when I, happening to look at the woods, saw a solitary figure walking toward us through the grass.

"Who's that?" I asked, pointing.

Everyone stopped and turned around. It felt so strange to have anyone in our midst who wasn't related to us that we all stood still.

A girl had come out of the woods. She looked to be about sixteen, with thick, light brown hair that fell in appealing waves on each side of her face. As she came forward she watched us intently, her eyes wide—and her eyes were enormous to begin with, their irises an unusual mixture of speckled blue and gray. They were her most noticeable feature, aside from the paleness of her skin. None of us could understand, once we learned who she was, how someone in her situation could be so fair. Her skin was not simply untanned but truly alabaster—there was not a freckle anywhere to mar its whiteness, and on the inside of her arms the blue veins were clear under the surface. When she first walked toward us she looked frightened, as if she were an animal drawn to something it knew was a trap.

At last she gave us a cautious smile. Isabella was the first to speak. "Hello!" she called. "Who are you?"

The girl waited until she had come nearer. Then, standing with her hands behind her back as if to present herself, she said, "Hello. Do all of you live here?"

"We're the Hatfields," Aunt Rose said. "This is Shorecliff, our family home. Where have you come from?"

"My name's Lorelei," said the girl. "I live on the farm beyond the woods, and I heard voices when I was walking. I thought maybe the house had been sold or rented for the summer."

"It's still our house, but you're right—we're only here for the summer," Isabella said. "During the school year we live in all different places."

"Do you mean you live at the old Stephenson place?" Aunt Edie broke in.

"I'm Lorelei Stephenson," the girl said, smiling shyly at Aunt Edie.

"Fred's daughter?"

"Yes, that's right."

"I used to play with Fred when I was a girl," Aunt Edie said.

"You minx," Tom whispered. Isabella and I were the only ones who heard. I looked up "minx" later in my dictionary—the definition was "a deceitful woman." I assumed from this that Tom thought Aunt Edie hadn't actually played with Fred.

"How many of you are there?" Lorelei asked, glancing around at us.

"Eleven cousins, eight adults," Tom said. He had stepped to the front of the small crowd that surrounded her. "We're playing croquet. Do you want to join us? You can play with me."

She looked at him, and it was as if we could see her heart fluttering in her chest. She was so transparent, physically and emotionally—so different from the Hatfields. "I'd like that very much," she said.

"You don't need to play anymore, Isabella," Tom said over his shoulder.

Isabella put her hands on her hips and opened her mouth to retort, but her eyes flickered to Lorelei, and she said nothing. That was one of the things I loved about her—she never did anything that might hurt someone else's feelings. When she said the wrong thing, which was often, it was usually because she was too enthusiastic or too confident that everyone would agree with her. But when she read situations correctly, she was always compassionate. "Go ahead," she said, nodding to Lorelei. "The game's almost over, but you can have a few shots."

"I've never played before," Lorelei said, raising her eyes to Tom's as he handed her the mallet. "I don't even know the rules."

"That's all right," he said. "You're just trying to hit this ball here through that wicket there with this mallet. That's all."

They were like two actors in a play; we were all watching them. Lorelei hit the ball feebly, and it bobbled off at an impossible angle. Charlie, who had no compunction about taking advantage of others' mistakes, roared with delight and plunged in to skunk the ball.

Philip and Fisher ended up winning the game. Their partnership was a strange one, though typical of their personalities. Philip always wielded the mallet, but Fisher would scout out the distance to be covered and the angle at which the ball needed to travel. He would stand next to Philip like a surveyor and murmur advice to him: "Try to put a left-handed spin on it" or "Be careful of the tussock halfway to the wicket." Philip and Fisher were the two quiet brains of the family, and their respectful friendship was one of the most understandable among us.

Charlie's thirst for glory having led him astray, the combined calculations of Philip and Fisher brought their ball to the stake, and the aunts, forgetting their own battle over mallet rights, congratulated them. Charlie stomped on his mallet with a good-natured bellow. Francesca, with an imperious toss of her hair, laid all the blame on his shoulders. As for Tom, he was still standing with Lorelei at the place where she had mishit the ball. Isabella, from a distance, watched them.

I wandered over to her, wanting her opinion on the new arrival.

"I think we've lost him," she said, speaking before I could say anything. "What do you think of her?"

"I think she's nice," I said. It delighted me that Isabella was treating me as someone with a worthy opinion, so I tried to sound grave. "But she's not like us."

"No, she's not like us."

Lorelei came often after that day, but we never knew when she would arrive or leave. Tom insisted that we hold croquet tournaments regularly, and he played with his head turned toward the woods. Being Tom, he continued to win often, in spite of being so obviously distracted, except for the times when Lorelei appeared. Then he would claim her as his partner and smile as she condemned him to second or third place. After that first tournament, the games were mostly between only five or six of us at a time. Pamela played only rarely, and the Delias usually bowed out. I tried to claim a mallet in every game but was frequently pushed aside by Philip or Francesca or Isabella. The aunts, probably because they knew how silly they had looked fighting over the mallet, never played again, though I often caught Aunt Edie observing our games with a gimlet eye.

For the most part, Lorelei remained for me a character in the distance, a figure complemented by Tom standing possessively beside her. Once or twice, though, I got to speak with her alone. One morning Tom slept late, and so we weren't dragged out onto the croquet field. I was on the lawn—by myself, since Pamela had opted to remain at the breakfast table—and, for lack of anything more interesting to do, I drifted in the direction of the woods. Lorelei appeared the way she always did, as if out of the grass. I waved and ran toward her. She wore clothes that emphasized her countryness—starched white blouses and skirts that flared out to well below her knees. Sometimes I thought they made her look old-fashioned, but most of the time she just seemed foreign—foreign to our family, our customs, our whole way of thinking.

"Hello, Richard," she said. She had needed to hear our names only once, and afterward she remembered them perfectly, never mixing any of us up.

"We're not playing croquet," I said, coming to a halt beside her. "Tom wanted to sleep late."

"That's all right," she said. "I'm not good at it anyway."

"Yes, you are. You're very good," I said dutifully.

"Liar," she replied, smiling at me. Even when Lorelei said things like that, she seemed to be asking permission to say them, showing with her big eyes what a harmless creature she was. She never told us much about her life, but the aunts had interrogated her early on and established that during the school year she went to a girls' boarding school in New Hampshire and that she wanted to go to college. My mother in particular was pleased that Lorelei was being "properly educated," but to me and I suspect to the rest of the cousins, including Tom, she seemed entirely unsophisticated and natural. Aunt Edie called her, with some sarcasm, "Tom's wood nymph."

"Do you think your family would mind if I came into the kitchen for a moment?" Lorelei asked. It was the first time she had ever requested anything or volunteered a wish of her own, and I was the one she had chosen to ask. This filled me with pride.

"Of course you can come in. We'll be happy to have you." With which grandiose remark I led her into the kitchen to exclamations of delight from its inhabitants. She stayed for several hours that day before flitting away, refusing offers of lunch, shy of wearing out her welcome.

All the cousins seemed to like her, though I sometimes thought Isabella begrudged her presence. I asked her about it once, having crept into her room when no one else was there. She was lying on her bed, looking at the ceiling, something she often did when she wanted to think. I sat at the foot of the bed and distracted her with idle chatter. When I mentioned Lorelei, a slight frown appeared on her face.

"Don't you like Lorelei?" I said.

"Why? Is she downstairs or something?"

"She and Tom went for a walk along the cliff."

Isabella propped herself on her elbows. "Yes, I like Lorelei," she said. "Don't you? She's friendly and modest and sweet. I like her a lot."

"Really?"

Isabella looked over the top of my head, which was usually the signal that she was going to unveil her innermost emotions. "The truth is, Richard, I like her a lot for herself, but I'm not sure I like her being here. It sort of takes Tom away from us, don't you think? He's preoccupied with her, and now he's having this big adventure, and we're...well..."

"What big adventure?"

It was the wrong question. Isabella burst out laughing and said, "An adventure into the unknown!" in her booming radio voice.

She never brought up the topic again, and I knew only that the inarticulate desperation which was always a part of her character intensified and began to shine in her eyes whenever Lorelei came and Tom fawned over her. Isabella would stand apart in one of her gawky postures and look at them with her eyebrows wrinkled in unconscious dismay.

She was not the only one displeased by Lorelei's presence. I'll never forget the croquet game when Yvette nearly killed Fisher. It was a five-man game—Tom, Isabella, Yvette, Fisher, and Philip. Fisher, with his usual earnestness, had advised me to stand on the sidelines and watch their strategies so I could improve my own skill.

Lorelei appeared from the woods, and I called out for Tom's benefit, "Here she is!"

Tom's face lit up. He waited, his mallet resting across his chest on one forearm, until she had walked up to us. She never ran. "Hi," he said, smiling. I had taken to watching his face when he spoke to her. Tom had a signature grin, a big, unrestrained flashing of teeth, but he never showed it to Lorelei. The smiles he gave to her were subdued, as if he were holding something back or waiting for her to do something. Her smile, on the other hand, was the same for everyone.

Tom said, as he always did after greeting her, "Do you want to be my partner for the rest of the game?"

Lorelei nodded and said, "I won't be any help to you."

From two wickets behind Tom, Yvette asked, "Why can't she take the sixth mallet? We only have five players."

"Because I want her to play with me," Tom said. He shielded his eyes to look at Yvette, who was standing with her back to the sun. "Besides, where would she start? We're almost halfway through."

Inconspicuously, I circled around so that I could be nearer to Yvette. I had sensed from her voice that she was more upset than she wanted to show.

"But she makes you lose," Yvette said. "You're always in the lead, and then you fall into last place because she's so terrible."

At first I thought that she was simply annoyed by Tom's indifference to victory. I had to agree that it was irritating to see Tom, our best player, consistently lagging behind mediocre talents like Philip and Fisher because Lorelei would send his ball shooting toward the fence or rolling off weakly toward the woods. But I was shocked that Yvette had called Lorelei terrible to her face.

Tom obviously thought the same. "I'm teaching her how to play," he said. "She'll get better." He put his arm protectively around Lorelei's shoulder, and Yvette's eyes widened.

"Fine, then!" she cried. "I'm not playing anymore. What's the point of playing when nobody's going to try to win?" She flung up one hand and hurled her mallet away from her, not looking to see where it would land. The mallet arced through the air, and Fisher, who was standing in a daydream, didn't see it coming. It slammed into his shoulder, and he gave a yell and fell to the ground. If it had hit his head, I think he might have been killed or at least badly hurt.

Yvette was not always cold. When she saw that she had inadvertently assaulted her brother, she dashed toward him. The aunts, who had a preternatural sense for detecting injury among the children, poured from the house like a flock of starlings, cawing and flapping. We crowded around Fisher, whose blue eyes were covered with a film of tears. I thought it was a sign of bravery that none of the tears spilled onto his cheeks. He was all right, though his shoulder was purple for weeks afterward. It must have hurt like hell, but after that first surprised cry he didn't say anything except "It's not that bad. It wasn't her fault."

Tom got the game going again. "Don't pay attention to her," he said to Lorelei. "She gets too wound up in the game for her own good."

I took Fisher's place while he was escorted into the house for treatment by the aunts, and in no time I was in last place. I never did pick up the finer points of croquet; the interactions between the players were always so much more interesting than the game itself. Tom, for instance, was gentler with Lorelei that morning than I had ever seen him be with anyone. It was a side of himself that he never brought out for his cousins.

At least for me, Tom continued to be an object of adoration throughout the summer. Lorelei didn't have enough courage to accompany us on family outings, and so our days at the seashore, our walks along the cliff, our game-filled evenings—all these were times when Tom escorted his cousins into whatever adventure he could think up for us. I liked best the times when I came across him in moments of quiet. He loved books, in spite of his questionable college record, and often he and Philip would spend rainy afternoons in their room, both reading on their beds. Tom read history and Philip philosophy, but they occasionally borrowed each other's volumes—I can't imagine how they managed to bring so many. I would peep in and watch their eyes moving across the pages. Philip read languidly, turning the page with an aristocratic hand while one leg dangled off the edge of the bed. Tom read with a scowl on his face, concentrating so hard that he would often sit scrunched up in a ball, his body curling around the book as if to absorb its information through osmosis.

Other times I would hear music coming from their room, and that meant Tom was dancing. Philip had thrilled us all by bringing an old wind-up Victrola to Shorecliff, along with an extensive collection of jazz records—King Oliver, Louis Armstrong, Duke Ellington. He himself never danced, but Francesca, after all her

Manhattan escapades, was an expert at the Charleston and the Shimmy, and she would dance with Tom, who capered along enthusiastically and managed to look handsome even while mixing up all the steps. Once they attempted the Lindy Hop, a dance requiring a flight through the air like Charles Lindbergh's. It ended with Francesca on the floor, laughing hysterically—the only time I ever saw her stumble. I found the sight of her dancing so dazzling that I could hardly watch her, and when other cousins joined in, the room became a magnificent pandemonium.

Yvette was a natural dancer, sleek and weightless. Her technique outshone even Francesca's, and she delighted us sometimes by wearing a beaded flapper dress for the occasion—an article of clothing she carefully concealed from the aunts. Isabella was as enthusiastic as Tom but far less skilled. She often let me jump around with her, to my joy. Charlie was all flash and exuberance and constantly tried to lure Francesca away from Tom, to the accompaniment of catcalls from the other cousins. The Delias liked to make up steps of their own, and Pamela sometimes tried to follow their lead, but she was too shy to dance energetically and often sat out. Fisher also sat on the sidelines next to Philip, who manned the Victrola with the air of a musical connoisseur. But Tom was the leader of these gatherings. In the early days at Shorecliff I would frequently hear music bursting into life in their room, and I would know that Tom had instructed Philip to put on some jazz and let him dance.

Some mornings I encountered Tom in the hall outside our rooms. He would be in his pajamas, his hair tousled from the pillow. "Hey there, buddy," he would say. "Why are you up so early? Don't you need your sleep?"

"What are we doing today?" I would ask.

"God knows!" he would say. "Don't ask me, buddy. I just live here."

Of course the truth was that he was a typical college freshman, cocksure and overeager, all too ready to put down his elders and place himself above the rest of us. But he was also intelligent and passionate, and a student in everything. He looked around him with an interest that was contagious, and that was why we followed him so willingly—he saw things in a more exciting light than we did. Francesca brought about the same effect, vivifying her midnight imagination for us with terrifying immediacy, but Tom's visions were bright and sun-filled, and the hint of vulnerability in him, which in Isabella dominated her character, put the finishing touch on his magnetism.

One day I was looking out the window of my bedroom with my telescope. I frequently scanned the horizon in this way, hoping in vain for battleships on the sea or strangers on the cliff, and I often saw things that captured my fancy. On this afternoon, I spotted Tom and Lorelei standing dangerously near the cliff's edge. He had his arm around her waist, and she was clasping his upper arm. The wind was blowing her hair out and making her skirt swirl. Tom had on the white dress shirt he always insisted on wearing. The two looked supremely romantic. His mouth was moving; I was sure he was saying something vitally important, something to make her swoon. She was listening to him with her eyes wide. There had been a storm the night before, and the waves were still so big that occasionally they threw a shower of spray over the top of the cliff.

I asked my mother that day whether Tom was in love with Lorelei.

"Why do you think so?" she asked.

I explained that they were always together when Lorelei came, that Tom wouldn't let the rest of us come near her, and that he looked at her in a way that he never used with anyone else.

"I think there's a good chance that if you asked him, he would say he was in love with her." My mother had a way of sidestepping questions she didn't want to answer.

"Do you like her?" I asked.

"I think she's a lovely girl. And, you know, Fred Stephenson has been a friend of our family for a long time. We should invite him to lunch."

The aunts repeated this sentiment many times that summer, but I have yet to lay eyes on Fred Stephenson. The truth was that the Hatfields, with one notable exception, were uninterested in their neighbors.

My mother remained adamantly in favor of Lorelei throughout the next three months. Some of the other aunts had doubts, however, and Edie was rabid on the subject.

"It's disgusting!" she said once during an impromptu Aunt Conference in the kitchen. I liked to eavesdrop on these discussions by lurking behind the stove. None of them could scold me for spying, since they knew I was there, but they were almost certain to forget my presence as their argument grew more heated. (The conferences always turned into arguments.) At the moment Aunt Edie held the floor, and she was conjuring up a demonic vision of Tom's activities with Lorelei. "You know young people," she snapped. "The way they lust after each other is revolting. It's positively morbid." This was one of Edie's pet words. "God knows what they do when they're alone. The mind boggles. Rose, you're letting that boy run into sin as if he were on a galloping horse. It's not good for him. You should keep them from seeing each other."

Rose opened her mouth to reply, but before she could begin my mother spoke. It was one of the few times I've heard her speak sharply to anyone. "Don't be ridiculous, Edie," she said. "The only times they're alone together are when they go on walks along the cliff. They're never out of sight of the house, or if they are, they're in the woods near Condor's cottage. I think the way you're talking is disgraceful. There's nothing wrong with young people spending time together. They're enjoying themselves."

"Tom is enjoying himself too much," Aunt Edie retorted.

"He's neglecting the family," Aunt Margery said.

"Rubbish," said my mother. "He's with us constantly. His cousins adore him. They all like Lorelei because he does, and besides, she's a sweet, innocent girl. I think she was very lonely at the farm with no one her age to talk to. It would be cruel to stop her from visiting."

I was stunned to hear my mother talking with such force, and I wondered if she ever spoke that way to my father. I doubted it then, and I doubt it now, but I respected her more after I heard her reprimanding Aunt Edie. It took nerve, the sort of nerve I could understand and admire, unlike the very different sort of nerve it must have taken to live with my father.

"Have it your way, Caroline," Aunt Edie said. "But just you watch them the next time they're playing one of their interminable croquet games. You watch the way they look at each other. I tell you, it's nearly obscene."

My mother laughed at that, and Margery joined in. The argument ended merrily, as they so often did. But I heard the phrase "it's nearly obscene" as if it were on a record playing over and over again. I knew what "obscene" meant, in a formless sort of way, and the next time I saw Tom and Lorelei together I watched them eagerly. It was, of course, during a morning croquet game. Lorelei strode over the grass, looking as usual as if she had emerged from a fairy tale, and Tom waited for her and offered her his mallet. I examined their eyes, but I didn't see a satyric expression on either face.

In the end I don't think Aunt Edie interpreted their relationship correctly. There was lust enough and to spare in that packed old house of ours, and Tom certainly felt his share of it, but I don't think his attraction to Lorelei was obscene, nor even entirely phys-ical. I believe that what had captured him in Lorelei was what had captured us in him—the living spirit of romance and the pos-sibility, so enchanting for all the cousins, of what might happen between the two of them. At the beginning of that summer, Tom seemed to hold on to Lorelei with the trembling excitement of a little boy sheltering a baby bird in his hands—hardly breathing, amazed that he has been given the privilege of holding all that life in his hands, feeling the bird's heart beating like a telegraph signal against his skin. The present then is so thrilling that it is impossible to reflect on it; one can only wait, panting, for the future to unfold.

3

War Stories

I broke my mother's injunction not to disturb Uncle Kurt in the mornings within days of it being issued. Before that summer I had never been in close quarters with Kurt for more than a day or two at a time, when he came to visit in New York, and during those weekends I had never found the opportunity for leisurely tête-à-têtes. Once I knew that he was holed up in his room at Shorecliff alone, it was impossible not to try to gain access to the inner sanctum. Accordingly, one morning, as Tom led a squadron onto the lawn for the morning croquet game, I slid out of my seat and darted from the kitchen. I waited for a few moments to see if someone would miss me, but I was more inconsequential than I imagined, and I crept all the way to Uncle Kurt's closed door on the second floor without anyone noticing my absence.

I knocked. There was a muffled cry of "Come in!" That was all I needed.

Uncle Kurt's room looked different from every other room in

the house, mostly because of the cream-colored curtains he had draped over the windows. His room was at the front of the house, overlooking the lawn and the end of the road. It didn't get much sun in the mornings, and what light did get in was filtered by the curtains into a yellow syrup that covered all the furniture. It made Uncle Kurt in his morning beard seem golden. The space was small and cluttered. His bed was shoved under the window, not quite at right angles, and the table he always sat at, fingers poised over the keys of the typewriter, was overflowing with books and papers and reams of typing paper. I asked him once why he knew how to type—an occupation, as far as I knew, reserved for women—and he told me it was one of the odd skills the army had taught him, like darning and bridge-building and how to tie a tourniquet. "Damn useful, all that stuff."

I often caught a waft of tobacco smoke in the air when I came in, though Uncle Kurt was careful to hide his cigarettes in case I was one of the aunts. The Hatfield women disapproved as strongly of smoking as they did of drinking.

That first morning I found Uncle Kurt at the table, staring at a sheet of paper in the typewriter. When he turned around and saw me, he took the paper out of the carriage with one fluid movement and laid it facedown on the table. I was so awed by the appearance of the room that I didn't think anything of this action, but if I had, I might have reconsidered my assumption that Uncle Kurt was always open with me.

"Mother told me not to bother you," I said by way of introduction.

"So you came right up here and pounded on the door," said Uncle Kurt, nodding. "That's good, my boy. Break the rules while you're young."

"What are you writing?"

"Oh, various things." He stretched and waved a hand at a chair next to the door. "Take a seat, Richard. Stay a while. Did you want anything in particular?"

"Are you writing about what happened to you in the war?"

Uncle Kurt laughed. He always met what I considered daring statements with an embracing laugh that was like a flood of warmth. "Is that what you came up here for? War stories? I've got hundreds of them stored up, you know. Mine, my company's, other companies'…"

From that moment it was inevitable that I beg to hear them, and Kurt always obliged. I heard about his training, his fellow soldiers, his officers, his first battle. For the most part he left out the graphic details, but I was relentless in my requests for fighting scenes, and though I cringed at the gore, I rejoiced in the excitement.

"What was the scariest thing that ever happened to you?" I asked one day, scooting forward to the edge of my seat.

"The scariest thing? Kiddo, I went through so many scary moments that I can't choose between them. There were far more than I ever want you to experience. But if you'd like to hear a scary story that didn't take place during a battle, I can give you one. I've never forgotten it. It was when we were walking through the woods in the northern part of France."

So it began. I sat rapt and motionless until the end.

"Our platoon had been cut off from the rest of the company, and we were trying to cut across in a southeastern diagonal to meet up with the others. My lieutenant—you remember him, Lieutenant Mange, the old Mangy Monster—had gotten us lost. That wasn't a surprise to any of us. What we really resented was that he was making us slog through the woods during a snowstorm. His getting us lost had cost us all the time he'd set aside for resting, so we kept walking, hour after hour. It was rough going, let me tell you. We were exhausted from trudging so far, and the wind blew right through our uniforms. I felt as if I wasn't wearing anything

at all—no overcoat, no khaki, no underwear even. It was just me
and the elements. The snow was the cold, wet, stinging kind that's
no fun to be in, not the Christmas kind everyone loves. The wind
drove it into a kind of slushy hailstorm, and the branches above
us kept getting overloaded with snow and dropping bucketfuls on
our heads. It was an awful night. I still dream about it sometimes.

"Hennessey, my best pal—I've told you about him too; he was
the one who stole that pair of boots from Old Mange, remember
that?—anyway, this was before he'd stolen the boots, so the ones
he was wearing still had holes in them on both sides. Poor old
Hennessey—it was awful for him, but he was one of the tough-
est guys you'll ever meet. He was a big blond giant, as friendly
and sweet as a kindergarten teacher, and he had a great laugh,
a big booming roar. He could set off a whole company when he
got started. He wasn't laughing that night, though. He kept slog-
ging along next to me with his mouth in a straight line across
his face and his eyes focused on the back of the man in front of
him. I can still hear his boots through the snow—clump, clump,
clump—and I knew with every step more snow was pouring in
and freezing his feet. He was a brave man, Richard, one of the
bravest I ever met.

"Anyway, we were walking along like that for what seemed
like years, and suddenly Hennessey, who was a bit of a practical
joker, leaned over and said, 'You know, they say this wood is
haunted.' Now, ordinarily I'm not the sort of guy to let supersti-
tions get to me. I'm not one of those guys who gets spooked in
an empty house. But after hours of walking in the dark and the
snow, ducking branches at every step and being so hungry—well,
I was susceptible to the oldest trick in the book. Hennessey kept
telling me about all the ghosts that were supposed to be in the forest—the ghosts of murdered men whose deaths had never been
solved, whose murderers walked the earth without punishment.

He laid it on pretty thick. And then suddenly he stopped in his tracks, grabbed my shoulder, and said, 'What's that?' He was pointing behind a tree some feet away from us. I looked over, trying to see something, and he shouted, 'Boo!' right in my ear. I jumped a foot. Can you believe it? A five-year-old wouldn't have taken that bait. But I took it, all right. The woods were beginning to get to me. Hennessey roared with laughter, and all the other men turned to look at us, to find out what was going on. Luckily Hennessey was laughing too hard to do anything except point at me, and then Old Mange shouted for us to keep walking.

"For the next hour or so Hennessey kept up a running narration for my benefit. He was almost enjoying himself by now. I bet he'd forgotten all about the holes in his boots. He was happiest when he was making a joke out of something, and now he kept pointing at bushes and trees and saying, 'That one, for instance. They like to keep low to the ground. Just imagine some ax murderer crouching behind that bush, watching us, waiting until we're right across from him before leaping out, right *now!*' Then he'd grab my shoulder, and I'd shy like a frightened horse. I don't know if it's ever happened to you, Richard, but when you get in the mood sometimes, everything can seem scary. You'd think I would have been too exhausted, too hungry, too plain old worn out for Hennessey's joking to have any effect, but I wasn't. And the way our lanterns were bobbing around, it seemed as if the shadows really were moving next to us, as if the wood were full of ghosts.

"Then something else happened. Hennessey was saying, 'Imagine a pair of eyes suddenly appearing from behind the tree—white, staring eyes looking at you as if they wanted to eat you up whole—eyes ready to kill you.' I was trying not to look at the tree, so he took hold of my head, turned it around, and pointed straight at the tree. And right as I looked, a pair of eyes *did* pop out from behind that tree—white staring eyes exactly the way he'd described. I tell you, I've never been so goddamn scared in all my life. I was so scared I didn't even scream, though it felt like my heart was about to explode. But the most terrifying thing of all was the sound Hennessey made. It wasn't a shriek or a yell—it was more like an intake of breath combined with a moan, very sudden and choked. And that told me Hennessey was so scared that even he, even such a big man as he was, couldn't scream out loud.

"Just as we thought we would die of fright, another pair of eyes popped out beside the first, and then another and another. They were all around us. The other men in our platoon noticed them, and then did we hear some screaming, let me tell you! It was a bunch of Germans—they'd been cut off from their company too, I guess, and now they'd discovered us and tried to surround us. We couldn't see their bodies; it was too dark. Only their wild eyes stared out, reflecting the light of our lanterns.

"God knows what would have happened if Lieutenant Mange hadn't shouted, 'Scatter!' at the top of his lungs. Boy, we scattered. We ran like hell. I even lost Hennessey in the crush. I dove forward between two pairs of eyes and galloped into the woods. Damn near poked my own eyes out because I kept running into branches. I heard shouts all around me, but after a while they became fainter, and when ten minutes had gone by I'd had enough aimless running. I stopped and looked around. I had one little lantern with me that I'd been hiding under my coat—that was all. Then I felt another type of fear, Richard. This wasn't the sudden terror you feel when something startles you, the way those eyes startled me. This was the sick, deadening apprehension you feel when you're all alone in the middle of a big snow-covered forest, cut off from your comrades. There's nothing like it. I hope you never experience it, kiddo, because it comes awfully close to—well, you could almost call it despair.

"I knew there was a good chance I would die if I didn't keep walking, and my only hope now was to find Hennessey and Lieutenant Mange and the others. So I wandered in a new direction. But I didn't dare call out because I knew the Germans were still nearby. I just walked on trying to make as little noise as possible. That part of the night I don't like to think about. The cold and snow and darkness seemed ten times more horrible now that I had to face them alone. I started missing Hennessey's silly jokes, even though I'd been about to throttle him earlier. I must have walked for about half an hour—or maybe it was less, twenty minutes, but it felt like years—when I heard someone crashing toward me from my left. Before I could think better of it, I cried, 'Is that you, Hennessey?' Then the man stepped into the circle of light my lantern cast, and I saw it was one of the Germans.

"He'd lost his helmet, and his blond hair was all spiked up and covered in snow. His face was white too because it was so cold, and there was snow in his eyebrows. He didn't have a light at all, poor devil. He'd been staggering along in complete darkness. But he was holding his gun out, aimed in front of him, so that when he came up to me the barrel almost touched my chest. Then I felt yet another type of fear. I guess I experienced all the colors in the fear rainbow that night, Richard. This was the gut-wrenching terror you feel when you know your life depends on another man's nerve. I could hear him panting—his breathing was ragged and hoarse, as if he'd been sprinting for miles—and I could tell he was scared practically out of his wits. That meant at any moment he might panic and pull the trigger. So I didn't say anything. I just stood there, looking into his big eyes. My stomach felt as if it were slithering out of me. I wanted to throw up my hands and shout, 'Stop, stop, I can't take it anymore!' But I didn't say a word.

"The German was getting more and more worked up. He was breathing faster, and his shoulders were heaving up and down. That's how scared men get in these types of situations, Richard. It's not the sort of thing you ever want to see. Finally he jerked the gun a little—making me jump, I can tell you—and he said, 'I'll shoot!' He didn't have a very strong accent.

"When he said that, I should have been even more scared. He was threatening me, after all. But for some reason it calmed me down. I think it was because I knew then what sort of scared he was—he was filled with the fear that's so paralyzing you can't do anything except shake. So I didn't panic. I raised my arms slowly, away from my gun to show that I wasn't going to attack him, and I asked, 'Where are the other American soldiers?' I figured he would at least understand the word 'American.'

"As it turns out, I think he must have known a lot of English because he pointed behind him and said, 'They're over there, not very far from here.' He turned back to face me, stared for a second with his eyes even wider, and then burst into tears. Yes, Richard, he just started sobbing right there, with the tears rolling down through the melted snow on his cheeks. He kept clutching his gun so that it pointed at me in a wobbly sort of way, but I wasn't scared of him at all anymore. I stepped to one side. That poor bastard—I felt the most god-awful pity for him then. German or not, enemy or not, he was a pathetic sight. I think he was younger than I was, and so frightened to be there facing me that he was about to lose his mind. And then, the shame of telling me what I wanted to know—I could tell that was the last straw. Being in that position and losing his nerve and giving the enemy information, the last scrap of his manliness thrown away... Richard, my boy, one of the worst things about war is the way it makes men feel about themselves. If he lived through it, I'll bet you a hundred bucks the memory of that moment still makes him shudder with self-loathing. Poor bastard.

"I wanted to say thank you. I even wanted to tell him everything would be all right. But anything I said would have made it worse. So I moved down alongside the barrel of his gun until I was standing next to him, met his eyes once more, and walked past him into the woods. I thought he might shoot me in the back just to get back his self-respect. But he didn't. I walked on for a little bit, and then I heard a thump. I looked back. As far as I could make out from the light of my lantern, he'd fallen onto his knees. Kneeling there...I wish I hadn't seen that."

Unexpectedly, Uncle Kurt stopped talking. He looked out the window and said nothing for a few moments.

"And then what happened?" I asked at last, unable to restrain myself.

"Well, then I found Hennessey and the others, and we dragged ourselves along until morning, and by that time we'd found the rest of the company."

"What happened to the German?"

"I don't know, buddy. I never found out. That's the end of the story."

That was all I got out of him that day. He had drifted away, it seemed reluctantly, into a pensive silence.

Not all of Kurt's stories were so grim and unsettling. Many of them would end with a punch line and a laugh. But all of them were riddled with comments about the awful things war did to people. They didn't stop me from glorifying him, but they did stop me from glorifying war itself. I admired him all the more for being so wise, for being able to criticize the very thing that had made him a god.

Once, later in the summer, my mother discovered me in Uncle Kurt's room. She opened the door right as Kurt was reaching the climax of one of his stories.

"Richard," she said, "what have I told you about bothering your Uncle Kurt in the mornings? I'm surprised at you. Run along now."

"Don't worry," Kurt said, smiling at me in a conspiratorial

way that filled me with pleasure and pride. "Richard here doesn't bother me at all. He comes up for news of the war."

My mother looked at him with a crease on her forehead. "But, Kurt," she said, "isn't it—well, troubling for you to think back over all those memories? Are you sure it's good for you?"

"Now, Caroline." Kurt laughed, but it was a soft, strained laugh that I didn't like at all. "I think about the war with or without Richard. At least when he's here I have a captivated audience rather than a captive one. I've relived my stories many times, but they're new for him. Aren't they, my boy?"

"Yes, Uncle Kurt," I whispered.

"But aren't you working?" My mother glanced at the typewriter and the facedown sheets of paper.

"Yes, I'm working," Kurt said. He gave her a level stare and added, "In all the many times Richard has come here, he has never once looked at my typewriter the way you just did. He's content to hear my stories directly from me, without prying."

My mother got the hint and left. I treasured Kurt's comment, though I felt guilty too, knowing how false it was. In fact I had shot many a furtive glance at his desk, wondering what he was writing and if it was anything like the stories he told me. He never noticed. I don't think Kurt realized how abstracted he became while telling those stories, how often he would look at the window, his eyes locked on something far away.

My mother never scolded me again about bothering Uncle Kurt, but I tried to keep my visits private anyway. It would have taken away half their excitement if I hadn't felt that I was on forbidden ground. Of course I often felt the urge to boast to my cousins about Kurt's stories, but I valiantly resisted mentioning them.

All too soon, however, it became clear that the cousins knew my secret and simply weren't interested, which meant that I could refer to my talks with Kurt freely, without fear of being usurped as his audience.

Once, on my way back to the beach, still sandy from previous exploits, I saw Isabella lying on her bed and tiptoed in to ask why she wasn't at the shore.

"The shore's not a good place for me right now, kid," she replied, her words muffled by the pillow. She had crushed her face into it so that I could see only one eye and half of her distorted mouth. She didn't seem to be crying or even particularly unhappy. She spoke in a bored monotone.

I was baffled. "Are you sick?" I asked.

"Not in any way that you'd understand."

"Are you sad?"

"I guess you could say so." This was said after a sizable pause.

I was frozen by an onslaught of pity and awe. It occurred to me that I might stroke her hair, the way my mother still stroked mine when I was upset, but I discarded the idea. A thirteen-year-old boy could not stroke a seventeen-year-old girl's hair—it would have been sacrilege of the most terrible kind. Nor could I present her with sympathy. She had rejected my offered ear, and clearly my ignorance made it an offense even to be standing in her room. "Do you want me to go get someone?" I ventured.

"No, there's no one I want to talk to."

That was when I had my flash of inspiration. "You could talk to Uncle Kurt!" I exclaimed. "He's so old and smart, he'll know exactly what to say."

Isabella smiled into the pillow. "Uncle Kurt's not a good person to talk to when you're upset. He has too many secrets of his own to worry about other people's."

"Uncle Kurt doesn't have any secrets!" I said, horrified. As soon as I said it I realized I was wrong. "Or at least, his secrets are all good secrets."

Isabella laughed again. "There's no such thing as a good secret, Richard."

Her statement was so sweeping that I couldn't help but stand there, squinting up my eyes, trying to prove her wrong. Of course there are good secrets—surprise birthday parties, for instance. I thought of that one in under ten seconds, but before I could say it, I heard a laugh in the doorway.

It was Francesca, tossing her long, curly hair away from her bathing suit. The suit was a rich green, with nothing but two thin straps to hold it up and an almost nonexistent skirt—more modest than the ones girls wear nowadays, but still shockingly revealing by our family's standards.

"No such thing as a good secret?" she echoed, her eyes sparkling. "I don't think that's true! I can think of a lot of good secrets." She laughed her throaty laugh again and said, "Right, Richard?"

"I was being serious, Francesca," Isabella said. She had sat up as soon as Francesca came into the room.

Francesca smiled at Isabella without malice, looked at me for a second or two, and left. From the hallway we heard, "Are you coming to the beach, Isabella?"

"You go on without me," Isabella called.

There was a moment of silence that I felt to be extremely awkward.

"Will you be all right?" I asked at last.

"Oh, yes, I'll be fine." She was still sitting up, waggling her feet at me. "Run away to the beach, little boy. Don't worry about me. What have you all been doing down there anyway?"

"Tom and Philip had a swimming race," I answered, ready to give her the full details in spite of her condescending tone. "Charlie was the judge, and he and Tom got into a water fight. Pamela and I went exploring down the shore by the cliff, and the Delias are building a sandcastle. Fisher decided to hunt for crabs—but only unusual ones, he said. Yvette is sunbathing. And that's everyone because Francesca came back here with me. I wanted to get my telescope."

"Can you see down to the shore from here with your telescope?"

"No, of course not." I laughed, thinking she was trying to be funny. "The shore is half a mile away and below the cliff. The furthest I can see from my window is to the edge of the woods. Sometimes I can see boats out at sea too, but not very well. I'm not good at focusing it." I was hitting my stride. Conversation with Isabella always seemed easy. "So are you going to come back with us?" I asked, assuming that, having heard the enticements of the beach, Isabella wouldn't be able to resist.

She said, "No, I'm going to stay here. You can tell me all about it when you get back. I'll be waiting for you."

I shrugged and left. My cousins spent a lot of time lying on their beds. Considering how dark and gloomy the third floor of Shorecliff was, even on the brightest days, it was impressive that they were so willing to give up the outdoors. But I guess misery is more satisfying when you wallow in darkness. Being sad in the sunlight is harder to pull off.

Francesca was loitering on the stairs, waiting for me. She surprised me sometimes by her consideration—I never expected any from her. "So she's not coming?" she asked. When I shook my head, she said, "Well, that's her choice. Come on."

4

Shore

We went to the seashore constantly, nearly every day. Most of the older cousins were intrepid swimmers and ventured into the freezing waves even on windy days that would have seen me huddling in bed were it not for the fact that I refused to be left behind. The water we swam in was cold enough to make our skin go numb after a few minutes, and the aunts and uncles never went in past their knees. But the children were fearless.

Francesca, in particular, would not be denied her daily swim. Probably this was largely for the purpose of wearing her green suit, but nevertheless she thrived in the water, hurling herself into oncoming rollers like a selkie. She boasted that Aunt Loretta was a magnificent swimmer and had taught her all the strokes, though in fact the boys were much more skilled at withstanding the waves than she was. She had a strange habit of crouching in the shallows, her black hair resting on the surface, and then exploding upward with her hands above her head as if she were diving into the air. The gesture seemed to embody our pleasure in the water. The boys also reveled in dodging waves and starting water fights. Pamela and I went in on occasion, usually when there were several aunts nearby and the ocean was so calm that the older cousins deemed it boring and sunbathed instead. I preferred to feel the water swishing gently against my legs, beckoning me onward. Conquering the sea as a foe felt like a distasteful and pointless exercise, but embracing it as a friend was a delight each time.

There was nothing between the house and the beach except the coarse grass that abounded around Shorecliff and a sprawling patch of wild roses and blueberries. We children thought nothing of trotting for ten minutes or so through this thicket and then bursting onto the sand, but for the aunts and uncles it was a chore—whenever they came, they brought lawn chairs and baskets of food and bags of books, as if they meant to be there all day. Then they would stay for an hour or two and depart, while we, who were constantly racing between the house and the beach, could spend all day there without thinking anything of it.

We went to the shore so often that for the most part our times there melted into one another, and maybe that's why my memory of it seems so magical, built as it is out of so many different mornings, so many lazy afternoons. But one event stands out from the collage, a fear-filled hour that formed one of the milestones of the summer.

The two Delias were fond of building sandcastles. They constructed forts, palaces, villas, once even the Taj Mahal. Proudly they pointed out similarities between their lumpy creations and the sources of their inspirations. Delia Ybarra insisted on using the wettest sand, and so the two of them could usually be found at the edge of the water, piling up bulwarks against the oncoming tide and shouting with happy dismay when the icy waves burst through their walls and flooded the castles' moats. The rest of us liked the Delias best when they were at the shore. Too often they retreated into their own world of giggles and gossip, but at the beach they played in our midst, and we could run up to tease them or throw water on them, knowing we would receive good-humored smiles in return. Occasionally they even let us dig a trench for them or strengthen a rampart.

One blustery morning, the day after a storm of near-hurricane proportions had kept us prisoners in the house for an entire afternoon, we trooped to the shore, hoping that the water would calm down after a few hours of sunlight. The older girls lay in decorous poses on the dry sand at the top of the beach, and the boys ran footraces and tossed a ball back and forth. Fisher wandered up onto the dunes, where the grass, tall and coarse, whipped against one's legs like birch canes. The two Delias, undaunted by the towering waves, headed toward the waterline to begin their latest project, a miniature version of the palace at Versailles. They made a picturesque couple as they trotted down the beach, Delia Ybarra in a bright red bathing suit that tied around her neck and contrasted with her black curls, Delia Robierre in a yellow suit barely distinguishable from her tan skin and light brown hair.

Versailles did not fare well under the Delias' hands. The force of the water was too strong for their sloppy walls, and the foundations they kept laying out dissolved with every fresh wave. The girls rapidly became frustrated, and Francesca chose that moment to turn on her matronly manner. It was clear to the rest of us that she acted the mother only for the pleasure of exerting authority. She was too absorbed in her own existence and too blithely confident that everything would turn out all right ever to be genuinely concerned that we might be injured or lost.

Catching sight of the Delias framed by a menacing wave, she propped herself up on her elbows and called, "Delia and Delia! The waves are too big. Come away from the water."

Delia Ybarra, without hesitation, armed herself for war. She stood over the feeble beginnings of Versailles, her hands on her hips, and shouted, "How would you know? You haven't been near the water, you sissy!" As part of her defiance she took several steps backward, and a wave nearly toppled her. Delia Robierre, remaining faithfully by her side, hung onto her arm and looked nervously behind them. Both of the girls were already shivering.

The ball game stopped, and the older cousins—with the exception of Fisher, who was still up on the hill—gathered around Francesca. A fight was cause to drop everything and watch.

"I'm not joking, Delia!" Francesca called, standing up and cupping her hand to her mouth. There was no need to do this—she was just theatrically emphasizing the strength of the wind.

"Neither am I!" Delia roared.

"Come here right now, you little brat! Or I'll come down there and drag you out by force!"

A mischievous smile crossed Delia's lips. "I'd like to see you try," she said, and turned around to splash as fast as she could into the next wave. There was a moment of confusion. Delia Robierre, after a useless lunge after her, retreated to the water's edge and started jumping up and down, calling, "Delia! Delia, come out!"

Delia Ybarra's head surfaced after a few seconds, her black hair dripping onto her forehead. The wave had dazed her. Then the undertow grabbed her legs and whirled her out to sea. Pamela and I, lurking behind the older cousins, were so terrified at the speed with which she rushed into the water that we joined hands and remained linked for the rest of the crisis. Beyond the breaking surf, we could see Delia's black head bobbing for an instant and a white hand flailing beside it. Then another wave engulfed her.

For one dull moment no one moved and our minds refused to work. It couldn't be true, we thought. It wasn't really happening. But it was, and Delia Robierre proved it by turning around with her face red and crumpled and her hands held out. "Somebody save her!" she sobbed, her teeth chattering. After that, the situation became sickeningly real.

Cordelia was whisked away so rapidly that within seconds her face was only a white blur, though even from the shore I could see her desperate efforts to swim toward us and then her head swiveling as the next gigantic wave rolled over her. Much of the time, because of these waves, she was lost to view. But Delia Robierre mirrored her panic, and her fear is what remains most vividly in my memory. She was in such agony that she kept dancing in and out of the water, as if she were being pulled by a cord toward her cousin. After her one plea for help, she kept her back to us, crying for Delia over and over again. Her pain was made all the more unbearable by the fact that she was screaming her own name.

I stared at her and at Cordelia's tossing hands, my whole body trembling with hysteria. Pamela stood beside me, her fingers digging into mine; later I discovered that she had drawn blood.

The older cousins had been thrown into confusion by Delia Robierre's cry. Yvette held her hands to her cheeks and shouted incessantly, "Come back, come back!" Francesca, suddenly plunging into action, took a few determined steps forward. But Isabella grabbed her arm. "You can't!" she said, her voice wobbly with distress. "You know you're terrible at swimming through big waves. We'll lose you too!" Then she turned to her brother. "Tom!" she cried. "Go on out there. You're our best swimmer. Go now—quickly!"

But Tom wore the same crumpled red face his sister Delia was wearing. He didn't show it to us at first. Then he turned his head, and we saw the tears streaming into his mouth. "I can't go!" he said, his voice cracking. "Somebody else save her. Please, somebody save her!"

Afterward I remembered this moment with awe—the great,

invincible Tom, who had honored us by giving up a walk with Lorelei to spend a day at the beach, collapsed in tears. He was so distraught that no one thought of pressing him further, but his appeal to the others made my terror rise to an intolerable pitch. I was convulsed by sobs when I heard Philip say, "It's okay, Tom. Don't worry about it. I'm going." He had stripped off his shirt and was already knee-deep in the water.

"But you're a worse swimmer than Tom!" Isabella exclaimed.

"Do you think I'm going to let my sister drown?" He spoke over his shoulder, his voice loaded with hostility. She didn't answer, and he stepped forward and was immediately buffeted by an oncoming wave.

Philip's lithe brown body was not built to withstand an ocean stirred up by a storm, and he lost his agility in the water. It made no sense that he, of all the older cousins, was the first to go out to Delia, but he had spoken with such assurance that the rest were temporarily immobilized. Isabella stared at him as he flailed in the waves and then put an arm around her sister, whose voice, hoarse and despairing, was still flying over the water.

In the end it was Charlie who rescued Cordelia. While Philip battled the surf in front of us, trying to break through into the trough where she was whirling, Charlie took off his shirt and ran down the beach so that he could take advantage of the undertow's current. Then he plunged in, forging through the water like an elephant shouldering its way through underbrush. He came to Delia, who had exhausted herself by fruitless struggling, and, wrapping one arm around her, dog-paddled to shore.

When he finally staggered with her onto the beach, we crowded toward them in such a rush that we almost knocked them down. Delia Robierre was the first. Even before Delia Ybarra's feet left the water, her counterpart had embraced her nearly to the point of suffocation. Charlie tugged them up onto dry sand and then let them fall over each other in earnest. They were soon swamped by the rest of us. Delia, still coughing water, was hugged by Francesca, Yvette, even Philip, who had splashed out of the waves with some difficulty. We were giddy from feeling so many emotions in such a short time and hardly knew what we were saying. I hung on to one of Delia's cold hands, unwilling to push myself forward but also unwilling to let go of my connection with her.

Through the uproar, however, released at last from the nauseating ache of fear, I kept an eye on Tom and Philip. Neither seemed to be embarrassed by their dramatic failures. After the initial clamor over the rescue, Philip wrapped a towel around his waist and rubbed another through his hair, staring at the sea. Tom, meanwhile, was directing the celebration of Delia's safety. His tears had disappeared as if they had never been, and the horrible squashed-tomato appearance of his face had vanished. He and Isabella, always the leaders in shows of emotion, were now heading the pack in hilarious joy. The Delias themselves were already laughing, the rush of relief making them all the more exuberant.

We encountered Fisher halfway to Shorecliff. He called out something about a kingfisher, but his ornithological surprises were lost in the explosion of explanations that greeted him. Unshaken by the emotions we had just lived through, he seemed like an alien creature, strangely calm even after hearing about Delia's ordeal. His cool blue eyes widened in surprise and sympathy, and he patted her shoulder, but it was nothing to the typhoon of love and relief the rest of us felt.

The aunts, on the other hand, reacted with a satisfactory amount of panic. They clutched at Delia, who was becoming displeased at so much manhandling, reprimanded Francesca for negligence, and scolded all of us for going to the beach so soon after a storm.

"It's a good thing Loretta wasn't here," Rose said to my mother over Delia's head. "She probably would have gone down there with them and been drowned herself."

My mother smiled and stroked Delia's hair. Francesca explained how manfully Charlie had plunged into the water to get Delia, and he stood to one side and blushed. It was odd—before we entered the house, I had been imagining how we would describe Philip's self-sacrificing efforts or Tom's flurry of tears. But adults can be disconcertingly concrete. The aunts were concerned with one thing only—Delia's safety—and they did not care about the other extraordinary events that had accompanied her brush with death. Charlie was the one who had saved her from the sea, and thus, in their eyes, he was the only other cousin who had played an important role. But I was already marshaling the bits and pieces from the shore that had imprinted themselves on my mind: the white smudge of Cordelia's face in the waves, Delia Robierre's piercing cries, Tom's tears, Philip's struggles—these isolated fragments became my memory of the disaster.

The aunts were so alarmed by Delia's near-calamity that they tried to ban us from the shore. The attempt led to a family argument of the type I had encountered on first arriving that summer. Once again the cousins lined themselves along the walls of the kitchen, and once again the aunts ranged themselves around the table. Aunt Edie, luckily for us, was confined to her bed with a headache, and the uncles were on another hunting trip—or maybe they were out visiting Condor.

Aunt Rose opened the discussion with typical bluntness. "It's obvious to us," she said, "that you children are not as responsible as we thought you were. Of course, as the oldest, Francesca ought to have been keeping an eye on you, but we can't put all the blame on her. You're all equally guilty—especially you, Cordelia—and none of you are allowed to go down to the shore again unless we're with you. Is that understood?"

"That's not fair!" Isabella cried, staring at her mother with horror in her eyes. "It was an accident—it doesn't mean we're not responsible."

"Charlie saved me," said Delia Ybarra. At this point she was enjoying the spotlight cast on her. The terror had worn off, and all that was left was the glamour of nearly dying.

"Yes, Charlie saved her, which proves that we are responsible," Francesca said. "Besides, you can't take the beach away from us. If we can't go down there and swim, we'll have absolutely nothing to do and we'll go insane."

"That's absurd," Rose snorted. "There are plenty of things to do here. You're all spoiled and willful, that's what the problem is. A more disgusting pack of children I never saw. You're not going."

"Now, Rose," my mother said. She glanced around at us, smiling. "Of course you're not disgusting, my dears. A little headstrong, perhaps."

"Some of us don't even go in the water," Yvette said from her corner. In fact Yvette swam often, but she was also skilled in debate and knew that the best tactic was to draw the aunts' attention away from the water. "I do nothing but sunbathe down there, and there's nothing dangerous in that."

"How about our games?" asked Tom. "The sand is the softest surface around. If we played catch on the grass, we'd get cut up in no time. The shore is the safest place."

"And what about Pamela and Richard?" Francesca added, bringing us in without compunction. "You know how they love to go off and collect shells or whatever it is they do. You never go in the water, do you, kids? You're too scared."

"As they should be," said Aunt Rose.

"That's my point," said Francesca. "They know better than to charge into the ocean. Just because Delia is an idiot doesn't mean the rest of us should suffer."

"I'm not an idiot!" Delia cried. "You were yelling at me, and I was trying to get away from you!"

"I was telling her not to play so close to the water—wasn't I? Wasn't I?" Francesca waved her hands at the other cousins, and they nodded. "If you tell us the beach is forbidden," she went on, "how are you going to keep us from going?"

"Let's not descend to the level of fighting dogs," Aunt Margery said, frowning at her. "It's not a question of us keeping you prisoner, Francesca. We're worried about your safety, as we have to be, being your aunts. You don't have to snap at us and be rude."

"If you don't want to keep us prisoners, then let us go to the goddamn beach!"

"Francesca, you are out of line." Rose stood up and put her hands on the table, looking at us from under lowered eyebrows. "The final word about the shore is that you have betrayed the trust we placed in you. If Loretta were here, she would be taking off her belt right now. Thank God she isn't and has been spared the terror of hearing that her own daughter nearly drowned."

"She wouldn't be taking off her belt," Cordelia interrupted.

Rose, disconcerted, broke off her speech. "What?"

"I said she wouldn't be taking off her belt. She never beats us."

"That was metaphorical, Delia. The point is I'm glad she's not here to witness how disgracefully her children are behaving. The final word on the beach—"

"The final word on the beach," said my mother, cutting in, "is that you must all give us your solemn words of honor not to go anywhere near the water when there's an undertow as bad as there was today. Do all of you swear?"

Aunt Rose was still gaping impotently as we raised our right hands and swore. I don't think my mother smoothed things over like that simply to gain our adoration, though that was a by-product of her diplomacy. She realized what Rose on her high ground couldn't see, which was that if the shore were denied us, a mutiny would not be long in the making. A vision had already sprung up in my head of Francesca sneaking down the stairs at night—or perhaps climbing down a ladder made of sheets from her bedroom window—and loping off to the beach by the light of the moon. The chaos resulting from such a rebellion would be irremediable. My mother the peacemaker had saved the day without allowing Aunt Rose to lose much face. We all admired her for that.

"Richard," she added, "it's especially important that you understand how serious this is. Do you know that if you go in the ocean after a storm, you could drown?"

I nodded, scowling at her implication that I was young enough to be so abysmally ignorant.

"Did you see what happened to Delia?"

"Yes, Mother, I saw it. I'm not a baby. I won't go near the water unless an older cousin is with me."

"The same goes for you, Pamela," Margery said.

Pamela nodded. "Richard and I prefer to go crabbing anyway," she said haughtily. There was something so assured in Pamela's poise that even though it was preposterously exaggerated, no one laughed when she made statements like that. I was grateful for her dignity because it allowed her to sail through difficult situations with ease, trailing me in her wake.

The conflict petered out after Pamela's remark, but I had been struck by my romantic image of Francesca skipping down to the beach in the moonlight. A week or so after the day Delia nearly drowned, I found myself in Tom and Philip's room, trying ineffectually to impress them. I had covered the topics of my telescope, my books, my position at school (beat-up dreamer, if the truth be known), and my dictionary. They remained unmoved. So I forged ahead: "Do you know what I think would be really neat? If Francesca and a bunch of you snuck out to the beach at night and went swimming in the moonlight. Wouldn't that be neat, guys? Wouldn't it?"

For the first time, Philip raised his head. Tom was more polite about appearing to pay attention to me, but now his eyes focused rather than remaining glazed in thought. "Sneak off to the shore and swim in the moonlight, you young delinquent?" he said. "It takes a criminal mind to think up shenanigans like that at your age."

"Sounds good to me," said Philip shortly.

"I wonder if Lorelei would come." Tom murmured this to himself, though both Philip and I heard him.

"I think that would be a two-person-only venture, then," Philip said.

"You're right. And Francesca has to be in on this. Meaning that Charlie has to be in on it"—they grinned—"and Isabella, of course. Who else?"

"Yvette's a priss."

"The Delias are unsafe."

"Fisher would be bored."

"No, he wouldn't be bored. I think the idea would appeal to him. And how about this guy?" Tom indicated me with his head.

"He thought of it," Philip said, shrugging. He didn't smile, but I had learned by this time that Philip didn't always express affection directly. His eyes were soft as he looked at me, and I beamed.

"How about Pamela?" Tom asked me. "She's your girlfriend, buddy. What do you say? Do we bring her?"

"She's not my *girlfriend*," I said, reddening and tapping the floor with one toe. "But I think she'd like to come."

"That's settled," said Tom. "We'll do it tonight. It's almost a full moon—that's good enough, isn't it, Richard?"

I was thrilled to have Tom asking for my advice, as if what I thought mattered. I told him that a near-full moon would be just as good, and Tom and Philip began discussing the details of the expedition. I preferred to gloat alone in my bedroom, glorying in being the creator of a daring plan.

The chosen cousins—handpicked in a private council at which I, for once, was present—were soon informed, and Tom decided on one o'clock in the morning as the best hour to start. The adults would have gone to bed by then. We would meet in the main hall by the phone booth.

Francesca, when Tom told her about it, turned to me with glowing eyes and said, "He's a boy after my own heart." Her enthusiasm, I suspect, was partly due to an incident from the day before that had provided great amusement for us and horror for the aunts. A bunch of cousins, including Pamela and me, had somehow washed up in the sunny ground-floor room at the back of the house where the aunts liked to read. We kids rarely wasted time in the house when we weren't in our bedrooms or in the kitchen, but today we had taken over the back room and were all laughing at Charlie's clowning.

On the spur of the moment, Francesca, who had been leaning on the back of Charlie's chair, skirted around and threw herself into his lap. She had no motivation for the move, other than an instant's whim. She settled herself like an affectionate kitten—though Charlie must have felt more as if he were handling a full-grown lynx—and twined her arms around his neck. Charlie kept his eyes locked on hers, a dazed smile on his face, afraid to move lest she dart away. It was all lighthearted, but with Francesca one could never quite predict what would happen. The rest of us were mesmerized. She stroked Charlie's hair, drew one finger down his throat to his collar, threw back her head as if she were in a Victorian melodrama, and then, with an impish giggle, curled over him so that her forehead was touching his, her wonderful hair falling down to hide their faces.

At this moment Aunt Edie and Aunt Margery entered the room. To be fair to them, Francesca's position was entirely brazen, and they had not seen her teasing expression before she engulfed Charlie. With a batlike screech, Aunt Edie clutched her throat and staggered backward—in her way she was as accomplished in melodrama as Francesca. Margery, with less show but more force, let out one shocked "Oh!" and marched up to the pair of them.

Francesca dissolved into gales of laughter. She exchanged a glance of incredulous delight with Charlie and then, leaping up from his lap, mimed embarrassment, replicating Aunt Edie's gestures with uncanny accuracy. The rest of us roared along with her.

Five minutes later, hauled before a tribunal of aunts in the kitchen, Francesca was no longer laughing.

"Your behavior is a disgrace!" Margery said. "You and Charlie are close relations, and intimacy of that kind is completely inappropriate."

"It's simply revolting!" Edie gasped from her chair in the corner.

"Oh, please," Francesca scoffed. "We weren't doing anything, for God's sake. We were just joking around."

"In front of the children?" Aunt Rose asked, taking command. "In front of Pamela and Richard? I don't want you acting as an example even for Isabella, who's old enough to realize that you believe you're 'just joking around,' as you say. I'm afraid to think what Charlie imagines about your intentions."

"The fact is you're utterly out of hand!" Margery exclaimed. She was getting more and more worked up. "Maybe you don't grasp the implications of your actions, but that's no excuse. It's not correct behavior for a young woman!"

"What's not correct," Francesca snapped back, "is boxing up eleven kids in an abandoned house in the middle of nowhere for an entire summer."

From my position outside the screen door, glued to the side of the house in my eagerness to hear every word, I blazed with admiration for her. She showed such magnificent bravery, standing up to the most fearsome aunts without a tremor. The scolding ended indecisively, but the confrontation left Francesca itching for further rebellion, and I was not surprised the next day when she threw herself into my scheme for a late-night visit to the shore.

The only hitch in our plans was a predictable one. Pamela did not succeed in leaving her bedroom without waking Yvette, and hisses of outrage broke out in consequence. The noise woke Delia and Delia, who appeared and demanded explanations. The boys, clad only in their bathing suits, with towels draped over their shoulders, paced back and forth and whispered to each other.

"What are the girls doing, anyway?"

"They blew it. Yvette and the Delias are coming."

"Who cares? Let's go."

"Sure you want to come, Fisher?"

"Yes, I think it will be exciting."

"Me too, buddy. Has someone gotten Francesca?"

"She's probably down by the phone booth."

"Shut up, you idiot! What the hell are you doing?"

"I stubbed my toe!"

"Shut up!"

"Both of you be quiet."

The girls emerged. Luckily Yvette, though quick to voice complaints, did not feel overly resentful at having been initially left out of the plan. The thrill of sneaking through the house spread even to her, and one of her rare smiles burst into bloom as we crept down the stairs. "Not bad, Richard," she whispered.

We found Francesca, as predicted, fidgeting by the phone booth. "It took you long enough," she growled, stalking to the door. "At this rate Aunt Edie will be coming down in her swimming tent, ready for a morning dip. Are you ready?"

We followed her. She set off at a run across the grass, reveling in the brisk, salty breeze that rushed in off the ocean. I had never been out so late before, and I was stunned by the transformation of the house, the lawn, the woods, the fence. The moon was rising and hovered, enormous, over the cliff, as if someone had cut out a gigantic circle of tinfoil and hung it in the sky. The light silvered all the blades of grass on the lawn. It changed Shorecliff from an old, peeling country house into a shining treasure box.

Pamela stayed with me; I think even she was overwhelmed. As we moved away from the house, she made a wide-eyed comment that I've always remembered. "It's like a different place," she said. "And what if it really is, and we've been magically transported here?"

The others galloped over the grass, exulting in the mystic sense of freedom that fast movement gains in darkness. I watched them, nine dark silhouettes fanning out over the grass like a handful of black spiders sent scurrying across a floor. Francesca's hair streamed behind her, Isabella's giraffe-like limbs could be recognized at a glance, and the two Delias ran hand in hand, urging each other to greater speeds. Eventually Pamela and I sprinted after them. There was no sound other than the wind blustering past us and the waves, as always, crashing against the cliff. We didn't want to speak until we had reached the safety of the shore, where even with their superhuman hearing the aunts wouldn't be able to detect our triumphant yells.

Once at the beach, the majority of the cousins careened, shouting, into the frigid water. Fisher stayed on the dunes and admired the scene from above. Yvette sat to one side and covered herself with sand. Pamela went to join her, but I was surrounded by my older cousins, lifted up, splashed with water, pounded until my back was sore, grinned at by Isabella, laughed at by Francesca. What heaven that night swim was! They were all so grateful to me for coming up with the plan, and so pleased and amused that I had been the one to think of it, that they showered me with praise. Of the nightly excursions that followed, there was not one that matched the innocent pleasure of our first venture into the nocturnal world, nor one that went so smoothly—with no discoveries, no recriminations, no lost secrets, no betrayals.

When at last we wandered back to the house—at a leisurely pace now; none of us was eager to return to bed—we found Shorecliff still undisturbed, the windows as dark as before and the door welcoming because it was closed. We had spent more than two hours at the shore, and the moon was a distant quarter dollar in the sky. The night was now simply your average summer night, splendid only in that it was warm and caressing on the skin.

We were covered in sand, and I'm sure that all of us suffered from sand in our beds for many days afterward, though Isabella kindly came to my room the next day and shook out my sheets for me. We had no idea what to do with our towels and suits, not wanting to hang them on the clothes line. Eventually we hung them out our windows, and Aunt Edie on her early morning walk found three crumpled towels at the back of the house, where they had landed after falling from the sills in the night. They were the only signs of our escapade, and she mentioned them at breakfast with the mildest of acerbic comments.

On our way up the stairs there was a moment of panic. From Uncle Kurt's room, the door of which was next to the stairwell, we suddenly heard a frantic shout. All of us froze, each on a different stair, a line of eleven sandy children. Finally Tom mouthed, "He talks in his sleep." We hovered uncertainly. Then the strange cry sounded again, and we were convinced: only sleep could distort his voice so much. Smiles rippled down the line, and we continued onward to the safety of our bedrooms.

This was when I first learned that Uncle Kurt talked in his sleep. Among the other cousins it became a joke to decipher his slurred and anxious cries. We knew he had been having a nightmare, but the word itself had been almost incomprehensible. Tom's hypothesis was that Uncle Kurt had been crying, "I can't see! I can't see!" Fisher suggested that it might have been "Tennessee!" but this possibility was discarded with great scorn and hilarity.

In fact only I knew the truth behind that scream, and I had known it at once, when I was standing on the stairs. I never told anyone, though, and I never felt any pleasure in possessing the key to Kurt's nightmare. As I stood by my window at the end of the night, replaying the events in my head, it bothered me that the expedition had ended on such an unsettling note. I didn't want to be reminded of Uncle Kurt's suffering when I was surrounded by my admiring and admired cousins. But I could not forget Uncle Kurt's voice as he shouted that word: "Hennessey! Hennessey!"

It was only when I heard him yelling his friend's name that I realized something must have happened to Hennessey. Uncle Kurt must have had a reason for never mentioning him in casual conversation, never bringing him, now that the war was over, to visit us at Shorecliff. I couldn't work up the courage to ask him for the story behind Hennessey's absence, the story in which his last illusions of war's glory must have been torn down, and he never told me about it. But I was convinced after that night that Hennessey had died an awful death and that Uncle Kurt felt responsible for it.

Over the course of the summer, Fisher's suggestion of "Tennessee!" became a sort of battle cry among the older cousins. They would bellow it at times of excitement, as a cheer or as a shout of derision. It became distorted even further as it passed into their vocabulary, and by the time it was an established joke, it had lost most of its similarity to Uncle Kurt's sleeping cry. But toward the end of the summer, when he heard them shouting it—by sheer chance he had never heard it before—Uncle Kurt looked up from the newspaper he was reading with a frantic, almost angry look in his eyes that changed after a moment to bewilderment and then to pain. Tom saw his expression and later mentioned it to the other cousins, and from that point on they always made certain Kurt wasn't within hearing distance before they shouted the word. With a constraint placed upon it, the joke lost its spontaneity, and "Tennessee!" died a rapid death. I never forgot it, though, and I'm sure Uncle Kurt didn't either. It must be strange to hear one's darkest nightmare revived in bright sunlight in a joyous cry.

5

A Day with Fisher

As one might imagine, since there were eleven children in the house, I never got much time alone with individual cousins. With Pamela, of course, I spent hours in that children's play that loses its flavor entirely when discussed in later years, and I would have occasional conversations with Tom or Philip and quiet moments with Isabella, but for the most part group activities were the order of the day. While this was exciting, it was also exhausting, and it made those rare hours with a single person times to remember. Fisher was an especially elusive cousin, and there was only one day that I spent with him alone.

Fisher initiated it. A fount of kindliness lurked behind those dreamy eyes, and it's possible he had noticed how frantically I tried to be part of the group, how ardently I admired my older cousins. That makes it sound as if he were condescendingly giving me some time with the great man, but Fisher would never have thought of himself that way. It's more likely that he simply felt like giving me a nice day with a friendly confidant. At any rate, one morning after we'd been at Shorecliff for about a month, he showed up at my bedroom door.

"Hi there, Richard," he said. "What's cooking?"

Tom had gone off with Lorelei for the day, and Francesca had decided to organize an outdoor game in which I was not invited to participate. I told him, sulkily no doubt, what Francesca's plans were, and he replied, "But what are your plans, boy scout?"

"I don't have any plans," I said, trying to make this sound deliberate. "I might find Pamela and go somewhere with her."

"Any interest in going somewhere with me?"

I stared at him. "What, you mean like a walk or something?"

"Yeah, that's right. I thought we could make a day of it. You know where I've been wanting to walk to? The Stephenson farm, where Lorelei lives. She's always talking about it"—an exaggeration; Lorelei didn't "always talk" about anything—"but we've never seen it. What do you say?"

"I'd love to. You mean just me?"

"I figured you'd make a good companion. You're a good walker, right? And you could bring that telescope of yours." He nodded to the telescope lying on my bedside table, and I clutched it eagerly. The offer was too good to be true, and my one thought was to set off immediately before he could change his mind.

When Fisher made plans, he made them well. He meant it when he said he wanted to make a day of it, and on our way out through the kitchen he asked my mother for a bag of sandwiches and some ice water in bottles. I was amazed. Picnics were usually huge expeditions, and here was a picnic being prepared for just the two of us.

"I think it's a lovely idea, Fisher," my mother said.

"I'll put some cookies in," Margery added.

They beamed at us. We had won full approval from the adult sector. This sort of activity—demure walks in small groups—was their rarely fulfilled ideal of cousinly exercise.

Fisher and I headed west over the grass toward the belt of woods separating Shorecliff from the Stephenson farm. Our rambling walk through the trees and into the fields beyond took much longer than I had anticipated, though Fisher probably had the day planned from the first minute. His leisurely pace covered more ground than it appeared to. He held the lunch bag in one hand, swinging it with every step, and most of the time he didn't talk to me. When we were in the woods he kept his head tilted upward to see any birds that might fly overhead. One time he grabbed my arm and stood stock-still, and we listened to a birdcall that sounded to me like all the other birdcalls surrounding us.

"Gosh!" he said, after we had stood for over a minute. "Wow!"

"What was it, Fisher?"

"I don't know. I've never heard it before. Wow! I'll have to ask Uncle Cedric. I bet he'll know." It was the first I'd heard about Uncle Cedric knowing birdcalls. Fisher spent a lot of the afternoon whistling under his breath and trying to imitate the string of notes we'd heard. By the evening he said he had messed it up so much that he would never be able to reproduce it, and sure enough when he whistled it for Uncle Cedric, all he got was a chuckle. "The call of a lesser nuthatch," Cedric said, "one Fisher Wight by name."

The woods between the Stephensons and us were mostly pine, but there were patches of maple and oak and a surprising number of enormous old beeches. The strip was wider than I had thought it would be, and when we were in the middle we couldn't see Condor's cottage, even though we knew it was only about a quarter mile north of us. That isn't surprising in a wood, but I had been convinced we would see it.

"Are we lost?" I asked.

"No, we're not lost. On our way back we'll stop at Condor's and say hello, what do you say? Maybe Uncle Eberhardt will be there too."

I nodded. Condor was an appealing but threatening proposition, and Uncle Eberhardt only increased the stakes, but if Fisher was game, then I was too.

We emerged beside the Stephenson fields close to noon. The woods were on slightly higher ground than the farm, so when we stood on the grassy strip beside them, we could see large swaths of cultivated land undulating into the distance. It was a disconcerting view, as if somehow it were being changed and expanded in a funhouse mirror but we couldn't see the trick. Right in front of us the crop was green and small, with wide dirt alleys between the rows that we could easily walk along. Further west was an impenetrable field of wheat rustling in the breeze, and to our right lay a plowed field dotted with haystacks. Across that was a little farmhouse next to a big barn complex with multiple silos.

"Isn't it wonderful?" Fisher said. "I love to see land unrolled like that, as if someone were showing me a giant map. Doesn't it make you feel powerful?" He glanced at me as I nodded. Then he said, "How's your head? Is the sun too strong?"

"No, I like it. Can we walk across the field?"

"Let's have lunch here."

We sat on the grass, half in the shade of two maples towering above us, and Fisher laid out our sandwiches and cookies on the linen napkin my mother had provided as if we were sitting down to a formal meal. He unscrewed the tops of both water bottles and put one in front of each of us.

"How's that for a meal?"

"The best I ever saw."

"I'm just as hungry, pal."

As we ate, Fisher and I had a philosophical conversation. Normally he wasn't one to talk, but that day he plied me with questions. No one could help being comfortable with Fisher, but at the same time I felt tense because I wanted so much to give him the right answers. I remember thinking, "I don't even know what he means," and then taking a stab at it, looking at him to make sure I'd said what he wanted. From his expression you would have thought I was the perfect companion, but I couldn't feel the same confidence in myself.

"What's your opinion of all this, Richard?" he asked, munching.

"All what?"

"Oh, all this—Shorecliff, the family, your crazy cousins. You like it?"

"Sure I do. I love it! Being here with all of you is the greatest thing that's ever happened to me."

"Really? Are you having fun?"

"Yes, every day!"

"You don't go to boarding school, do you?"

"No." I knew he did, but I was too shy to ask him about it. I couldn't tell whether his question meant that I didn't know what I was missing or that I didn't know how much I should appreciate the summer.

"I wish I could remember that birdcall." He spent a few minutes whistling and then glanced at me again with the endearing, hangdog smile that charmed everyone. "Sometimes I wish I could stay in the woods all day with some kind of sound recorder and get all the calls. Wouldn't that be great?"

"I guess," I said. "I don't know a lot of birdcalls."

"But doing something like that is just an example. I mean really focusing on something until you understand it—even if it's just a little thing."

I had no idea what he meant and offered only silence as an answer. After a few moments, looking around the fields, I was inspired to ask what I thought was an adult question. "So what do you think of Lorelei?" I asked, taking a manly sip of water.

"Lorelei? I think she's very nice. I'm glad Tom is friends with her."

"She doesn't talk much."

"Neither do I. Neither do you, for that matter." He smiled at me, and I pondered the idea that I might be a silent type.

"Richard, doesn't it seem like this summer is going by too fast?"

"How many more weeks?"

"Oh, thousands. But I mean, here we are, and the days keep going by. I always think the future is so far away, but one day I'll wake up and there it will be. What then, buddy?"

"I don't know. What do you think will happen?"

"Well, you know, one day I made this carving in Dad's workshop. At least, I wanted to do this carving, and of course it didn't look at all the way I wanted, but it was supposed to be this man stepping out of a patch of woods and coming up against a big wall—bam, right in front of him. Sort of like us coming out of these woods, only instead of fields you have to picture a wall. A nice wall, maybe a brick wall or one of those Italian walls that you can picture around a villa or something. And in the wall there was supposed to be a door, a little curved door in the wall. Can you picture it?"

"Yes," I said, mystified.

"Well, there you go. The future seems like that to me sometimes, a mysterious door in a wall. You don't have to open it now, but someday you'll have to because there won't be anywhere else to go, and who knows what's on the other side? It might even be disappointing." He paused. "Of course the carving didn't come out. Dad says you have to be trained to carve pictures like that. He says it's a form of sculpture. I think he likes me to do it, but he also says it would be more practical for me to stick to furniture. I hate the lathe, though. Have you ever used a lathe?"

"No."

"Everyone says it's so satisfying and smooth. I think it feels like cheating."

"Oh."

"But it's no good telling you that if you've never used one. Someday you'll have to come visit, and then Dad and Charlie and I can show you around the shop. Charlie's really good, you know. Better than I am."

"I bet he's not."

Fisher grinned at me. "He's got four more years of experience, so of course he is. You want to keep going?"

"Where are we going to go?"

"Oh, I thought we could wander through this field toward the farmhouse. Maybe we could go visit Lorelei."

"She's with Tom. I saw them by the cliff when we were leaving the house."

"Oh, that's right, I remember. Well, let's go through the field anyway, to explore." Fisher stood up, packed up our lunch materials, and headed down one of the dirt alleys in the field nearest us. I was quiet, thinking about our conversation. It didn't make much sense to me, but nevertheless it left a vivid impression, as if I had been presented with a view into a box that had always before been locked. I couldn't understand what I'd seen, but I had still gotten the chance to look, and it made me feel grown-up and unsettled.

We'd walked about halfway through the field, and I was wondering if it would be acceptable for me to say that I felt like going back, when Fisher turned to me and said, "Let's give that old telescope a try. Since we have it, we might as well use it."

I had been carrying the telescope in my hand, its brass cylinder becoming warm and sweaty in my grasp. I gave it to him now, after wiping it on my shirt. He swept the far horizon over the wheat field and then gave it to me.

"It's an excellent instrument. Did your father give it to you?"

"My mother," I replied, holding the telescope to my eye.

"Is your father ever coming up here to visit?"

"I hope not." I didn't want to talk about my father, but I also didn't want to tell Fisher not to talk about him, so I remained silent and hoped he would get the message.

I examined the farmhouse through the telescope and then moved it in a long arc across the plowed field to look at the haystacks. At the base of one of them, indiscernible to us without the aid of the telescope, Tom and Lorelei were sitting side by side, huddling together to keep in the shade of the stack. Tom had his arm around Lorelei, and she was half looking at him and half looking down. She had on a bright green peasant skirt. As I got them into focus, Tom leaned over and started kissing her. I watched for five seconds and then felt scared. My heart started pounding.

"There are Tom and Lorelei," I said, handing the telescope to Fisher as if including him in the viewing would make it less of a violation. "They're over there under that haystack. We can't see them without the telescope because of the sun."

"I don't see them," said Fisher, swinging the telescope. "Where are—oh, I see. Look at that! I didn't know they were coming back to the farm." He watched in silence for a moment and then let out a low, knowing laugh that made me instantly jealous. I wanted to take the telescope, and I also wanted to interrogate him. I had never thought of Fisher in connection with sex before.

"I guess we should leave them alone, boy scout. Let's go back, what do you say?"

He gave me the telescope. Of course after he had said we should leave them alone, I couldn't use it again, but I kept my eyes riveted on the haystack in question.

"Let's go visit Condor. Come on, Richard."

On our return to the woods we walked in single file. I couldn't bring myself to forget about Tom and Lorelei, and I kept turning around in a futile effort to see them. My interest in Fisher, however, revived once we reached the trees. As we strolled toward Condor's cottage, he entertained me with an extensive nature lesson, sometimes jokingly imitating a naturalist instructing his pupil, sometimes lapsing into his normal tones and telling me about the lives of birds and insects with as much excitement as I would have used when telling my friends about my cousins. The lesson made me love Fisher more than ever. I was filled with envy at the fact that he had another, fully satisfactory world to retire into when ours became too troublesome.

Condor's cottage was a dark building of weathered wood and black roof shingles. It was one story, and though it had many windows, it stood in the midst of a dense group of tall pines and thus was always shadowy inside. The cottage was an ideal setting for Condor, not to mention Uncle Eberhardt. The two men were about the same age and entirely disparate in size. Whereas Uncle Eberhardt, with the voluminous black cape on his back, seemed like a withered bat about to drop from its perch, Condor was a giant with the chest of an ox. He had so many muscles, and they were so crabbed from years of labor, that he appeared to have no neck, an enormous humpback, and spindly legs under his gargantuan torso. Yet in spite of these deformities he did not look like a hideous monster but rather like a mythic hero, aged now and not well enough to go on the road in search of hydras and sea monsters, but still a man of unlimited physical ability. His face was reddened and cracked, his features squashed into the center of it. His eyes were a penetrating blue. Francesca once surprised me by saying that Condor as a young man must have been devastatingly handsome. I'm sure he was, but to me it seemed like sacrilege, even in thought, to deprive him of his age and wisdom.

Condor and Uncle Eberhardt were inseparable. They were almost as bad as the Delias, and from what my mother told me, they had been like that for decades. She could not remember a summer when it had not been most probable for Eberhardt to be found in Condor's cottage. Condor had been hired by my grandparents when he was still a young man and they were a newly married couple, giddily wealthy, thrilled to be buying an extravagant summerhouse. In that same conversation about Condor, Francesca declared that Grandmother Hatfield had had an affair with him and that Uncle Kurt and my mother were the result. This was patently absurd, since both of them were Hatfields to the bone, but the suggestion unnerved me, so much so that Isabella beckoned me away to assure me that Francesca was an oversexed maniac who thought about nothing but her own insatiable lust. Not surprisingly, this explanation did not enlighten me. The word "oversexed" wasn't even in my dictionary, though at that point in the summer any word with "sex" in it triggered an alarm bell in my mind.

When Fisher and I arrived at the cottage, we found the door locked and the curtains drawn across the windows. Fisher knocked at the door, and from within we heard Eberhardt's cracked, shrill voice shouting at us. "Keep away, whoever you are! If it's one of you damn kids, go shove your snout somewhere else. You're not wanted." A low rumble sounded in response to this—Condor's voice was unintelligible through the closed door. Then the knob rattled, the bolt shot back, and Condor appeared in the doorframe, bending to fit his head under the lintel, squinting from the sunlight. He was wearing, as he always wore, a spotlessly pressed dress shirt of a delicate pastel hue; that day it was mint green. I have no idea why Condor insisted on wearing the clothes a rich tycoon might have worn on his yacht in the Caribbean, but whenever he wasn't working, he changed into his duck trousers and Oxford shirts. He had a Panama hat for the sun and a sporty fisherman's sweater for colder days.

"Hello, boys," he growled. "How are you today?"

"We're very well, thank you," said Fisher. "We just came to visit you and Uncle Eberhardt. If you're busy, we can leave."

"We're not exactly busy, but we have a surprise that I'm sure you'll like."

Condor gestured us into the room. In the far corner, lit by a feeble desk lamp, Eberhardt crouched on a rickety stool, staring into a box on the floor. He looked more like a bat than ever, his knees sticking up to his chest and his elbows out at his sides.

"Well, you're in now, aren't you?" he sneered when Condor shut the door behind us, cutting out almost all the light. "You'll have to share in our little surprise. You like surprises, boy?" he asked me.

I couldn't decide whether or not he had really forgotten my name. "Yes, Uncle Eberhardt," I said.

"You'll love this one. Condor found it in the woods. It's not a good sign. A very bad sign. We're going to have to kill it." He leaned forward when he said these last words and grinned at us, revealing teeth which, in spite of the fact that he showed enthusiasm about food only during the dessert course, had remained straight and healthy into his old age. The combination of his thin, cracked lips and gleaming horse teeth was very disconcerting.

Even Fisher was taken aback by Eberhardt's latest pronouncement. He stuttered, "K-kill what, Uncle Eberhardt?"

Eberhardt let out a high-pitched chuckle and bent over the box. "Kids!" he muttered.

"We're not going to kill it," Condor reassured us. "Eberhardt knows that perfectly well. Would you like to see? I found it in the woods. I think its mother and siblings have all been killed or starved to death. Old Farmer Stephenson may have shot the mother."

He gestured toward the box, and Fisher and I, sidling around to avoid touching Eberhardt's cape, peered in. Cowering at the bottom was a minuscule red fox, clearly a young kit, its huge, sail-like ears flattened over its back; you could see the blood vessels in them through the skin. The kit was staring up at us with widened yellow eyes, terrified to the point of petrification. I didn't think it was cute at all. I had no impulse to pet it or goggle over it. The expression in its eyes made me feel lost and angry. Uncle Kurt had recently told me the story of being surrounded in the forest by German soldiers, and it occurred to me that he and his companions must have felt the way the little fox felt now.

"Are you going to set him free?" I said. I had to speak around a lump in my throat, which was extremely embarrassing, and I backed away so that I wouldn't have to look into the fox's eyes anymore.

"Of course not!" Eberhardt snapped. "We've only just caught it!"

"It would starve in the wild," Condor said. "And besides, Farmer Stephenson is quick on the trigger and just as likely to shoot kits as vixens. It's better if we keep it here and raise it as a tame fox. People do, you know. I've always wanted one."

I would have been more touched by this revelation of sentimentality in Condor if I hadn't bent forward just then to look at the fox again. "He's like..."

"Yes, what is he like, Richard?"

"He's like—a little lost soldier," I said, stammering because I was about to cry.

Fisher put his hand on my shoulder.

"Little Lost Soldier," Eberhardt repeated, scrutinizing me. "An interesting epithet. Little Lost Soldier. His name is Barnavelt—I named him the moment I saw him—but you've come up with a good secondary name. You may be a more worthwhile child than the rest of those louts." Fisher smiled at this, and Eberhardt, with his usual perspicacity, saw him do it. "You're not included," he said. "I've always known you were a bright boy. Don't think I don't notice just because I don't care."

"Thanks for that," Fisher answered. Sometimes he trod a surprising line between awkwardness and self-assurance.

"Now then, Richard," Condor said. "You were right in saying he's like a little soldier. That fox is a fighter, and he's not going to die of fright. He's scared now, but he's not going to be scared for long. You don't have to worry about that."

"But he's young!" I said. I wanted to add, "Like me."

"All soldiers are young," said Eberhardt. "Look at your Uncle Harold—picked off before he was out of his diapers, practically. Kurt came back still talking baby talk."

Condor took me by the hand—his own hand, the size of a small ham, engulfing mine—and led me into the tiny bedroom that opened off the main room. "You too, Fisher. And you, Eberhardt. Come in here. I'm going to show Richard something that I think will reassure him."

Eberhardt flapped a hand, but Condor repeated his request, and eventually the old man staggered into the bedroom with us and sat down on the bed. The fox was left alone in the living room. Condor went to the kitchen and came back with a saucer of milk. "I'm going to put this on the floor," he said to me, "and then I'm going to tip the box gently on its side. You see how long it takes the fox to find the milk. Hide behind the doorframe now."

We hid, and Condor in the main room set down the saucer and slowly tilted the box until it was lying on its side. I imagined the fox slithering down and watching his view change. Condor retreated into the bedroom, and we watched. For a few minutes nothing happened. Then we saw a little black nose surrounded by whiskers poking out of the box. It was followed by the whole foxy face, complete with outsized ears. The fox sniffed, still quivering, looking disproportionately small in the dark room. Another few minutes passed before it emerged from the box, but soon after that it crept up to the saucer, nudged at the blue china, and then lapped cautiously at the milk. After the first few laps it set to work in earnest, and we could see its little sides heaving. When it was finished and looking around the room, I said, "Now it will be cold."

"You're a natural caretaker, Richard. I'm planning to put a blanket on the bottom of that box so he can curl up at night. Are you satisfied now?"

"I guess so," I said, shrugging. But I wasn't really. I still thought there was something not very nice about the whole business. On the other hand, I had seen that the fox was eating on its own and becoming curious about its surroundings. The blank fear was gone, and I relaxed.

Fisher had been more impressed than I'd realized by the incident. "That was something!" he breathed, staring at the fox in awe. "That was something, all right! Did you see him lap up that milk? How old is he?"

"Oh, he's not an infant," said Condor. "I would say he's old enough to live without his mother but young enough to appreciate our help. How's that?"

"Ah, Barnavelt, my friend, you'll go far!" said Eberhardt, leaping off the bed. "You boys think I went round the bend long ago, but who has the fox now, eh? Who has the fox? That's what counts."

Eberhardt must have been experiencing senility that summer, but no one talked about it at the time, neither the children nor the adults. He was just Great-Uncle Eberhardt, difficult and eccentric and part of the family.

"Wait until the rest of them hear about this," said Fisher.

His comment brought back the complex world of cousins that we had left behind at Shorecliff. The day with Fisher and its discoveries—the fields, the haystack with its hidden occupants, the woods, the fox—had cleansed my mind momentarily of familial intrigue. But after he spoke I was enchanted by the idea of reporting our findings.

"Should we go back?" I asked.

"We'll go right now, if that's all right. Condor, Uncle Eberhardt?"

They waved us out. Barnavelt raced back to his box when we went through the room, and Condor insisted that we wait to open the door until he had lifted the box upright. In time, he said, he would arrange matters so that the fox would not have to be imprisoned every time someone wanted to use the door.

Our return through the woods and over the grass to Shorecliff held none of the peacefulness of the beginning of our expedition. Fisher was talking so fast about the fox that his words piled up on themselves—I'd never heard him so excited. I desperately wanted to be the one to tell the news, but I suspected that he wouldn't give me the chance. I was organizing the day in my mind and breaking it up into memorable episodes so that I could keep it all vivid. The lawn, abandoned in the languid hour before dinner, seemed mysterious and unfamiliar—our own private territory. As we walked the last stretch to the house, looking at the figures in the kitchen through the windows, I was filled with a sense of satisfaction. I had just had a marvelous time with someone I liked immensely. This was what a good day felt like.

I broke into a run, and Fisher obligingly followed suit. We galloped toward the back door, laughing in our exhilaration.

That was the last moment of the good day. The minute I stepped inside, I knew our timing was horribly off. Tension was crackling in the kitchen. All the aunts were there, but only a small assortment of cousins. Standing by the table were Pamela and Aunt Margery. It was strange enough for these two to be the focus of a crisis, but at Margery's first words I felt utterly bewildered. As she spoke Fisher skidded up behind me, almost pushing me into the room, and we stood like that, with the door open and mosquitoes buzzing in.

"You're ungrateful," Aunt Margery was saying. Her tone hit me like a ruler across the knuckles, and I felt my limbs tighten. All children recognize the feeling. It doesn't matter which adult is angry or why or at whom—your heart speeds up, your mood is shattered, and you feel dismal.

"I'm not ungrateful. Don't boss me around in front of everyone!" Pamela's face was pale, and there were tears in her eyes. I had never seen her emotional before, and I was astonished by the sight. I would almost not have recognized her except that she still held on to her overstated dignity.

"If you're not ungrateful, then why don't you eat your pie quietly without making offensive remarks?"

"I don't want to eat your stupid pie! I hate this family and all of its endless pies and dinners and lunches and breakfasts. Everything's awful!"

She turned and ran from the room. Everyone else tried to relax but couldn't. The fight wouldn't have seemed so terrible if it had involved someone other than Pamela, but it was painfully obvious that for her becoming upset was a self-betrayal.

"Does Pamela often get into states like this?" my mother asked Aunt Margery.

"Almost never," said Margery. "I don't know, Caroline." She sat down, and the cousins in the room—Isabella, Francesca, and Delia Robierre, if I remember correctly—beckoned for us to follow them out.

"What happened?" Fisher asked as we went up the stairs.

"Pamela started getting strange about Aunt Margery's pie," Isabella whispered. "She said she wouldn't eat it and that she hated the way Aunt Margery was always shoving sweets at us. I don't know what she was talking about."

"And then?"

"That's it. Then you came in and heard the rest."

"But that wasn't anything," said Fisher.

"I know, but that's all there was."

"You'd better go to her, Richard," said Francesca.

I thought I hadn't heard correctly. "Me?" I asked.

"Yes, of course. You two are always together. Go on up to her. Make sure Yvette isn't in the room—Yvette is sure to say something wrong—and then drag it out of her. She'll tell you what's going on."

"Maybe it's something serious," Delia said, her eyes wide. She was still too young to act older and wiser.

"Don't worry, Deals," said Isabella. "She'll be okay. Richard will see to it."

The responsibility had been placed on my shoulders, and they made an aisle so I could go up the stairs ahead of them. I hadn't had time yet to feel bitter about my obliterated good mood. I had a mission, and I hurried to carry it out. When I got to the room where Pamela and Yvette slept, I found the door partly open. Pamela was alone, crying facedown on her bed. I pushed past the door and crept up to her.

"Pamela?" I said.

"Go away," she replied, her voice muffled in blankets. There is something intolerable about hearing a sad voice muffled by a blanket. It makes you want to roll the person over and free the voice from its misery.

"What's wrong? Will you tell me?"

"No. You won't understand. Go away."

"Can't you explain it?" I ventured to sit on the bed, and she inched away from me toward the pillow.

"I'll be better in the morning," she said. Her voice now sounded snuffly and resigned.

I was itching to leave. "Did any of us do anything wrong?"

"Well, you obviously didn't. You were gone all day with Fisher."

"Did something happen today?"

"*No.* Go away."

"Should I bring someone in to apologize?"

"No! No one's done anything. It's me. I'm fine. Go away."

"Are you sure you won't tell me what happened?"

Abruptly she lifted her head so that I could see her face, now blotchy with tears, and shouted, "Isn't it obvious that I want to be left alone?"

That was enough to send me scuttling to the door, but it also wrung a flood of useless sympathy from me. I would have given anything to be able to comfort her. Seeing her ugly face was like a punch to the solar plexus.

There was nothing left to say, however. I slipped out, closing the door behind me, and went straight to my own room. The other cousins were waiting like sentinels at their bedroom doors, but I didn't say a word to them. It was clear that they had heard the interaction from the hall. I was embarrassed and defeated, and all I wanted was to get away from inquiring eyes.

My mother didn't come up to bid me good night that evening after dinner—an awkward and uncharacteristically quiet gathering—and I didn't go down to her room. I think the aunts had decided it was best to leave all of us alone. Consequently, I stood for nearly an hour at my open window, looking through my telescope at the moon, which was pale and uninteresting but better than the ceiling. What I resented most was that Pamela's inexplicable outburst had ruined my day with Fisher. Inevitably, whenever I thought of walking in the woods with him and seeing the Stephensons' farm, I would also remember Pamela and her tear-covered face. Her one little outburst had as much emotional clout as an entire day of happiness—that's what was so unfair. I suppose I wouldn't remember that summer at Shorecliff so well if it hadn't been for the bad times, but I wish I could remember only the moments of glory. Would they be any less glorious if they weren't shadowed by misery?

Luckily for my peace of mind, there were many days at Shorecliff—at least in the first half of the summer—that didn't end unsettlingly. On one marvelous occasion, not long after my walk with Fisher, the cousins closed the evening with a dance of joy, though we had dawdled through the earlier hours in ignorance of the holiday we were missing.

It was difficult to keep track of the days at Shorecliff. We had a number of clocks, some of them notoriously unreliable, but no calendars, and newspapers always arrived in a bunch a week late, when Aunt Margery drove to Pensbottom for supplies. The adults were usually better at remembering the date, but they were equally baffled when Uncle Kurt, one evening at the dinner table, said with a sudden grin, "Is anyone here aware of what day it is?" There was a chorus of "Well, let me see…" from the aunts and uncles. Then Kurt answered his own question: "The Fourth of July, of course!"

The room broke out in a deafening clamor. The Fourth of July, and we had wasted the whole day! Shock and chagrin rolled through the cousins. In New York the day was one of my favorites—swelteringly hot but filled with cheering crowds, the patter of firecrackers, and the rousing melodies of brass bands. At night fireworks would light up the sky over both rivers, so that nearly everyone in the city could catch a glimpse now and again.

Here in Shorecliff, we had heard not a peep. It had been a day like any other. Disappointment threatened to overwhelm me. Uncle Kurt was still talking, however. "The day may be over, but we've still got the evening. What's for dessert?" He glanced at the aunts.

"Ice cream," said Aunt Margery. "Caroline and I made it this morning."

"Fine. We'll take it out on the lawn. Go on, kids."

Obediently we trooped outside into the dusk, not sure what we were supposed to do when we got there other than slap mosquitoes. Aunt Margery and my mother scooped out the ice cream and handed bowls through the kitchen's screen door. We ate in a gloomy silence, broken every once in a while by Tom or Philip thinking of things we could have done that day but hadn't.

"I bet they were selling firecrackers in Pensbottom," said Tom.

"Hell, I bet they were selling bangsnaps and flags and watermelons and the whole works. Even a sleepy town like Pensbottom celebrates Independence Day."

Uncle Kurt emerged to find eleven long faces drooping over empty bowls. "Well, boys and girls," he said, still grinning. "Don't look so down. See what I've got?"

He held out a slim box. It took us several seconds to realize it held sparklers. Our moods revived as if we had taken a miracle cure. To a background of shouts and clucks from the aunts, we threw down the bowls and held out our hands.

I lurked in the rear of the crowd. I had seen sparklers, of course, but never held one, and the thought of handling a live firework gave me a sinking feeling. Nevertheless, the older boys were delighted, so of course I had to be too. With a succession of pops and sputterings, sparkler after sparkler bloomed into life. The cousins raced and jumped over the grass, the stars in their hands tracing red tangles in the air.

"Ready, Richard?" said Kurt. He bent down, gave me a stick,

and held a match to its end. "Keep it away from your face," he said, and my mother called out, "Don't go too close to the others, Richard!" I could hear the aunts murmuring more and more fearfully, though even they couldn't help commenting on the beauty of the scene—eleven giant fireflies dancing across the lawn.

Mine was the lowest to the ground and the shakiest. I was mesmerized by the bright, joyful violence of it, but visions of a burnt hand haunted me. I leaped here and there, wondering how long sparklers stayed lit and what would happen if I dropped mine.

Fortunately Uncle Kurt, as he so often did, divined what I was thinking. He came over and said, "How about letting me have a try, kiddo? Cedric and Frank are battling over the last one, so there's none for me." Gratefully I handed it over, and for the last three or four minutes of the fireworks' short lives, I could watch the cousins in peace as they twirled through the darkness, lit by showers of sparks.

6

Pensbottom

We had been at Shorecliff for a little over a month when an event occurred that involved, at first, only Charlie and Francesca. When I heard about it, I both hoped and feared that it had been inspired by the moonlight swim I had thought up. Neither Charlie nor Francesca would have deigned to tell me about it, but Isabella was in on the plan from its inception, and after it happened I came to her room and asked what it had all been about. Obligingly she gave me a spirited account of the night before, and I spent most of the day filling in the blanks with my own fabricated speeches and scenes—for it was certainly an adventure to excite the imagination.

Francesca and Charlie had wandered into Isabella's bedroom one night in search of a remedy for their boredom. Isabella's room often served as a council chamber—she possessed the rare combination of being both an excellent listener and an unbeatable enthusiast. The other cousins were all in bed, with the exception of Fisher, who frequently went outside after dark to look at the stars and listen for night birds.

Charlie and Francesca flopped down on the spare bed, treating Isabella as a Complaints Bureau to whom they could air their grievances.

"There's not one damn thing to see or person to talk to in this hellhole, and I want to get out and revive my dying life," Francesca announced.

Isabella replied, "Why don't you?" which caused momentary confusion but was soon taken as a suggestion to leave Shorecliff. Within minutes the plan had been born.

"Where would we go?" Charlie asked. His was always the voice of practicality, probably because he had so much experience in carrying out college pranks.

"Anywhere!" Francesca replied, eyes sparkling.

"Pensbottom is really your only choice, unless you want to go for more than one night," Isabella said. From the first she assumed that only Charlie and Francesca would be involved in the escape—they were the oldest and thus the most immune to parental retribution.

"Not more than one night," Charlie said. "We don't want to lose our beds here or anything like that."

"Who cares how long it's for as long as we get out in the first place?" Francesca said. "We'll go to Pensbottom if there's nowhere else. How do we get there?"

"It's obvious," said Charlie, and they exclaimed at the same time, "The rattletrap!"

This was when Charlie became fully invested in the plan. Driving the rattletrap, no matter the destination, was something he yearned for as much as Francesca yearned for a new setting. They decided on the following night as the best time for their escape and spent the next hour talking excitedly about the details.

For some time they toyed with the idea of inviting Tom and Philip to join them. "The more the merrier!" Francesca cried at first. But they concluded that Philip would not be a good man for the job. "He's too introspective for games like that," Isabella told me afterward. "He's much too serious. He wouldn't see the point."

"I don't think he's serious all the time," I answered.

"Of course he has a lighter side," Isabella said sharply. "All geniuses do."

Tom's candidacy lasted longer, but eventually they decided that he would rather dream about Lorelei than go with them. This was said half in jest, but I think it arose from a feeling of jealousy. Tom, after all, was already having an adventure. The question ended when Charlie sighed, "Lucky bastard." Having heard Uncle Kurt as well as Charlie use the word, I looked up "bastard" in the dictionary later and found "illegitimate child." When I looked up "illegitimate," it gave a series of definitions, one of which was "when pertaining to children, born out of wedlock." I looked up "wedlock" and found "marriage." With these clues my infant brain deduced that I should be having doubts about Aunt Rose and her husband. This will show what a sheltered life I led. The possibility that Rose and Cedric had never been properly married occupied me for a while, but in the end I decided that "lucky bastard" must be simply affectionate slang.

Finally Francesca said it would be better with just the two of them anyway, and I can easily imagine in what manner she said it, her eyebrows raised, that unforgettable feline expression creeping across her face.

The next night began smoothly. At one o'clock, the hour they had appointed as the earliest at which all aunts and uncles would be asleep, Francesca and Charlie tiptoed down to the front door. Isabella waved good-bye from the top of the stairs. Charlie was wearing his usual outfit of brown slacks and light shirt, but Francesca had on a black skirt, a black blouse, and a black shawl around her shoulders. Isabella was particularly struck by the shawl. We had no idea where Francesca had found it—we guessed one of Shorecliff's many closets—and we couldn't figure out why she would want to wear it. Nevertheless, it added to the mood. "She looked like a gypsy!" Isabella told me, and that, I suspect, was the desired effect.

Francesca and Charlie galloped across the yard to the fence, where the rattletrap was languishing from lack of use. They hopped in, and Charlie, who had lifted the key from its hook in the kitchen, started the car. The rattletrap always made a terrific noise when the engine first came to life, and they must have spent a good few moments frozen with apprehension as the car cleared its throat and prepared for action. No one emerged from the house, however, and soon Charlie and Francesca were bouncing along on the road to Pensbottom, giddy with the success of their departure.

God knows what they talked about on that half-hour drive to town. When I imagined Charlie and Francesca in the rattletrap, I could picture their faces and postures and expressions, but the words themselves were inaudible. Charlie was in the driver's seat, his big athlete's hands clasping the wheel in what was meant to be a casual, experienced way, though inside he must have been thrilled by driving, not to mention by the beauty in the passenger seat. Francesca would have been lounging beside him, stretching her glorious legs, insinuating herself all over the seat, maybe even putting her arm across his shoulders, and then ruining her own effect with the spontaneous, rippling laugh that was such an essential part of her seductive powers. The contrast between her attempts to be an enchantress and her mockery of those same attempts made her absolutely irresistible. Certainly Charlie couldn't withstand her. His blond hair plastered to his red face, he laughed at her, egged her on, and reveled in every second of her attention—though he probably didn't take it any more seriously than she did, at least not in those early days.

In spite of Francesca's enthusiasm, Pensbottom was not the ideal scene for excitement, and a letdown was inevitable. Besides the train station, the town boasted a cluster of residential houses, a post office, a market, a general goods store, a church, and one strange and pathetic attempt at a museum that was nothing more than a converted colonial house. The place had none of the invigorating fresh air of a seaside village and none of the clean, wholesome friendliness of a Midwestern settlement. It was just a backwoods town, filled with uninteresting inhabitants—though my view, of course, was colored by years of Hatfield scorn. In any case, there was nothing for two young adventurers to do there. In that respect it was greatly inferior to the beach.

When Charlie and Francesca arrived in Pensbottom, they drove to the train station, partly out of habit and partly because it was the first turnoff when coming from Shorecliff. They rattled along until they had reached the tracks, and then, somewhat uncertainly, Charlie switched off the engine. They listened for a while to the total silence that enveloped the town. The stationhouse was dark and abandoned, the platform equally so. Not a single person roamed the village.

"Well," said Francesca, turning to Charlie, "what do we do?" At that moment, Francesca later reported, they both felt like "incredible idiots." Nevertheless, they held on to enough of their enthusiasm to get out and explore. They left the rattletrap by the station, thinking it would be the best place to stage a getaway if one became necessary, and went into town on foot.

"If only there were a nightclub—or a speakeasy," Francesca sighed.

"Why, what would you do if there was one?" Charlie asked.

"I'd stroll up and say, 'Give me a martini with a twist, bartender.'" She smiled and sashayed to Charlie's side. Then she broke the pose, chuckling. "That's my mother's drink of choice."

"My mother doesn't drink," replied Charlie.

"What a surprise—Aunt Margery isn't a drinker. Let's go, Charlie."

When Isabella was telling me the story, she said, "Of course they wouldn't really have gone into a speakeasy." But I wasn't so sure. Alcohol loomed large in our family as a vice abhorred by the aunts above all others—I wasn't sure why, except that they disapproved of intemperance in general. But Francesca, I knew, was capable of anything, so the fact that Prohibition was still in place made the story much more comfortable.

The destination Charlie and Francesca finally decided on was comic in its contrast with illegal drinking establishments. When they turned onto Main Street, they saw the steeple of the church, and Charlie said, "Do you want to see if it's open?"

"Are you planning to desecrate the altar?" Francesca asked.

"Of course not." Charlie was genuinely insulted at her question. "I just want to see what it's like inside."

"Does that count as breaking in?"

"You can't break into a church. They're open to everybody. I think."

"But what if we're caught?"

"We'll say we wanted to come in to find shelter and pray."

"For our lost parents," Francesca giggled.

The church was a typical Protestant house of worship, an austere white building that looked gray in the darkness, with a squat steeple and wide front steps leading up to double doors. The doors weren't locked, and Charlie and Francesca slipped in without making a sound. The inside was lit only by the faint glow coming through the windows, and since the moon was a crescent that night, it was almost impossible to see anything. They walked slowly down the aisle, keeping their hands on the pews to guide them and getting an impression of a lot of open space over their heads. Their eyes adjusted eventually, but Francesca said there wasn't much to see. By the far wall was a white altar.

According to Isabella, Francesca told this part of the story very seriously, as if something important and meaningful had happened in the church. "She said it was as if a woolen quilt had fallen all around them, muffling them from the outside world. A great peace settled on her soul, and she felt a contentment she had never felt before. At the same time she felt uplifted, as if she were expanding to fill the church, and a light seemed to shine in her mind!"

"Did she really say all that?" I knew perfectly well Francesca would never have said anything of the sort.

"Well, no," said Isabella, breaking from her narration. "I got that from a book I read once where the character converts to the Catholic Church. That's exactly what it feels like when you convert, at least according to that book."

"But Francesca wasn't converting. What did she actually say?"

"She just said that it was silent and peaceful and that it killed their mood completely, but she still didn't want to leave."

"That's more like it."

"You have no flair for the dramatic, Richard."

After a moment or two Charlie turned to Francesca and said, "It's pretty solemn in here, isn't it? Sort of gives me the creeps."

Francesca smiled ruefully. "It's certainly put a damper on the night anyway. Should we leave?"

"No. I like it in here."

"So do I. But," she added with an effort, "we can't stand around here all night doing nothing. What would we tell the others?"

When Charlie and Francesca closed the door behind them and stood on the church portico, they felt as one does after emerging from a cave or a musty old house—as if the outside air has never been so fresh. All their excitement came rushing back redoubled.

"Let's take the town by storm!" Charlie said.

Francesca was laughing at this idea as they made their way down the steps, and so she didn't notice the man standing at the bottom. Neither cousin had seen him. He took her arm with the abruptness of a ghost appearing in a movie.

"Hey, you kids!" he said. "What are you doing in the church at this hour?"

First Francesca screamed—"like a stupid schoolgirl," she told Isabella. But then her better nature recovered itself. She jerked her arm out of the man's grasp and said, "We were praying for our dead parents!" before breaking into a storm of laughter.

"Run!" roared Charlie, and they pelted down the street.

The man ran after them, shouting at them to stop, and lights started flicking on in a few windows over the shops. At first the man called them "kids," but then Charlie heard him shout, "Church vandals!" and started to get worried.

"We didn't take anything—honest!" he yelled, not slowing down. He told Francesca to hold her hands out so the man could see there was nothing in them.

"We looked like two chickens who had just been axed," Francesca told Isabella. "There we were, running with our heads down and our hands waving on either side of us. We looked like a couple of ninnies." Her eyes were shining as she said it. That chase down Main Street had made the whole trip worthwhile. "It's not every night you're accused of vandalizing a church," she said.

When the man saw their empty hands he slowed down, and then another man appeared in a doorway and called, "What's going on, Charlie?"

"That nearly foiled us," Francesca said later. "Charlie, idiot that he is, skids to a halt. It never occurred to him that he has a ridiculously common name. I don't think the men noticed, though. So I grabbed him and kept on running."

As they turned the corner to go to the train station, they heard the other Charlie saying, "A couple of kids goofing around in the church, damn their eyes. It's shameless behavior, shameless."

"Did you see their faces?" said the second man.

"No, I didn't get a good look at them. The girl has a head of dark curly hair, though. And the boy's blond."

That was all Charlie and Francesca heard before the buildings cut them off from the street, but in all likelihood the next words were "Some of the Hatfield crew, I'd bet. Good-for-nothing rich brats."

They arrived at the rattletrap panting and laughing. The night had been a success, and all they needed now was a clean getaway. They leapt into the car, the doors screeching on their hinges as they banged them shut, and Charlie started the engine.

Francesca told Isabella that they laughed like lunatics all the way back, and I was even more envious of that ride home than I had been of their ride toward Pensbottom. There are few things more satisfying than reliving danger when it is safely over. No car followed them on the road out to Shorecliff, no shouts or horns threatened to cut short their victory. Indeed they passed no car on the road at all—the route to Shorecliff almost never saw any traffic. Charlie drove at a slick pace. He was so wound up that he pressed hard on the accelerator and made it to Shorecliff in a record twenty-five minutes.

But when they pulled up at the fence and turned the engine off, they weren't laughing anymore. The lights in Shorecliff were ablaze, and they knew they hadn't gotten away with anything.

"It was the most crushing disappointment," Francesca said later, and as Isabella told me the story I could feel the apprehension that must have hit Francesca and Charlie when they saw the lights shining over the lawn. It was not as if they were going to face one or two angry parents: up to nine adults might be waiting for them, reprimands at the ready.

"The first thing I wondered," said Francesca, "was how they could have found out. I assumed that someone had checked our beds—or maybe that someone had ratted." Here she gave Isabella a murderous glance and then laughed. "Not really, of course. I didn't think for a moment of what it actually was. And that made it ten times more awful. Especially when Aunt Caroline described going downstairs. But anyway," she added, pounding her fist on the bed, "let them scream! It was worth it. We had a wonderful night."

What had happened at Shorecliff was as follows. No one had woken up to check on Francesca or Charlie. Isabella, after lying in bed for half an hour thinking of all the adventures they might have, had fallen into delightful dreams. The house got bigger at night, in the darkness and the silence. The rooms expanded into gargantuan caverns, and time moved more slowly. Even the curtains in the open windows seemed to billow against the sills at half speed. Everyone was asleep.

Then, in all that silence, the phone began to ring. Only the adults could hear it; the children on the third floor were too far away. Even imagining that shrill sound in the dead of night gave me the creeps. The number at Shorecliff was, of course, private. But the fact that the house had only one phone and that it was situated in the ornate wooden booth in the hall gave the illusion of its being a public phone. Everyone knows how mysterious it is to hear a public phone ring on the street, and when we received calls at Shorecliff the effect was reproduced on an only slightly less startling scale. During the day, we could easily laugh off the sensation that the outside world was reaching in to disrupt us; most of the time one cousin or another would dash over and snatch up the receiver after the second ring. But to hear that phantom phone ringing in the middle of the night was another matter. My mother said it jerked her out of a sound sleep. She lay rigid, willing it to stop. In a few minutes Aunt Margery appeared in her doorway and whispered, "Caroline? Who could be calling us at this hour?"

"I'll answer it," said my mother. She was very brave, that summer and always. I've never known her to turn from a crisis. But the ringing phone rattled her all the way to her bones. She couldn't get rid of a dread that flooded through her from the first ring. As she walked down the stairs, her fears crystallized into a certainty that the phone was ringing to inform her of my father's death. It was even more courageous of her to keep walking toward what she thought was her own bereavement, but she did, faster than ever so she could get the shock over with.

She felt an overpowering relief when she picked up the receiver and heard, after the operator's mumbled introduction, an angry man's voice saying, "Is that the Hatfields' place? This is Charlie Ballantine. Two of your brood have just broken into our church." It took her several moments and more than one repetition before she grasped what he was talking about, but at last she understood. The relief she felt at my father's still being alive quelled most of the anger she would have felt toward Francesca and Charlie. For a long time after she hung up the phone, having apologized profusely and promised an in-person apology from the children the next day, she sat on the bench in the phone booth and rested her head against the glass.

But it occurred to her, while she was sitting there, that she had fallen in with Charlie Ballantine's accusations without making any attempt to defend her own family. This realization energized her. She raced up the stairs, knocked on Francesca's door, and flung it open. When she saw the empty bed, she knew at once that Mr. Ballantine's description—"two young hooligans, the girl dark-haired, the boy blond, obviously Hatfields!"—had been correct. "The most awful thing," she told Francesca later, "was that it didn't occur to me to doubt what he'd said. I knew you were so careless and reckless that it was not only possible but probable that you'd gone off to Pensbottom in the middle of the night."

My mother had just enough time to rouse the other adults—with the exception of Uncle Eberhardt, who refused to leave his bed—and gather them in the kitchen before the rattle-trap returned. Even Uncle Kurt was there, sleepy and resentful in his blue pajamas, his hair sticking straight up. He told me later that it had taken "a hell of a long time" for Francesca and Charlie to enter the house after they'd gotten out of the car. "But I'm not sur-prised," he said with a grin. "Something like that happened to me once in the army, and when you're heading toward trouble from a superior, nothing can speed up your feet."

With half-frightened, half-defensive expressions, the two delin-quents finally slunk into the kitchen. By this time most of the chil-dren had woken up, and they were ranged on the second floor by the stairwell, listening with all their might. The only ones still in bed were Yvette and the Delias, who sometimes slept through uproars, much to their dismay. I was there, clutching the railings of the banis-ter. As soon as I woke up I gravitated toward Isabella as the person most likely to tell me what was going on. In a moment she had ac-quainted me with the main points of the case, and I strained to hear the rise and fall of the rebukes for so heinous an offense.

Aunt Rose was the one who began the scolding. Aunt Margery had tried to claim the role of spokesperson, but it had been de-cided in a hurried colloquy that she would overstate the case and become too agitated. Aunt Edie was rejected for the same reasons, to her annoyance. Charlie told Tom later that even though he had been "terrified" during that hour in the kitchen, the sight of Aunt Edie's embroidered nightcap was so absurd that he kept wanting to burst out laughing. "I guess it was mostly just nervousness," he said, "but, my God, she looked like a bad-tempered mushroom in that cap!"

The first question Aunt Rose asked was "Did you just drive to Pensbottom and break into the church?"

Both cousins had too much sense to deny the charge, and they nodded. Francesca said, "We didn't break in. The door was open." Then she asked what both of them had been dying to know ever since they'd seen the lights: "How did you find out?" She told Isabella that it had seemed for an awful moment as if the aunts had witchcraft on their side.

My mother answered. "Charlie Ballantine called just now and said he saw two Hatfield children emerging from the church and acting very disrespectfully on the steps. Do you know Mr. Ballantine?"

After a moment Francesca shuffled her feet and said, "He must have been that other Charlie, Charlie. The one who was running after us."

"Running after you?" Aunt Margery repeated, her voice rising. "You started a chase?"

"Not on purpose!" Francesca protested. "We weren't doing anything—really! We just wanted to go into Pensbottom, and we stepped into the church, but we didn't mean to do anything wrong."

"You haven't even begun to get into trouble about the car," Rose said.

Her warning started a barrage of adult commentary. "You've been unbelievably irresponsible," wailed Aunt Margery.

"Do you think we make up rules just to bother you?" asked my mother.

"I'm disappointed in you, Charlie," Uncle Frank said, adding the first man's voice to the clamor.

"Damn stupid," said Uncle Cedric.

"If you're going to do something dumb, at least don't get caught," Uncle Kurt said, and he couldn't resist smiling. That turned the scolding onto him. The adults shushed him violently, and for a few moments Francesca and Charlie thought they were going to get off lightly.

Finally Rose waved a hand. "Let's get the facts straight," she said. "Charlie Ballantine said that you, Francesca, claimed to have been praying for your dead parents in the church. Is this true?"

"I was only joking," Francesca said, her voice breaking.

"Thank God Loretta isn't here," Aunt Rose muttered.

It was then that my mother told Francesca and Charlie about how frightened she had been when the phone rang. My mother could be shattering when she was upset or angry, mostly because she never lightened the solemnity by even the hint of a smile. Francesca felt a wave of guilt and started to cry.

"I'm sorry, Aunt Caroline!" she blurted out. "I didn't know that would happen. I didn't mean to scare you!"

"Of course you didn't know it would happen," said my mother, "but that's exactly why it's dangerous to act so thoughtlessly. You can never tell what will happen because of impetuous behavior."

There was a moment of silence, during which Francesca sobbed dramatically. I suspected her of enjoying her position as the penitent maiden—one never knew how much guilt Francesca truly felt, and it seemed unlike her to cry so easily.

Then the silence was broken in an unexpected and, for us eavesdroppers, a thrilling way. Aunt Edie, who had said nothing up to this point, suddenly burst out, "I want to speak! I'm just as much related to these children as all of you are, and I ought to get a say in what happens."

Aunt Rose snapped, "What are you talking about, Edie? Don't be absurd."

"Don't get excited, Edie," said Uncle Cedric. "They're both safe—that's the main thing."

Edie, however, paid no attention. "None of you understand!"

she exclaimed. "I'm apparently the only one who can see what's happening. And if you think I'm going to stand by while that shameless jezebel leads the other children into sin, you can think again. It's clear to me that Charlie has been seduced by this girl here, who is an exact replica of Loretta as far as I'm concerned. And I won't have it in this house!"

On the stairs, we were all impressed by her tirade. But, as was usual with Edie's rants, we couldn't take her outrage seriously. No one would deny that Francesca was a seductress—even I knew she was, though I didn't understand the more sordid implications of the term, and when I looked up "jezebel," the definition was "wife of Ahab, Phoenician"—but it was an insult to Charlie to suppose he had no choice in the matter.

He was the first to say it. "That's not true, Aunt Edie," he protested. "I'm as much to blame as Francesca is. I drove the car, after all." A tinge of pride crept into his voice.

"She lured you into it," Aunt Edie proclaimed. "And I'm not surprised. That girl has been on the warpath of lust ever since she got here. What did I say in the first week? What did I say about a house filled with children at this age?"

"That's enough, Edie," said my mother.

At the same time Uncle Frank said, "Edie, you're being positively indecent. Let's not blame Francesca for anything more than what actually happened. Charlie's my son, but I'm clearheaded enough to see when he's at fault. You made a mistake, son, and I hope you regret it."

"I do," said Charlie. In reaction to Edie's hysteria, everyone else was acting very upright and reasonable and man-to-man.

"I promised Mr. Ballantine that we would take you to Pensbottom so you could apologize to him personally," said my mother. "Are you willing to go?"

"Of course," said Francesca angelically. Inwardly, she later reported to Isabella, she was seething. "That stupid, snotty little man," she said. "The day I apologize to him with any sincerity is the day I die."

Nevertheless, Aunt Margery and my mother drove Charlie and Francesca into town the next morning. By daylight, Pensbottom lost its last meager trappings of romance. The main street was covered in dust because of a recent heat wave, and the buildings that huddled on either side looked like two rows of the proverbial small potatoes. "Uncle Harold was right," Charlie said when they came back. "Pensbottom is obscene. It wasn't worth it." But Francesca said, "Oh, what did Uncle Harold know?"

Charlie Ballantine was standing on the steps of the church, self-importance pouring out of him. "So here are the Hatfields," he said. "I'm glad you saw fit to come and apologize—not too high and mighty after all. As the church warden for Pensbottom, I will be very happy to accept your apology for trespassing on this sacred property."

"That will do, Mr. Ballantine," said Aunt Margery. From the moment he started talking, she had bristled with indignation. "My son and niece are here to say they're sorry, and that's all. We're not here to listen to your comments."

"Well, I see that turning out destructive children hasn't affected your pride. But perhaps the children themselves will be more polite?"

My mother took Aunt Margery's arm to prevent her from saying anything.

"First of all, we didn't vandalize the church," Francesca said.

"But," said Charlie, "we apologize for entering it at night."

"Even though we didn't know it wasn't permitted."

"And we're sorry we were rude to you."

"It won't happen again," said Francesca. She was openly wearing a malicious grin at this point, but Aunt Margery and my mother were so offended by Charlie Ballantine's manner that they didn't scold her.

Mr. Ballantine stared at Francesca and Charlie in disbelief. "You call that an apology?" he asked. Then he turned to the aunts. "Are you going to let them get away with that? If you do, you're as bad as they are."

"They both said they were sorry and that it wouldn't happen again!" Aunt Margery burst out. "And that's all we can expect. After all, entering an open church isn't a crime. They didn't really do anything wrong. What punishment they receive will come from us—not from you!" The last word she essentially spat. Charlie Ballantine responded by spitting in the usual sense at her feet. From that moment there was war—albeit a cold war—between Shorecliff and Pensbottom.

On the ride home Aunt Margery was too outraged at Mr. Ballantine's behavior to comment on anything else. "To think the townspeople feel that way," she gasped, "and we've been in total ignorance! All our lives we've thought of Pensbottom as a welcoming place. And the people there are like vipers in the grass! They've struck our heel, Caroline—they've stabbed us in the back. They've given us the Judas kiss!"

"Now, Margery," said my mother, "Charlie Ballantine is one man. I'm sure the rest of the town doesn't feel the way he does. He's clearly obsessed with the church and thinks of it as his private property."

"That's another thing!" Margery fumed. "What I said was true. A church is a house of God. It's open to all comers. If they didn't want people to come in, they should have locked the door at night. What sort of security is that?"

"I agree he seemed very unreasonable. And it's disgraceful to spit before children, or before anyone for that matter. He was abominably rude."

"What did you two do in the church, anyway?" Aunt Margery asked, twisting her head around to see into the backseat.

"We just walked in and stood quietly in the aisle," Francesca said. "Honest."

"We were very respectful," Charlie said.

They didn't say anything more, but I'll bet they had a more meaningful experience in the church that night than Charlie Ballantine ever had.

"I hope you realize," my mother said as they pulled up to Shorecliff, "that what you two said to Mr. Ballantine doesn't pass as an apology. We allowed it because we were as horrified by him as you were. But if you ever apologize to one of us like that, you'll find we aren't as forgiving. Is that clear?"

"Yes, Aunt Caroline," they answered. They suspected that they had escaped a severe punishment thanks to Mr. Ballantine, and they were right. They were confined to the house for a week and required to eat meals in the kitchen while we ate in the dining room. But for Francesca and Charlie, eating alone was more of a present than a punishment, and after two dinners of segregation Uncle Kurt, a smile stretching across his face, came into the kitchen where the two cousins were roaring with laughter over some joke and said, "All right, kids. You win. Come on back to the dining room and quit that braying—you sound like donkeys."

The morning after the escapade, Francesca narrated the whole story to Isabella. I wanted to know what had happened so badly that as Francesca was finishing the story I burst into the room and said, "Can I just sit in the corner?"

The girls laughed. Isabella patted the bed next to her and said, "You don't have to sit in the corner. You can have the seat of honor."

I'd missed most of it, of course, but I did hear Francesca talking about apologizing to Charlie Ballantine. "The biggest reason it made me so mad," she said, "was that he was horning in on a wonderful night. We'd had an adventure, Charlie and I, and then this weasel of a man—who I would shoot without hesitation, if I had a rifle—had to wreck everything with his stupid arrogance. But the only thing that really matters is how excited we were, driving to Pensbottom." She dissolved into laughter. "And then driving home feeling as if we'd really done something, even in Pensbottom, even in that dead little town. It was great—I'd never take it back! And I'm sorry I frightened Aunt Caroline, I really am," she added, turning to me, "but that wasn't my fault, was it? It was Charlie Ballantine's fault, that son of a bitch. I feel guilty about it, but I'm not going to let him ruin my fun." She was standing in front of us, and now she threw up her arms in a stage-actress gesture and said with a triumphant grin, "I got out, kids! I escaped from this old prison of a house, and I had a night on the town!"

7

Fox

Nearly a week after the Pensbottom incident, when the uproar resulting from it was dying down, I woke up early one morning. Usually I awoke around seven o'clock, which was two hours earlier than any of my cousins but half an hour later than most of my aunts and uncles. This gave me the opportunity to have all the adults to myself over breakfast, a privilege that seemed daunting every morning when I stepped into the kitchen but lent me a feeling of superiority when the older cousins wandered down hours later to face leftovers and dishes in the sink. The mornings also gave me the chance to hear treasured gossip and to test the wind of adult opinion. Perhaps assuming, as so many adults do, that children are either not interested in or not capable of understanding their conversation—an assumption fatal to secrecy but vital to the education of children—the aunts and uncles would often discuss their offspring in front of me, giving me clues not only to their own attitudes but also to the true natures of my cousins.

That morning I found the sun shining on me at six o'clock

rather than seven. I don't know what woke me—perhaps an un-settling dream—but I felt disoriented and lay in bed for a while staring at the window, waiting for familiarity to return. Eventually I decided to get out of bed and go downstairs. Tiptoeing down when no one else was awake was a new and pleasant experience. I surveyed the ground floor awash with virgin sunlight, and all thought of my dream was swept away by exhilaration.

As soon as I got into the kitchen, the audacious idea struck me of making my own breakfast. I loved pancakes, but I knew they would be too difficult—I had never followed a recipe—so I decided on eggs and began to rummage through the icebox. I re-member noticing that the kitchen door to the outside was open, only the screen door remaining closed to keep out mosquitoes, but Shorecliff was so isolated that there was no fear of thieves, and we often kept the doors open all night.

I was so startled that I nearly dropped an egg when the screen door banged behind me and a voice said, "What are you doing up so early?"

Tom was standing by the door, wearing nothing but pajama bot-toms covered in grass stains and soaked through at his ankles. He was barefoot, and his chest was heaving slightly. I think he had been running. The sunlight cascading through the door gave his tanned skin an almost molten glow. His hair was ruffled, and his torso, lean and muscular from months of exercise, seemed to me a paragon of manliness. After the first shock of his entrance, I was struck dumb by the glory of his appearance. I knew I would never look like that.

"Well, pal," he said, grinning at me, "cat got your tongue? Sneaking something to eat before anyone else comes down? What are you up to?"

The way he spoke, the way he was holding his hands at his sides, the way he stood with his feet apart, not lounging but as if he were filled with some private excitement—all these things showed me that he had been doing something thrilling.

I answered, "I'm getting breakfast. Where have you been?"

Tom laughed and folded his arms. He didn't seem to know what to do with his hands. "I've been spending some time on the couch of Venus, my friend. I've been experiencing connubial bliss."

"Connubial" was beyond me (I later looked it up in my trusty dictionary and found "pertaining to marriage," which was no help since Tom wasn't married). I did know, however, what bliss was. It went without question, furthermore, that Tom had been with Lorelei, and though I couldn't fill in the details, I had learned on my walk with Fisher what kind of activities Tom and Lorelei engaged in. So I asked with ravenous curiosity, "Did you like it?"

He laughed again in the same way, uncertain and a little distracted, as if he too were experiencing the disorientation I had felt on waking. "It was great stuff, kid," he said. "Great stuff. You ever hear anyone running down connubial bliss, you tell them they've got it wrong. Have you got that?"

I was nodding when I heard a snort of derision from the doorway leading into the rest of the house. Yvette was standing there in a sleeveless blue nightgown. Her ash-blond hair hung all the way down her back, and her arms were bare. She had lovely arms, skinny and rounded, the muscles well defined because she was so slim. Whenever I saw them I wanted to wrap my fingers around the flesh just above her elbow, and even during this early-morning confrontation I admired her. She would have looked beautiful in the sunlight except that she was obviously burning with a constrained emotion I couldn't identify.

"Is that what you like to tell little boys, Tom?" she said. "All about 'connubial bliss'? That's pretty low, if the best audience you can get is your youngest cousin. Why don't you announce it at the dinner table? I'm sure your mother would love to hear what you've been doing."

"Leave it alone, Yvette," Tom said. I could tell he was trying to hang on to his earlier mood of triumph. "It's got nothing to do with you."

In an instant I became an invisible watcher. What I saw now was that Yvette couldn't keep her eyes off Tom's body; they wandered over his hair, his hands, his chest, his bare feet. She avoided his eyes, probably because they were now staring at her with mounting irritation, but even I in my ignorance could feel the force pulling Yvette toward him.

There was a long pause in the conversation, and during that pause I did some rapid thinking. I saw that Yvette was angry with Tom, and I remembered Lorelei kissing Tom under the haystack, and I deduced that Yvette wished she had been in Lorelei's place. In this way I came to my first understanding of the many layers beneath my cousins' behavior toward each other.

"Aren't you going to tell Richard what you did with Lorelei?" Yvette asked.

"No. I think he knows all he needs to know, don't you, pal?" Tom turned to me, and I shrugged, trying to look inconspicuous.

"Don't you feel bad?" Yvette burst out. I knew she was losing her hold over her anger. "Don't you feel bad sneaking out at night like that, lying to your parents, lying to all of us?"

"I'm not doing anything wrong," said Tom. There was a shade of defensiveness in his voice.

"If you're not doing anything wrong, then why are you hiding it? Why don't you tell Aunt Rose you'll be running over to the Stephensons' farm to make love with their daughter every night? If it's not wrong."

"Look," said Tom, shifting on one foot, "how do you know about all this anyway? What have you got to do with it?"

"I happened to wake up early, and I looked out my window and saw you racing across the yard from the direction of the farm." Yvette was on her moral high horse now. She had regained her self-control and was lording it over Tom, confident that her knowledge gave her power. "It was a logical conclusion," she added. "After all, it's no secret that you're swooning over Lorelei. It's disgusting, the way you drop everything and run for her. I bet you'd do anything for her." The way she said it made it sound like an accusation.

"Look, Yvette, seriously—you're not going to tell anyone, are you? You have to agree it's not really wrong. Where's the harm in it?"

"Don't you feel bad that you've abandoned us for so long? That you're constantly running over to see her and leaving us all behind?" She tried to make the last phrase sarcastic and failed.

"I haven't abandoned all of you. Don't be silly. Anyway, half the time Lorelei comes over here to spend time with us. So you can't really be angry about that."

"What do you know about me being angry? I'm not angry."

"Well…If you're not angry, you won't say anything, right? Come on, Yvette, this is important. We both know my mother would blow up if she found out about it."

"I don't think it's nice to lie to your mother."

"Nice or not!" Tom exclaimed, slapping his hand on the doorframe. "I'd rather you didn't tell anyone, all right? Is that so much to ask?"

"What do you think, Richard?" Yvette asked, turning to me. "Do you think it's a lot to ask?"

In spite of my realizations during the discussion, I was still floundering for a foothold, and their rapid exchange had bewildered me. "A lot to ask?" I repeated, looking to Tom for help.

"You know how it is, buddy," he said. "My mother wouldn't be happy if she knew I had been out at night."

"Doing what?" prompted Yvette.

"I was visiting Lorelei. And it's sort of secret. You won't tell, will you?"

"No, I won't tell," I said. For me there was no question—cousins' secrets were sacred. As long as they considered me trustworthy, I could serve as a confidant.

"He doesn't think there's anything wrong with it," Tom said, pointing at me.

"What does he know?" Yvette scoffed. "He's only a child."

She was heading down an insulting path, but the conversation was brought to a halt by Pamela padding into the kitchen in her slippers. "Why are you all awake?" she asked sleepily. "Yvette, you woke me up. Do you have to thump around like that? I couldn't get back to sleep."

"Sorry, Pamela," Yvette said. "Tom and I were just having a fascinating conversation about—"

"I've now heard three sets of little feet coming down the stairs. What are you all doing down here?" This was Aunt Margery, wrapped in a floral dressing gown and finally restoring the sense of normality that I had missed ever since waking up. Her presence ended the debate between Tom and Yvette, and from that point on the morning continued the way most Shorecliff mornings did. About five minutes after Margery's arrival, Aunt Edie appeared at the screen door. I had forgotten that she was the earliest of early risers and frequently walked by the cliff at five in the morning as the sun came up. Tom jumped several inches when she rattled the screen behind him and asked him to move aside.

Aunt Margery never commented on the fact that she had heard three sets of feet but found four cousins standing in the kitchen. Maybe the inconsistency escaped her.

Tom shot Yvette a last pleading look as Aunt Margery began to whip up some pancake batter for me, and she responded with a slow, inscrutable nod. I didn't know what she meant by that, since it certainly wasn't acquiescence. Poor Yvette—she probably didn't know herself. But she didn't say anything that day and for several days afterward about Tom's escapades with Lorelei.

The day of their confrontation was also the one on which Barnavelt escaped—one of the many events which, though they seemed innocent at the time, laid the groundwork for the summer's final disaster. The fox's escape sparked an idea in the minds of the Delias that germinated for a long time before the rest of us became aware of it.

Since the day of my walk with Fisher, the fox had become a celebrity in the family. Uncle Eberhardt was outraged by the frequent invasions of the cottage and tried ineffectually to prevent them. Condor was secretly pleased—he was a more sociable person. But even he must have been unnerved to receive daily visitors after years of seeing no one but old Eberhardt.

After two or three episodes of delirious amusement at being in close quarters with a fox, the older cousins lost interest. The more devoted visitors were Fisher, the two Delias, and me. Isabella was enchanted, but she felt so sorry for Barnavelt, who for the first week stared out of the box with his yellow eyes glazed and his ears laid back, that she stopped going after three visits. "I can't stand seeing him all crouched down like that," she said. "It's awful. I don't think any of us should go." I thought this was one of the noblest comments I'd ever heard, and after she said it I deprived myself of seeing the fox for two whole days. Then I caved in and returned to the cottage.

The fox was not ill treated. Though a stream of visitors came to see him during the day, he spent long evening hours and most of each morning alone with Condor and Eberhardt. Eberhardt returned to Shorecliff to sleep, so only Condor knew of Barnavelt's nocturnal activities. The fox, though it was cautious with the rest of us, learned to love Condor, who had established from the first that Barnavelt was to be a tame fox—he could not help him survive and still allow him to maintain his wildness. So after the first few weeks Condor could hold Barnavelt and stroke him. He said that he was working on training Barnavelt to respond to a call. Condor would sit in his bedroom and say, "Barnavelt, come here, boy. Come here, Barnavelt!" (No one ever called him Barney.) Thus far Barnavelt had once wandered into the bedroom, where Condor promptly rewarded him with a bowl of milk. Condor didn't know whether the fox had come in response to his calling or not, but he was hopeful.

The two Delias, Fisher, and I listened to these reports as if they were necessary for our survival. As far as we were concerned, Condor had suddenly become one of the most important and fascinating figures at Shorecliff. I never tired of seeing him, an enormous man buttoned up in a pale pink Oxford shirt, with a tiny fox on his arm.

Barnavelt was never so relaxed when we were in the cottage. The moment Condor saw us through the window, he would wave and send the little fox back to his box. He was constructing a wooden house for Barnavelt, but it wasn't completed yet. Condor claimed that when none of us was around, Barnavelt would run to the wooden house, investigating everything with his twitchy black nose and occasionally forgetting even to pretend to be afraid. There was no pretending with us, though—every time we stared into the box, his ears went back and his eyes took on the petrified look I had seen on the first day. After Isabella's outburst I felt guilty whenever I saw that look, but the Delias were undaunted. Condor would open the door and try to look fierce, but we could see from the smile in his eyes that he was pleased by our interest in his new project. Of course we weren't allowed to do anything more than look on from a distance. Condor sometimes showed us how he could pat Barnavelt, the fox cringing away from the meaty hand and then suddenly rubbing against it, making us squirm with envy.

About a week after Condor found him, we made another unexpected discovery connected with Barnavelt. Lorelei had come over to Shorecliff for one of our morning croquet matches, which Tom was still organizing assiduously. Diffident and meek and un-Hatfield-like as she was, Lorelei had become a fixture at our house. Tom had exclusive rights over her, and she seemed willing to follow his direction. Sometimes, though, she was left alone with a group of us, and it was enchanting to watch the impulsive Hatfield girls deferring to her slow, uncertain manner. They would listen with the utmost respect, their mouths open, as if they were worried she might stumble over a word. I caught Francesca once nodding unconsciously in time to Lorelei's hesitant voice. Not one of the girls was exempt from this involuntary soft-stepping around her. The Delias would stop giggling, Yvette would thaw, Pamela would come close to pandering. Maybe this was the sort of extreme politeness that results when two alien beings come into contact, or maybe the Hatfields admired qualities in Lorelei that they knew they could never attain. In any case, we were not averse when Tom suggested that Lorelei come to visit Condor and Barnavelt.

We knew, moreover, that Great-Uncle Eberhardt was safely out of our way. Earlier that day we had noticed him, in one of his unusual morning appearances, stalking across the lawn, grumbling something about lemonade. He had one of the most bizarre gaits I've ever seen: with every step he swayed from side to side as if each foot were coming down much lower than the level of the grass. To balance himself, he would hold his arms out under his black cape in a position I've seen ballerinas use, elbows bent and forearms hanging down. With his gray hair springing out on either side of his head, he looked like a scarecrow covered by a black tarpaulin and swaying in the wind.

As Eberhardt passed, Isabella commented, a little too loudly, "I think Uncle Eberhardt has a peg leg!" The minute she said this we could imagine it perfectly. There he was, wobbling past us over the yard, lifting up each leg as if he were pulling a weight with it. But now he froze in his tracks, his arms still held out from his sides, and turned to Isabella. The cousins roared with laughter and then tittered into silence.

"Well!" he said in his grating voice. "So you think I have a peg leg, do you? I suppose you think I'm an old retired pirate? Is that your idea?"

He began to stump toward her. Isabella essayed a smile but failed to produce one. The uncles, who had ranged themselves by the side of our croquet court, were enjoying themselves immensely.

"You're in for it, Isabella!" Uncle Frank cried.

"You've got her now, Uncle Eberhardt. That will teach you to make accusations about your elders, Bella!"

We children were too afraid to say anything. Eberhardt bore down on her, swaying and clumping.

"I didn't mean it, Uncle Eberhardt!" Isabella squeaked. Her stance seemed to increase tenfold in its gangliness. The phrase "every which way" defines her at that age.

"You want to see my peg leg, Isabella?" Eberhardt demanded. "I'll show it to you!" He staggered up until he was standing two feet in front of her. Isabella was taller than he was, but he was by far the more powerful figure. He stared at her, his round eyes glinting, and then kicked out a leg to the side. There was a black boot on the end of it. Then he kicked out his other leg, also black-booted. He might have been dancing in very slow motion. "Happy?" he barked.

"It was just a joke, Uncle Eberhardt," Isabella said with an effort.

"You children," Eberhardt said, sweeping all of us with a beady-eyed stare. "You think I'm nothing but a figure of fun, don't you? You'd be surprised at what I know—things about you, things about your parents, things about your family and your past. I wouldn't underestimate the older generation if I were you. It's fouled up this family before, and it can foul it up again."

"What are you telling them?" Uncle Frank called from the side-lines.

"You keep out of this, Frank!" Eberhardt said, waving a hand. He fixed each of us with a long stare. Finally he reached Lorelei, who was hovering in the protection of Tom's shadow.

"And you?" he said. "What do you say to all this?"

"I'm very glad you don't have a peg leg, Mr. Hatfield," Lorelei replied.

We agreed afterward that she had found the perfect answer. Eberhardt grunted, almost smiled—Tom swore he saw teeth—and headed for the house.

Uncle Frank gave Lorelei a round of applause and claimed that she'd slain the beast, but she put her head down and seemed uncomfortable at being the center of attention. We obeyed her un-spoken request. The croquet game was resumed, and when later on Tom made his suggestion about going to visit Barnavelt, we knew that the coast would be clear of great-uncles.

It was when we arrived at the cottage—Tom, Lorelei, the two Delias, Fisher, Pamela, and I—that we made our discovery.

Condor had Barnavelt on his arm, but when he saw us at the door he tipped the fox back into his shelter. He greeted us with the words "I've redesigned his house," and we saw that the frame for Barnavelt's more permanent home had been demolished.

"What are you doing with it?" Fisher asked, intrigued. His architectural streak came to the fore, and for a while we heard of nothing but angles and supporting beams.

The two Delias crept to the box and peered in, kneeling side by side on the floor, giggling to each other, their brown and black heads touching. The charm of Barnavelt never wore off for those two—it was enough for them simply to see his silky fur. Pamela and I hung back, waiting our turn. Pamela liked the fox but never said anything about him. Since her inexplicable tantrum she had been acting more inscrutably than ever, but she spent no less time with me, so I didn't resent her moodiness.

Tom waited for the Delias to finish their worship session and then said, "Move aside, girls. I want to introduce Lorelei to the fox."

Obediently, the Delias moved away. We stood around the walls of the cottage, even Tom, and watched as Lorelei knelt down next to the box. She hooked a hand over one of the sides, and then she became perfectly motionless, staring into the box with her back to us.

After a minute or two, the rest of us began to get edgy. None of us wanted to speak to her; her stillness was as intimidating a barrier as a physical wall. So we waited for Tom to say something. The minute I looked at him, though, I knew he was content just feasting his eyes on her as she crouched on the floor, her soft hair falling around her shoulders. He wasn't going to say anything.

Soon after that Fisher and Condor moved into Condor's bedroom so Fisher could see the blueprints for Barnavelt's new house. There was a cry of surprise, and we trooped into the bedroom, leaving Lorelei and Barnavelt to their own devices.

Fisher had discovered that Condor was planning a sliding door for the house, and the structural intricacies of this luxury distracted us for almost ten minutes. Condor handed the plan to

Fisher, and while all of us clustered around him, for once the center of attention, Condor crept back into the living room. I prided myself on being the only one who heard his exclamation when he saw Lorelei and the fox. He said, "Well, string me up for the bears!"—an expression I have never heard before or since. Lorelei, he told us afterward, was patting the fox, stroking him from the top of his head to the tip of his tail, and Barnavelt's ears were sticking straight up. Condor said he had never seen the little fox so comfortable with anyone, not even him, let alone a stranger.

"What it was," he said, "was that at first she kept perfectly still. She didn't make a single move, that girl. I've known her since she was a little mite, and she's always been like that—good with animals, good at spotting birds." Fisher looked up at this and later asked Lorelei about it, but she denied all knowledge of birds, to his disappointment. "None of you Hatfields," Condor went on, "could stand still for more than five seconds at a time. You're like candle flames, all of you. But that Lorelei—well, she's like a statue, that's all. Calm and still. Animals like that."

We resented his crack about the Hatfields, but it was accurate, of course. Not even the Wight children could stand still for more than a minute without stretching or rearranging themselves, and as for the more volatile members of the family, Francesca or Isabella or Cordelia, they couldn't be motionless to save their lives.

We were more impressed by Lorelei than ever after the incident with Barnavelt. When Condor said, "There's a look in her eye that Barnavelt understood right away," we all knew what he meant. Tom nearly burst with pride, and I was annoyed by how proud he was, as if he could take credit for Lorelei's talents. After that day she became, for me at least, more than simply "Tom's girl."

The day Barnavelt ran away, Lorelei was with us at the cottage. She came often after her initial visit, and Condor welcomed her more warmly than any of us. Pamela told me once that she thought Lorelei visited Condor in the evenings, when we were having dinner, and she may have been right. Certainly Lorelei seemed more comfortable in Condor's cottage than in Shorecliff.

The more unexpected participant was Philip, who almost never accompanied us. I don't know why he came that day. He was standing in the cottage, looking out the window and apparently bored by the whole idea of the fox. I would have been more fascinated by his presence had I not been mesmerized by Lorelei. Armed with my memory of the confrontation between Tom and Yvette in the kitchen that morning, I watched her with new eyes. She had become an object of lust, fantasy, jealousy. A cloud of sexual intrigue surrounded her. I felt guiltily that by thinking of her in this way I was defiling her purity—for there was something pure about Lorelei—but at the same time I knew, or thought I knew, that she had been anything but pure with Tom. Though hazy about the idea of sex itself, I was well aware that Tom's actions with her had been of the illicit and highly secret kind that yields the direst consequences when discovered by adults.

Now there was Lorelei, crouching by Barnavelt's box with the Delias, and there was Tom, standing over her with God knows what knowledge of her in his head. Yvette had declined to join our expedition. I assumed she did not want to be near Tom after the altercation of the morning.

Delia Ybarra suggested that we let Barnavelt out of the box while all of us were in the room. "You said yourself he's getting more and more comfortable in the cottage," she pleaded. "And we wouldn't move. Really, we wouldn't!"

"Hatfields always move," Condor grunted, but he was close to yielding.

Fisher, who thought of it, as of most things connected with Barnavelt, as a naturalist's experiment, suggested that we stand in the bedroom doorway so the fox would have the main room to himself. Condor assented to this idea after some hesitation, and we crowded into the bedroom. Philip remained by the window until Condor called him away, and as he turned he said, "Uncle Eberhardt is coming." But we were all so excited about seeing Barnavelt come out of the cramped cardboard box, which seemed horribly small and rundown after nearly three weeks, that we didn't pay attention to him.

Condor tipped the box onto its side and came to join us. I was reminded of the first day when he had shown us Barnavelt lapping milk, but the fox that emerged from the box today was a far cry from that tiny, ragged, terrified creature. Sleek and fat from Condor's careful treatment, Barnavelt trotted out after only a minute or two. He looked at us and then moved toward the skeleton of his wooden house as if he were quite familiar with his surroundings.

"He likes to explore it," Condor said in a Paul Bunyan whisper. "He's going to love living there."

Barnavelt was sniffing the planks that would one day be his walls and roof. He avoided the doorway to the bedroom where we were all squashed together, watching him, but the rest of the room he treated as his own territory. He was slinking along the wall beneath Condor's table when the door slammed open and Uncle Eberhardt stomped into the room.

"Stop!" we roared.

Barnavelt took advantage of the opportunity almost instantly. It was astounding that he wasn't more terrified by the banging door. He froze for only a second and then flew outside in a flash of orange fur.

Wails of grief rose from the Delias. "Oh, he's gone, he's gone! You let him get away!"

"Uncle Eberhardt," Delia Ybarra cried, stamping her foot, "how could you do that!"

It took a moment for Eberhardt to figure out what was happening, and by then Condor was already taking action. "All of you kids stay in the cottage," he said. "Our only hope is that Barnavelt will come when he's called. I've been training him, after all. Don't move, any of you."

For once we Hatfields obeyed that order, staying almost as still as Lorelei did. Eberhardt retreated to one corner. Tom said later, "Thank the Lord it was old Eberhardt and not one of us," and when he said it I realized how awful it would have been to be responsible for Barnavelt's escape. Even Eberhardt felt guilty about it—in his codgerish way he was fond of the little fox.

Condor went to the doorway and called, "Barnavelt! Come here, boy, come here, Barnavelt! Come back!" He repeated this call several times without success. Then he came back into the cottage, rubbing his head, obviously distressed. "He may have already rushed off too far to hear me calling. I can't decide whether it would be better to wait until dark, when he'll want food, or to send you out in different directions, calling to him."

"Oh, do that, Condor!" said Delia Robierre.

"He won't recognize your voices, though," Condor answered. "Who knows if it's his name he responds to or just the sound of my voice."

"But if you wait until dark," Fisher said, "he may get frightened or confused. He may wander too far from the cottage and not be able to find his way back."

"He might be just as scared if he suddenly heard all of you galumphing around bellowing his name."

"We won't galumph around, and we won't bellow," Delia Robierre begged. "We'll tiptoe as quietly as we can, and we'll call very gently and softly, just the way you did." She gave an imitation of

Condor's call, which sounded so inviting that Condor in his desperation was convinced.

"Go on out then," he said. "But only for twenty minutes! After that we'll let him be. I don't want him frightened to death."

Tom divvied us up, and I was pleased, in an obscure way, that he paid more attention to his cousins than to Lorelei in those few minutes before the search began. It seemed to me that it meant his loyalties were still in the right order. We all fanned out, crouched down like footpads next to a highway, and called Barnavelt's name over and over again. I was totally unsuccessful and never believed I would be anything else, though of course I imagined a victorious return, Barnavelt draped across my arm, a new bond forged between us so that eventually he would sleep in my bedroom and become my constant companion.

The other Hatfields had the same experience I did. Philip bowed out from the beginning, explaining to Condor that he would be of no use because he was too liable to be distracted by his own thoughts. Condor sent him back to Shorecliff, relieved to have fewer people cluttering up the woods around the cottage. Eberhardt remained, grouchy and scowling, on his stool in the corner, and Condor stood at the door of the cottage, an emblem of familiarity should the fox look back.

Delia, Delia, Tom, Fisher, and I spread out through the woods and found nothing. Lorelei moved rapidly toward the lawn surrounding Shorecliff. She didn't call Barnavelt's name or crouch down as if she were an outlaw. She whisked through the trees, making less sound than any of us, as if she knew exactly where she was going. When she reached the edge of the trees she stopped. That was the last I saw of her before I veered off to another portion of the woods. Delia Robierre said she saw her taking a few steps forward onto the grass, her head turning this way and that. And Lorelei herself told us about seeing Barnavelt sitting as dogs sit, on his hind legs, his tongue out, panting. He was so little that in the uncut grass he was nearly hidden; but his ears were sticking straight up, and that's what gave him away.

None of us was really surprised when Lorelei came back with him in her arms, but it was hard not to feel crestfallen, as if we had somehow let the family honor down. We watched her lower the fox into his box and give him a final pat, and each of us imagined doing the same thing.

Then she stood up and told us what he had looked like when she found him, and she had such a lovely, shy smile on her face that we forgave her. "He was just sitting there, waiting for us," she said. She used "us" out of politeness. It was clear that none of the Hatfields would ever have found him. "He knew we would come, and there he was, with his pointy ears just showing above the grass. When I came to pick him up, he looked right at me, as if he were expecting me. He didn't try to run away at all. I think he was playing a game." She beamed at us. None of us, with the possible exception of Tom, had ever heard her say so much at once.

One of the Delias, I think Delia Ybarra, said, "Maybe he wanted to be free." But we didn't pay any attention to her. It was so obvious that no fox would want to be free when he could be rescued by Lorelei.

I thought for a moment of her dealings with Tom and tried to feel angry at their secret intimacy, but I couldn't call up any disapproval. Lorelei was an amazing girl and a fox-catcher. Tom was lucky to have her. All of us were.

Unfortunately his possession of her carried ramifications well beyond the simple issue of loyalty to the rest of us. A week after Barnavelt's short-lived escape, when I had become almost accustomed to the idea of Tom's nightly visits to Lorelei, several of the older cousins and I were sitting in Isabella's room. A desultory card game was in progress, but for the most part they were all just chatting. It was one of those evenings in which everyone seemed full of wit, and with much delighted laughter the cousins were tossing around ideas for shocking Aunt Edie. I drank in the innuendo, more desperate to learn than I ever was in school. Every night with the cousins was an education, even when, as on this night, their love of absurdity outweighed their inclination to pursue scandal with any seriousness.

Yvette appeared in the doorway in the midst of one of Francesca's most outrageous and comical descriptions—it involved an elaborately staged series of silhouettes for Aunt Edie to catch sight of through Shorecliff's windows as she took her morning walk. The words were almost unintelligible because Francesca, watching Isabella's disbelieving face, was laughing so hard as she spoke. But Yvette deciphered the gist and raised her eyebrows.

"Who would it be?" she said. "You, Francesca? Charlie? Don't you ever get bored with your own jokes?"

"If you're in a bad mood, don't stick around," said Tom.

"I'm not in a bad mood. I just don't see why Francesca wastes her time teasing Charlie and making things up when there's a much better story right here in this room." She stared at Tom. I don't know why she picked that night for a fight. Maybe she had been sitting in her room, listening to the laughter from down the hall, working herself into a fury. At any rate, her intention was unmistakable. Tom, who had been lolling on the floor, slowly rose to his feet.

"What do you mean by that?" he asked.

The comic atmosphere died. We all stared, even Francesca, who—I was proud to remind myself—knew less than I did about the secret tensions between Tom and Yvette. Or perhaps that was only wishful thinking on my part. The older cousins rarely missed a trick, and in retrospect it seems unlikely that Francesca or Philip or any of them would have failed to notice Yvette's infatuation.

"Well?" he said, when Yvette didn't respond. He took a step closer to her. "Well? Aren't you going to explain? They don't know what you're talking about."

"Of course they do," she said, tossing her head. "Everyone knows. It's obvious. The aunts know too."

For a brief second Tom was startled. "They do? Why—did you tell them?" Then he looked at her face, and his eyes narrowed. "You're lying. They don't know. You just think everyone knows because you can't stop thinking about it, can you? I bet you imagine it."

Yvette winced, and the rest of us stirred uncomfortably. "Take it easy, Tom," Philip said. I glanced at him. He was watching Tom from the spare bed, but he was poised for motion. I could see that he was debating whether or not to break up the fight by stepping between them. The rest had similar expressions on their faces, both horrified and expectant. They were wondering if Tom was going to tear down the barrier of implication, if he was going to come right out and say something that would make it impossible to smooth things over.

Yvette's eyes were locked on Tom's. They were staring at each other with an intensity that, if truth be told, held no place between family members. "You're just scared," she said. "You're scared every day that people will find out. That you won't get to have her anymore. That she won't want you anymore."

She was obviously casting around for any remark that would sting Tom. Nevertheless, her words hit home. For the first and nearly the last time, I saw Tom lose his temper. He bridged the remaining distance between them in one stride and with his body inches from hers looked her slowly up and down. "Would you like this better?" he said. "You're just trying to hurt me—I know that. But it won't work. I can hurt you much more, any day. Can't I?"

The electricity between them was palpable. The rest of us felt it, and it nailed us to our seats. Whether it was resentment or attraction or simply the excitement of possibility, it made Yvette tremble. She was breathing so quickly that her chest heaved. Tom lifted his hand. It seemed for an instant as if he were actually going to touch her, and in that moment I saw his expression falter. He had begun in anger, but a devoted admirer, even a jealous one, can be compelling. I think it was the first time he considered Yvette as a girl he could actually caress.

Isabella saved us from disaster. With a clumsy bound she stood up and slipped her arm around Yvette's waist. "That's okay, Yvette," she said, tugging her away from Tom. "He doesn't mean it. He's just joking around." She glared at Tom, surprise and hurt patent in her face. I can imagine that it would be disconcerting to see one's own brother so unmistakably tempted by desire.

Yvette, freed from the magnetism of Tom's stare, kept her eyes on the ground, and Isabella ushered her back to her room like a nurse with a patient. From the rest of the cousins came several audible sighs of relief.

"Jesus, Tom," Philip said.

Tom looked around at us, saying nothing.

"I think—" Charlie began hesitantly. "You know, maybe we should all just—you know, tone it down. All of us, I mean." He smiled hopefully at Tom but could not help glancing at Francesca. Fascinated as Charlie was by her, there was no frightening intensity in their flirtation. But Tom's intimidation of Yvette had cast a shadow of risk over the rest of us. For a few moments it seemed necessary to take Francesca's salacious teasing seriously, something no one—least of all Charlie—wanted to do. He was, I believe, genuinely innocent in his appreciation of Francesca, and she, in those early days, was simply amusing herself out of boredom. For Yvette and Tom the stakes were higher, the feelings deeper—passion and longing edged their impulses.

I think Isabella felt a similar intensity, but it lacked, at first, a defined focus.

It should also be noted that Delia and Delia, without any hint of sexuality, were experiencing emotions of an equivalent power. Their immense adventure of the summer, however, was in the bond of friendship—a bond equally deep, equally magical, equally passionate, and yet how much less dangerous and destructive than the attractions and jealousies that rocketed back and forth among the older cousins!

Charlie, in his good-natured, blundering way, was trying to bring us back into the comfort of the family circle. We all appreciated his effort, especially me. I was dreading the moment, near to inevitable, when one of them would remember I was in the room and send me away.

Tom, smiling sheepishly, said, "Yeah, you're right." He was still standing. Awkwardness prevented him from sitting down.

"We all know just how far you've gone with Lorelei," Francesca said. "In case there was any doubt on that score."

"Pretty hard to miss at this point," Philip said with his inimitable sneer, half mocking, half comradely.

"In fact," Francesca said, beginning to grin, "Yvette was right, in a way—it's too good not to be put to use. If our aim is to give Aunt Edie a heart attack, what better way than to lead her over to the Stephensons' one morning. 'Don't worry, Aunt Edie,' we'll say, 'we're just going to get some jam from Old Farmer Stephenson.' And then, when we bring her into the barn..." She dove into the story, embroidering it with her velvet voice, skirting around the details, covering up the nakedness of Tom's emotions. In ten minutes they were all as uproarious as they had been before the fight.

The next day at the shore Tom—urged by Isabella—walked over to Yvette as she sunbathed and said, standing above her, "Will you play racquetball with us? We need a fourth player."

She squinted up at him, shielding her eyes with one tense hand, searching his face.

"Really," he said, and he smiled. "We do."

It was an apology, as clear as any apology could be. Yvette stood up in a fluid, long-legged movement and said, "Okay." She smiled back at him. "Thanks."

They were friends again. But we had seen the confrontation between them. We had felt the waves of emotion rolling out from where they stood, as if a boulder had been thrown into a pool. Their restored friendliness was genuine on one level, but the menace of that other level—the level where true alliances are made and broken—lurked beneath their interactions from then on. It lurked beneath us all, tied together as we were.

8

New York

Toward the end of July, my mother fell into step with what was destined to be a long line of family betrayals. I was in her bedroom, visiting her in the evening as I sometimes did. She had asked me to come there especially that day, but I suspected nothing. We sat on her white bed, looking out at the yard that was glowing in the last of the sunlight, and chatted about the day's events.

My mother liked to wear dresses that set off her figure—usually they had flowers on them, blue or green or yellow. Aunt Margery wore wide-brimmed sunhats, but my mother never wore anything on her head except when traveling, for which she always donned a maroon cloche hat. Shorecliff was good for her, in spite of the constant noise of children and their escapades, and her skin by this time had tanned to a warm brown that I loved.

I was feeling vividly and consciously happy when she said, "I have something to tell you, Richard."

"What is it, Mother?" I asked.

"Your father called yesterday while all of you were out at Condor's cottage. He's going to come up for the weekend. Won't that be nice?"

She knew I would think it was anything but nice, and I couldn't believe she looked forward to his visit either. Theirs was not precisely an unhappy marriage—my mother would not have scrupled at divorce had my father been cruel—but she stuck by him through what seemed to me to be cruel coldness. When I was older, my mother told me my father was made of pure honor and that was why I didn't like him. "His honor is untinged by mercy," she told me, "or humor or understanding for human mistakes."

"That's not my type of honor," I growled, then in college.

"No, but it's a sort the world needs in some men," she replied. I failed to see the truth of that statement, and I failed even more to understand why she would marry such a stony pillar of honor. She said that she had wanted to find the man behind the principles, but when I asked her if she'd had any luck, she dodged the question. I hope she did find the man. At any rate, I can truly say that my father has never lied, never stolen, never connived for his own gain, and never betrayed any man's trust. It occurs to me that I should value this last trait, given the events of that summer. And I do value it. You could and still can depend on my father always to be himself. He is never absent when he says he will be present; he never startles anyone with an unexpected smile or joke. Everyone who knows him can be certain that when they speak to Richard Killing the First, they will be speaking to the same dour, thin-lipped, iron-clad man they have always known.

But I would like to ask my father if he has ever burst out of his protective shell, if he has ever thrown away his high-flown morals and raced out on some shocking, thrilling adventure. Did he ever disobey his elders? Did he ever break a rule? Has his heart ever pounded? Has he ever turned red? Has he ever let out a real burst of laughter, one lasting longer than his usual humph of amusement?

I've never asked my father those questions. He is still alive; I could still ask him. But I know that I won't, just as I wouldn't and couldn't as a child. Even then I wanted to ask my mother whether my father allowed any crack to appear in the mask he wore, if only to show her that he loved her. I worried often that he didn't appreciate her. But I didn't ask her that summer or ever, so I can only hope that he did.

At thirteen, my thoughts of him were permeated by fear. I knew he would never beat me, but his reprimands were worse than blows—they were so unbending, so mercilessly stern and distant, that I felt as if I were being given a glimpse of some hell where human feeling had been eradicated. When my mother told me he was coming, I was horrified. Shorecliff, my haven, was being invaded by the outside world's most dreaded agent.

"Why is he coming?" I cried.

"Why, to see you and me and all of our family," my mother replied. She didn't pretend not to know why I had asked, though. "Don't worry, Richard. Your father loves you very much"—she never ceased trying to convince me of that—"and besides, he won't be staying long."

My cousins weren't excited to hear of my father's visit either, but they were courteous about not showing it in front of me.

"Uncle Richard is coming?" Tom said with a glance at Philip, when I came into their bedroom and told them. "That's fine. It's just for the weekend, right?"

"We'll survive," Philip said, looking at me. "You will too, buddy," he added.

"I don't want him to come," I announced. It was important that my cousins be aware of my own dislike of him. I didn't want them to think I was on his side, in the enemy camp.

"You know what your father's got going for him?" Philip asked.

I expected him to say something about how he never lied or never let down a client, and I said, "What?" resentfully.

"He's really smart," Philip said. "I've only spoken to him a few times, but he's really, really smart. He's maybe the smartest man I know. I think he's even smarter than Uncle Cedric." Tom threw a pillow at him, but he ignored it. "Anyway, I think that's worth something," he told me.

I had never thought of my father that way, but Philip was right. He was extremely intelligent—it was what made him such a successful lawyer. And though Philip was trying to be nice, he was also sincere, and that made me feel a little better.

Pamela also offered me an unexpected bit of comfort. We were dawdling in my room, and I must have hinted at how worried I was. She was looking out the window—I wasn't sure she was even paying attention—but eventually she said without turning around, "Well, at least you never have to feel embarrassed by him. Uncle Richard never acts like an idiot." It was a perspective on my father I had never considered—up to that time fear and resentment had pushed out any possibility of embarrassment. But like Philip's observation, it was undeniably true.

The next two days were spent in unpleasant anticipation. My father was arriving on Friday evening. Aunt Margery, the official driver of the rattletrap, my mother, and I were all going to Pensbottom to meet him. The prospect of entering the town, scene of Francesca and Charlie's glorious escape, enlivened me somewhat, but I found that the closer we got, the more anxious I became. I was sitting alone in the backseat. Halfway there, after some intense calculation, I said, "Mother, I'll let you sit in the backseat with Father on the ride back, so that you can talk with him." Mother laughed and said it was sweet of me.

The train arrived ten minutes after we reached the station. My mother insisted that we get out of the car and line up alongside it, the way Pamela and Aunt Margery had when my mother and I came. My father was the fifth person off the train. He was wearing a black, pinstriped suit, undoubtedly the one he had worn to the office, and a homburg hat. He looked distinguished and very tall. My mother came up only to his shoulder, and she wasn't particularly short for a woman. When she saw him stepping down from the car, she ran forward with a bright smile and said, "I'm so glad to see you, Richard!" Then she put her arms around him, and he kissed her. I couldn't analyze the emotion in that greeting because my father was approaching the car. First he said hello to Margery, and she said, "It's nice to see you, Richard." Then he said, "Hello, Richard. How have you been?" He never called me Junior—a mark in his favor.

"Hello, Father," I said, swallowing. It was a terrible, awkward hello.

He ruffled my hair but didn't smile or hug me. "You'll have to tell me what you've been doing."

"Playing with the cousins, mostly."

"Had some fun?"

"Yes, lots."

"Been a good boy? Been a good son to your mother?"

"Richard has been a delightful son, as he always is." My mother smiled at me with her special smile, signifying our membership in a private, two-person club.

"Well, I'm famished," my father said. "Let's drive home." I resented his calling Shorecliff home.

Thanks to my preemptive strike on the ride down, I had the comfort of Aunt Margery's cushiony body next to mine on the ride back. Mother and Father spent nearly the whole thirty minutes mute, and Aunt Margery, usually garrulous to a fault, was cowed into silence.

When we arrived at home, the same formal greetings were handed out on all sides. My father shook hands with the other men, smiled a lips-only smile at the women, nodded at all his nieces and nephews, and considered his duty done. Aunt Rose—for once taking on the role of chef—gave him a wonderful meal that he acknowledged with conventional compliments, and then he sat back at the dinner table and engaged in shop talk with Uncle Frank and Uncle Cedric.

I was relieved to see that Uncle Kurt, though appearing to pay attention to their conversation, contributed very little and at times glanced over and winked at me. Sometimes, when I went to his room in the mornings, instead of launching into a story about his wartime adventures he would ask me for advice on some unimportant matter or probe my feelings on a certain topic. When Francesca and Charlie ran away to Pensbottom, Uncle Kurt and I had a man-to-man talk about it, weighing the pros and cons. In hindsight, it was maybe hypocritical of Uncle Kurt to indulge me in these discussions, but at the time I felt privileged and, for once, valued for my intelligence. That night I knew I would find solace in his room the next morning, when I could complain to him, in an adult manner of course, about my father's visit.

During that first evening, my cousins walked around as if they had taken a vow of silence. Normally our dinners, held at the enormous table in the dining room, were rowdy to say the least. Food fights had been known to break out, riotous arguments raged from the salad through dessert, jokes were told, secrets were revealed. Dinnertime was one of my favorite times of each day. But when my father ate with us, my cousins were replaced by lifeless replicas of themselves. They all remembered to put their napkins in their laps. They spoke when they were spoken to and not before. They were so subdued that they didn't even smile or exchange rebellious glances. I looked at them with despair in my heart. Would the rest of the summer be like this? Would my father, with one three-day visit, kill the life of Shorecliff altogether? I felt not only horror but guilt—he was, after all, my father, and I was convinced that my cousins condemned me on account of his presence.

As soon as they had been released from the bondage of the dinner table—and Aunt Rose, in an unexpected show of compassion, exempted the two children on kitchen patrol from their duties—the cousins raced as one to the third floor. My father's tentacles of sobriety did not reach up two flights of stairs.

I had been held longer at the table as The Son, an additional punishment, and when I finally arrived upstairs, I went immediately to Pamela. I found her and Yvette sitting on their beds, talking. The rest of us never knew what the Wight girls said to each other. They got along well and almost never quarreled, possibly because their decorum prevented them from anything but passive aggression. I respected their sisterly bond, and I also found their combined reserve hard to face. Therefore, though they both politely turned to look at me when I entered the room, I didn't ask Pamela to come with me. I just said, "I've gotten away."

"That's good," Pamela said.

They waited; I left. The next door to try was Isabella's. I found not only her but also Charlie, Francesca, and Tom. They were, I assume, having a meeting about how to fight the dragon. When Isabella called for me to come in, I closed the door and stood in front of it, feeling as if I were facing a panel of judges in a courthouse. Their stares, though not accusing, seemed as intimidating as my father's cold gaze. Finally I exclaimed, "I don't want my father to be here!" Then I burst into tears.

Isabella leaped up and enfolded me in her gawky embrace. It was the first time she returned to her old habit of hugging me, and in the midst of my tears I thrilled at her touch. She dragged me to her bed as a sort of trophy, and as I sobbed on her bony shoulder I could feel Francesca rubbing my back. The boys patted my shoulders and told me not to worry. We Hatfields excel at empathy, though all four cousins must have known that my misery was exaggerated. My father, after all, was leaving that Sunday, and he was not deliberately attempting to spoil our fun. It would be easy to head out to Condor's cottage or the shore the next day and avoid all contact with him. Nevertheless, they felt the magnitude of the situation as I saw it and suffered with me, and I was grateful to them for doing so.

I was also grateful that they didn't try to comfort me by vilifying my father. Tom kept saying, "He's really not that bad, Richard. He's just not like the rest of us, but that's okay. After two months with us, you'd think you'd want someone who didn't fly off the handle about everything."

"None of us mind that he's here," Isabella said, which was a blatant lie.

"And remember what Philip said," Tom added.

"What did Philip say?" Isabella asked.

"He said that Uncle Richard was incredibly smart, which he is. Richard here ought to be proud of him. He's one of the best lawyers in New York."

"The main thing, Richard," Francesca told me, "is that you love your mother, and she chose to marry your father. You have to trust her about that. We all love Aunt Caroline, and we know she's just as smart as Uncle Richard. She wouldn't have married him if he weren't a great man." Francesca's phrasing was a little odd, but her insights were sound, and her comfort was the most effective, though their pats and hugs all helped to quiet me.

I went at last to bed sedated after an hour of crying and coddling. The next day we played our traditional morning game of croquet, and Lorelei appeared. I watched with trepidation as Tom led her up to my father, but Lorelei never lost her poise. She was wearing a blue skirt and a white blouse, and her feet were bare. "Good morning, Mr. Killing," she said. A smile fluttered on her lips without quite coming into existence. "It's very nice to meet you." That was all. We returned to the game, and my father returned to his conversation with Uncle Cedric and Uncle Frank at the sidelines. Though they both took up their usual posts in lawn chairs—sagging, moldy chairs that were ragged after years of steady use—my father stood beside them, wearing clothes that would have gone unremarked in his legal office, sipping a glass of lemonade and shading his eyes to watch us play.

In the afternoon we went to visit Barnavelt. All eleven cousins stuck together that day, and Lorelei remained with us. Condor had never received such a large visitation. Soon after we arrived, though, we switched tactics and went to the shore—we were feeling restless and uncertain. It was one of Lorelei's only appearances on the beach. She wasn't wearing a bathing suit, but she picked up her skirt and dabbled in the shallows with Pamela and me while Tom cavorted farther out to show off for her.

Dinner was a reenactment of the previous night's meal. My father asked us for a report of the day's events, and in the halting summaries we gave him, the fun and exuberance drained out of our activities, making us seem like colorless, uninteresting children. Other than this alarming loss of personality, we got through the meal unscathed, and eventually Aunt Rose nodded once again at whoever was on kitchen patrol and said, "Not tonight, you two. Go on upstairs."

It was later that night, when it was dark outside and we were retiring for bed, that my father showed his powers of destruction. He and my mother had ended up in the kitchen alone. I was with them for a while—it would have been a cozy family scene had different actors been playing the parts—but after I had suffered for fifteen minutes, they sent me to bed.

It must be obvious by now that I spent half my time at Shorecliff in shameless eavesdropping. When I left the kitchen, I did not trot straight upstairs but instead lingered in the rarely used morning room adjacent to the kitchen. Tucked into the shadows and the dust, one could hear perfectly what was said in the kitchen. I wasn't sure what I was listening for, perhaps a clue to my parents' relationship, but I stood there, pressed against the wall, feeling the rapidly beating heart that spying invariably produces, even before anything has been discovered.

"Well," my father said. "Richard seems to have been staying out of trouble pretty well."

"He adores it here. Being with his cousins has done wonders for him," my mother replied—ever loyal.

"Yes, apparently he's been enjoying the summer, though I wonder what influence those children can have on him. You know what I think of the Ybarras."

"They're good children, all of them, Richard. You've seen for yourself."

"I've seen the look in Francesca's eye, that's what I've seen. Cedric and Frank told me about her incident with Charlie Wight. That boy is no better, it would seem, though I'm sure she dragged him along."

As my father said this I glanced at the doorway to the parlor and through that into the main entryway of Shorecliff, and I saw Francesca coming down the stairs. She walked noiselessly to the morning room where I was standing, acknowledging what I was doing with a mere lift of the head, and then froze when she heard my father's voice. I assumed she had come down for a glass of water, or perhaps to see if the coast was clear for a late-night swim—one never knew with her. But she had not expected my parents to be on the ground floor. It was uncanny that she arrived directly before my father revealed the reason he had come up to

Shorecliff, thus ensuring that she heard his story from beginning to end. Coincidence can be very cruel.

"Caroline, it's about the Ybarra family, or what's left of it, that I wanted to talk to you," he said. "I came up here to see you, of course, but also because I've been hearing ugly rumors about Loretta."

"Rumors?" echoed my mother, instantly on the alert. She had her fair share of Hatfield family pride, and her battle blood rose whenever someone hinted at an insult to the tribe.

"Yes, rumors. The most disturbing part is that I've heard them from my own clients. I was mortified, as you can imagine, though naturally the most important thing is to save Loretta."

"Well, what are the rumors?" My mother's voice was hard.

"It's difficult to say this, but the gist of it is that she's become utterly brazen in her affairs. We've always known she was promiscuous—look at her marriage, for God's sake. And it's been no secret to her family that she has the tendencies of a nymphomaniac—"

"If by 'her family' you mean her children, they certainly are not aware."

This made me look at Francesca, whose connection with Loretta I had almost forgotten in my eagerness to memorize every word I didn't recognize for later research in my dictionary. The definition for "nymphomaniac" was unexpectedly frank: "a person obsessed with sexual relations." Afterward I was never able to think of my Aunt Loretta without remembering that word.

One glance at Francesca, however, drove all vocabulary questions out of my head. She wasn't trying to hide herself. She was standing in the doorway to the parlor, and I'm sure if my parents had craned their heads they could have seen her. Her hands clutched the doorframe on either side of her, and her coquettish little nightie, pale blue with lace around the neck and ruffles on the shoulders, barely reached mid-thigh. With her black curls tumbling loose, she looked like a seductress herself, but her face wore an expression of such heartbreaking shock that it destroyed any suggestion of sexuality. Francesca occasionally seemed much older than twenty-one, mature in her manners, her knowledge, her language. But when she heard of her mother's habits, her face showed the innocence of a seven-year-old whose world has been demolished, and I, looking on from my corner, felt as if I were witnessing something no one should be allowed to see.

Nor did the horror stop there. My father had merely been laying the groundwork for his story. "In any event," he went on, "whether or not her children knew, the rest of us did, and we were prepared to accept her behavior, or at least resign ourselves to it, as long as she remained discreet."

"Your method of resigning yourself was to forbid me to see her in New York," my mother interrupted.

"Caroline, that is not the point. I didn't want to cut you off from your own sister, but we are not a rich family, and my business is sensitive to reputation. In any case, Mr. Karlevich—you remember him, the man with the fraud case against his uncle—told me a few days ago that someone had mentioned Loretta to him in frankly revolting terms. As he related them to me, this other man's words were 'that slut Loretta Ybarra, apparently an in-law of Mr. Killing's.' You can imagine my dismay."

There was a pause. My mother didn't say anything. Francesca had jerked her head back at the word "slut," so I knew it was important. Tears began to roll down her cheeks, but she kept her head thrown back with her neck rigid, so that it looked oddly as if she were bound to the doorframe, her hands clutching the wooden posts. She was waiting for more, and it came.

"I don't know what Loretta wants or what she's thinking when she gets herself into these situations, but it seems she's not only involved herself with several different prominent men, she's done it publicly. If she'd set out to become the town harlot, she couldn't have done a better job. And I can't have my practice suffering from this woman's behavior. Really, Caroline, whether or not she's your sister, it's little better than prostitution."

"That's enough, Richard!" my mother said, and from the way she said it I knew she was crying. Apparently she hadn't known the extent to which Loretta's passions ruled her life.

"If she's acting this way to support her children, surely she knows that we would gladly lend her money rather than see her throw herself and her family away in this manner. In any case, it's time you all got her in hand. If she keeps it up—"

"Stop, Richard! I've heard what you had to say."

I dared another glance at Francesca. My position had become intolerably embarrassing, but since Francesca was blocking my one avenue of escape, I could do nothing except cower in my corner, trying not to look at her too often and striving both to hear and not to hear the conversation in the kitchen. By this time Francesca was crying in the stifled way that causes one's face to swell up and become bright red. She kept half bending over, as if she were being attacked by bouts of nausea—maybe she was.

What made it so unbearable was that Francesca had always adored her mother. Her conversation was sprinkled with constant references to Loretta: she could learn to speak a language fluently in two months; she had turned heads all over Europe; she wasn't afraid to stand up to anybody. Francesca modeled much of her arrogance and wildness on what she believed her mother's behavior to be, but whereas Francesca's unruliness was rooted in her innocence, Loretta's had been born of experience and cynicism and God knows what else. As I watched Francesca in the doorway, it seemed as if a great weight descended on her, and I imagined it to be not disgust with her mother but rather an overwhelming helplessness, for nothing now could save Loretta from humiliation.

My parents' conversation did not last much longer. Francesca's sobs became audible, and my mother, hearing them, let out a gasp and rushed to her. In her worry that Francesca had overheard the conversation, she didn't notice me in the corner, and when they found me later it didn't matter anymore. Francesca became hysterical when my mother wrapped her arms around her. My father came to the doorway of the kitchen and looked at the two of them huddled on the floor. It was one of the few times I've seen a look resembling remorse on his face. After a moment he turned around, and I heard the screen door of the kitchen slam shut. He had gone outside to escape.

Aunt Margery heard the commotion soon enough, and within a few minutes the first floor was swarming with so many relatives that Francesca suddenly rose like a missile from her heap on the floor, shrieked wordlessly, and flew up the stairs. The children wandered from room to room, weaving in and out among the adults and asking what had happened. My mother refused to tell them, but at the same time she needed to let the aunts and uncles know of Loretta's disgrace. For a few minutes there was an impasse. Then Tom and Philip caught sight of me. They knew my talents as an eavesdropper, and they quickly realized that I knew all there was to know. I was hustled upstairs, followed by a pack of cousins.

Yet after they had placed me on Philip's bed, when I saw him and Cordelia gazing at me, thirsting for knowledge, I refused to say anything. "Ask Francesca!" I hiccupped, nearly crying myself and wrapping my arms over my face so I wouldn't have to see them anymore. "I won't tell you. Ask Francesca." Though I didn't understand fully what had happened with Aunt Loretta, I had seen Francesca's reaction, and I had no intention of witnessing a repeat performance from her siblings.

At first Francesca refused to speak to anyone, but after an hour she let Philip into her room. In any case, before the night was over everyone knew the secret. It was inevitable in a house filled with so many loud talkers. Aunt Margery soon worked herself into one of her semi-hysterical states, and her exclamations, combined with Aunt Rose's booming tirades, broadcast Loretta's scandal through the house.

I might as well set the record straight now regarding Loretta's activities. My mother had a long talk with her at the end of that summer, and Loretta told her the story of her disgrace. No one except my father questioned her confession. She had never, in fact, gone around with more than one man at once, and only one had brought her into the public eye. Unfortunately he was a notorious celebrity, a forty-year-old bachelor named Joel Ambersen, known for his conquests of women, his twin penchants for extravagant clothing and exotic animals, and his endless funds. Loretta, once connected to him, was helpless against the flood of gossip. I don't believe she was such a scarlet woman as the press and society circles painted her. No one could question her fondness for men, but it was her equal fondness for glamour and excitement that struck the finishing blow. Loretta could never resist a man who lived on the edge, and this particular tycoon, the heir to his father's hard-earned millions, had lived with ostentatious recklessness since he was eighteen. So people laughed and sneered at Loretta and marveled at what she would do for money. That was part of what Francesca resented. I remember her crying at one point that night, "She wouldn't do it for money! She doesn't care about money!" And she was right—Loretta acted only out of love, though she loved the thrill of passion as much as the man himself.

The worst part was that it soon became clear, from snippets we read in week-old gossip columns, that Loretta's millionaire had thought of her as no more than a passing indulgence. There were claims that Loretta had called the scorn of society upon herself by trying to win her lover back when he had obviously left her. Rumors flew that she had stood in the rain on his street corner, that she had screamed at him and his new date in a restaurant, that she had offered herself again and again and been rejected. Who could hear such stories about her mother and not feel that her touchstone had been unveiled and derided as a sham?

When Philip heard the news he didn't say anything informative. I was lurking in the corridor when he came out of Francesca's bedroom, and I knew that he knew, but his eyes passed over me as if barely registering my existence, and he said, "If anyone wants to know where I am, I've gone for a walk." Then he went down the stairs and out the front door. It was after midnight, but no one cared about rules that night.

I never found out what Philip thought about the whole thing. As far as I knew, he never discussed it with anyone, not even Tom. I suspect, however, that his mental life saved him from the full blow of his family coming to pieces. Francesca, after all, had patterned her life on her mother's—Philip had always turned away from it. Now he simply averted his face yet further. Cordelia's reaction showed itself only later, but from the first, Delia Robierre mourned with her. So did we all.

As for Francesca, after my father's revelation her lightheartedness abandoned her. Maybe she had been trying to live the romantic dream she had of her mother's life, and now, equipped with her new knowledge, every jokingly wanton move seemed like a step toward her mother's fate. Maybe she was overcome with self-loathing at the possibility that she had been living off money raised by her mother's affairs. Whatever the reason, Francesca's fire was smothered in a stroke by my father's words, and all that remained were its smoldering, angry coals. The extent to which we, her cousins, relied on Francesca's energy, the extent to which we reveled in her mischief, her defiance, her throaty laugh, we learned only after we had been deprived of them and given her ghost.

Yes, it was indeed a sad day when my father came to Shorecliff. Our grief focused not simply on Loretta's action but also on the plant we knew would grow from that seed—the humiliation she would feel, the sidelong jabs from newspapers, the eyebrows that would soar at every mention of her. Most poignant was the fact that within her own family her position had changed. From being the embodiment of romance and daring, she fell to being an object of regret and uncertainty. Had I discovered that one of my cousins was no longer worthy of admiration but instead deserved only pity and a touch of contempt, then maybe I would have felt what Loretta's children felt.

The depression that now settled on our family, though it didn't last in its full force for more than a week, was augmented by the simple fact that we were at Shorecliff. My father's bomb of a story might not have been so earth-shattering if he hadn't dropped it in the midst of our summer bliss. Regardless of the bickering and tantrums that so often interrupted our games, Shorecliff previously had seemed like an impregnable fortress. For the first two months we lived in an oasis, away from the fears and surprises of the real world. Even Yvette's passion for Tom and his dalliance with Lorelei, though they set our pulses racing, were contained in the isolation of summertime, a portion of the year bracketed off from the rest of life. Shorecliff offered us an unshakable sense of safety—until my father came. After that all of our passions gripped more tightly, and there was no safety anymore.

My father, who had caused this tumult, left almost unnoticed the following day. Francesca never blamed him; she told me as much before the end of the summer. After all, he had not been responsible for Loretta's actions, and in his own reptilian way, for his own self-preserving motives, he had been trying to save her from further humiliation by asking her family to put a stop to her antics. Still I lay on my bed that night, after climbing into it at last at three in the morning, and I stared at the ceiling and planned his punishment. I never contemplated violent punishments for my father—they seemed out of place for him, and besides, violence wasn't cutting enough. Instead I planned elaborate public humiliations, grandiose versions of what I so often felt in his presence. Often, with vindictive pleasure, I imagined him realizing that he had been making a fool of himself in front of thousands of people he wanted to impress.

That night I imagined him feeling every ounce of what Aunt Loretta must have felt when she read the first snide remark about herself in the society columns, and never had his humiliation seemed more deserved. It was his toneless, emotionless voice that most enraged me. I kept hearing him say, "It's no better than prostitution." I had looked up "prostitution" in my ancient dictionary and found "the practice of selling sexual favors for money," which, once again, proved unexpectedly comprehensible. The idea that my father could speak so impassively about what he considered the prostitution of his own wife's sister—that revolted me, especially with the image of Francesca's reaction fresh in my mind. In my fantasy, I imagined a rock-hard voice just like his own blaring in his ear, "Richard Killing thinks he's the most talented lawyer in New York. It's a shame he doesn't know what everyone's saying about him, that he's a deluded, incompetent, run-of-the-mill amateur. Pitiful, really. They're all laughing at him down at the club." Yes, I knew even then what would hurt him most.

9

One Delia

The day after my father dropped the bomb, the day he left, my mother tried to call Aunt Loretta and bring her up to Shore-cliff, partly so that she could get away from New York and partly to show her children that she hadn't turned into an ogre as a result of her sins. The aunts were more upset than one might imagine given that they, unlike Loretta's children, had been aware of her promiscuous tendencies. They had not known, however, that she was continuing to indulge them.

There was a family story, so familiar that all of us knew it, of how Loretta had first met Rodrigo. She had been in Barcelona, shopping for trinkets to send home to her brothers and sisters, when a man bumped into her from behind. Loretta's bags went flying. Cheap necklaces clattered along the plaza, tangling around women's ankles and dogs' legs. Loretta's temper always simmered just below boiling point, and it now exploded. Leaving the inno-cent passersby to pick up her dropped belongings, she whirled around and attacked the tall, dark stranger with a barrage of

American-accented Spanish. At once she attracted a ring of rub-berneckers, and merchants came from behind their stalls to calm her. The stranger grabbed hold of her, putting his hands on her shoulders, and said, "My God, you are the most beautiful woman I've ever seen. Come to dinner with me." When I was young, this struck me as a ridiculous thing to say, and I thought Loretta was even more ridiculous to accept his offer, but that's what she did.

Aunt Rose claimed that when Loretta told her later about the meeting, she spoke with her eyes glazed and her lips parted. "Rose," she said, clutching her sister's hand, "the minute he looked at me, I knew I would never want another man. Rodrigo is the man of my life." It poses a problem when the man of your life dies after only twelve years of marriage. Since his death Loretta had been involved with nearly a dozen men, but her sisters only found out about the strength of her desires on the day when my father revealed her public shame.

The aunts, therefore, were in favor of calling Loretta. Aunt Margery was particularly incensed. "It's not the thing itself I mind," she exclaimed, "it's what she's doing to her own children. Let her play whatever godforsaken games she likes. But at least let the children keep their self-respect! Don't let them think that on top of being a wild woman, their mother would sell herself for money! It's a damned shame is what it is." That was the one time I ever heard Aunt Margery swear.

Aunt Edie was the only adult in the house who minded Loretta's behavior in itself. Most of them were angry, as Margery was, because they were worried about the Ybarra children. But Aunt Edie was horrified that her sister was still heading down the road to sin—a journey that Edie seemed to think Loretta had begun with her mar-riage to Rodrigo, if not before. The morning after my father's reve-lation, Aunt Edie cornered a handful of cousins—Isabella, Charlie, Yvette, and Fisher—and lectured them for a good twenty minutes about the dangers of promiscuous sex, though she used archaic euphemisms rather than direct explanations. Her arguments might have been more convincing if she hadn't explicitly warned Charlie away from Francesca. As soon as the four cousins escaped, they thundered upstairs and reported the lecture to the rest of us. My worldly knowledge was expanding in leaps and bounds.

While the cousins were marveling over Aunt Edie's paranoia, my mother was in the kitchen debating with Margery and Uncle Cedric the advantages of a phone call to Loretta. Edie lurked outside the closed door, still puffed up from her lecture.

When I went downstairs, I found her pacing back and forth like a sentry. "Children aren't allowed in there," she rapped, shooing me away.

"I need to speak to Mother," I replied.

"What has happened in this family is not fit for a child's ears," she announced. "Your mother is engaged in the missionary work of rescuing a lost soul. A soul that in my opinion is irrevocably lost."

"Aunt Loretta's not lost at all. She's in New York. We all know where she is."

"You missed my metaphor, Richard. I meant lost in a figurative sense."

I had not missed her metaphor; I was attempting to lure her attention away from the door, and at this point I succeeded. Darting past her, I burst into the kitchen to hear Cedric saying, " —if only to get her away from the newspapers and gossipmongers."

"Richard, didn't Aunt Edie tell you not to come in here?" My mother was standing up. She made her way to the hall without further comment—a sign that she was truly distracted, since under normal circumstances she would never have let me be so rude without a more extensive reprimand—and disappeared into the phone booth.

"Who is she calling?" I asked.

"Your Aunt Loretta," Uncle Cedric said.

"But she didn't listen to what I had to say."

"Well, what did you have to say?"

"I wanted to tell her that Delia is crying. She's in her room and won't let anyone in, not even the other Delia. None of us know what to—" I looked up, hearing a crash. There Cordelia was, hurtling down the stairs, her face distorted into ugliness.

Under normal circumstances, it would have been against all of my private rules to report a cousin's crying to the adults. Not only would the older cousins have flayed me alive, but I would have been consumed by my own guilt. This, however, was a different matter. Most of us, at one time or another during that turbulent summer, had been seen to cry. I myself, just two nights ago, had been nearly hysterical in Isabella's room about my father's arrival. Pamela had gone through her temper tantrum, and Yvette, while rarely gushing tears, had been upset many times. The Delias, however, had been so delightedly wrapped up in each other that I had never seen either of them look more than passingly solemn, except for the crisis of Cordelia's near-drowning. Even then, Delia Robierre had been the one in tears. It was shocking now to see Delia Ybarra cry, and unthinkable that either Delia would lock the other out.

We had been laughing over Francesca's irreverent plans for a future with Charlie. "We'll name our first child Edie," she had declared, "and Aunt Edie will shriek and faint at the baptismal ceremony. The child will be a drooling idiot, and when it gets older we'll make my mother her godmother." I didn't understand any of this—I was laughing partly from relief and partly from nervousness. It was reassuring that Francesca was no longer hysterical, but the way she spoke now differed from the way she had spoken in the past when making her wilder remarks. Before she found out about her mother, she would wear a little half-smile of excitement and raise her eyebrows until she reached the high point of the joke, then burst into a gale of laughter. Now she spoke with a flat, humorless smile on her face, and her voice was bitter, as if she were trying to wound herself with her words.

Isabella and I laughed out of a sense of duty, not from real appreciation, and our lame, thin giggles were still hovering in the air when a strange sound came from the spare bed. We looked over and saw Cordelia's head hanging over her lap. Her short curls hid her eyes, but we could hear well enough. She was crying in a painful, donkeylike way. Beside her, Delia Robierre dissolved at once into sympathetic tears, but when she put her hand on Cordelia's shoulder, Cordelia shrugged her off. Francesca's hard face changed then into a look of horror.

"How—could—you!" Cordelia gulped, drawing in ragged breaths and letting them out with her shoulders heaving. I was worried that she would throw up in her lap, but she was simply sobbing with the body-shaking heaves of a person who rarely cries but who abandons herself utterly when she does.

Francesca stood in a rush and moved toward her. She obviously wanted to comfort her sister, but even for Francesca Delia was too daunting at that moment. Instead she hovered, exchanging glances with Delia Robierre. It was one of the few times I saw her hesitate. Charlie had been sitting on the spare bed too, and he had to force himself not to move away. I saw him inching toward the footboard.

"When Mother is all alone in New York, and everyone is making fun of her, and now you're mocking her like all the rest of them. Her own daughter…"

After that, Francesca never made another joke to us about her mother's antics. It was a long time before I heard her make a joke about anything.

"Right now," Delia went on, "she thinks that no one loves her at all. But I'm going to get on the train back to New York, and she'll see…" Here she broke down beyond the power of speech, and then, before any of us could stop her, she bolted from the room and ran down the hall to her own bedroom. Delia Robierre was a few steps behind, but when she tried the door it was locked, and in spite of all her pleas, the other Delia remained silent and the door stayed ominously shut. In the ensuing confusion I slipped downstairs, where I found my mother about to call Aunt Loretta.

Cordelia seemed to know what my mother was doing by instinct. Having burst out of her room and raced down the stairs, she didn't even glance at me or Uncle Cedric or Aunt Edie. She flung open the folding door of the phone booth and took my mother's arm, not violently but with enough force that my mother looked up in alarm and put the receiver back on the hook.

"Aunt Caroline," Delia said. She had stopped sobbing, but her eyes were glistening, and her voice was higher than usual and slurred, as if someone had distorted a recording of it. "Don't call my mother. Don't bring her up here. The last thing she needs is more people making fun of her and telling her she's done something wrong. Please don't bring her up here now!"

"But Delia," my mother said, sitting on the bench in the phone booth, "I wanted to invite her here so that she could have a rest from everything that's happening in New York. Don't you think she might want to come up here and be with the people who love her most? We don't condemn her, Delia," she added, holding Delia's hand and looking into her red face with what I thought was admirable steadiness. "Your mother has led a difficult life and made many mistakes, as all of us have. I'm only worried now that she may be feeling lost and alone."

"I worry about that too," Delia faltered, and I thought how strange it was to hear a Delia say "I" instead of "we." She was teetering on the verge of tears again. "I don't want her to see our faces. We won't be able to help it, but we'll be lined up—Francesca, Philip, and me—and we'll look at her. She won't be able to bear it!" That was enough to send her off again. The last intelligible thing she said was "Call her up and tell her we love her, but don't let her come up here. Don't let her come!"

My mother shot Aunt Margery a look that pleaded for help. The adults were as unnerved as we were by seeing a solitary Delia bursting with emotion.

"Delia, darling, I think you should lie down," Aunt Margery said, putting her arm around Delia's shoulders.

Delia didn't shrug off Aunt Margery the way she had the other Delia, but she accepted the caress as if she were a sack of vegetables. She seemed to be immune to everyone's words and gestures. Soon she ran upstairs and returned to her room, and Delia Robierre drifted into Isabella's room to wait disconsolately with the rest of us.

Neither she nor Francesca nor any of the other girls succeeded in persuading Cordelia to open the door that day. Eventually, when we were all nearing tears at hearing Delia Robierre's endless pleading, Cordelia called out, "I'm sorry, Lia, I just want to be alone for a while." That night, still shut out, Delia Robierre slept in the spare bed in Isabella's room, taking refuge in Isabella's sisterly concern. My mother said later, "I never knew Cordelia felt for other people so strongly," and we agreed. Until then we had seen her only as one of a pair, directing all her emotion toward her counterpart. Now, standing alone and upset, she seemed both more vulnerable and more formidable. We all yearned to help her, but no one knew how.

When Delia disappeared once more into her room, my mother turned to Uncle Cedric. They were still so wound up in the catastrophe that they didn't notice me hanging on the stair railing. Aunt Edie scowled at me, but her authority was negligible.

"The most terrible thing is that I think she has a point," my mother said. "We know they love her, but all Loretta will see when she gets here are their horrified faces. Francesca has been completely shattered. Who knows how Philip has taken it. Margery said she heard him coming in from his walk after five this morning. And now Delia."

"Delia is the most troublesome one of all," Aunt Edie said. It was typical of her to say "troublesome" rather than "troubling," but there was sympathy in her tone.

"I'm afraid we would end up torturing Loretta if we invited her up here," my mother said. "Don't you agree, Cedric?"

Cedric had maintained an air of regal reserve throughout this crisis. Probably it was his method of keeping his emotions in check, or maybe it was an attempt to take on the commanding manner of Aunt Rose, who unusually had not made an appearance that morning. Of all the Hatfield sisters, she was the most closely bound to Loretta, both by affection and by clashing tempers. Uncle Cedric now pronounced his judgment in the decisive tone we usually heard from his wife. "Delia said you should call Loretta and give her a message. Under the circumstances, we ought to obey her wishes."

"I agree," my mother said with a slight smile, "though you don't have to act as if Delia has died and left a will. I'm sure they'll be all right eventually."

"Will they?" Aunt Edie asked darkly, as Uncle Cedric retreated into the dining room. "I don't suppose anyone has considered what this situation will do to the children's prospects in New York. Do you imagine they'll be able to waltz back into their old life as if nothing has happened? Who will see them? Who will invite them into their homes? You know as well as I do that the children of a loose woman are a favorite subject for the scandalmongers."

My mother frowned, which meant that Edie's questions

couldn't be brushed off as we did so many of her comments. "Well...Delia is still in school and Philip will be going off to Harvard in the fall. I don't think they'll have much trouble."

"But Francesca?" Edie insisted.

My mother sighed. "I don't know. Loretta's own set is generous about these things, I believe. They won't have been the ones spreading the rumors, so maybe they'll be polite enough to ignore the whole business. The more sensible women might even be especially kind to Francesca—I'd like to think so. But one thing's certain," she added as Edie opened her mouth to speak. "The last thing Francesca is worried about right now is her position in society. She's grieving over her mother, not herself. Hearing the story the way she did must have been an awful experience, especially for someone like Francesca—so headstrong and wholehearted about everything. She doesn't need anything more to worry about, and you shouldn't add to her burden by bringing this up with her."

"Of course not," said Edie. "But someone needs to think about it."

"I'll talk to Loretta, and we'll see what can be done. In any case, I hope we're not the type of hidebound family who thinks Francesca's life will be made or broken by the number of names on her dance card." She cocked an eyebrow at Edie and in doing so caught sight of me hanging over the railing. "Run away, Richard," she said.

She spoke affectionately but firmly, and as a result I didn't hear a word of her phone conversation with Loretta. Instead I went upstairs to ponder the array of ominous phrases I had picked up from Edie's remarks.

For the next few days I felt so shaken by the typhoon of emotions in the house that I, like Cordelia, spent a great deal of time alone in my room. Interacting with the cousins frightened me. The Ybarra children were set apart, and the other cousins tiptoed around them for fear of saying something out of place. Our jazz parties were a thing of the past, and when I went into Tom and Philip's room one evening, I saw that Philip had dismantled his Victrola. We could not listen to music, much less dance, when Aunt Loretta was in such straits. Everyone who had heard Delia's halting description of her mother alone in New York was tormented by the thought that no one was comforting Loretta. Pamela was especially dismayed by the idea. She would come to my room and sit wordlessly next to me on the bed, and after a while she would say, "It's so horrible. Just horrible. Imagine everyone laughing at her, and she's all by herself, and there's nothing she can say to make them understand."

Our solemnity infected all of Shorecliff. Even the air seemed tamped down, as if the house had been muffled. Uncle Kurt, who had returned from hunting with Frank and Cedric only the day before my father arrived, said one evening at the dinner table that he was afraid they had made a mistake and come back to the wrong address. The joke didn't go over well. Uncle Kurt's gaze traveled to each of the Ybarra children in turn as they picked at their food. I usually treasured the fact that he limited his niece-and-nephew attention to me, but when I saw him eyeing the Ybarras, I felt relieved. Uncle Kurt, of all the adults, seemed most well equipped to handle sadness.

I was thus only momentarily surprised when, four or five days later, I knocked on Uncle Kurt's door and found Cordelia sitting by his desk. I stared at her, thinking how novel it was to encounter her without another Delia by her side. Her grief had redefined her as an individual, and by doing so it had made her once again a stranger.

"Good morning, Richard," Uncle Kurt said. "Delia and I were just having a talk. Would you mind coming back later?" Delia didn't look at me.

"No, I don't mind," I said.

"Thanks, buddy," said Uncle Kurt. He had picked up the habit of calling me "buddy" from hearing Tom and Philip say it so often.

An hour later, when Delia came out, I happened to be on the stairs. She didn't seem as if she were about to cry, so I risked a question. "What did you talk about?"

"Lots of things," she said. I felt almost happy at hearing her disdainful voice. She spoke as if she considered me infinitely younger and more ignorant than she was, but it sounded wonderful because that was the way she always spoke to me—her voice was no longer plangent with tears.

"Did Uncle Kurt tell you a story?"

"Yes, he did."

"Did he mention Hennessey?"

"Who's Hennessey?"

"What did he tell you about?"

"Let him tell you if he wants to. I'm not going to say it all over again."

I was painfully jealous that Uncle Kurt had told her a story I had not yet heard, but I couldn't get up the courage to ask him about it. Instead I waited on tenterhooks for the cousin grapevine to pull through. Eventually, it did. Cordelia, coming across Delia Robierre sitting sadly in their room, at last relented and sat down next to her. Hearing their voices, Isabella ran down to find them talking earnestly, gazing into each other's faces the way they always did when wrapped up in a story or a plan. Another cousin might have discreetly slipped away, but Isabella burst in, declaring how happy she was to see them together again. As soon as she heard that Delia Ybarra had been conversing with Uncle Kurt, she ran to find Francesca, and together the two older girls demanded all the details of the story Kurt had told. Soon afterward, with her usual dramatic flair, Isabella told the story to me.

One of Uncle Kurt's most beloved officers had been named Captain Kerrigan. Delia couldn't remember where Kurt had been stationed at the time or what his company was doing there—details I would never have neglected—but she knew that Uncle Kurt idolized Captain Kerrigan. All the men loved him. Through the heaviest gunfire he not only kept his cool but remained compassionate toward the men in his charge. Many of the officers, at least according to Uncle Kurt, were monsters of discipline who considered kindness a flaw in an officer's character. But Captain Kerrigan didn't subscribe to that mindset, and he gained almost perfect obedience from his company.

Their devotion was augmented by his unflinching bravery. Apparently he was once sitting in an empty lookout post, comforting a private who had been frightened into gibberish by a recent attack, when an unexploded shell hurtled down and thumped into the mud right next to them. The private shrieked and scrambled down the trench in a panic, but Captain Kerrigan glanced at the shell, stood up as casually as if he were getting out of bed, and walked away without looking back. The private described this incident to the rest of the company, and from that point on Captain Kerrigan had the loyalty of every man under his command.

One day another private was making Captain Kerrigan's bed—really just an army cot. When he lifted up the mattress—an old, moldy, hay-filled mattress plundered from an abandoned peasant's cottage—he found a stack of photographs held together with a piece of string. They were pornographic photographs, showing naked women in all sorts of horrible positions and doing things, as Uncle Kurt told Delia, that no one would ever want to see a woman doing. "Of course," Kurt said, "nine out of every ten soldiers had pictures of women tucked away somewhere, lots of them racy enough to lay your Aunt Edie out flat. But these were different. They weren't just racy—they made you sick." Delia reported this statement word for word, upon Francesca's request, but that was as much detail as we got about the photographs, and for a long time I had to make do with Philip's curt definition of pornography—"sex pictures." My own dictionary, in a return to nineteenth-century vagueness, defined it as "books or photographs of an explicit and compromising nature."

The private who found the pictures felt horribly guilty at discovering Captain Kerrigan's secret weakness. He was so bewildered that he walked straight out and showed the pictures to Uncle Kurt, who also felt that Captain Kerrigan had been defiled. How could they respect him, knowing that every night he was lusting over disgusting images? Uncle Kurt made his friend put the photographs back, and when Captain Kerrigan went into the dugout that night, neither Kurt nor his friend made any comment. They didn't tell the other men in the company. It was heartbreaking enough that they themselves wouldn't be able to think of him anymore without connecting him to pornography of the vilest sort.

Uncle Kurt told Delia that for a long time he didn't even like to speak to Captain Kerrigan because he felt too guilty knowing the captain's secret and too disgusted by the secret itself. But Captain Kerrigan was Kurt's commanding officer, and he had to interact with him every day, whether he wanted to or not. Captain Kerrigan never guessed that anyone had discovered the pictures, and eventually Uncle Kurt found himself pretending that he didn't know about them, or at least forgetting their existence for long stretches of time. He ended up feeling more affectionate toward Captain Kerrigan than before, simply because he knew that underneath the captain's godlike exterior was a man as fallible as the rest of them.

"No one," Uncle Kurt told Delia, "is so courageous and so strong that he has no weaknesses. Your mother is no different from anyone else. All of us are upset by her situation because so many people know about her weakness. But all of us also know what a magnificent woman she is. Just because she has a weakness doesn't mean she's any less the person we love." Then he asked her, "Do you think she's done anything wrong?" and Delia said, "I wish she wouldn't do it for the money." Uncle Kurt said, "Do you know for sure that's why she's doing it?" Delia agreed that she didn't, and Uncle Kurt told her to withhold judgment until they had more information. He was wise in this suggestion, for as I said, we later found out that Aunt Loretta had been involved notoriously with only one man, and she had refused to accept presents from him.

Delia said that Uncle Kurt had spoken to her in a way no one else ever had. Francesca didn't find his story nearly as comforting as Delia did and was scornful at how much faith her sister put in his reassurances. But I understood why Delia had been relieved. It was not so much what he said as how he said it, the way he looked at you while he was speaking, that made Uncle Kurt's stories so magical. He could deliver a riveting tale and all the while make you feel that his attention was riveted on you.

The day after I found Delia in his room, I knocked on his door. The first thing he asked was "How are you feeling, trooper?"

I told him I didn't like seeing all the cousins so upset, and he said, "I couldn't agree with you more, Richard. I couldn't agree with you more. Are you upset?"

In all honesty, I hadn't been hit as hard as they had been, and after a moment of deliberation I said, "Only because they are."

Uncle Kurt laughed and said, "That's the way of the world, kiddo." He was full of taglines like that. No matter how hackneyed, they seemed profound when he said them, and once again I felt bowled over by his infinite knowledge.

The Aunt Loretta Incident, as I thought of it, never really went away. Francesca permanently lost her earlier manner, and we could all feel the remnants of shock lurking underneath our daily routine, as if a poisonous gas were leaking up to us from New York. But gradually things went more or less back to normal. The adults were eager to bury the incident and pretend it had never happened. I sympathized with them, since I believed their determination stemmed from an anxiety not to have their summer ruined any further. The Ybarra children took longer than the aunts and uncles, but eventually they too seemed to make a decision not to think about their mother unless forced to do so.

About a week after my father's visit, we woke up to an overcast day, gray and cloudy. On such days Shorecliff fell victim to a cruelly cold wind off the ocean, a wind that felt impossible during the summertime, as if just beyond our sight a winter storm had whipped itself up over the waves and were blowing toward us. No one did anything that afternoon. The older cousins shut themselves in their rooms. They often did this, excluding me and Pamela. The aunts were in the dining room, surrounding a pile of mending like a flock of hens gathered around a heap of seed. Pamela, with what I considered snooty disdain, declined to play with me. In desperation I decided to go out. My mother was surprised and alarmed. She became almost like Aunt Edie during bad weather—it called up unreasonable fears that I would catch cold. I swathed myself in a sweater and jacket and insisted on stepping out the front door. Once beyond her grasp, I was glad I had insisted. The cold air slapped at me, but it was a refreshing slap, and I felt wide awake. After a few moments of deliberation I stumped off, a lone intrepid explorer, toward the cliff.

The cliff played a central role in our life at Shorecliff. We used it as a path to walk along, a lookout place, a focal point for our daily play. The adults were not happy about this, for the cliff, though it descended down to the surf in great rocky ledges rather than one sheer face, remained dangerous. There are limits to the powers of adult regulation, however, and with the cliff only forty yards from the house, they couldn't keep us away from it. Of course, it was the danger that drew us. The risk joined with the possibility of exploring was a combination no child could resist.

Near Shorecliff the coast turned sharply. If you walked west along it, you could trace a line above the patch of woods hiding Condor's cottage and see a glimpse of the Stephenson farm before the coast swung northward again. I had found Tom meandering along that elbow of the coastline more than once. He would grin sheepishly and assume I knew why he was there, which I did. Tom's visits to Lorelei had tapered off drastically during the week after my father's visit—he must have felt uncomfortable enjoying himself when his cousins were unhappy. After a few days, though, his enforced celibacy became too difficult, and when Lorelei appeared at the screen door of the kitchen one day, he swooped down on her, becoming once again an ephemeral figure in our lives.

The afternoon of my bad-weather walk, I assumed the cliff would be deserted, and indeed the stretch I initially approached, the portion behind Shorecliff, seemed utterly desolate. I watched the gray sea for a while—it was singularly unappetizing in its overcast state and melted into the clouds not far out from shore. I decided to walk east toward the beach where we swam, and after five minutes of desultory strolling I was surprised to see two figures coming into view above the brambles and blueberries.

By the time I was within fifteen yards, I could see by their dark heads that they were Ybarras, and a few more feet revealed Philip and Delia. The pairing was an unexpected one, as odd as Tom with Pamela or Francesca with Fisher. In my experience, Philip and Delia treated each other with the distant respect of siblings who have nothing in common but also no grounds for quarreling. Now, watching their backs as they stared out to sea, I realized they did have something in common. For all her usual sparkle and flash, Cordelia had within her the same smoldering passion that Philip had, and she possessed, like him, a fierce and deep-rooted loyalty. It made sense for the two of them to seek each other out during an Ybarra catastrophe, and even more sense that they would do so privately, in accordance with Philip's penchant for secrecy. I felt on seeing them a ripple of the pleasure one gains at discovering something logical, a piece that enhances rather than destroys the puzzle.

The sight also made me think of Philip in his capacity as a brother, a role I did not often consider where he was concerned. I imagined what it would be like to be the middle Ybarra child, with Francesca on one side and Cordelia on the other. The position seemed more intimidating than appealing—I couldn't picture myself standing up to either girl. Later that evening, during dinner, I watched Tom and Delia Robierre as they giggled together across the table, and I realized that Tom too was an older brother and had grown up with an adoring Delia. This time I was seized with envy. I had spent a great deal of time that summer wishing I could insinuate myself into another branch of the Hatfield family, but it had always been as the youngest and most insignificant member. To have a younger sibling of my own—someone who would look up to me, respect me, perhaps even admire me—this was a fantasy I had never woven before.

We all knew, moreover, that Delia Robierre took Tom's word as law, no matter what absurdities he produced. Her gullibility was a running joke among the cousins. Whenever Tom elicited from her an awed "Really?" and the rest of the cousins roared with laughter, I stayed in the background, congratulating myself on having avoided their mockery. But now I imagined myself in Tom's place as the worldly-wise brother leading his younger sister down the garden path. It was a new aspect of family life for me to explore, and I daydreamed about it from that time onward.

Of course, no one could live with the extended Hatfield family for a summer and not realize that having younger siblings can also be a disadvantage. When I found Philip and Cordelia on the cliff, I soon saw the drawbacks in action.

It was impossible to approach anyone along that stretch of cliff without being seen, so I didn't attempt to hide. Instead I strode through the brambles, breaking branches at every step and raising a hand in greeting—the image of an innocent walker, free of all intention to eavesdrop. When Philip and Delia finally turned around, I smiled and trotted across the remaining distance. "Hello," I said. "I was just taking a walk. I didn't know you were out here."

Philip laughed. "Richard finds his way everywhere," he said. "People who aren't in the loop think there can be privacy at Shorecliff—in their bedrooms or outside. But we know better, don't we, Richard? No matter where we are, you'll find a way to be there too, a few steps behind."

"He could be Shorecliff's ghost," said Delia. Her comments to me were usually dismissive, but today she seemed to be including me in the joke.

"Richard," Philip said, beginning to walk along the cliff. He obviously expected me to fall into step beside him, so I did. Delia strolled along a pace or two behind us. "I've just been telling Delia that we should devote ourselves to higher learning and the examination of man. What do you think of that?"

"I don't know," I said. This was usually the most acceptable as well as the most honest answer.

"It's ironic, isn't it, Delia," he went on, tossing the words over his shoulder, "since the foibles of man are what we're trying to avoid."

"You'll make a great professor one day," she replied. "You love to hear yourself talk. I think it's stupid. You're not saying anything at all."

There lay the peril of a younger sister—she was apt to be sarcastic just when you most wanted unquestioning support. But I too thought Philip sounded pompous, and it spoiled the glamour of his loftiness. Even though I didn't understand what he was saying, I recognized pretension when I heard it.

"The uncles are planning another hunting trip in a few days," I said, rescuing him by changing the subject.

"That's great for them. They have an escape."

"But they said we could do something exciting tomorrow, if the sun comes out."

"That would be a nice change."

"I think it would be neat if we all went somewhere together—the aunts and uncles too."

"Maybe we should devote ourselves to what Richard wants for the rest of the summer. What do you think, Delia?"

"It would probably be the best thing we could do," she said.

She didn't seem to be speaking sarcastically, and I was so startled to hear something friendly from her that I didn't say anything more. Of all the cousins, Cordelia was normally the last to be interested in my wants and welfare. But she was also the one most liable to bring out surprises, as I had discovered in the past week. For several minutes I felt buoyed up invincibly. I was relieved to see her outside, seeking the solace of Philip's wisdom, even if she did reply to it with barbed remarks. It seemed proof that the Ybarras were once more prepared to philosophize and bicker and offer me the snatches of camaraderie I found so thrilling. Though certainly not carefree, they were no longer acting as if their mother's disgrace had crushed them into complete dejection, and I dared to hope that their willingness to talk to me heralded a return to cheerful days.

10

Picnic

The exciting thing that my uncles had planned was a surprise picnic dinner. Unexpectedly, it was Uncle Cedric who spearheaded the venture. Emerging from his cocoon of silent observation, he announced his plan, organized the trip, ordered picnic foods from the aunts, suggested that we bring the tools of both athletes and naturalists, and selected the path we were to follow—west along the cliff until it curved northward and then inland to a small meadow that he had discovered on a hunting trip several years ago. Eberhardt and Edie declined to accompany us, and Uncle Kurt, to my disappointment, begged off, using his writing as an excuse. The other aunts and Uncle Frank laughingly agreed to come along, but Cedric was the leader. It was the first time that summer that either he or Frank played any sort of role in family events. As if to give its blessing to the expedition, the sun shone brightly and dispelled, at least for a while, the shadows my father had cast around the house.

Francesca didn't come with us that afternoon, but the other

cousins were all there: Fisher, bursting with delight at the thought of conversing scientifically with Uncle Cedric on our several-mile hike; Delia and Delia, appearing together for the first time after Delia Ybarra's days of invisibility; Charlie and Tom, eager to walk with the uncles; Yvette, Pamela, and Isabella in a trio, looking beautiful against the green grass and sunny sky; and Philip, as so often, walking alone.

Pamela was exceptionally agreeable on this expedition, and I spent most of my time with her after we arrived at the hidden field. During the hike I stayed by my mother's side, where I could observe my cousins unnoticed. Once we got to the meadow, the aunts formed a cluster on a blanket in one sunlit corner, the uncles spread out a miniature camp in another, and the cousins claimed all the territory in between, racing back and forth for sheer joy at being in an alien field. This field had the additional advantage of being situated in an unexpected location within a depressingly dark forest. When Uncle Cedric first led us into the wood, we all groaned in unison, but the abrupt transition from damp pine needles to cushion-soft grass made the gloomy interlude worth it. It would have been impossible to predict the meadow's existence had Uncle Cedric not promised it to us ahead of time. We stood on its edge, feasting our eyes on the sunlight over the sloping expanse, and Uncle Cedric said, "It's all ours. There's no one else around for miles."

Charlie and Tom arranged a game of badminton, and Fisher, who had belied his frail figure by heroically lugging the bocce balls all the way from Shorecliff, began to coax various cousins into the game. Yvette proved surprisingly adept, and soon the badminton players abandoned their tournament to contest her superiority. Charlie could never resist an athletic challenge. Philip and Isabella and even Uncle Frank joined in. I was debating the pros and cons of taking part—the possible glory of making a hit balanced by the shame of being unable to throw a bocce ball more than a few feet—when Pamela appeared at my side and said, "Let's explore the border." She often made suggestions of this sort, giving me a kernel of an idea to work with and then looking on as I nourished it to life. Now she walked by my side as I instructed her on the proper way to conduct a border patrol, using the terminology Uncle Kurt had been feeding me all summer. We discovered that the underbrush was especially thick around the edge of the field—part of its allure, since it made the place seem more private—and that if you hid in the bushes only a few yards away from someone else, you became very difficult to find. Much of the afternoon was spent analyzing this phenomenon.

We were still at it when we observed the most interesting aspect of Uncle Cedric's picnic. I was crouched in a holly bush, trying to ignore the pokes and jabs from its serrated leaves and waiting for Pamela's bland face to stare into mine when she finally found my hiding place. Through the branches I could catch glimpses of the field, sunlit cracks that yielded fleeting views of the cousins. In one light-filled slice I suddenly caught sight of Philip and Isabella, walking together toward the meadow's edge. This was an unusual combination and an intriguing one. I knew of Isabella's fascination with Philip, of course. Ever since the day Delia Ybarra had almost drowned, Isabella had been drawn to the lofty secrecy that hung around him. Philip, however, never seemed to have much time for her, at least not more time than he had for any of the cousins except Tom. Other than tossing me a word or two during a game or joking with me in the evenings as I passed his door to brush my teeth, Philip had hardly spoken to me, and I suspected that for most of us the story was the same. Yet here he was with Isabella, trailing off toward the far end of the field.

Luckily for me, the trajectory of my game of Hide and Seek with Pamela led in their direction, so I didn't have to point them out when her blond head appeared. I wasn't sure how she would take a confidence of this sort—one that verged on being gossip. I suspected she would look at me with half-closed eyes and say in her best impersonation of Yvette, "I don't know why you would mention that."

If Pamela noticed that our game was speeding up, she didn't say anything. I found her with record speed and concealed myself in absurdly ill-chosen spots. We advanced around the edge of the field, and eventually, as I leaned against the soft bark of a beech tree, I could crane my head and see Philip and Isabella walking aimlessly back and forth by the border, like sheep presented with a picket fence. It was obvious that they were using the walk as an excuse to talk—their heads, one black and one brown, like the Delias' heads when they conversed, were bent intimately toward each other. I saw a flash of Isabella's wide eyes as she stared at Philip's face.

Pretense at this point had to be abandoned. When Pamela found me and said, "That wasn't a very good hiding place at all," I replied, "Never mind that now. I want to hear what they're saying."

Pamela attempted to see the cousins in question and crashed into a bush with unpardonable carelessness. "It's just Philip and Isabella."

"Quiet!" I hissed. "I'm going to crawl forward and listen. You don't have to come."

"I wouldn't want to," she sniffed. "It would be eavesdropping."

"Tell it to your sister," I said, turning away. I had picked up retorts like that from the older cousins, especially Tom.

Thanks to the thick undergrowth, I was able to weasel my way to within a few feet of Philip and Isabella without being noticed.

"Do you really think that's the way it should be, though?" Isabella was saying, sounding more serious than I had ever heard her.

"That's the way it is, like it or not," answered Philip.

A shout erupted from the other end of the field. "Philip! Isabella! Come back here. It's time for dinner."

Philip turned to Isabella, and for a fraction of a second he looked awkward. "I guess we should go back," he said.

Isabella answered with a shy smile and a shrug. "Guess so." They turned toward the others, Isabella with studied casualness. I could see her smile growing irresistibly into a grin. As they walked back, her legs became more and more unruly, until she was bouncing along at Philip's side like a puppy. Philip glanced at her and laughed his philosopher's laugh. Isabella laughed too and steadied herself, but I had read everything from her limbs.

What surprised me, however, was that, different as Isabella's goofy gestures were from Yvette's icy stares at Tom, they conveyed the same message. It disconcerted me to realize that I now understood something about Isabella because of my earlier observation of Yvette. As for Philip, I had never seen him behave awkwardly before, but there had been uncertainty in his manner with Isabella, as if he didn't know quite how he had landed there and was not willing to admit how much it pleased him.

"Do you know where Pamela and Richard are?" Uncle Cedric bellowed.

"Let's go. They're calling us," Pamela said from behind me.

I turned around, gloating that she had followed me after prissily refusing to eavesdrop. But my gloating soon turned to alarm—she was preparing to plunge out into the open at exactly the point where Philip and Isabella had been standing.

"Not there," I said, grabbing her arm. "It will be obvious we've been listening to them. We have to go farther on."

"I wasn't listening to them."

"Yes, you were. You were right behind me."

"I just came to pull you away."

"It's obvious that you came to hear what they were saying."

We were still arguing when we emerged at last onto the grass, and at once we were confronted by the searching faces of the two people I had been trying to avoid. Isabella almost cannoned into us. "There you are!" she said. "It's time for dinner."

She tossed her head and, to my immense satisfaction, left Philip to Pamela in favor of racing me down to the other end of the field, where the aunts had spread a luxurious repast on a red gingham cloth. Aunt Margery was responsible for the little details that made our expeditions seem like entries in a booklet of American traditions. There were sandwiches for all, each according to our tastes, and several types of pies for dessert—blueberry, rhubarb, lemon.

While we were eating Charlie related the events of the bocce game. Yvette, to everyone's surprise, had held her own against the onslaught of more than half a dozen relatives and carried her team to victory. Charlie was still in shock.

"And what were you two doing?" my mother asked me.

"We were exploring the border," I replied.

I didn't say anything more; I had no intention of revealing our whereabouts or allowing Pamela to say anything about my tendency to overhear things. Instead I watched Philip and Isabella closely. Philip had returned to Tom's side, and Isabella was sitting by herself at one corner of the gingham cloth, apparently lost in contemplation of her sandwich. I inched my way over to her, and she smiled at me absentmindedly. Clearly I would learn nothing more until I could talk to her in private.

For a while we concentrated on the business of eating, enjoying a leisurely meal. At last, however, as Aunt Margery sliced up the pies, conversation revived, and the talk drifted to the subject of dancing. A few of the cousins stood up to prance over the field, and Yvette soaked up some praise from the adults for her unaccompanied Charleston. We were not a musical family, in spite of our penchant for jazz, and all of us that evening regretted not being able to complement our outbursts of energy with melodies. Isabella and Tom cavorted around the circle, and then my mother said, "Rose has told me about your talent in that direction, Cedric. Won't you show us a step or two?"

Cedric smiled into his mustache and shook his head. "Certainly not. I couldn't do it now. It's been years," he said.

Aunt Rose glared at him. She had been in her element, lording over the picnic baskets and doling out food with the exactitude of a drill sergeant. Consequently her color was up, her eyes were glittering, and she would not tolerate rebellion in her mate. "Of course you'll remember it," she said. "Cedric," she added to Uncle Frank, "won several prizes for his Irish step dancing when we were newlyweds."

The Hatfields have no Irish blood in them, nor have the Robierres, who as far as I know are wholly French in origin. I had no idea where Cedric could have picked up the art of step dancing, but after a few more moments of hesitation, he got to his feet amid applause from the cousins. Tom, Isabella, and Delia Robierre were laughing—they had seen their father in action many times. "Just you wait," Tom said to Philip. "This is one of Dad's greatest talents."

Cedric stood in front of us, his shirt and trousers hanging loosely on his thin frame. The field was bathed in the last of the daylight, the almost blue glow that comes before the sun disappears. Uncle Cedric's face as he looked down at us was in shadow, and because he was standing with his back to the sun, we had to squint to see him.

"I haven't done this for years," he repeated. Then he added, with a sidelong glance at us, "It's been known to some as the French step dance." He kicked out a leg and raised one arm above his head, curling the other arm in front of him the way a ballerina might before the orchestra begins. Immediately he was transformed into a man I had never seen before. Under his breath, he began to say, "Da da da. Da da da da." He didn't say it with any tune, or even with any voice. He was simply whispering the rhythm to himself. Then he launched into his dance, jumping and spinning and waving his arms. When I saw Irish step dancing in later years I could think only of Uncle Cedric, even though his dance bore almost no resemblance to it. His extravagant moves were, I suspect, entirely his own creation. As soon as I saw him in action, I began to doubt Rose's claim that he had won prizes. Nevertheless, we were all mesmerized, partly by his jerky movements and exuberant leaps, partly by his total lack of self-consciousness, partly by the almost bored tone in which he whispered, "Da da da da da. Da da." His own children continued to laugh softly, not derisively but in support, forming a sort of background chorus. The rest of us sat in silence, our eyes following every dash and twirl. As Cedric danced, the field became darker, and he became a more and more mysterious figure as the edge of his silhouette sharpened into a black line against the sky.

The dance went on for quite a while, and I had time to think, "Isn't it strange that this is the man I've always known, the man who is married to Aunt Rose?" This brought to mind my most formidable aunt, whose breath I could feel on my neck as she watched her husband. It struck me for the first time as more than a genealogical fact that Rose and Cedric were a married couple, that they shared a house and children and presumably loved each other, that in all particulars they lived as man and wife. This seemed incredible, and the gap between them seemed to widen as I watched Cedric's dance. Given her sense of dignity, I knew Aunt Rose would not be caught dead in such a compromising position, one vulnerable to the attacks of ridicule. It was surprising enough that she had encouraged her husband to dance in the first place. I had thought Cedric possessed a similar sense of dignity, an insistence on the sobriety of his person, but in ten seconds of French step dancing, he had obliterated that impression beyond recall. The Robierre marriage, therefore, seemed more inexplicable than ever.

At this point in my reverie, Uncle Cedric performed an impressive gallop from one end of our picnic cloth to the other, and I was reminded of Isabella's chaotic movements. I saw his children in him—Tom's unstoppable enthusiasm, Isabella's long limbs, even Delia's sturdy balance. Amiable, quiet Delia Robierre, who that summer lived in the shadow of Delia Ybarra, often adopted Cedric's unflappable demeanor. Both he and his youngest daughter could project an air of being as unexcitable as a boulder, so assured in their movements and calm in their decisions that their competence seemed unassailable and their judgments, when they came, irrevocable. Delia held less of this power at fifteen, but whenever it appeared no one could deny the resemblance between her and her father.

On the other hand, Tom's insistence on getting his own way—indeed, on his right to get his own way—came from his mother. So did Isabella's tornadoes of passion, equal in size whether they stormed over a game of croquet or the rights of women, and Delia's unswerving loyalty to her friends. These characteristics were unmistakably the legacy of Aunt Rose, who commanded us with the assurance of Napoleon and flew into rages over late sleepers but who would, I knew, unhesitatingly defend any member of her large family. These Rose traits—Hatfield traits, really—melded so lovably, so seamlessly, with the Robierre traits in her three children that I seemed to see, in a brief flash of emotional clarity, the bonds that joined her so closely with them and with her husband.

My thoughts raced in this way all through Cedric's dance. But when he finally pulled himself to a halt and sat down on the gingham cloth, I simply said to myself that I liked Aunt Rose much more than I had before. With his ridiculous parody of a step dance, Cedric had placed his wife in a far more favorable light.

After the dance it was obvious that the party was over. Nothing could eclipse Cedric's triumph, and we packed up the baskets and gathered the bocce balls with the sated languor that is nearly, though not quite, the best part of any picnic. Night was falling rapidly, and my mother and Aunt Margery began to voice some concerns that we would lose our way in the dark, that we might (this in a whisper) lose someone over the cliff. Uncle Cedric waved a hand. "Don't worry, girls," he said. "Frank and I have that all figured out. We're going to cut across the Stephenson farm and avoid the cliff altogether. We'll strike for Shorecliff inland."

At the mention of the Stephenson farm my eyes swiveled to find Tom. I knew he would be alert and poised, listening for more fragments of Lorelei's name. I discovered him, however, looking away into the trees by the edge of the meadow. Only the tips of his ears burned in the dying sunlight. The Robierres' extremities tended to give them away—Isabella's legs, Tom's ears, Delia's hands, which she clasped and unclasped when she was nervous.

The aunts were in favor of the alternate route home, especially since the sun soon disappeared; they were eager to get back to the homestead. Cedric struck a course through the belt of trees girdling the hidden meadow and led us south. The moon rose over the tops of the pines, and though it wasn't as big as it had seemed on the night of our nocturnal jaunt to the shore, we all admired it. The time passed quickly, and we hardly noticed when we crossed the line from gentle wilderness to farmland.

As usual, I was keeping a close eye on the cousins. The Delias and Pamela walked behind Uncle Cedric. Pamela occasionally changed allegiances and traveled with the two Delias when she got bored with me. I didn't mind much because I knew they would soon turn her away, and her absences gave me time to track the other cousins. Fisher was walking by himself, his shoulders sagging from the weight of the bocce balls, though he did not voice a single complaint about having to carrying them. He was probably comforting himself by listening for owls, something he did often that summer with great enthusiasm. The three aunts walked in the middle, serving as the center of a straggling family web. Then came Yvette and Isabella and finally, lagging behind everyone, Tom and Philip.

Isabella was near the aunts, but she was walking in a bizarre fashion—lolloping forward and backward. Eventually I realized that the reason for her gait was that she was trying to walk with Philip and Tom but couldn't get up the nerve to break into their conversation. All my efforts to overhear their discussion were in vain. They were used to my exploits by this time, and whenever I neared they grew quiet and grinned at me. I knew they wouldn't have minded much if I had heard them—on Tom's side, for one thing, it would be all Lorelei, an intrigue I knew about already. No, they liked to frustrate me out of adolescent sadism, a trait I recognized and understood. I didn't mind, either. The night was too warm and peaceful to be annoyed about anything. For long stretches of the walk I strolled alongside my mother, who was sharing the task of carrying the picnic basket with Margery and Rose. The three of them passed the time by talking about the good old days when they had been girls at Shorecliff.

More than an hour had passed when Cedric stopped. We were walking in a field that had recently been mown, and the chaff crept up my legs and itched horribly. I hopped on one foot and scratched while the aunts inquired about the halt.

"Well, Cedric?" Rose asked. "What's going on?"

"I'm not sure," said Cedric, pausing between each word. He was turning in a circle, peering into the darkness.

"You're lost," said Rose. "This is wonderful. So much for your navigating skills. I would have thought you'd know this whole area like the back of your hand! Do you realize we have young children here who need to be in bed?" I took this as a personal insult. "Who came up with the idea for this shortcut anyway?"

"It was me, darling, and I still think it was a good idea," said Cedric. "It's just a matter of orientation. Fisher, you don't know where we are, do you?"

"I don't have a good sense of direction," Fisher confessed.

"Anyone here got an inner compass?" Uncle Frank asked. He said it jokingly, as he said most things, but I sensed a note of genuine concern in his voice. Grown men hate being lost, and it makes it worse when there are women and children hanging around, demanding solutions.

No one, it appeared, had an inner compass. I have never been able to distinguish the cardinal directions, and at the time, as the youngest of the group, it hadn't crossed my mind that I should pay attention to where we were going. At that age you are led everywhere; the responsibility for knowing where you're going has not yet crashed onto your shoulders, and you live in happy ignorance of road maps, wrong directions, and faulty estimates of time.

"It seems to me Shorecliff is this way," Uncle Frank said, waving a hand.

"No, no, that's dead west, Frank," Cedric replied. "You've gotten turned around as we walked. I'm almost positive it's that way." He pointed in another direction, not quite opposite to the one Frank had chosen.

"You're both wrong. It's this way," said Charlie. As the oldest male cousin, he often took part in the uncles' discussions. He was pointing in a third direction.

"Who knew the Stephensons had all these damn fields?" Frank said irritably.

I glanced at Tom—he would know. Philip nudged him, and Tom winked at me, pulling his mouth down so he looked like a clown. But he didn't have enough brazenness to flaunt his knowledge in front of the adults, and throughout their baffled conversation he remained silent. The rest of the cousins organized a game of freeze tag, and I joined in with vigor, though it meant losing track of what the uncles were saying.

After ten minutes of debate, my mother interrupted them. "It seems to me that not one of you has any idea where to go," she said. They fell silent and looked at her. "The one thing we do know," she went on, "is that we're on the Stephenson property. I suggest we continue walking until we find a familiar landmark. As long as we're on harvested fields, we can't be too far off. Isn't that right, Cedric? Sooner or later we've got to hit either the farmhouse or the woods next to Shorecliff."

"But the Craddock farm borders the Stephenson fields," Cedric said. "What if we wander into those?"

"We could go this way," Tom suggested, guilt finally getting the better of him.

But his father asked dismissively, "What makes you say that?" and of course Tom didn't have an answer.

"Sooner or later we'll hit a farmhouse," my mother repeated.

"In any case," Margery added, butting in, "it's not doing us any good to stand here doing nothing. Richard and Pamela are exhausted. They should have been in bed hours ago."

Since I was at this moment sprinting after Isabella in the game of freeze tag, Aunt Margery's words seemed unjust, and I skidded to a halt to object to them, allowing Isabella to skip out of harm's way. Cedric had agreed, however, and in a moment we were marching along again, this time behind a blind leader. Now that it was clear we didn't know where we were going, the darkness around us seemed thicker, the distances longer, the stars further away. The group pulled more and more tightly together, until we were walking in a small huddle. I had a firm grip on my mother's hand, and Pamela had found Aunt Margery. The Delias lurked by Aunt Rose, which was a measure of their nervousness. The only person at ease was Tom. He swung along behind us, his hands brushing audibly against his shorts. He wasn't exactly relaxed, for I noticed that he was holding himself straight and glancing from side to side over the fields; but he didn't look as if he were walking in a strange place. I knew he must have been there many times before.

Another ten minutes passed, and we hadn't found anything resembling a farmhouse or a stretch of woods. Our humor had died at this point, and we trudged in silence. The warmth of the night had lost its charm. The moon was merely a hard white pebble in the sky. This night taught me how big the world was: I realized that if one farm could encompass such never-ending tracts of land, then the world itself must be unfathomably enormous. How many countless farms were there, in how many countless countries and continents? I felt dizzy trying to think about them all at once.

"You look concerned, Richard," Uncle Cedric said. "Are you scared? We'll get home all right."

"I'm not scared," I answered. "There are just too many farms in the world."

Uncle Cedric quoted my reply for the rest of the summer. The older cousins too found plenty of opportunities to make fun of me for it. Tom in particular liked to race up and say, "Richard, Richard! They've just discovered another farm in Bolivia! Are you all right? Can you still stand?" Regardless of these jibes, however, the number of farms in the world seemed to me a reasonable cause for metaphysical concern, and Uncle Cedric knew what I was talking about, underneath his teasing.

In spite of his laughter, he was beginning to be frustrated; I could tell by his stiff-legged walk and the way his neck jerked when he turned his head. As soon as I noticed his distress, I felt sorry for him. I knew he was worried that his glorious picnic might end as a failure. I wanted to tell him that the first part of the day would still be good, that a bad ending doesn't mean a bad whole. This was one of the summer's most valuable lessons to me, and I thought he might benefit from it.

I never had a chance to tell him, though. Yvette was looking across what must have been the seventeenth field we had traversed and said, "There's someone walking over there. Look!"

Instantly Tom was by her side. "Where?" he said. "I don't see anything. Are you sure?"

A wave of laughter rolled through us, and I knew that if it had still been light I would have seen the backs of Tom's ears glowing a sheepish red.

"I think it's a man," Yvette said vindictively, glaring at Tom.

Tom paid no attention to her. He had caught sight of the silhouette striding across the field, and he waved at it, yelling like a banshee. Then we all saw it and began to wave and shout, and after a few minutes the figure resolved into Lorelei. The sight of her walking toward us in the darkness is one of my favorite images of her. She looked absolutely tranquil, as if her proper place in the world were among fallen stalks of grain in a midnight field. Her white blouse glowed silver in the moonlight, and her skirt swished around her legs. She was barefoot, as always. Her hair, falling in thick tresses on either side of her face, made her face look paler than ever.

She smiled at us shyly when she got near enough to see our expressions. "Hel-hello, everybody," she stammered. She got nervous when she had to talk to more than two people at once.

"Thank God you're here," Tom said, stepping out to meet her.

He didn't kiss her or even touch her, but we knew he was claiming possession.

"We're lost, Lorelei," said Aunt Margery. "Could you point us in the direction of home? We've been walking for hours."

"Of course we know it's ridiculous to be lost within a half mile of our own house," Cedric added. "But these fields—they turn you around."

"I used to get lost all the time at night, when I was little," said Lorelei. She was trying to make Uncle Cedric feel better, and she succeeded, though coming from anybody else what she said might have sounded condescending. "You're walking south now," she continued, "but Shorecliff is east of here. You've been walking just out of sight of the woods where Condor's cottage is. But you would have hit the road soon. So you would have made it home on your own in less than an hour." I thought it was gallant of her to refuse any credit for putting us on the right path.

"Are you having a nice walk?" Tom asked. At once I detected an inaudible second conversation. He was speaking in a constrained manner that could only indicate the use of code.

"Very pleasant, thank you," she responded. She was always polite to everyone, even Tom. I'm sure she was equally polite to him when they were alone. "I often walk around the farm at night. I'm not a very good sleeper."

"My dear girl, you must try to fix that," said Cedric. "Sleep is essential for a sound mind in a sound body."

"She's fine, Dad," Tom said, scowling at Uncle Cedric. "Night walks are good for the soul."

"They're good for something more than the soul in Tom's case," Philip said, and the cousins burst out laughing.

I thought it was rude to laugh at jokes like that in Lorelei's presence. I wanted to say hello to her so I could receive a personalized version of her angelic smile, but shyness prevented me. The most

I could do was edge toward her, inadvertently bringing my mother along with me.

With her usual perceptiveness, Lorelei spotted me in spite of my silence. "Hello, Richard," she said. "Are you enjoying yourself?"

I nodded.

"It's time he was in bed," my mother said, joining the traitorous forces. "I'm so glad you're here to tell us where to go. It felt absurd to be lost, knowing how close we must be. Would you like to walk back with us? I'm sure it's very late."

"After midnight," said Lorelei. "I should be going home myself. But I'll walk with you as far as the wood."

Within five minutes we could make out a smudge of black trees against the deep blue of the sky, and soon we were crunching twigs and leaves underfoot. Cedric slapped his thigh and burst into self-recrimination. He couldn't believe he hadn't been able to find the wood himself.

"I should go back," said Lorelei. She had been walking with Tom, who had taken her hand as soon as we were on the move.

"I'll walk you home," said Tom.

This recalled Cedric from his frustration. "Certainly not, young man!" he cried, putting an arm around Tom's shoulder and forcing him to walk forward. "Plenty of time for all that in later years. I'm sorry to deprive you of your guardian, my dear," he added over his shoulder to Lorelei, "but as you've just shown us, you know your way around better than we do."

"Please come and have lunch with us tomorrow," my mother said. Before my father's visit, Lorelei had come almost every day to our house, but it seemed since then as if she had been deliberately staying away.

"I will," said Lorelei, smiling. "Good night, everyone. Good night, Tom." She waved at us and walked quickly back across the fields. Within moments she had blended into the darkness.

As I turned to follow my mother through the woods, I caught sight of Yvette's face, staring after Lorelei. I had permitted myself an inner smirk of satisfaction when I heard Cedric's naiveté—as if anything he could say would prevent Tom from slipping out and returning to the farm as soon as we were all in bed! To me, however, the secret was something glamorous, something exciting that I could admire from a distance. I had forgotten the intensity of Yvette's feelings until I saw the look on her face as she gazed over the field. There was jealousy, of course, but also exasperation, as if she wanted to leap up and scream and throw her arms out and be as un-Wight-like as possible. She didn't do any of these things, but it would have been better if she had. As it was, all her frustration stayed bottled inside, and when it finally found expression, it did much more harm than her previous outbursts.

One more thing happened that night before I climbed into bed. Exercising great stealth, I kept watch from behind my bedroom door, and at last I was able to corner Isabella as she came out of the bathroom. "What did you and Philip talk about this afternoon?" I asked.

"What do you mean?" she said, but there was a grin spreading over her face. Isabella knew she was a terrible liar. "We were just talking," she went on without a pause.

"About what? What was Philip saying?"

"Why would you care?"

"I always want to know what Philip says. I think he's very interesting."

"So do I," she said. "But as a matter of fact, we weren't talking about anything. At least nothing I can say again. Philip has theories, you know, about the world, and he was telling them to me, I guess. I don't remember."

"But why did you go walking in the first place?"

Isabella shrugged. "We're cousins," she said, which seemed to me the most unhelpful explanation I had ever received—though, in its way, it held everything. She returned to her bedroom, leaving me alone in the bathroom doorway with my toothbrush. That was all I ever heard about their conversation. I think really it was the enchantment of the walk, rather than the substance of the talk, that mattered to Isabella. She had extracted what she wanted from the interaction without bothering over the superficialities. People never gave Isabella's insight enough credit—they became distracted by her awkward extremities and forgot the grace that lurked at the center of her. But it was her helpless honesty that I loved most, the way her feelings shone out whether she liked it or not. That night she was overjoyed. I could read it in every gesture, and it made me love her more than ever.

Yet thinking about her talk with Philip filled me with another feeling that I had difficulty analyzing. I was all too familiar with envy—I had spent much of that summer wishing I could be part of every interaction I witnessed. This time, though, I knew that simply being part of Isabella's conversation with Philip wouldn't have been enough. I imagined myself in Philip's place, next to her on the field. She would talk to me, I would watch her face…But what would she say? How would I act? I couldn't picture any of the details. The picnic taught me to covet something more, not just her company but her attention, her delight—even, unarticulated though it was, her yearning.

After a moment or two of standing alone in the hallway and wading through these thoughts, I remembered how happy she had been, and I reasoned that—putting aside all question of attraction—I too would be overjoyed if Philip had picked me as a confidant. I slowed down as I passed his bedroom, peering in as if taking casual stock of the room. Tom was sitting cross-legged on his bed without a shirt on. He waved to me. Philip was lying on his back with his hands behind his head. Neither of them was reading, but they hadn't been talking either. I wondered how often they sat together saying nothing. When Tom beckoned me in, Philip sat up, got his toothbrush, and disappeared for the bathroom.

"Who are you looking for?" Tom asked me.

"I don't know. No one."

"Did you have a good time today?"

"I sure did. That field was the perfect place to play games."

"You've got that right. And it got everyone's mind off things—don't you agree?"

"Yes, it did." I was thrilled. Tom had deigned to ask my opinion of a serious matter, as if I were his equal.

Then he added, grinning, "The end of the night was pretty entertaining, too." I knew he was talking about Lorelei, but I couldn't think of a way to respond, so with a quick "Good night," I retreated.

I almost ran into Philip in the hall. Toothbrush still in hand, he trotted down the staircase, and I leaned over the banister so that I could see his back as he knocked on Francesca's door.

"Francesca? Are you in there? Can I come in?" he called. A moment later he said, "Just for a minute." Then he opened the door and slipped inside.

In the excitement of the day, I had almost forgotten Francesca. I decided it was no use waiting for Philip to come back upstairs, since I wouldn't have the courage to ask him what they had been talking about anyway. Instead I got into bed and tried to imagine Francesca all alone in Shorecliff that day, with only Aunt Edie and Great-Uncle Eberhardt for company, rebuffed by Uncle Kurt as he worked in his room, whiling away the hours until we came back.

Later, when I had fallen asleep, I was visited by a dream that haunted me for many days. As I drifted off I had been thinking of Francesca's sadness, but the dream was about something quite different. At first I was walking with Isabella in the field, just as

I had imagined earlier that evening, replacing Philip. Isabella was beaming at me. It seemed natural to reach out to her, and then she was hugging me, crushing me with a delicious fierceness that I recognized from the years before that summer. This time, though, I hugged her back, and it was not the same, for I sensed her body against mine—and from there the dream hurtled forward, both frightening and exhilarating, as if I were inhaling a forbidden drug.

For a time I stroked Isabella's back and sides, reveling in a heavenly but misty pleasure. Then I discovered she was Lorelei, and I felt horrified, but, logically it seemed, I realized I was Tom, which made everything all right. Being Tom, I moved my hands in experienced passes over Lorelei's body and thought to myself, "So this is how it's done." Then, abruptly, Lorelei was Isabella again, submitting to my caresses. At this point I was floundering back to reality, yet for one unforgettable instant the vividness of the dream increased, as happens sometimes when dreams continue to the point of wakefulness. My hands were on Isabella's waist, and I could feel the heat of her body beneath her shirt. Then I awoke, my hands tingling, and I lay there thinking desperately that I should not have had the dream. I tried to forget it, but it remained a burning image in my mind, and I could not help savoring it, reliving the feeling of her warmth. It had never occurred to me that her body would be hot to the touch. That was what made the dream so real, for it showed me something entirely new but unquestionably accurate.

When Isabella came down to the kitchen that morning, I took one look at her, and my dream, which was rapidly becoming a malignant entity in my brain, leaped up as if it were mocking me. I stared at her, and though I tried to stop myself, I knew I was looking at her body in a way I never had before.

11

Hike

On the day before the uncles had arranged to leave for their hunting expedition, Uncle Frank announced at breakfast that he had devised a scheme to rival Cedric's picnic. The intervening days had witnessed a return to the moping pessimism that had clouded Shorecliff since my father's visit. We attempted a few halfhearted games of croquet, and Philip and Isabella, testing out their new comradeship, spearheaded a trip to the shore, but the day was cloudy, and they did not meet with much success. Uncle Frank, I think, wanted to be the hero who brought back the lightheartedness Uncle Cedric had briefly captured at the picnic. Pamela and I were the only cousins in the kitchen when Frank made his announcement, but the aunts listened politely, and as he talked a few of the older kids straggled in, drawn by the volume of his voice, which tended toward the deafening when he was excited.

"We went north with Cedric," he said. "I propose a journey south. We've been living for months now alongside that cliff, and we've never followed it. Who wants to map the coastline with me?" He swung around to Charlie and Fisher, who had appeared in the doorway. "What do you say, boys?" he asked. "A hike along the coastline. We'll see how long it takes before the cliff peters out."

"But we know where it peters out, Dad," said Charlie. "We go to the shore all the time, remember?"

"Don't be silly, Charlie. That's only a little gap in the line of the cliff. It starts again half a mile further on. Didn't you know that?"

Charlie shrugged, uninterested, but Pamela and I were intrigued. I had been bitten by the exploration bug since the picnic. The idea of heading out from Shorecliff into the unknown was enormously appealing, and I treasured the long hours of enforced proximity to my cousins.

"Let's go!" I said. "Pamela, don't you want to go?"

"I guess so," said Pamela.

Poor Uncle Frank looked crestfallen. The aunts, however, settled the matter.

"Today is cleaning day," said Aunt Rose. "We were going to kick all of you out of the house anyway. A hike sounds like the ideal solution. Richard, go wake up the other children and tell them they're going on a hike with Uncle Frank."

Aunt Rose frequently gave me the unpleasant task of awakening my cousins, a task sure to end in insults and thrown pillows. But I did it with relish, simply for the sake of staring in awe at Tom and Philip still asleep, their sheets tangled, their feet hanging off the beds, both of them bigger and more masculine than I imagined I would ever be. I liked also to wake Isabella because, unlike the other cousins, she didn't meet my whispers with abuse but with sleepy smiles and a chuckle muffled by the pillow. Then she would gaze at me, her eyes glazed by sleep, until she pulled herself into wakefulness.

On the rare occasions when Charlie and Fisher were still asleep when I made my rounds, they welcomed my entrance with polite thank-yous that made me feel guilty. The two Delias were the easiest to wake because as soon as one of them opened her eyes and saw the other in the opposite bed, she was sure to begin making faces and giggling. Yvette, on the other hand, was especially acidic in the mornings. I would come into her room, admire her river of hair, and say, "Yvette, Aunt Rose says everyone has to wake up." I'm sure she always heard me the first time, but she never deigned to answer, so I would repeat myself five or six times. There was no possibility of shaking Yvette awake—I would never have dared to touch her. After countless repetitions of my request, she would explode from the covers, her hair flying around her face, shoot me a poisonous look, and snap, "*Fine!* I heard you." Then she would fall back onto the pillow. She was always the last one to make her way downstairs, but I figured that my task was done when I got her response.

The cousin I most feared waking was Francesca. Not only did I have to enter her bedroom, which was nerve-racking enough, I then had to jerk her out of her dreams. Francesca was one of those people who look like aliens when they're asleep. She slept on her back with her head thrown to one side, so that I had to circle the bed to find her face. Then I would look at her for a few minutes, marveling at the stranger living in Francesca's body. Her hair tumbled onto the pillow in so many curls that it looked knotted, and her hands often crept up to her face in the night, her knuckles pressing against her chin. Her mouth would be open the tiniest bit, and her irises would be rampaging around under her eyelids. After my father's visit, I found the prospect of waking Francesca almost unbearably intimidating, but I knew that if I came downstairs without doing so, Aunt Rose would send me back up, so I slipped through her door and tiptoed around the bed. For a long time I simply watched her dream, imagining that her face looked sadder than usual, that her mouth was turned down at the corners, and that there were traces of tear lines along her nose.

Finally I said in a reedy whisper, "Francesca, it's time to wake up." Of course that did nothing. The worst thing about the whole procedure was that she slept so deeply I was often forced to shake her. This morning was one of those times. After repeated whispers that rose in volume without effect, I gathered my courage and found one of her shoulders. When at last she did waken, her eyes sprang open like window shades hurtling upward. "Yes?" she said frantically, as if I were about to tell her something of the utmost importance. She always said that. I think her mind woke a few moments after her body, so the urgency of her question arose from her dream emotions.

"Francesca, it's time to wake up," I quavered for the hundredth time.

There was a long pause while her wide eyes searched my face, her hands gripping the covers. Then she relaxed, and her head sank back into her hair. "Okay, Richard," she sighed. "I'll get up."

Eventually, that morning, we were all shepherded out the front door. Because no aunts were coming with us, we had to stand around while Cedric, Frank, and Kurt received extensive instructions as to our safekeeping. Not one of the cousins was left behind. Several of them were still rubbing their eyes and yawning, and none of them looked happy to be awake before nine.

The hike was ill-omened from the beginning. Most of us, by then, were yearning for something we couldn't have: Isabella watched Philip, I watched Isabella, Yvette watched Tom, Charlie watched Francesca. As for Francesca herself, I suspect it was our hike by the cliff that pushed her into true desperation—I can remember her so well, straining at her fetters as she stalked along, impelled by the irksome, meaningless duty of enforced family activities.

For unknown reasons, Great-Uncle Eberhardt was flapping around by the door, waiting for us to leave. Uncle Kurt, who always tried to be courteous to Eberhardt, said, "Are you coming with us? It looks like it will be a nice day to walk."

"Certainly not when you have all these children with you," Eberhardt replied. "Besides, I'm going to spend the day with Condor. Today is an important day for Barnavelt." He glared with one eye half closed at the younger cousins—Pamela and me, the two Delias, and Fisher—knowing that any mention of the fox would grab our attention.

"What's going to happen to him?" asked Fisher.

"He's going for a walk too," Uncle Eberhardt said after a dramatic pause.

"A walk?" I repeated. "By himself?"

"Of course not, you stupid boy!" cried Eberhardt. "Condor and I are going with him. He'll be on a leash."

"A leash?" shrieked Delia Ybarra. "But that's cruel! He's a wild animal. You can't tie him up like that—he'll go crazy!"

"Can't you let him go now that he's old enough to take care of himself?" asked Delia Robierre. "You wouldn't want him to spend his whole life in Condor's cottage."

"Of course I wouldn't," said Eberhardt. "That's why we're taking him on a walk. He's going to see the world…just like you." He grinned, showing us his elephantine teeth, and stalked away toward the woods before the Delias could continue their campaign for Barnavelt's freedom.

Uncle Frank and Uncle Cedric took the lead for the hike. They strode to the cliff's edge, a long tail of children weaving lackadaisically behind them, with Uncle Kurt bringing up the rear. "Are you ready, kids?" roared Uncle Frank. "We're off!"

Uncle Kurt had predicted a nice day, which did later turn out to be the case, but at that hour of the morning the sky was whitish gray, and none of us could respond to Uncle Frank's shout with enthusiasm. For more than an hour, we trailed along without saying much at all. We passed the shore where we went to swim and, as Frank had predicted, found the cliff again half a mile south of it. Uncle Kurt walked next to me and Pamela and told us stories of his leaves in London, the older cousins surreptitiously listening as eagerly as we were. Gradually the sun broke through the sheet of clouds and turned the day cheerful. The cousins woke up in the warmth and began to talk and joke—mostly about pushing each other off the cliff.

As we progressed further south, the land to our right remained wild, showing us nothing but long stretches of desolate dune grass. The cliff itself, however, became more formidable. The ledges that we often thought of as safety nets disappeared and left a sheer drop to the rocks and surf below. Around noon Uncle Frank strode to the edge, looked down, staggered back, and told us we were to keep at least ten feet between us and the cliff at all times. Naturally this provoked a wave of interest. The boys, openly disobeying his order, rushed to the edge and teetered there, gazing down in ebullient confrontation of the danger. I saw terror on the uncles' faces. They were afraid to go and pull the boys back for fear they would lose their balance.

"Boys!" Cedric called. "Step back. This is no time to joke around. There aren't any ledges here—it's a straight drop if you fall. Boys!"

Uncle Frank tried to coax them back too, with no success. Charlie, Tom, and Philip, with Fisher only a few inches behind them, stared as if mesmerized by the waves crashing against the gray face of the cliff. Finally Uncle Kurt said, "Boys, you're being stupid. Smart men don't flirt with danger when they don't have to. Step back now. Save your courage for some other day—right now you're just being foolhardy."

The rebuke roused them, and they stepped back to where I was standing, a good fifteen feet from the edge. I watched Cedric wipe the sweat off his forehead and his neck. None of the boys realized how awful those few moments had been for everyone watching them. After that summer I never dared to go near a cliff's edge, not because of the height itself but because of the fear and shock that I associated with cliffs, background as they were to everything at Shorecliff.

Still I was intrigued when Philip said, "I bet someone has jumped off this cliff and lived."

"Don't be ridiculous," said Cedric. "The water isn't deep enough. The force of a person's fall would carry him to the bottom, and he'd be smashed on the rocks."

"Let's not talk about it," said Uncle Frank. "It's time to keep walking, kids."

"No, I bet someone's done it," Philip said. I saw then, by the way he was staring out over the cliff, that he was fixated on the idea. "I bet they went far back there in the grass and sprinted up and flew over the edge."

"Sorry, Philip," said Cedric. "It can't be done."

The other cousins hovered to one side in various degrees of abstraction, but Isabella and Tom listened with interest to Philip's comments. He could always count on those two as an audience. Tom moved one step closer to the cliff and said, "Wouldn't that be great, to dive over the edge and soar out over the water? I bet it would be a good place for hang gliding, Philip. I bet you could do it that way, if you had the things they use in the mountains."

"Hey, that's right," said Philip.

"I'd jump," said Isabella, stepping up to him. "I bet I could make it if there were a deep enough place in the water."

Philip looked at her and said, "You would never have the nerve to do that." He turned away to Tom, and Isabella stared after him with her mouth open.

"It's not a question of nerve," said Uncle Kurt sharply. "It's a question of common sense. None of you are going to be jumping off a cliff any time soon. If I didn't know you better, I'd think you were suicidal. Now come on."

Pamela, standing next to me, decided it was time to join forces with the adults. "I agree with Uncle Kurt," she said. "It's stupid to do something unsafe." The other cousins ignored her. I pretended that she and I had no connection. Sometimes Pamela was infuriatingly obtuse about what made our older cousins wonderful.

After that the walk couldn't recover its former cheerfulness. Though the sun was beating down on us, we walked in silence, well away from the cliff. In half an hour the grassy hills to our right melted into woods, and the strip of open land we walked on became narrower, only ten yards between the edge of the cliff and the line of trees. Uncle Frank called a halt for lunch, and we investigated the baskets the aunts had hurriedly prepared for us. Eating was the most enjoyable part of the expedition.

While I was munching my way through a turkey sandwich, I noticed that Francesca had retreated to the underbrush at the edge of the woods and was eating there by herself. Uncle Kurt noticed at the same time and called out to her, but she just waved a hand and kept eating, her eyes turned away from us.

"I'm worried about that girl," Kurt said in an undertone to Frank and Cedric.

After we had packed up the baskets, we continued to head south for about fifteen minutes. Then Charlie and Yvette, in an unusual alliance, went up to Uncle Frank. Charlie said, "Look, Dad, maybe we should turn around and head back. We don't want to be walking by the cliff when it gets dark."

"But we haven't gone so far that we can't be back before nightfall," Frank protested. "I was going to keep going south until at least two or three."

Charlie hesitated and then said, "The truth is we're all pretty bored, Dad. I don't think anyone is having such a great time walking along doing nothing."

"Can't we go back now, Daddy?" Yvette broke in. "Maybe we could go for a swim or play croquet or bocce or something…"

I could see that his two children understood Frank's desire to give everyone a good day and felt guilty about cutting it short. But the hike was a failure. For whatever reason, while Cedric's picnic had been redolent with summer romance, Frank's hike was just a dreary trudge out and back, one of those warm-weather activities that leave you tired and sweaty and annoyed that you agreed to it in the first place. Maybe it was the lack of a destination. After all, as Charlie was quick to point out as soon as Uncle Frank had commanded an about-face—a command met with exaggerated cheers from the cousins—it was impossible to tell how long the cliff would continue in its present state. For all we knew it might stretch along the whole Maine coast. Sooner or later we would have had to turn back, and after we had retraced our steps for twenty minutes even Frank seemed relieved.

On the walk back Francesca stayed as close to the woods as possible, and when the trees ended she drifted even further away onto the grassland. Uncle Kurt, by whose side I had stayed throughout the day, kept lifting his head and searching her out, his brow more and more wrinkled. Finally he changed his pace and strode toward her. In a moment of daring, I followed him. He didn't seem to notice me, and neither did Francesca when he finally reached her.

"Hello, kiddo," said Uncle Kurt.

Francesca shot him a quick smile. "Hi, Uncle Kurt," she said.

"You've been walking by yourself an awful lot. Are you happy out here, or do you want some company?"

Francesca shrugged. In my puppy dog's position three feet behind them, I couldn't see her face, so I imagined her bleak expression. I knew she was wearing one, but I was hazy on the exact
reasons for her bleakness; it seemed to me, from my heartless
thirteen-year-old's vantage point, that the shock of my father's revelation about Aunt Loretta should be wearing off. After all, as
I reasoned, we only had a few more weeks of summer, and it
would be stupid to let them be ruined by news from a faraway city.
The Ybarra children would have time enough to deal with their
mother's scandal when they got home. Why did they need to think
about it at Shorecliff?

As I had suspected when I met her on the cliff with Philip,
Delia Ybarra was slowly coming around to a similar way of thinking. A few mornings before the hike, I had even seen her smile. It
happened on the first day after my father's visit that she emerged
early enough to have breakfast with the rest of us. I watched her
sitting at the kitchen table while she ate a bowl of cereal, her rambunctious hair limper than usual, as if it too were depressed. Delia
Robierre stood next to her, eyeing the black curls as they drooped
over the cereal. "Come on, Eel," she said. "Are you coming out to
Condor's with me?"

"I don't know," said Cordelia. She bent lower over her cereal.

"Are you going to stay like this for the rest of the summer?"
Delia cried.

There was a note of desperation in her voice that made
Cordelia raise her head. "That would be pretty horrible, wouldn't
it?" she said, and for a moment her lips curved upward. Her normal smile was an infectious grin, but while this one made me
think of a crown with the jewels stripped off, it was a smile none-
theless.

"Look," said Delia, bending confidentially over Cordelia's head
(a useless exercise, since she still didn't whisper and I was one

chair away). "I know things are bad right now for Aunt Loretta, but you aren't helping her by sitting here moping. Do you think she'd be happy that you're acting this way?"

"How should I know, when she's so far away?"

"Well, all right. Do you think I'm happy that you're sitting here moping?"

This was a much better question to ask. Cordelia looked up guiltily and said, "I guess not."

Triumphantly, Delia played her final card: "So why don't you just *let* yourself be in a good mood? We're going to visit Barnavelt. Isn't that what you've been wanting to do?"

Twenty minutes later I saw both of them hurtling at top speed across the lawn toward the woods where Condor's cottage stood. And that, I felt, was a sensible way of dealing with disappointment, resentment, and all the other emotions that my father had brought uninvited to Shorecliff.

Francesca, however, couldn't shake off the demons so easily.

Her silence didn't stop Uncle Kurt from walking with her. "I'll just stay here, if you don't mind," he said. Francesca did not reply, and he went on, "You've been pretty unhappy lately."

Francesca tossed her hair. "Let's not beat around the bush, Uncle Kurt. My mother is a whore, and I'm a little upset about it. Does that satisfy you?"

"No. She's not a whore, and if your Uncle Richard implied that she was, he was exaggerating—you know that as well as I do. His story came as a shock to all of us, but it seems to me you're upset about more than that."

"Did you ever find out that your mother was no better than a dolled-up prostitute? That she wasn't anything like the person you thought she was?"

To me her voice sounded like a whiplash, but Uncle Kurt remained unruffled. He looked into the distance and said, "No, it wasn't my mother." This was a classic Uncle Kurt answer—cryptic, unexpected, and unanswerable.

Francesca certainly couldn't think of a response. It was obvious he hadn't meant Loretta. I could see Francesca almost speaking, twice jerking her head around and opening her mouth, but she never came out with her question.

Finally he spoke again. "So you're upset about Loretta. That's okay—the rest of us are shaken too. We're still trying to have a good time, though."

"Right," Francesca broke in. "Dance the night away while they're murdering the hostages upstairs."

Uncle Kurt nodded slowly, as if considering the merits of the comparison. "Is that the way you think of it?" he asked at last.

"Oh...no, of course it's not!" she said. "There's just no point in anything anymore. I've been bored all summer, but now it's a thousand times worse because I know it won't get better when I go back to New York. What's the point of doing anything there either? You know how it is—parties, dancing, dressing up. It all seemed new and exciting last year, but really it's just more people being fake and hypocritical. Everyone runs around pretending they don't care about the rules, but they still do. And I know now that if I ever do anything—anything that isn't dull and conventional—they'll be watching me, and *this* is how it will end up: with people saying horrible things about me and accusing me of being the town harlot."

She broke off, and Uncle Kurt began to say something, then stopped. Francesca had spoken more in these few minutes than she had in all the days since my father's visit, and Kurt must have thought it would be good for her to keep talking. Already the rush of indignation had brought back her lost sparkle.

"Mother always says I shouldn't worry about what will happen later," she went on. "'Dive into each day.' 'Grab the bull by the horns.' But she's wrong. She's wrong! Now when I go to parties people will whisper and ask me about her and make comments. That's if I'm even invited to parties anymore. Either way, I can't stand the idea of anyone talking about her! And I don't want to go anywhere at all if it means I'll end up regretting everything in twenty years." She took a deep breath and let it out in a ferocious sigh. "So what's left? If you don't go out and find excitement, life isn't worth living. The people who stay inside being proper and polite may be safe, but they don't know anything—and I refuse to be one of them. I'd rather die!"

There was a long pause. Then she stopped walking and scowled at Uncle Kurt. "Does that satisfy you? Am I heartless enough now? No, I'm not ashamed of my sex-crazed mother. I'm not shocked that she's not an angel. I just wish she had told me about it herself, that's all, instead of letting me hear it from Uncle Richard." She spat the name, and I didn't spare a shred of pity for him. To my mind, he deserved all her loathing. "If you ask me the world is sordid and disgusting and mercenary and perverted!" she burst out. "And I don't see why Mother made me come up here. I don't see how living in this sunshiny, falsely cheerful summerhouse is fixing anything."

She had finished her speech at last, and now she waited for a reply, but Uncle Kurt didn't offer one. Eventually she broke her pose and kept walking. Then he said, "You're right, it's not fixing anything."

"So what's the point?"

"We're all having a good time. Or most of us, anyway."

"I'm not. And besides, what's the point of having a good time if everything is going to end in misery? Don't you feel worried, Uncle Kurt?"

Uncle Kurt surprised me by laughing. "Not a bit," he said. "And I don't see any reason not to have some fun while you can. Why not? What else is there to do?"

"Oh, I don't know." She feigned sulking, but I could see from her profile that the conversation was putting her in a good mood. "You know what I really want? I want something exciting to happen! Something I could really care about, something I could feel passionate about. Then I would be all right. But I don't even know what it would be. And the days keep going by, and nothing happens, and I can't stand having to wait and wait and *wait!*" She shrieked the last word loudly enough for the other cousins to look at her in surprise.

"Now you've gotten that out of your system," Kurt said.

Francesca sped ahead, not wanting to show that she was enjoying herself for the first time in more than a week. By the time Kurt caught up with her, her smile had faded. "What's the good of talking to you, anyway?" she said. "You're an adult. You can go where you want, do what you want."

"Even adults can be frustrated. And I too was once twenty-one."

"When you were twenty-one you were in the army!"

"And there were other things to worry about."

"Yes. You're right. I'm sorry. I know I don't have any right to complain. I know I'm sounding like a spoiled brat. That's the point, don't you understand? I know I'm being an idiot, but I can't help it. It's this place, and these people—all my wholesome family members, and not one of them will say anything to me about my mother being the opposite of wholesome. They just tiptoe around pretending nothing has happened. Doesn't it make you sick?"

"Now I think you're being unjust to your family, which I can't accept. And, you know, I can understand feeling bored and out of place here." She looked at him incredulously and saw that he was being sincere. "I know what it's like to be your age, to want to be out there doing something—anything. Right now you don't know how to value what you have here because you don't know what to compare it with. But you have your family! Do you know what some people would give for that? I'm being serious. Look at me, Francesca."

I had never seen Uncle Kurt so solemn, and neither had Francesca. She was as unnerved as I was. And I knew Kurt had made a mistake in springing that sermon on her. It wiped the levity from her face and brought back the dreary straight line to her lips, the line that made it seem impossible that she would ever smile again. "I'm looking at you, Uncle Kurt," she said. "I know what you're saying." Then she turned her head away and muttered, "But I'm still bored."

At this point I proved my age by doing something moronic. I stepped forward and said, "My mother told me intelligent people are never bored."

Francesca stiffened and turned. Incredible though it seemed to me, she hadn't realized I was there until that moment. She looked at me without speaking and then, loading her voice with contempt, replied, "On the contrary, Richard, it's stupid people who are never bored. Their minds are so empty they can stand like sheep and let their brains rot. But imagine some genius like—like Isaac Newton, or Aristotle—in a cage. Imagine telling him to play with a rubber ball in a corner. Or imagine putting Shakespeare in a prison cell. Don't you think they would be bored, Richard? Don't you think they would go crazy with their minds running around in circles?"

Uncle Kurt gave her a round of applause and said, "Now where does that put you? Are you before or after Isaac Newton?"

Francesca laughed out of the side of her mouth. "I was just trying to prove him wrong," she said. "They're the extreme cases."

"Well, anyway," he said, jerking his head in my direction. "It seems like Richard's onto something. Maybe you should listen to him."

"Yeah. Maybe I should." For a second I thought she might smile, but she didn't, and when she walked away from us this time, Uncle Kurt didn't follow her.

Instead he patted my shoulder and said, "I guess our effort to cheer her up didn't work, did it, pal?"

Morosely, I shook my head. The full idiocy of my interruption was only then hitting me. "I shouldn't have said anything," I said in a monotone.

"Sure you should have. Why not? I wasn't getting anywhere with her. She's at a difficult age, Richard. You'll know what I mean when you get there. And she's going through a rough time too, right now."

I didn't say anything. I didn't feel up to discussing with Uncle Kurt such an obviously forbidden topic as Aunt Loretta.

After a pause he said, "Do you think she was right?"

"Right about what?"

"About intelligent people being bored. Newton in a cage, Shakespeare in a cell. Do you agree with her?"

"Oh." I thought about it and then said, "No. If you put Shakespeare in a prison cell, he would just write another play."

"What if he didn't have paper and a pen?"

I shrugged. "He'd ask for some. Or he'd memorize it and write it down when he got out."

"I think so too. But Francesca's answer is her all over, isn't it? She's more of an actress than a playwright." He walked away to re-join the uncles, and I was left wondering what he had meant by his last remark.

We were within sight of our familiar shore by this time, and Francesca went to the beach to look at the water. We all followed her, but not closely enough to be in speaking range. Half an hour later, while the rest of us were still splashing in the surf, she headed across the dunes toward the house.

I discovered later that my presence during Kurt's talk with Francesca had made me an object of interest to the older cousins. I was heading for my bedroom that night, dawdling past the doorway of Philip and Tom's room on the chance of catching their attention, when my hopes were answered by a call from within. It was Isabella, not one of the boys, who would never have deigned to show their curiosity. When I came in she asked with shining eyes, "Well? What did Uncle Kurt say to Francesca? We all saw you—you were right there with them. You must have heard everything!"

Charlie was in the room too, and one of the other cousins. Yvette probably, or Fisher. Charlie was pretending not to pay attention to what Isabella was saying, but his eyes kept coming back to me. He was finding Francesca's withdrawal from Shorecliff life very disconcerting.

"They just—you know—talked about stuff," I replied lamely. I realized then that I couldn't possibly reproduce the conversation, and moreover that I had no desire to. It was something private between Francesca and Uncle Kurt, which I had been clever enough to overhear and could therefore analyze at my leisure. I needed no interference from my know-it-all cousins.

"Very descriptive," Tom said, grinning at me.

"Did she seem upset?" asked Charlie.

"You must remember something they said!" Isabella insisted. "Give us a few lines. We've all been worried about her, Richard. Did Uncle Kurt cheer her up?"

"He made her mad," I offered.

"Made her mad?" Isabella repeated, shocked. "How? What did he say, Richard? Now you have to tell us!"

She clutched my arms and shook me, only half-jokingly. I now imagined touching her at least twenty times a day, but her assault unnerved me. I would have preferred a safety zone between us.

"Knock it off, Isabella," Philip said. It was his first contribution to the conversation. "Richard doesn't have to say anything. He shouldn't have been there in the first place."

With that comment he annoyed both me and Isabella, who felt he was missing the point. "Whether or not he ought to have been there, he was," she said.

"That still doesn't mean we should ask him about it," Tom replied.

"Exactly," said Philip. "It was a private conversation, and I don't want to hear it. It's pretty low to interrogate a little boy about people he was eavesdropping on."

Once again he had offended both of us in one sentence. Isabella's face grew bright red. I was overcome by sympathy and daringly brushed her arm with my hand. She said, "Come on, Richard—let's go," and I felt a sudden overwhelming need to protect her. But I was proud of her as well for not responding to Philip's comment. His manner was infuriatingly arrogant, as if he were standing on a platform above us and prodding us with a long stick.

Isabella slammed the door behind us and stood in the hall, her cheeks burning. "I hate it when he does that!" She stomped her foot. "Of course I know it was a private conversation, but I wasn't trying to eavesdrop, and neither were you. We're both worried about Francesca, that's all. He's so obnoxious! And Tom is just as bad."

"Really, they didn't say anything important," I burst out, trying to be comforting. "Uncle Kurt was just trying to make her feel better." I was lying shamelessly, since to my mind the conversation had been one of the most significant I'd ever heard, but I wanted Isabella to stop shouting.

"Of course, of course." She bent over me, her body impossibly gangly but at the same time tantalizingly near, so that I could concentrate only on the patch of skin showing where her shirt lifted above the hemline of her skirt. In another moment I would put my hand on it. "And," she said more quietly, "we have to remember that Philip has been upset recently too. He can't be responsible for everything he says. Don't be too angry with him, will you, Richard?"

The door swung open, and Tom, doing his Adonis act with only his pajama bottoms on, swung into the hall. "Everyone okay out here?" he asked.

"Yes, Richard and I are both fine," Isabella said, putting her nose in the air. She prepared to stalk away to her bedroom, but the effect was ruined because she almost lost her balance as she turned.

"Sure you're okay?" Tom said, laughing.

"Yes!" she snapped.

He knew she was angry then and stood in silence for a moment. But right before she reached her bedroom, he said, "Hey, Bella. Croquet tomorrow?" When she turned he was smiling in inquiry.

"All right," she said, smiling too. She and Tom got into many spats, but they always declared peace moments after they had begun to argue. They were so similar that it was impossible for them to maintain full-blown anger against each other—the slightest hint of reconciliation on one side would bring the other skipping forward to make up.

I went to my room intending to ponder the meaning of Francesca's discussion with Kurt. Once in the confines of my bed, however, my mind began to circle like a jackal around certain images I had picked up during the day: Francesca's face as she glared at Uncle Kurt, her black eyebrows drawn low; the grace of her hands, which swung a little higher than other people's when she was walking determinedly; Charlie's gaze, which I had followed once on the hike to find that it was directed at Francesca's calves, flashing in the sunlight. Her beauty, of course, was a magnet for everyone's eyes, but lately I had been focusing on odd little bits of it, for reasons I couldn't understand—it was as if I were observing a gemstone one facet at a time. The same held true for Isabella, but in her case fantasy was interwoven with the images. I dropped off to sleep at last, wondering why I hadn't put my arms around her when she was upset about Philip. It would have been so easy, and then she would have been there, close and lovable, with all those long limbs hot beneath my hands.

12

Aunt Edie's Birthday

The day after our unsuccessful hike, the uncles departed on their hunting trip and I discovered why they had chosen to leave then and not later. Aunt Edie's birthday had appeared on the horizon.

The truth was that Aunt Edie had been a disappointment to us kids. We were so used to her scandalized outbursts when she visited our families that we had expected her to continue her performance throughout the summer. In fact, however, Aunt Edie viewed Shorecliff as a place of rest, where she could retire into herself and speak only to whichever of her sisters happened to be there at the same time. The presence of eleven nieces and nephews disgusted her. We were a nuisance and a bore, and our foibles and rowdy antics horrified her. Nevertheless, she remained loyal to her idea of Shorecliff as a sacred place of quietude, and for the most part she kept away from us. I'm sure she had no idea what disappointment she caused us by her silence. Tom went so far as to say that Aunt Edie had conceived a new tactic for infuriating us, which was simply to say nothing and thus deprive us of her astounding statements. When her reserve did crack and an acrid comment came flying out, we would respond with grins of delight.

The day of Aunt Edie's birthday, however, was a different matter altogether. I had been present for only one other of these hallowed occasions, when she made an appearance in New York for the great day. All I remember from that event was Edie's wrath-filled face as she surveyed the inadequate restaurant to which my mother had escorted her. This year, secure in her dominance at Shorecliff, Aunt Edie would tolerate no such mediocrity. Of course she did not dictate her wishes for the celebration in so many words—that would have been indecorous. But the way she began to eye Aunt Rose as soon as the uncles trudged off in search of game; the way her thin lips smirked when Aunt Margery called an impromptu family gathering in the kitchen, excepting Edie; the way she strode around the house with a new sense of ownership—all these signs demonstrated Aunt Edie's insistence that her party be successful.

To the cousins, the news came as a shock. Aunt Margery closed us into the kitchen and announced without preamble that in two days Aunt Edie's birthday would be upon us. "This is the most important day of the summer, as far as Edie is concerned," she said, "and we must all work very hard to make it a properly festive celebration. That means I'll need help from all of you. Is that clear?"

Francesca was seated at the table, outlining designs on the soft wood with a fork. "What exactly will this help entail, Aunt Margery?" she asked. I was not alone in hearing rebellion in her words.

"'Help' in this case means anything we ask of you, Francesca," said Aunt Rose. She leveled her hawklike stare at Francesca. "It's our responsibility to make Aunt Edie's day a happy one—one she feels is worthy of her. Do you understand?"

Pamela said, "Are we all going to give her presents?" and re-

ceived the glares of eight outraged cousins. Fisher never got outraged at anyone, and I withheld my glare out of loyalty, though
I was struck by the same alarm at her comment—what on earth
could I give to Aunt Edie?

"There's no way we can all give her presents," Yvette said.
"There's nothing here we can give her, and if we went to Pensbottom we wouldn't find anything either."

"You will not be giving her presents," my mother broke in.
"Your present—the present from all of you children—will be the
lovely way you decorate the house for the occasion. You will gather
flowers and put up streamers and perhaps make little cards for
her—anything you think is appropriate."

"Streamers?" Charlie repeated skeptically.

"We thought ahead," said Aunt Rose. She lifted two large canvas bags onto the table with the air of a magician completing
a trick, and we saw that they were jammed with party supplies—streamers, balloons, party hats, place cards, fancy napkins,
colored candles—all the trappings of an American birthday. I remember thinking how strange it was that the person for whom all
these decorations had been bought was turning not four but forty-
seven.

"But she'll know about it beforehand," Isabella objected.
"She'll see us setting everything up."

"We plan to keep her occupied," said Aunt Margery. "We'll take
it in shifts while the rest of us prepare. Tomorrow is the set-up day,
and the day after is the birthday itself. The main thing to remember is that Aunt Edie not only knows this is coming, she expects it
to be as grand as we can make it."

"I wish I'd taken up hunting," Tom said.

"With a little help from all of you," my mother replied, "I'm
sure everyone will have fun. After all, it's only two days, and we'll
be providing you with lots of cake."

We filed out of the kitchen, subdued by the knowledge that we had only that afternoon and evening before the slavery commenced.

"This summer has gone to hell," Charlie said as we spilled out onto the lawn. He glanced at Francesca, a habit he found unbreakable.

"I wasn't aware that it had ever been anywhere else," she answered.

Isabella and Tom loitered by the croquet mallets, considering a possible game. Isabella was in her thoughtful pose, meaning that she was resting her cheek on one fist and had twisted her legs around each other so that her feet stuck out at odd angles. She assumed this position, entirely unconsciously, whenever she was preoccupied by an idea. Lately she had taken to twisting herself into her thinker's knot nearly every hour. I often stood in front of her and tried to meet her gaze, which she directed toward the ground during these meditative interludes. At the beginning of the summer I usually found laughter or incipient joy in her round brown eyes, but in the past week I had twice surprised a look of distress. This time I was pleased to see her face suffused with excitement, and as soon as she caught sight of me she raised her head and looked at Tom.

"We have to do this birthday, right?" she said. "There's no way we can get out of it. So let's really do it properly. Don't you think, Tom? Let's give Aunt Edie a birthday she'll never forget. And we can transform the house! We'll plan out the whole day. It will be spectacular. You have to imagine" — here she bounded onto the lawn and turned to gesture at the house — "the entire front of Shorecliff covered in a curtain of flowers, and we'll tie candles in among them so that at night we can light up the whole lawn."

"You'll burn down the house," Charlie interrupted.

"Do you see any flowers around here?" Delia Ybarra asked, craning her neck as if searching the grass.

"That's not the point," said Isabella. It was difficult, when she got excited like this, to bring her down from the plane of fantasy. "We could have the party out here on the lawn, on a long table, with torches all around. We could bring out the Victrola and put flowers everywhere—maybe a path of flowers leading to Aunt Edie's chair!—and there would be a different flower for each person at every place. What do you think, Tom?" In the end it was always Tom's approval she sought out.

This time, Tom turned to Philip. "Do you think we could make a tent?" he asked. "I mean like one of those big marquees they use for weddings and things?"

"Well," said Philip, surveying the lawn with a designer's eye, "we might be able to, if it didn't have to be too big. How long would the table be?" He asked the question of Isabella, and right then we knew that the plan was happening and that there were three masterminds in charge of the affair.

The following day, which we spent scurrying here and there on absurd missions entrusted to us by these three, was one of my favorites of the summer. It came after my father's visit, after Francesca's withdrawal from cousinly camaraderie, after Uncle Frank's strange hike, after the beginning of Isabella's moodiness, and only one day before the evening that heralded catastrophe—yet somehow it still managed to be filled with boisterous anticipation and a delight in the company of cousins and siblings.

Perhaps the thrill arose partly because we were preparing for the only holiday we celebrated properly that summer. On the Fourth of July the family had been struck by a collective forgetfulness, but for Aunt Edie's birthday we had time to get ready, to soak for twenty-four hours in anticipation. That, as far as I was concerned, made it far superior to our Independence Day.

Isabella, Philip, and Tom spent much of the morning standing in a triangle on the lawn, speaking with the greatest seriousness about the preparations. Charlie and Francesca thought they were being ludicrously childish, and their own bond was renewed by the sarcastic remarks they tossed back and forth. Yet they showed as much good humor as the rest of us in complying with the orders our three leaders barked at us. Everyone was relieved to be engaged in something harmless and silly, not to mention generous—for we bathed in a pleasant sense that our latest game was also a charitable act. Aunt Edie must have sensed the same thing. She would never have admitted how much it touched her to see us careening around the house all day, our arms loaded with paints and flowers and bedsheets (these for the tent), but I saw her face once through a window as we were trying to make the tent stay up and caught an expression of almost girlish joy.

Tom's idea for the tent was the main point of interest for most of the cousins. The fripperies of streamers and flowers left the majority of them cold, but the tent appealed to all of us. On the day before the birthday, those of us who came down to the kitchen early found Fisher, surrounded by flour-covered aunts and fluttering recipes, sketching a plan for the tent's erection complete with angle measurements and strategies for wind resistance. I was so excited by the professional appearance of his design that I raced upstairs to rouse Tom and Philip. On the landing I encountered Isabella peering down the stairwell, still in her nightgown, enthralled by a vision of what the house would look like by the evening.

"Fisher has a sketch!" I cried, pounding on Tom's and Philip's doors.

"A what?" said Isabella.

"He's sketching out the tent!"

At this moment Fisher himself came up the stairs, gazing at the piece of paper in his hands. The aunts had banished him from the kitchen, and for the rest of the day, whenever we wanted food, we had to stand at one of the kitchen's two doors and accept whatever scraps they handed to us.

"I'll need poles," Fisher said. "We'll need to have six poles of equal length, and they'll need to be very tall. I would prefer eight, but that's probably too much to ask."

His request resulted in a surprising discovery. In the top-to-bottom hunt that followed, we unearthed countless artifacts from the days of the aunts' and uncles' childhoods, and eventually, in a dust-filled closet we had previously ignored, Philip discovered six weathered oars. Never had I seen him so excited as when he backed out of the closet, an oar in each hand and the dust in his hair so thick it looked as if he had suddenly gone gray. He was grinning one of those grins that are painful to the cheek muscles, and when he shouted to Isabella and Tom, his voice rose in an unexpected squeak. Part of his excitement over the oars was simply the pleasure of finding something that exactly fit his requirements. But all that day I was surprised by his enthusiasm. It seemed unlike him to become so involved in the mundane matter of someone's birthday. On the other hand, one can't be a philosopher every day.

Armed with two oars each, Tom, Isabella, and Philip lumbered out the front door, banging the walls with oar heads and oar handles and leaving Charlie to muse over the absence of a boat. Fisher was outside pacing the ground and looking at his sketch. Luckily it was a beautiful day, sunny but not enervatingly hot, and garnished, every once in a while, with an elusive salty breeze off the ocean.

"Look what we found!" Philip crowed, depositing his oars with a clatter at Fisher's feet. The oars, once white, were now brown with filth and covered in cobwebs. Fisher's raised eyebrows were not unreasonable. However, when Tom and Isabella had thrown theirs too onto the heap and stood back in triumph, it did seem harsh that Fisher's only comment was "But they're much too short."

Philip's grin disappeared. He looked at Fisher for a moment with his usual eyes-half-closed expression, indicating the unspeakable superiority of the philosopher to the common man. Then he glanced at Tom and Isabella, saw that they were trying not to laugh, and burst out laughing himself.

"That's true, Fisher," he said. "Mathematically, you're correct. But don't you think it's incredible that we found six poles an hour after you asked for them?"

"Couldn't we tie them onto other things and make them taller?" Isabella asked.

"Chairs!" bellowed Tom. He turned around, preparing to storm the house and remove all the dining room chairs. Just as he took off, he collided with the two Delias and Pamela, who had trekked across from the woods with armfuls of flowers. Behind them stood Lorelei, bearing a similar load.

"Lorelei knows all about flowers," Delia Robierre said.

Isabella had sent the Delias and Pamela on a flower-hunting mission, and we were impressed with their resourcefulness in going to Lorelei. It didn't come as a surprise that Lorelei was a botanical authority. She seemed to be an expert on all aspects of nature, though except for her bond with Barnavelt she had rarely shown us her talents. Today she had led Pamela and the Delias to all the right spots for wildflowers, and Tom beamed like a proud husband.

"Bring the flowers to Yvette," Isabella instructed. Yvette had volunteered to do the flower arrangements but refused to go hunting for the flowers.

Francesca had announced that she would set up the table in the dining room for the next day's luncheon—prelude to the grand finale of the outdoor dinner. She had nothing but skepticism for the plan of the tent, but with her new muted behavior came an unexpected vein of malleability. She said that she would take care of the table settings and follow Yvette's advice on the place cards—both very uncharacteristic statements. Remembering her comments to Uncle Kurt on the hike, I suspected her offer arose from an overwhelming sense of emptiness. It didn't matter to her what she or anyone did at Shorecliff, since all our activities were painted for her in the same dreary shade.

Nevertheless, once she had assumed responsibility for the dining room, Francesca's sizable bossy streak resurfaced, and she did not, in the end, allow Yvette to say a single word about the place cards. She refused to listen to any advice from anyone, and when Delia Robierre suggested that the streamers could stretch across the dining room ceiling, Francesca dismissed her at once. "You've got to be kidding," she said. "That doesn't fit in with the plan at all. I'll call you when I'm ready." The streamers ended up in swags across the windows, the flowers loomed in enormous bouquets on the side tables, the place cards were decorated with enchanting watercolor swirls, and all of these sprang from Francesca's imagination. I saw a glint of pride in her eyes when I returned a chair Tom had purloined before Francesca could stop him. Yet when at last we all came in to admire her work, the glint had died out. She looked at her dazzling creation and said, "Is everyone happy?" and then walked out of the room. During our buffet dinner in the kitchen that evening, she appeared for only ten minutes before vanishing into her room again.

Charlie and I were the only cousins not assigned specific tasks by the trio of designers, but they soon commandeered Charlie as a means of transporting heavy objects, and I served equally well as a messenger and vehicle of excitement. I felt almost delirious as I raced from cousin to cousin, shouting urgent messages, carrying flowers here and there, pulling oars and tugging ropes. It was the time pressure that got to me and to all of us. Only one day, and the aunts were waiting! When Tom burst into the kitchen, against orders, to ask for all the chairs, the aunts feigned indignation only for a second or two. Aunt Rose, mixing batter at the counter, told us to get out—cooking and baking made her mad, and she fought frustration by adopting a martinet's discipline. Aunt Margery, however, waved us in. My mother had taken the Edie shift, and they were off on a long walk to the shore.

"What are you children doing out there?" Aunt Margery said, smiling at us. Charlie and I had come with Tom as a moving crew.

"You'll see tomorrow," said Tom. "We'll need all the chairs." He scanned the room. Four of the chairs were the same size, with high wooden backs. Two were old and wicker-bottomed and had lived in the kitchen for years. "Those won't work," he said as Charlie picked one up. "We'll take the four high-backed ones and search for two other things the same height."

"Aren't there enough chairs in the dining room?" Margery asked. She knew perfectly well we were planning something on the lawn.

"Francesca won't let us in there," said Tom. "Besides, we need more."

I myself located the last two chairs for the tent. They were in my room, burdened by my long-forgotten adventure novels. While Tom and Charlie searched the house, I went straight to my room to examine them, and when I had lugged one downstairs, Tom clapped me on the back and said, "It's perfect, pal," which made my day.

The erection of the tent took two hours and strained everyone's patience. First we had to lash the oars upright to the chair backs, a task that seemed simple when Fisher told us what to do but proved to be Herculean. At one point Tom hurled down a length of twine and said, "This goddamn oar is giving me hell!" Ten minutes later, when my oar had slid down for the thousandth time onto the seat,

I said, "I can't get the damn oar to stay on!" Philip chuckled and came over to me. "That's the stuff, buddy," he said. His oar was securely lashed, and Fisher was already maneuvering the chair into place. "What you have to do is make sure the rope crosses itself, see?" He leaned over to show me the right tying method, and I inwardly gloated that my first venture into profanity had been met with equanimity, as if such language were only to be expected from a grown man of thirteen.

Once we had positioned all six chairs, the oars poking into the sky above them exactly according to Fisher's measurements, we were faced with the problem of the tent itself.

"Haven't you been figuring that out?" Tom asked Isabella.

"No, I thought you were going to deal with it," she said. "I've been working on the table problem."

The tent proved a stumper for some time. The only thing we could think of that would be even remotely large enough was all of our bedsheets put together. Tom and Isabella ran up to strip the beds and came out ten minutes later, their arms overflowing with fabric—white, blue, flowered. Each sheet looked ludicrously small when we spread them all on the grass.

"What are we going to sleep on tonight?" asked Charlie.

"It's the middle of summer," Isabella retorted. "We're hardy—we'll do without."

"This is ridiculous," said Yvette, who had come to view our incompetence. "Are we going to have a patchwork quilt over our heads?"

"Think of it as a parquet ceiling," Philip said, grinning.

I asked, "What's parquet?"

No one answered because at that moment Aunt Rose exploded from the kitchen with a rolling pin in her hand. "None of you will be defacing our bedsheets!" she shouted.

"No one's going to deface anything, Mom," Tom answered.

"We're just working on the tent. Have you got any ideas? Or any large bedspreads or anything like that?"

"Tent?" Aunt Rose repeated, staring in bewilderment at the oars on the chairs. "What are you children doing?"

"We're making a tent for Aunt Edie," Tom explained with elaborate patience. "You told us to make it a special day for her, and that's what we're doing."

"How much of the house have you ruined already?" she asked.

"None of it," said Tom. "It's all going to be sparkling clean for tomorrow."

Eventually we made the tent out of the bedsheets by tying the corners wherever they came together. The knots gave the tent a lumpy look, as if it had contracted a strange disease, but the technique was surprisingly effective. When we lashed the sheets to the oars, the tent, though small, low, and rickety, was still unmistakably a tent.

Tom and Charlie did the lion's share of the lashing. Philip, his aesthete's nature reasserting itself, stood back and directed them. When Tom and Charlie, panting and sweating, finally wrestled the enormous cloth mosaic into position over our heads, Philip smiled up at it and said, "It looks like we've got ourselves a tent, fellas."

"I like that 'we,'" Charlie answered.

Isabella came racing over to us. At this point the sun was setting, polishing her with a red-bronze gleam, and most of us were secretly wishing we'd never heard of Aunt Edie's birthday. But Isabella remained as chipper as she'd been when she woke up that morning. Her capacity for enthusiasm was incredible. "Yvette wants torches," she announced. "Oh, the tent looks perfect! Everything is working out!"

"What do you mean, torches?" Tom said. "Is she going to burn down Shorecliff?"

"No, she wants to put a ring of torches around the tent so that it will glow with poetic fires while we eat."

"Poetic fires?" echoed Philip.

"She said that part, but I can see what she meant. The whole family sitting around a table set with a white cloth and endless cakes, while the torches flicker in the ocean breeze!" Isabella leaped around us.

Tom and Philip stared at her and said in unison, "I'm not looking for them."

Pamela, who had come on the same mission, said, "I'll ask Mother."

It turned out that Yvette had inherited her love of torches from Aunt Margery. "Don't you remember?" said my mother, when we asked the aunts. "We had that summer evening party, and Margery insisted that we have it outside with torches all around the edge of the lawn. We wouldn't have thrown them out."

No one in the Hatfield family had ever thrown anything out. The torches were no exception, though tracking them down took some doing. Early in the hunt, Delia and Delia suggested Condor's cottage as a potential location. After they had set off I said, "That's unfair. They're just going to visit Barnavelt."

"Who cares, buddy?" Tom replied, throwing himself onto the grass under the tent. (We had not yet constructed the table—that was part of the flurry of the next day while Aunt Edie finished her breakfast in bed.) "This has been a crazy afternoon," he went on, "and I'm already starting to feel like an idiot. God knows what I'll feel like tomorrow."

"The tent looks nice," I commented, trying to make him feel better.

"Yeah, it does," he said. "'What did you do with your summer, Tom?' 'Well, you'll be impressed, boys—I built a tent.'"

"Who would you say that to?"

"I hope to God no one at all."

I was standing over him, admiring the length of his legs and mentally comparing my stubby arms with his muscular ones, when I glanced up and discovered four figures hurrying across the twilit lawn. I recognized them immediately—the two Delias, Uncle Eberhardt, and Condor—but their arms were full of bulky objects, and with a delighted shock I saw a flash of orange moving by their heels. When they saw me looking, Delia and Delia made quiet signals and gestured at Tom, so I didn't say anything.

"What are you looking at, buddy?" he asked from below.

"Uh...nothing." I wasn't very good at deception.

"No?" Tom propped himself on one elbow. "Who is that?" he asked. His view was hampered by the ring of chairs forming the bottom of the tent.

The four arrivals burst in on us. The bulky objects proved to be Aunt Margery's torches, and the flash of orange at their ankles resolved itself into Barnavelt on a leash. Someone must have seen them from the house because in seconds the doors poured with exiting cousins, and Barnavelt received the tribute he deserved.

"It's a shame he's on a leash, though," said Isabella. We had formed a circle around Condor and the fox.

"More than a shame," said Delia Ybarra. "He's a wild animal in captivity!"

Condor rolled his eyes. Though the moldy torches on their long sticks had muddied his shirt—pale blue with shiny white buttons—he looked as dignified and oversized as ever. "I've heard that one before, Delia," he said.

"Well, it's true!" she said.

The argument that ensued over the morality of putting Barnavelt on a leash was the last event of the evening, at least for me. My mother came to whisk me off to a quick supper and bed.

After a long night of fox-filled dreams on a bare mattress, I was awoken by Isabella hurling me bodily out of bed. "It's time!" she shouted, throwing clothes at me so hurriedly that I didn't have time to be embarrassed by her handling my underwear. "Come on, hurry up! We still haven't made the outdoor table!"

During the sunlit portion of the day, everything happened as planned. The aunts presented Aunt Edie with a lavish breakfast in bed, which she accepted as her due. After one look at her black hair, sticking out in stringy spikes all over her head, I fled from this ritual and devoted myself to running around outside with the rest of the cousins.

Tom and Charlie were battling the quandary of the outdoor table. They had met the challenge by the time Edie was dressed, but only by means of a titanic struggle with five bed boards my grandmother had insisted on installing in the Shorecliff beds years ago. They laid the boards atop four small tables appropriated from the house. Every tablecloth in the linen cupboard was in action by the time we had finished, and when Yvette positioned the flower vases, the giant table began to wobble.

"If this tips over…" she said, glaring at Tom.

"Nothing's going to tip over, Yvette. Have faith."

And nothing did tip over. We had lunch in the dining room, and Francesca's decorating efforts elicited a smile of pleasure from Aunt Edie's usually lemon-pursed lips. Francesca was wearing her fanciest pleated skirt for the occasion—none of the rest of us had thought to dress up—but her face retained its listless, absent expression. "I'm glad you like it," she said, barely looking at Aunt Edie.

Nevertheless, the meal was cheery: the scent from the flowers was intoxicating, the place cards sparked much exclamation, and the food, prepared by the aunts the day before, received rave reviews. Aunt Edie in a party hat was a strange sight. Her horsey face registered gaiety only with difficulty, but she wore the hat at a jaunty angle far back on her head. Tom said later that the way she looked made him think of a gargoyle on stilts, which was a perfect comparison though not entirely logical.

The afternoon was taken up by another aunts-only stroll to the shore. Philip said this change of pace showed the plethora of activities possible at Shorecliff. I didn't know what "plethora" meant, but there was no need for the dictionary because the sarcasm in his voice explained it all.

While they were gone, Yvette and Isabella joined forces to prepare the outdoor table for the evening feast. These few hours of preparation saw Yvette at her best. She flitted here and there like a beam of light, darting from the house to the tent and back again, carrying chairs so delicately that they seemed weightless in her hands. In comparison with Isabella, who preferred to gallop whenever she was carrying out a task she found exciting, Yvette seemed incorporeal. When she placed something on the table, a flower or a plate or a place card, she put it down exactly where she thought it should go, looked at it for a second, and went on to the next task. Isabella would plunk something down with a thud, stare at it, wander around it, reposition it, stare at it again, and so forth. Together, however, the two of them formed an efficient partnership.

Philip planted the torches for them. Isabella stood at his side and pointed at the ground where she wanted each one, and he drove the end of the shaft into the ground and twisted it until it was standing reasonably upright.

"If we start a brushfire, I'm blaming you," he told her.

"We'll be safe," she said. "I trust you."

Often, since Uncle Cedric's picnic, I had seen Philip and Isabella chatting together, each showing such newborn interest that the other might have been a stranger at Shorecliff. Their march around the tent as they set up the torches progressed more and more slowly and involved more and more discussion. Normally, of course, I would have crept close enough to hear, but I found myself captured by unexpected emotion. I could imagine so vividly Isabella's face from Philip's vantage point, how enchanting her smile would be at close range.

Yet it gave me an odd feeling, this imagining. In the bright light of day, so merciless compared to the forgiving darkness of my bedroom at night, I knew how ridiculous it would be for me, at thirteen, to receive a delighted gaze from a seventeen-year-old girl. I pictured myself, therefore, not only in Philip's place but as Philip himself, or perhaps as myself grown by four or five years. The sensation was confusing and distressing, and I tried to push it from my mind. I preferred my earlier, uncomplicated adoration of Isabella to this discontented fixation, though it held me in a grip I couldn't shake off.

Luckily, when Yvette reappeared from the kitchen with the last of the cutlery, Isabella flashed me an enormous grin and suggested a race across the lawn. I forgot my confusion in the straightforward excitement of speed. She beat me by yards and then turned around, laughing, to canter back to me.

At last Aunt Edie and her convoy of aunts returned from the shore. The table was set, the torches were lit, and flowers were strewn liberally over the grass, chairs, and tent. The lawn seemed almost as magical as Isabella's imagination had painted it. We stood looking at it in awe. The aunts found us in a ceremonial ring around the tent when they approached the house. Even Francesca came outside to take it all in. She wandered over to the older cousins as they admired their handiwork and said, "I'm impressed, kids. This is even better than the dining room."

Francesca looked wonderful by the light of the torches. Her black hair picked up their shine, so that each curl held a gleam of red. In the half-light, her face acquired the soulful expression of a medieval beauty. Francesca's personality was all military march and victory verse—or else pounding funeral dirge, depending on her mood—but sometimes the way she looked made one think of the most heartbreaking poetry.

Isabella's appearance had none of that poetry, but her personality easily outstripped Francesca's in its potential for romance. In my somewhat fanatical interest in both girls, I once mused that each would work better in the other's body. But instantly I recognized how faulty this reasoning was: Isabella's artlessness was matched by her flailing, exuberant limbs, and Francesca's volcanic emotions added a passion to her classical beauty that made her irresistible. I have not since met any women who so perfectly embody themselves.

Aunt Edie was led to the place of honor at the head of the table, her chair barely fitting under the tent's boundary. Then the rest of us, with the exception of my mother and Aunt Margery, who were acting temporarily as servers, found our places. For the occasion, Condor and Lorelei had been invited, and Uncle Eberhardt had been warned that he had no choice but to attend. Barnavelt remained at Condor's cottage. All together we were eighteen people around the table, seven on a side and two on each end, sitting on chairs transferred from the dining room. Aunt Rose sat beside Aunt Edie at the head of the table. It was a cramped meal, and Delia Robierre, whom I sat next to, elbowed me at least five times, once knocking a forkful of food into my lap.

While we ate, the evening seemed to be an unadulterated success. The aunts were astounded by how skillfully we had transformed the lawn. Isabella glowed at their compliments, Yvette smirked, Tom laughed, Philip nodded. Pamela gravely inclined her head and said, "Yes, that did work well, didn't it?" and implied that she had been behind it all. We told the aunts about Fisher's architectural genius in planning the tent, and that caused Uncle

Eberhardt to narrate the story of his youthful dream to build a bridge.

This story came from so far out of left field that not even the aunts had heard it before. Apparently, while still a college student, Uncle Eberhardt had conceived a vision of a bridge across the English Channel. In his first years at Dartmouth he had taken several engineering courses, and this bridge was to have been the culmination of a long and glorious engineering career. The thought of Uncle Eberhardt in college took all of his great-nieces and -nephews by surprise. We sat silent for several minutes while he ranted on, each of us trying to picture him as a young man.

"So why didn't you become an engineer?" Isabella asked at last.

"I didn't become an engineer, child," he growled, "because a boy I knew introduced me to poker. That's why."

Condor, from further down the table, said, "I would leave it, Eberhardt," and at the same time Aunt Margery said, "Now, Uncle Eberhardt, we don't have to go into that ancient history now."

"And why not?" Eberhardt exclaimed, slamming the table with a gnarled fist.

He was sitting kitty-corner to me at the end of the table, and I gaped at his fist as it came crashing down. The thumbnail was thick and yellow, cracked with deep whitish fissures. The veins were so purple and prominent that they seemed to have been placed on top of his skin. His knuckles were like beads on his bony fingers.

"Why do you call it ancient history?" Uncle Eberhardt continued, pounding the fist again. "Am I so old? Is my story not worth telling anymore? Is that it, Margery? You may wish," he added, glaring at all of us, "to hide the history of this family, but I'm responsible for it, and by God I'm going to tell it."

"But we know the story, Uncle Eberhardt," said my mother.

"We don't," said Tom, and I was glad he spoke up, since I was thinking the same thing.

Ignoring my mother, Uncle Eberhardt turned to Tom and the rest of us in the younger generation, who were gazing at him in astonishment. "I will now relate to you the downfall of a promising young man," he began. "All you young men, listen carefully—it could happen to you! Like you, I was a handsome young Hatfield, a favorite with the ladies—yes!—and convinced that I would be famous one day, renowned for my achievements. I might have been, too, if it hadn't been for Peter Cavendish. That was the name of the boy who introduced me to poker. He found me one night, while I was looking for fun in the streets of Hanover." He glowered at us from under his bushy beetle brows. "I'm sure all of you have the same urge. Resist it! It leads to no good. Peter Cavendish took me to his room and introduced me to the other boys there. They were sitting around a table, flipping cards and calling their bets. The sound of the chips clicking down on the table was strange to me then, but even now I sometimes wake up with it in my ears."

By this time silence had dropped over the table. The aunts themselves were enthralled by his story. Eberhardt hadn't had so much attention in years.

"Peter Cavendish invited me to play. I told him I didn't even know the rules, but that didn't matter. He wasn't playing for the rules; he was playing for the money—cold, hard cash! In those days the Hatfields were a rich family. He knew that as well as I did. Why not bring a young man like me to the table, wet behind the ears and primed for a fleecing! Yes, children, that is what happened to me. I was fleeced, trounced, taken. I lost three hundred dollars that night, and what is worse, I gained in return a thirst for the game. I went home rehearsing the cards I had played, wondering how I could have played them better. I read books on poker, I asked friends about it—and the next time Peter Cavendish invited me to his room, I said yes. A fatal mistake, children! And an even more horrible mistake was that my studying had paid off—I won. Hand after hand, I pulled the chips to my corner. I thought Peter Cavendish would be impressed, but he looked at me with a cunning smile. Yes, he knew he had hooked me well!

"When I lost to him that night, I thought it was a fluke—simply bad luck and bad cards. I kept playing, not only with him but with others. Before long I was asking my older brother for money—that was your grandfather. He gave it to me, not knowing why I needed it. I never graduated from college. I was sent away for gambling! And what did I do after that? I gambled more! I supported myself on the ruin of my family. The savings were drained. I finagled a letter out of your grandfather that authorized me to draw on his account, and I took the money myself. I traveled the world—Asia, Africa, South America, the Caribbean, more places than you've ever dreamed of! And what did I see? Nothing but green felt, children. Green felt and poker chips and money passing from hand to hand—usually from my hand to someone else's.

"What kept me going, you might ask. Yes, I see your mothers' faces—they know all too well what became my constant companion during those long years. Gin, children! Gin and plenty of it. A godsend, it seemed at first. I needed energy to stay alert through game after game, loss after loss. But devil-sent would be more accurate! How well I remember waving my empty glass—another, and another! Anything to keep me awake, though the cards were swimming in front of me. Of course your grandparents were horrified. It was the last straw, they said. Yet they welcomed me into their home again and again, hoping I would give it all up.

"I didn't—not for years. Oh, I came back here every summer, mooching off your grandfather's generosity, but I could never resist taking the first ship out in September. What did I care how long the journey was, as long as I found a poker game at the end of it! That was my life for thirty years before the funds ran out, and I came home for good to see all these beauties here deprived of their wealth."

He waved a claw at the aunts, and they, released from the sound of his voice, tried to shut him up. "We lived a happy enough life without the wealth," my mother said. "So there's no need to harp on the past."

"Yes, yes, you think I'm the only villain in the family!" he shouted. "You think I'm the only one with a past to hide. But the worst of what I started in this family wasn't losing money—it was losing dignity! Look at you!"

"Don't start naming names, Uncle Eberhardt," Aunt Rose said, frowning.

"And why not? You've all been very coy, but I know what's going on. Of course the worst ones are absent. This boy's father is so heartless he wouldn't hesitate to sacrifice his own wife's sister to the rabble."

He waved his hand in my direction, and what felt like a bucket of cold water splashed over me. It was then that the evening lost its glow. We sat with our shoulders hunched, waiting for what he would say next. None of the cousins dared to look at me, and even my mother was so taken aback that she just said, "Oh!" and couldn't manage anything more.

"Harold may be dead, but we all saw the path he was heading down," Eberhardt continued. "It's a good thing in the end that German bomb blew his head off. God knows where he'd be now if he were alive!"

"There's no need to defame the dead, Uncle Eberhardt," my mother said.

"But reason enough to defame the living, Caroline!" he cried.

"Loretta was a slut from the age of twelve. She probably got it from hearing about all the things I was doing. She ran off with that Spanish thief and came back with you three, ready for more! I know what she's doing now, I've heard the talk! It's a disgrace to the Hatfield line, but it's all part of the trail of corruption. The trail of corruption that I began!"

"I don't see why I have to listen to this," Francesca said, pushing back her chair. "I'll be in my room if someone wants me." She walked out of the tent before anyone could think of stopping her.

"Eberhardt, that's enough," said Condor.

But Eberhardt plowed ahead. He seemed unstoppable, and we sat as if frozen, watching as he wheeled and shot at each of us in turn. "That child," he said, nodding at Francesca's retreating form, "is headed for the same fate as her mother, and not one of you is lifting a finger to stop her. God knows where the rest of you children will end up. If it isn't sex, it will be drink, or gambling the way it was with me, or something far worse!"

My mother drew back her shoulders. "I will not stand for this any longer," she said. "Uncle Eberhardt, please apologize to all of us."

"Apologize, my foot, Caroline!" he snapped. "Besides, I don't see what you're upset about. They haven't started yet, these little innocents." He leered at us.

Then, to our complete shock, Yvette said, "I wouldn't be so sure." She was staring at Tom as she spoke. At first I couldn't understand what had provoked her outburst, but later I remembered the seating arrangement. Yvette was sitting across from Tom, and Lorelei was on her right. The entire meal, therefore, she had been looking at Tom while he looked at Lorelei. Lorelei herself was unaware of the cloud of anger next to her. She had been cowering under the blows Eberhardt was delivering to our family and was probably glancing at Tom out of fear.

"What did you say, child?" Eberhardt asked Yvette.

"Some of us have started, haven't they, Tom?" she said, smiling maliciously.

"Yvette, what are you talking about?" Aunt Margery said.

"She's being an idiot," Tom said. "Don't listen to her. At any rate, we can be sure she'll never cause any trouble. She's going to be a spinster for life."

This was an unfortunate thing to say because it caused Yvette to throw caution to the winds. She stood up, her chair toppling behind her, pointed at Lorelei, and yelled, "Even if I am a spinster, it will be better than being a whore like her!"

Lorelei's face flushed red. She stared at her plate, and through all the acrimony that followed she didn't look up or say a single word.

"Yvette! Apologize at once for insulting one of our guests!" Aunt Margery exclaimed.

"A more unfounded accusation I have never heard," my mother said. Her lips were trembling, and I was terrified that she was about to cry. "The idea is absurd."

"You think so?" said Yvette. "Why don't you ask your nephew about that, Aunt Caroline? You all think Tom is so wonderful. Well, Uncle Eberhardt has the right idea about this family. You ask Tom whether he's been sleeping in his bed half the nights we've been here, or whether he's been out with Lorelei in the nearest haystack!"

"Fuck you, Yvette," Tom said, pushing back his chair. It was the first time I had ever heard the word. Not surprisingly, it wasn't in my dictionary.

Aunt Edie shrieked, but no one paid any attention to her. Her birthday had been eclipsed by family scandal.

"How dare you say that to me!" screamed Yvette. She had begun to cry, but she was so angry that she ignored her own sobs, which made for a strange sight, as if she were fighting through a curtain of tears that someone else had dropped over her. "You know it's true. You've been sleeping with her every night for months!"

"You're disgusting!" Tom shouted. "I know why you're so angry—because you're jealous! You're green with envy because Lorelei is so much better than you are. But let me tell you, even if you weren't my cousin, I wouldn't sleep with you. You're a block of ice, that's all. A block of mean, jealous, underhanded ice!"

"I don't want you to sleep with me!" Yvette screeched.

The party was in shambles. The shouting match between Tom and Yvette had been held against a background of cries and gasps. Half the chairs were overturned, and most of us were standing openmouthed in a circle around the table. I had retreated to my mother's arms when Tom stood up. Only Uncle Eberhardt and Lorelei remained seated. Eberhardt was watching the chaos with an enigmatic half-smile on his face. Lorelei was still staring at the food on her plate, but she was trembling violently.

I don't have a clear memory of how everyone left the scene of the disaster. I can't remember Lorelei going home or Condor returning to his cottage. I don't know who ended up clearing away the debris from the party. The aunts took Tom and Yvette into the kitchen and left the rest of us to our own devices. My mother dried my tears and told me to go to bed, and I was so shaken that for once I obeyed. On my way into the house I encountered Francesca standing by the front door. I waited for her to move aside so I could go in, but for a long time she didn't—she just stared down at me, her face in darkness. Then she said, "What a terrible summer this has been, Richard. What a horrible, awful summer this has been."

It was one of the most chilling remarks I've ever heard. I felt as if she were passing a final judgment, not only taking away any chance of future enjoyment but also destroying the magical days we had already experienced. I became afraid that night, after I got into bed, that what I had believed to be an exciting and joyous summer had in fact been a bleak journey into despair. I worried that my memory itself wasn't valid—that all this time it had been presenting me with lies.

13

Phone Booth

The next morning I felt a confused sympathy for Aunt Edie. Of course I had no idea what she thought about the shambles that was supposed to have been her birthday dinner, but anything less than outrage over the neglect of someone's birthday rights seemed to me unthinkable.

Aunt Edie usually went out at dawn for a walk, ate a muffin with orange juice in the kitchen, and then returned to her room to read until ten o'clock. Once she closed the door, her bedroom became an inviolable haven. No one, on pain of her extreme displeasure, was ever to enter, and on the one occasion when Tom, during a lively game of Hide and Seek, barged into the room with a shout of "I've got you now!" he had to endure a forty-five-minute lecture on the etiquette of closed doors. The line he quoted to us for many days afterward was "You might have caught me in my drawers," a possibility that struck him as both hilarious and horrifying.

That morning I spent twenty minutes giving myself a pep talk and then tiptoed downstairs to Aunt Edie's bedroom. Thanks to Tom, I had a vivid image of her in voluminous white underwear trimmed with lace. As it happened, however, when she barked, "Come in!" and I entered the room, I found her wrapped in a bathrobe, sitting in a chair by the window. She had not yet fixed her hair, and it flew out from her head as if trying to escape. Other than that, she looked presentable.

"What do you have to say for yourself?" she snapped. I had never seen her lips so thin or her eyebrows so angular. All her features seemed to be focused into one accusing finger, pointing straight at me. "Do you think now is a good time to disturb me, Richard?" she went on. "I have no interest in seeing any of you reprobates."

Not stopping to wonder what "reprobate" meant, I said, "I've come to apologize, Aunt Edie." I spoke in a small voice. My apology was genuine, but the fact that I didn't think I was to blame for what had happened put me in a puzzling position.

At least, however, I had caught Aunt Edie's attention. "An apology, eh?" she said. "I'll admit I didn't expect that. Go on."

"Well, it wasn't very nice to have that big fight at your birthday dinner," I said. "It wouldn't have been nice anyway, but it was especially bad because we were supposed to be celebrating your birthday, and we'd worked so hard on getting the tent ready and setting up the table that it was horrible to ruin everything by shouting at each other."

Surprisingly, Aunt Edie smiled—a dry, vengeful smile. "What you really mean, Richard, is that you'd like to demand an apology from Tom and Yvette, is that it? Maybe one from Uncle Eberhardt too, for that remark he made about your father—which, by the way, I don't believe is true. Your father would protect Loretta if it became necessary." I was grateful to her for saying that, though I wasn't sure she was right. "In any case," Aunt Edie continued,

"I accept your apology for what it's worth, which isn't much since all you're really saying is that you feel guilty for other people's bad behavior. Most people would say that's a laudable feeling, but I think it's a waste of time. You should be angry at them, not trying to cover their tracks by making apologies they should be making for themselves."

"I—I could go get them…" I faltered.

"Nonsense." She waved a hand. "They wouldn't come. The point is I'm pleased you came even if it doesn't mean anything. Your cousins, Richard, are a disgraceful pack of hooligans engaged in worse activities than you know how to imagine. But I have sense enough not to lump you in with them. I've always thought your mother was the best of us. Rose is too domineering—she has been all her life. Harold was a featherbrain—you never met him, so you don't know. Loretta—well, no need to say what went wrong with *her*. Margery is a big pushover, though she pretends to be a strict mother. Kurt is too secretive for his own good. But your mother, Richard, she got the best of the Hatfield qualities. A little quiet, maybe, and she married a hard man, but in spite of that Caroline has what it takes. I know that when I look at you."

After this pronouncement she was silent and looked out the window. She seemed embarrassed at having made a compassionate speech, shadowed though it had been with her usual bitterness. I didn't know what to think of it. I was proud of what she had said about me and my mother, but half the things she had said about her other siblings seemed untrue. I never stopped to consider whether my virtues were as questionable as their vices.

"All right, run along now," she said, turning back to me. "Go to your filthy cousins. After the way they carried on yesterday, I'm not surprised they don't dare show their faces. It's horrifying to find that the younger generation is rotten through and through, but we have to face it. There's no use being an ostrich. God knows how the summer will end, but I predicted it. Don't forget that, Richard—I predicted this from the start. No good can come of locking up boys and girls together. Not with the wickedness of young people being what it is!"

I fled. Whenever she started making doomsday predictions about the evils of youth, I felt as if she were turning into the witch who tried to eat Hansel and Gretel.

Tom and Yvette never apologized to her for ruining her birthday, and Uncle Eberhardt never even considered apologizing to any of us. No doubt he viewed the evening as a good night's work on his part, though he was as shocked as the other adults by the fight between Tom and Yvette, so shocked that for the rest of the summer he eschewed all contact with us. He now spent almost all of his time at Condor's cottage, and whenever he encountered one of the cousins he would look as if a loathsome insect had crossed his path.

The aunts, as far as I could tell, were utterly dismayed. The incident on Aunt Edie's birthday scandalized them far more than it upset us children. The shock we felt stemmed from the fact that we knew how much the shouted words would upset the adults. Even I, with my vague knowledge of what "sleep with" meant (I pictured Tom and Lorelei writhing in a field), was more concerned with the inevitable repercussions from such a public display than with the implications of the fight itself. After all, we cousins had already known about Tom's visits to Lorelei and the tension between him and Yvette. The violence of their confrontation scared me, but in spite of Yvette's horrendous behavior, I felt some small sympathy for her. Tom was so magnetic that it was hard not to feel possessive about him—I did myself sometimes, when I saw him disappearing from our games to go off with Lorelei. He was one of those people you can't bear to lose, even if it's only for an afternoon.

Nevertheless, Uncle Eberhardt's harangue had upset us. Delia Robierre had begun to cry when Francesca left the table, and Isabella joined her for moral support. The noise of their sobs was part of what had made the fight between Tom and Yvette so horrible. Pamela and Fisher kept their eyes locked on their sister during her tirade, wearing such horrified faces that I never dared to ask them afterward what they thought of Yvette's behavior. Charlie bowed his head, unmoving. As for the Ybarra children, Eberhardt's comments about Aunt Loretta and Francesca renewed their misery over their mother's position. I doubt if they even paid attention to Yvette's outburst. Philip stared straight ahead through the entire fiasco with a stony expression. Isabella tried to say something to him at one point, but he shook her off. Cordelia too remained silent. None of the three Ybarras spoke much during the last two weeks at Shorecliff. It became unthinkable that Philip even owned any jazz records, and all inclination to dance seemed to have left Francesca's body.

There was one memorable occasion after Aunt Edie's birthday, however, when the cousins—or most of them, anyway—forgot their troubles and had fun again for one fleeting evening. It came about through a suggestion from me, which was only fitting since at the end of the night the fun died through my treachery. It was the day the uncles were expected home from their extended hunting trip, the last day in the long, dull week after Aunt Edie's birthday. Tom and Yvette had been confined to the house for seven days and were both, in their separate rooms, on the point of hysteria. The fact that they refused to speak to each other and thus could not even keep each other company compounded the torment. Perversely the weather had been beautiful that week, and I spent many agonized moments imagining their frustration as they looked out their bedroom windows onto gleaming sunshine and bright waves.

Lorelei made no appearance during the week, knowing that she had become an enemy in the aunts' eyes. Rose made many comments, which I resented wholeheartedly and did not consider disputing, about Lorelei's dishonest nature and promiscuous ways. I suspected that my mother and Margery secretly sympathized with Tom and Lorelei, but not one of the aunts was willing to condone unmarried sex at such a young age. Even more shocking, as far as they were concerned, was Tom's deceitfulness. "After all," Aunt Margery said, "if that's been going on, who knows what else has been happening in our own house all these months?"

Though I was desperate to know, I never had the courage to ask Tom what he felt about Lorelei being effectively banned from the Shorecliff property. Years later I discovered that he had sent Philip and Fisher on a secret mission to the Stephenson farm to explain his absence and apologize for the scene at the birthday dinner. At the time, though, the mission was so well protected—its agents were the two most discreet cousins among us—that I had no idea it was being carried out.

I spent most of every day with Pamela. The events of the past week brought us even closer together, though I don't remember discussing them with her. We accompanied Delia and Delia on their expeditions to visit Barnavelt and trailed after small packs of cousins going to the shore, gathering seashells in silence on the beach. Pamela liked to search for hours for polished sea glass, which was not common on that portion of the Maine coast. She was equally fond of searching for rare mushrooms in the woods. On those occasions when we actually did find a piece of sea glass or some form of fungal growth, she would beam with delight—they were among the few times when I have seen her look unreservedly happy.

In spite of these peaceful walks with Pamela, however, I was depressed knowing that so many of us were feeling miserable. This was why I suggested that we play a night game.

Our night games had been a tradition from the beginning of the summer. They did not take place in the small hours—that was when our secret expeditions out of the house would begin—but rather between nine and midnight, when the adults were in their rooms preparing to go to bed. The aunts and uncles tolerated our night games as long as we didn't come into their rooms. They even allowed us to turn off all the lights in the house, which both Hide and Seek and Sardines required.

We also played a game not well known nowadays, though in my opinion it is far superior, called Piggy Wants a Signal. The game is simple: one player is the farmer while the other players are runaway pigs. The farmer tries to capture the pigs, and when he catches sight of one and sings out, "I see So-and-So," that pig must go to the designated pigpen—usually a room with several entrances—and wait until another pig rescues him. This is where the name of the game comes from, for the captured pigs call, "Piggy wants a signal!" When they receive any kind of signal from a free pig—a shout, a hand wave, a blinking light—they are free to escape from the pigpen.

Because there were so many of us, it was almost impossible for the farmer to win by catching every pig and securing them all in the pen, but winning, in this game, is irrelevant. To be enjoyable, Piggy requires simply a devoted farmer willing to dash up and down staircases and lurk in corners for unsuspecting pigs. With a string of such farmers, the game can provide hours of entertainment. Luckily for us, most of the cousins became deeply committed to our night games. Tom used to claim that it was fun to have Yvette, who did not believe in running, act as farmer, but in truth a sleepy farmer resulted in bored pigs and the end of the game.

The two best farmers were Fisher and Tom, and indeed they were the most talented players in all our night games—Fisher because he was skilled at moving in total silence and patient enough to sit for long minutes behind a door or in a cupboard, and Tom because his dedication to the game bordered on the fanatical. When he was a pig he would instruct his fellow pigs with military discipline, ordering everyone into "position" and advocating "undercover tactics." At one point he even tried to elicit Uncle Kurt's advice on the best way to creep through the house undetected, but Uncle Kurt laughed and said he was sure Tom knew how to do it better than he did.

The game we played on the night of my great betrayal, the night the uncles came back from their hunting trip, was Piggy Wants a Signal. But games that involved running around were not the only type of night game we played. Equally beloved were the marathon card games held in Isabella's room. Most of the older cousins were good at cards, but the two older Ybarras were almost unbeatable—Philip could bluff anyone in poker, and Francesca never seemed more like a hunting cat than when she played spoons. There were too many of us for everyone to take part, but for me it was enough to loll on Isabella's pillow and watch them play on the floor between the two beds, Tom resting his chin on one knee, curled into a ball, Charlie sprawled out with his legs disappearing under the spare bed, Francesca cross-legged, Isabella crouching on her feet, too excited to sit down.

Isabella and Tom used to make each other laugh, often so hard that the game had to be put on hold while they fell over the cards. Tom could never resist making faces at her at crucial moments. It drove Philip crazy—some of his best bluffs were ruined by the inopportune raising of Tom's eyebrows. Fisher was unexpectedly an adept card player, eager to predict the probabilities of winning tricks and picking up valuable cards. Yvette also played well and ruthlessly. Pamela would usually sit out the games with me, and the Delias would gossip on the spare bed. Sometimes Isabella would call me down and say I could be her partner, which always thrilled me, though I never gave her any help.

Afterward I remembered those evenings with a painful pleasure. They held none of the sun-washed brightness of Shorecliff's days, none of the excitement of setting out for Condor's cottage or swimming at the beach, but they captured the coziness of living in a house with ten other children, and that closeness was one of the things I treasured most about our summer at Shorecliff. I never felt it anywhere else or with any other people. My cousins alone created this warm world, to which I undeniably belonged, privy even to the splendor of poker until midnight.

The number of night games declined dramatically after my father's visit, since the Ybarras were the predominant driving force behind them, and they stopped altogether after Aunt Edie's birthday. For five or six nights we filed gloomily into our respective bedrooms without any evening entertainment at all, so I was surprised when my suggestion of a game of Piggy met with enthusiasm.

"Why not?" said Tom, hurling himself onto Isabella's bed. "There's nothing else to do in this godforsaken place." He mused for a moment and then added, "Let's make this the best game of Piggy we've ever played. Are you up for it?" He looked at Isabella.

Francesca was absent, and Yvette, of course, was not welcome in any room that held Tom. But the rest of us were there, and we agreed to his challenge. Charlie was chosen as a reliable if uninspired farmer. Tom and Fisher were always so excited at the prospect of being pigs that they refused to be the first farmer. As for me, I was such an incompetent farmer that I was never called upon to be anything but a pig—infrequently caught, I'm proud to say, but only because I was often forgotten in the pursuit of a more exciting quarry.

Isabella and I ran downstairs to inform the adults that a Piggy game was about to commence. They were surprised, considering the recent upheaval, but it was clear from their faces that they were pleased; Piggy was a safely innocent activity. We then scurried through the house, turning off lights, and returned to Isabella's bedroom. Before going up the last flight of stairs, I hesitated outside Francesca's door and finally knocked.

"Who is it?" she said. I could barely make out the words.

"Richard," I called back after a moment. I poked my head in. She was reading in bed. "What do you want?" she asked.

"We're playing Piggy. Do you want to play?"

"Oh. No, thanks."

"Okay." I closed the door and leaned against it for a moment. Speaking with Francesca gave me a horrible sense of inadequacy. I felt as if I were so far from being able to please her that the mere sight of me filled her with disappointment.

On returning to Isabella's room, I regained my anticipation for the coming game. Tom was giving the pigs a brief lecture before we dispersed. Charlie was sitting on the spare bed pretending not to listen. Finally he counted down from ten, and the house was filled with silent pigs scampering to their favorite hiding places. The kitchen served as our pigpen. Because Shorecliff had no back staircase, restricting the pigs' movement considerably, we were allowed to use the kitchen's screen door as an escape route, provided we immediately circled around to the front door and came back into the house.

The life of a pig, if you were not in full stealth mode, was often boring. It was tempting, indeed wise, to remain in one well-considered hiding place and while away the time. I frequently wedged myself into a corner only to discover half an hour later that I had been daydreaming and forgotten the game completely. To forestall this piggy ennui, Tom encouraged each pig to pick a destination and try to reach it without getting caught. It was a pointless exercise as far as the aim of the game was concerned, but it kept the pigs entertained.

That night, however, I wanted some time to gloat over the success of my suggestion. To the sound of Charlie's voice counting down from ten, I raced down the stairs and crawled noisily into the closet where we had found the bocce balls at the beginning of the summer. There I settled myself on a pile of moldy tennis rackets and replayed the last quarter hour to myself. Within five minutes Charlie found me. I went to the kitchen and was surprised to find that I had not been Charlie's first victim: Isabella was already there. We bellowed, "Piggy wants a signal!" a few times, and Isabella added, "Piggy *needs* a signal!" for good measure. Then we sat down to wait. A few minutes later Pamela appeared at one of the kitchen windows and turned a flashlight on and off while waving. Isabella and I scooted through the screen door, and while she ran around the corner of the house to parley with Pamela, I circled to the front door and reentered the game.

An hour later I was racing down the stairs, narrowly avoiding my fourth capture of the evening. The farmer was close by, so I flung myself into the phone booth. The booth was such an obvious hiding place that it had no long-term value, but it was useful as a temporary shelter if the farmer was running by in search of another pig. I liked it because if you sat on the ground and leaned against the bench inside, it felt as if you were shut up in an underground burrow, cut off from the rest of the house. Only the top half of the booth was glassed in—the bottom half and the ornate framework had been constructed out of cherry wood, and the result was an attractive fixture in the hall, as well as a convenient way station for pigs.

Lying half underneath the bench, I made sure the door was fastened and then allowed myself to relax and catch my breath. Soft footfalls padded into the hall, and through the booth's glass windows I watched the shadow of a lone pig as it traveled across the moonlit wall. Then all was quiet. I settled in to wait until Tom, the present farmer, found me.

As it turned out, however, Tom was occupied in a battle of near misses with Isabella on the top floor, and for a long time I lay undisturbed. I was still in the booth when the uncles arrived home. Nearly asleep, I heard the latch of the front door open and saw a splash of moonlight washing over the hall ceiling. At first I thought it was a pig escaping from the pen, but then I heard the thud of heavy footsteps and a subdued male chuckle, and I realized who it was. Uncle Cedric, Uncle Frank, and Uncle Kurt crowded into the front hall, weighed down by their hunting gear. The moment passed when I could innocently present myself, and I remained in the phone booth, listening with growing apprehension to their talk, not allowing myself to breathe.

"Damn it, that was a devil of a walk," Uncle Cedric said. His words were muffled by the clanking of boots and guns as they dropped their bags onto the floor. "Kurt, you have to stop getting in so late. These evening hikes from town are too much for me."

"I'm sorry, Cedric," Kurt replied. My heart thrilled when I heard his voice. I had felt starved for stories in his absence. "You know I try as hard as I can to make the early train, but waking up at five in the morning is hell. I wish there were a midday train, but there isn't."

That was when I first sensed something was wrong. As far as we knew, trains played no part in the uncles' hunting trips. It sounded, moreover, as if Uncle Kurt had taken a train by himself. I tensed up, as listeners do when they hear something unexpected, and checked to make sure the phone booth's door was fastened.

"You must have outdone yourself in Portland this time, my

boy," Frank was saying. "Normally a man like you wouldn't think twice about waking up for a six o'clock train."

"Well, you know." Uncle Kurt chuckled, and there was something strange in the laugh, a bit of shame, a bit of discomfort. I recognized the sound I would have made if I had done something bad in school and were trying to laugh it off.

"I just don't see how you couldn't have done better than ten with my money," Uncle Cedric said after a pause. "That was a precious fifty dollars I gave you, especially since I had to snatch it from under Rose's nose. Where was your legendary skill?"

"I did the best I could, all right?"

"Well, it seems like a lot of trouble to go through just for ten bucks."

"I'm content with getting sixty back for my fifty," Uncle Frank said. "After all, it's easy enough for us, Cedric. Give the man some slack."

"I always keep your money in the small but safe games." Kurt cleared his throat, and I felt even more acutely that he was experiencing some species of discomfort—regret or remorse or humiliation.

"What is it, Kurt?" Cedric asked. "Where's your own money?"

"To tell you the truth, fellows, I lost it all. And then some." The last phrase he added in an undertone. "With my own money I just can't resist the big chance. After all, a dollar here and a dollar there...The long and short of it is I got myself into a high-stakes game."

I heard an intake of breath. "Have you got anything left?" Uncle Frank asked.

"Not a cent." False heartiness laced Kurt's voice. "But don't worry. A little debt never hurt anyone. I'll win it all back soon enough. I think I've found a good place now—reliable and honest, which is the important thing. If I hadn't been so distracted, I wouldn't have lost it in the first place. But it doesn't matter. I'll—"

"Distracted by what?"

"Oh, well…There's a girl involved with the place, and I—well, I got distracted. You know how it is."

"You lost your money because you were messing around with some floozy? Exactly what kind of a place was it?" Uncle Cedric said.

"Cedric, I hear that tone of disapproval. The day has been too long for me to be told I've been a bad boy."

There was a silence. Then Cedric said, "You're right. I worry about you, but in the end it's none of my business. A man your age has the right to do what he wants."

"I wish I knew why you've been staying cooped up here all summer—" Uncle Frank began.

Uncle Kurt cut him off. "We've been over this before, Frank. There are the kids to think about, and the fact that I like being at Shorecliff, and the importance of my work and how much I get done here. But the main point is that if I weren't here the girls would want to know why. They'd find out somehow—you know how they are. And can you imagine Rose condoning all this? Certainly not. She'd remember Eberhardt. She'd compare me with Loretta. She'd run the whole gamut of accusation, and Margery and Caroline would back her up."

"Where are they all, anyway?" Frank said. "I thought they'd stay up to tell us how late it is."

"The real truth is you're ashamed," Cedric broke in. "And I am too, God knows. I wish I'd never gone along with it."

"No more sermons, I said!"

I had been shivering for a good while, and now I felt as if I were about to cry. My heart was pounding so loudly I was sure it would rattle the bench of the phone booth, but the uncles continued talking until their conversation dwindled into the mundane, and eventually they plodded upstairs. As they went, a scattering of pigs emerged from the upper floors. I discovered later that I had been the only pig on the first floor and thus the only person close enough to hear their conversation. Bedroom lights flicked on, and Tom, peering down from the third floor and seeing the uncles, bellowed that the game was over and tore down to greet them.

I emerged from the phone booth, trying not to listen as Uncle Kurt described the deer that got away. Cedric and Frank were loaded down with rabbits and pheasants, and when I got upstairs I found that Uncle Kurt was holding a bag of game too. I didn't speak, even when Kurt smiled at me and said hello. The other cousins ignored me. I went to my mother, who had come out of her bedroom in her wonderful yellow nightgown, and told her I was very tired and wanted to go to bed right away. My face must have matched my words, for she felt my forehead and agreed that sleep was the best solution. Accordingly, I retired to the third floor and sat on my bed.

A huge choice now presented itself to me. In a few seconds, I had learned that Uncle Kurt, my hero, my upright soldier, spent his time away from Shorecliff at a gambling house in Portland in the company of loose women—"messing around with floozies," in Cedric's unforgettable words. At the time, of course, I didn't know the term "floozy," but I had recently gained a remarkable perspicuity about the influence of sex, and I had a good idea of what Uncle Kurt meant when he spoke about being distracted by a girl. The image I had created of Tom and Lorelei writhing in a field reappeared in my mind, only now Uncle Kurt was writhing with her, and the scene transformed into a red room with lots of tables, gilt chairs, and a glittering chandelier, and Lorelei became a woman with dark hair and blue eye shadow. I didn't know what a gambling house looked like, but I borrowed freely from hotel lobbies I had seen—these being the most decadent places I had ever visited.

What crushed me, though, was not the gaudy cheapness of gambling halls and their denizens—as I say, I knew almost nothing about them—but the fact that I had heard in Kurt's words his creeping shame. My uncle Kurt was someone who always told the truth; he was never afraid, and so he never had to lie. Yet here he was, lying to everyone, sneaking around because he was too embarrassed to tell us what he was really doing. That was what broke my heart.

Just thinking about him made it hard for me to breathe. I sat and heaved like a landed fish for about fifteen minutes, but the looming choice refused to leave my mind. The burden of knowledge was crushing me, and I knew that if I shared it, the weight would lessen. Yet by eavesdropping and overhearing Kurt's secret, devastating though it was, I had acquired an obligation not to betray him. I had been so outraged by Yvette's betrayal of Tom and Lorelei that I had vowed, while still quivering at the makeshift birthday table, never to be guilty of such treachery. Now, only a few days later, I was faced with the same temptation.

The truth was that on one level I wanted to tell simply because it would be such an astonishing revelation. I had just chanced upon what was easily the greatest remaining family secret, which would unseat one of the most adored Hatfields from his throne of virtue. How could I resist being the bearer of such stunning news? I imagined the shock on the cousins' faces, the eagerness with which they would listen, the insistence with which they would ask for details. I knew I held in my hand a ticket for almost unlimited attention.

Yet that made the choice worse. The fact that if I did betray Kurt's secret I would be doing it partly for glory made the treachery even more despicable. "No," I said to myself. "I can't do it. It's my secret now too." Having made the decision, I got into my paja-

mas, darted down the hall and back again in record toothbrushing
time, and climbed into bed. My mother had given me her good-
night kiss downstairs, so I expected no visitors. I lay on my back
and waited to fall asleep.

As soon as I stopped moving, the uncles' conversation replayed
itself in my head. I heard again Kurt saying, "I got myself into a
high-stakes game." A month before, I wouldn't necessarily have
associated gambling with the family's ruin, but now that Uncle
Eberhardt had revealed his story, Kurt's secret called to mind our
straitened circumstances, our lost fortune and reputation, our in-
glorious descent from the great days of old.

Uncle Kurt himself seemed to have been replaced by another
person. I couldn't convince my mind to register his new character,
to match the man I had revered for years with the sheepish gambler I had heard in the hall. Lying rigid in bed, I clutched the
sheets with my fists. After a while I said out loud, "It can't be
true! It isn't true!" I told myself that I had had a strange dream
but had just woken up or—even better—was still in the dream.
I looked at the bureau on the other side of the room and tried to
believe that it was out of proportion, that my dreaming mind was
distorting it. But it looked the way it always did in the moonlight,
and I couldn't persuade myself that I was asleep. Once again I
heard Kurt's awkward chuckle and pictured the scene of him with
the eye-shadowed girl, surrounded by sordid luxury. "Not Uncle
Kurt," I thought. "It was someone else. Uncle Frank. I got their
voices confused."

Suddenly I thrashed under the bedspread, kicked it off, and
leaped into a standing position. I threw open the door and raced
down the hall, gripped by the feeling that if I didn't tell Isabella
immediately, my mind would be overwhelmed. I had forgotten
that the cousins liked to congregate in her room at the end of the
day, and when I burst in I found Tom, Charlie, Philip, Fisher, and

the two Delias, in addition to Isabella. Pamela had gone off to join Yvette, and Francesca was cloistered in her bedroom. Desperately I sought out Isabella, who was standing by her bed, and ran to her, wanting to throw my arms around her but even in this crisis not quite daring to cross that line. Still, my entrance and frantic expression took her by surprise. The other cousins stopped talking and stared. I was breathing as raggedly as if I had run a mile down the hallway.

"What is it, Richard?" Isabella asked.

She sat on the bed and took my arm, forcing me to sit down next to her. Philip and Delia Robierre moved to one side so I could find space. I sat awkwardly, refusing to look at anyone. Isabella, sensing my distress, had taken my hand, and her touch lessened my desperation. Already I was recovering from my panic and taking a furtive pleasure in sitting so close to her and being the center of attention. I felt abruptly that this was a once-in-a-lifetime opportunity, since I would never again find the courage to clutch her hand, and I abandoned myself to an exaggerated performance of distress.

"Do you have something to tell me?" she asked.

I nodded. Then I remembered what I was agreeing to and said, raising my head, "But I shouldn't tell you."

"Would you like the others to leave? We can ask them to go away."

Fisher was the only one who made any move to depart. The others glanced at him in surprise. Then Tom said, "Oh! right." He got up too, but he couldn't stop himself from hesitating. Watching him from under my eyelids, I saw that he wanted to hear what I was going to say. From that moment, the secret was doomed.

"No," I said hurriedly. "No, they don't have to leave."

"Well, what is it then, darling?"

"It's . . . a secret," I stammered after a pause.

"Your secret?"

"No, not my secret." I was impressed by her interrogation skills.

"Are you supposed to know about it?"

"No. I heard it by…accident. It wasn't my fault! I couldn't get out fast enough."

"No one's blaming you," Isabella said, stroking my hair. "You'd better tell us, and then we'll tell you what we think about it. Won't that be best?"

I gave myself up to her coaxing. "Uncle Kurt didn't go hunting," I began.

That caught their attention.

"What are you talking about?" Tom asked, and I went from there. Still holding Isabella's hand, I told them every horrible detail. I forgot that I was speaking about Uncle Kurt. I simply constructed the most suspenseful story I could manage, and the cousins repaid me with open mouths and raised eyebrows. By the end I was so enchanted at being the focal point of the room that I forgot to be upset.

"It can't be true," Isabella said when I had run out of things to say. I was pleased to note that her reaction was exactly what mine had been.

"Of course it's true. Don't be stupid," said Philip. "It makes perfect sense. Uncle Kurt has always seemed strange, and now we know why."

"Don't you remember?" Delia Ybarra cut in. "That story he told me about Captain Kerrigan and the pornography. Remember how he said everyone has weaknesses? I bet he was thinking of himself."

"It's just as bad," Isabella said. "Just as bad as Captain Kerrigan. It's disgusting. It's awful! How could he do it?"

"It's not that bad," said Tom, taking the part of the worldly young man. "When there are pretty girls around…"

"I'm not talking about that!" she snapped. "The point is he's been lying all this time to our parents and to us—to everyone in the family! He's one great big deceiver."

"He didn't lie to everyone," Philip said. "Your father and Uncle Frank both knew about it. If you want to get angry, don't forget to be mad at them too."

Isabella shot him a furious look. "It's not the same," she said.

"It's pretty rotten," said Charlie. "Dad and Uncle Cedric must head out from Pensbottom instead of from here, after dropping Uncle Kurt at the train. It's a long way to go, just to help Uncle Kurt lie to all of us."

We found out later that Charlie was more or less correct: the uncles would depart from Shorecliff with a flourish, heading northwest past Cedric's hidden meadow, and then spend the day circling over to Pensbottom so that Kurt could catch the evening train to Portland. For the next few days Cedric and Frank would hunt in the wilderness near the town, and on the last day of each trip they would return to Pensbottom, pick up Kurt, and walk along the road back to Shorecliff. The loneliness of the route served them well—none of the townspeople remarked on their brief appearances in town, and they never met anyone on their three-hour trek home. To us, however, the smoothness of their subterfuge made it even more horrifying. We were forced to view all three men as practiced liars—and Uncle Kurt as the worst of all.

"I don't understand what Uncle Kurt was doing at the gambling house," said Delia Robierre. "I mean, of course"—she blushed—"I know what he was doing, but where did he get the money? Why did he go? What's the...well, what's the point?"

"The point is he was bored," said Philip sharply. "That's what Francesca would say, and she's right. They understand each other. Uncle Kurt was bored here, and he went to Portland to make sure he was still alive."

I didn't know how to interpret that statement, and I felt it was a little shocking to join Francesca and Uncle Kurt together. The day before I would have felt it was doing Uncle Kurt an injustice. Now the situation had been reversed.

"Should we tell Francesca?" Tom asked after a tense silence.

"No," said Isabella. "No. We shouldn't tell anyone. You were right, Richard dear, this is too horrible a secret."

"Of course we're going to tell Francesca," Philip retorted, glaring at her. "I'd tell her now, but I don't want to wake her up if she's asleep. Furthermore, Isabella, what right do you have to keep this a secret? I think it's something the aunts should know."

"The aunts!" Isabella repeated, horrified. "But we can't tell them!"

"Have you considered where he's getting the money?" Philip asked. "He's in debt right now! He doesn't have any money of his own. He must be borrowing from the aunts and pretending it's for something else. He's doing just what Uncle Eberhardt did when he was young, and we can't let him keep going!"

"But it's not our place to tell them," Isabella said, sounding frightened.

"How would you like to be the one to break the news to my mother?" Tom asked, more practically. "I think we should keep this to ourselves for now."

"But we will tell Francesca," Cordelia said. It was a moment of Ybarran tribal unity.

"Should I wake her up?" Philip asked, half rising.

"No," said Delia. "Tell her in the morning. You know she almost never sleeps."

That was news to me. I would have thought more about it, but with the weight of knowledge off my shoulders, I began to feel exhausted. The exhilaration of being the messenger had waned. They knew the secret now, and my status shrank back down to irrelevant youngest in the room. I wanted to lean my head on Isabella's shoulder but didn't dare. The moment for dramatic movement had passed.

"Richard's tired," she said. "I'm going to tuck him into bed."

Charlie laughed, which I thought was insulting. I appreciated her gesture, childlike as it made me seem. And besides, any moment alone with her was one to be treasured.

"Everyone else should go to bed too," she went on. Her voice shook a little. She was even more upset than I was, since she was able to grasp more clearly the ramifications of my discovery.

When she had escorted me to my room and tucked the covers around me, I asked, "Is everything ruined even more now? Will everyone be even more miserable?"

"Of course not," she answered, sitting down next to me. "Everything will be all right. After all," she added, in an attempt to comfort herself as well as me, "Uncle Kurt hasn't changed completely. He's still the kind, good man he was before. He just has some worse secrets than we thought. But everyone has their weaknesses."

"You told me," I said, remembering an incident that had happened several weeks before, "that Uncle Kurt had too many secrets of his own to have time for yours. Remember?"

Isabella laughed. "Yes, I remember. I didn't think his secrets would be like this, though. I was thinking more of the war."

"What are your secrets, Bella?" I asked, trying to come closer to her by using the nickname.

She looked down at me. "They're nothing. Nothing important. They don't really mean anything. Good night, Richard."

"Isabella," I said as she rose from the bed. "Should I stop going to visit Uncle Kurt in the mornings, to listen to his stories? I was looking forward— " I broke off, feeling only now, selfish brute that I was, as if tears were truly imminent.

"If you still want to," she said, "of course you can go."

She left the room, and I was left to ponder the wry sadness with which she had spoken her last words. It took me some time to realize that now, when I imagined listening to Kurt's war stories, I felt not excitement but unease.

14

Woods

Francesca cornered me an hour after she woke up the next morning. Philip hadn't lost any time in telling her about Uncle Kurt, and when she came after me, her black hair unbrushed and even more wild than usual, she looked terrifying. I was by myself near the cliff, going for a stroll before coming back to visit my mother in her bedroom. I hadn't been expecting company, and when I turned around after gazing for a while at the flat, gray sea, I was startled to see her bearing down on me. She was wearing a skirt with her little nightdress on top, and I concluded that Philip had sprung the news on her while she was dressing.

"All right, Richard," she said when she had gotten close enough to speak. "Tell me exactly what they said. Come on, right now."

"What do you mean, Francesca?" I was so alarmed that my instincts regressed to those of a five-year-old: I thought I could buy time by playing innocent.

"You know exactly what I mean. None of you creeps last night bothered to wake me up, so I didn't hear the story. Tell me exactly what they said."

"About Uncle Kurt?" I faltered. I had been trying, without much success, not to think about him on my morning walk.

"Who the hell else!"

I paused, looked out to sea again, and mumbled, "I don't want to talk about it."

Francesca grabbed my shoulders. She was so grim I thought she might slap me. In a strange way, with a thirteen-year-old's thirst for violence and sensation, I hoped she would. But she restricted herself to shaking me.

"Tell me now, you little brat!" she cried. "He's been going to Portland all this time. He's been lying to all of us. He's slept with prostitutes and gambled away our family money and been a cheating, poker-playing charlatan. Tell me the whole story! What did he say? What did Uncle Cedric and Uncle Frank say?"

"But you know everything already," I quavered.

"I want the details!" she roared.

"I—I don't remember them. Really, Francesca, I can't remember!"

"Well, try."

She let go of my shoulders and crossed her arms, presenting me with a fearsome display of a woman on the rampage. Surreptitiously I drank her in while I thought up various imaginary details to give to her, since it was true that I couldn't remember what the uncles had said. I had been so shocked by the content of their discussion and afterward so horrified while brooding over Uncle Kurt's treachery that most of their precise words had flown from my memory. But Francesca was standing there, staring at me with stormy eyes. Her crossed arms pushed up her normally near-flat chest, and I was mesmerized by the perfection of the smooth olive skin below her throat. The nightdress was quite revealing and on a more buxom woman would have been risqué. On Francesca, slender and willowy as she was, it merely emphasized the grace of her figure. Her black hair, pressed by her night's sleep into an enormous crown of waving curls, completed the picture of an Amazon ready for battle. I had to tell her something.

"Uncle Kurt told them he had been distracted by a girl," I began. "Uncle Cedric called her a floozy." So far it was the truth. "She was one of the women at the gambling house, and she played poker." This was pure invention. "He played with her the whole time he was there, and she stole all his money. He went dancing with her, too." I felt this was an inspiration. "There was a dance floor in the gambling house. They danced all night and played poker and...and..."

"Yes?" said Francesca. Her eyes glittered. I could almost see her stretching out her hands, trying to reach the noisy, flashing chaos of the imaginary place I was describing.

"And there was drinking," I whispered, adding the finishing touch.

Unexpectedly Francesca laughed. "Of course there was drinking, you idiot. You don't understand half of what you heard."

That was the sort of statement that made me resent Francesca. I waited for a few moments, but she was lost in thought. She stared out beyond the cliff, her arms still crossed. Eventually I asked, "So what do you think?"

"Think? What do I think?" She turned to me. "I think they're all a bunch of goddamned hypocrites. And I can't believe he's been having the time of his life all summer while we've been rotting here in this shit-hole."

I tried to display my debonair acceptance of her cursing—an attempt that probably made me look apoplectic—and said, "Well, this is only the fifth hunting trip they've been on."

"That's five more hunting trips than I've been on," she retorted. "And don't call them hunting trips, Richard. Call them whoring trips. Call them gambling trips. Call them lying trips. That high-and-mighty bastard."

She glanced at me, realized she was speaking to a thirteen-year-old, and strode off toward the house. I stayed behind, mouthing some of her more shocking turns of phrase and feeling daring for almost using my vocal chords when I said them.

There now remained only one and a half more weeks at Shore-cliff before we all dispersed to our respective homes. If our naked souls had been revealed, I suspect we all would have shown a longing to return to our humdrum lives, if only to escape what had become a nightmarish cycle of revelations concerning our family members.

I remember Philip lounging on Isabella's spare bed a few days after my encounter with Francesca. Isabella, Tom, and I were the only other people in the room. Philip glanced at us, his dark eyes full of playful malice, and without warning he raised a hand and began to count. "My lovely mother—a painted whore," he said, ticking one finger. "Great-Uncle Eberhardt—a wandering gambler. Darling Yvette—a lust-filled sex fiend. Old Tommy here—a lust-filled satyr. Gentle Lorelei—a lust-filled seductress. Uncle Kurt—a lying, promiscuous poker player." He looked at us.

Tom was grinning, not even pretending to appear shamefaced. When he wasn't grinding his teeth over Yvette's treachery, he was patting himself on the back for being such an accomplished ladies' man.

"Who's next?" said Philip, staring at each of us. "Who will be the next family member to reveal a dark and loathsome secret?

Richard?" He whipped his head toward me. "What have you been doing with Pamela all these weeks?"

"Stop that," said Isabella. She smacked Philip on the shoulder, but at the same time she looked at me with worried eyes.

"Don't worry about it, Isabella," I said, feigning nonchalance. I had been doing that a lot, now that I was so frequently allowed to hear the older cousins' discussions.

"Well, what about you, Isabella?" Philip went on. "Any secrets you'd like to share with us? Anything deep and dark and shocking?" His eyes locked with hers as he said this. He was in an unusually humorous mood, but I shivered at the aggression in his words. Half afraid and half intrigued, I was sure there was more to the conversation than I could understand.

Isabella, reddening slightly, slid off the bed and went to stand in the corner, the farthest point in the room from Philip. "I don't like this game," she said. "Tell us what you're getting at and stop joking around. Richard doesn't like it, and neither do I. You're being unpleasant."

"Richard likes it, don't you, pal?" he asked, widening his eyes.

I said nothing. I had learned, over the summer, that the best policy when confronted by a confusing cousin was to remain silent.

Abruptly Philip dropped his persona. He looked at Isabella, his face grave, and said, "I'm just pointing out how many awful things we've learned this summer. I'm wondering if we're going to get out of here with any of us unscathed."

"I hope we do," said Isabella. "I don't want to learn anymore. I want everyone to keep whatever secrets they have."

"Really, Bella?" Tom gave her a friendly smile.

"Yes," she replied. She stomped out of the room, and Tom and Philip grinned at each other. Isabella's mood swings had grown extreme. After my revelation about Uncle Kurt, she became completely erratic. In my head I compared her to a metronome with the weight at its tip, which flops all the way down and then rises up only to hurtle down again on the other side.

The morning following this conversation, the uncles announced that they had had such success on their last hunting trip—their bags, all three of them, had been loaded with game for the aunts to cook—that they were planning one more jaunt before we left Shorecliff. They would return the day before moving day, since the aunts required their presence for the endless hours of cleaning and packing that brought each stay at Shorecliff to a close.

The news that the uncles were going on yet another trip—"Number six!" Francesca exclaimed in outrage—caused a flurry of conversation among the cousins. Many speculations were voiced as to why they were planning another trip so soon after the last one. Philip was of the opinion that Uncle Kurt's debt was becoming unmanageable and that he was planning to chance the last of the family money in one wild, all-night poker game. Tom said it was obviously a case of infatuation: the girl who had distracted Kurt on the previous trip held him in her clutches, and he couldn't get her out of his mind. Francesca suggested that Kurt simply couldn't stand the sight of Shorecliff anymore and was escaping once and for all. No one entertained for an instant the idea that the uncles might actually want to go hunting. Among us, naiveté on that scale had been eradicated.

We watched their preparations warily, from doorways and windows. Not one of us dared to come too close. The uncles had become untouchable. Cedric and Frank had lied to us all summer, and Uncle Kurt had deceived us on a grander scale than any of us could have previously believed possible.

I stayed away from him altogether. The afternoon after my eavesdropping from the phone booth, he had discovered me in the kitchen and said cheerily, "Why didn't you come for a story this morning, kiddo? I was looking forward to one of our nostalgic sessions. Gotten bored with me, have you?" The truth was I had stood outside his door for five minutes debating whether or not to knock. I could picture so well the excitement of the story he would tell, the smile on his face, the thoughtful questions he would ask me. And I imagined sitting in front of him on the little chair, knowing he had been in Portland. Eventually I walked back down the stairs and went out to the cliff, where Francesca cornered me. That afternoon, when he asked why I hadn't come, I replied, "I guess I forgot. You've been away for the last couple days, after all." He ruffled my hair and left the room, and I breathed a sigh of relief, as if I had overcome an obstacle. Then I almost burst into tears at the thought of my beloved Uncle Kurt being an obstacle.

After Philip's speech about family members' secrets, I began to wonder which cousin or aunt or uncle would be the next to reveal a scandalous past. So many secrets had been uncovered that more seemed inevitable. I began to look expectantly at each person I came across—and, as often happens, the more I looked around the more I saw.

Like the inhabitants of a bombed city, the Shorecliff population had scattered under the shock of disillusionment. Morning croquet games were a thing of the past, and after my experience in the phone booth, none of us felt like playing Piggy Wants a Signal. The aunts had been driven into near silence by the fiasco of Aunt Edie's birthday. For the most part they kept to themselves, holding murmured conversations in the kitchen, their perennial stronghold. Whenever we came in, they would glance sideways at us and stop talking. Then they would wait with open impatience for us to leave. Even my mother seemed distant, and during my visits to her room she would often simply stroke my hair, sigh, and continue reading her book.

The uncles too kept a low profile, though this was nothing new. Uncle Eberhardt sensed the cloud of disgrace descending on him whenever he neared the main house and retired permanently to Condor's cottage. In spite of his presence there, we spent hours at the cottage in those last few weeks. Barnavelt was growing into a gleaming, strong, adolescent fox with an adorable temperament and a keen nose for mischief. He was allowed to run free in the cottage and divided his time between his own wooden house and Condor's ankles. Outside he stayed on his leash. Condor rarely left the cottage without him, and we often came across them in the woods, tracking an animal or tearing up brambles or planting saplings.

Delia and Delia spent the majority of their time with Condor and Barnavelt. I wondered what Condor thought about their shadowing of him. Having been a solitary man all his life, he must have thought it strange to acquire two young girls as constant companions, especially since they often didn't speak, instead communicating with each other simply through expressive glances. They were as devoted to Barnavelt as Condor was and cooed over him constantly. Whenever Condor slipped on the collar at the end of the leash, they would cringe as if Barnavelt were being whipped. They still believed that Condor should return the fox to the wild, though he had explained many times how unfit Barnavelt was now for anything except posh living among humans. Uncle Eberhardt was openly infuriated by the Delias' incessant comings and goings, and he usually greeted their entrance with a barrage of complaints. The two Delias and Condor ignored him. Condor, ever the gentleman, would shoot his pastel cuffs and say, "Good morning, girls," as if they had not been dropping by every day.

Isabella, Philip, and Tom spent most of their time together. Although, a week after Aunt Edie's party, both he and Yvette were allowed out of the house in the company of cousins, Tom still chafed under the close supervision of the aunts, and visits to

Lorelei were out of the question. Isabella and Philip would go for walks on occasion, and there was one swimming expedition in those final days, when the air was so humid that not to be in the water would have been torture. Otherwise the three of them lolled on the lawn or in the boys' room, talking idly or playing listless card games. I divided my time between them and Pamela, who remained primly uninterested in scandal and pretended she knew nothing of the goings-on that had fragmented the family. I found her company, as always, soothing but unsatisfying.

Yvette, disdaining the aunts' announcement that she could once more go outside, lurked in her room, visited only by Pamela, Fisher, and Isabella, whose powers of empathy sometimes got the better of her. We all considered that Yvette had behaved unpardonably to Tom, and I suspected that the other cousins were, like me, too frightened to approach her. She reminded me of an untamed beast at the circus who cannot be groomed into a presentable show animal because there is no circus hand willing to enter its cage. On a certain level, as I've said, I sympathized with her. But wounding Lorelei, who had borne a large part of Yvette's accusation, seemed unforgivable. Lorelei was to me the epitome of blameless purity. It didn't matter that she and Tom were sleeping together—she remained a quiet, gentle spirit, and neither I nor the other cousins could tolerate the callousness with which Yvette had thrown her to the wolves.

The wolves, in this case, were our aunts. Had Lorelei not tactfully disappeared from Shorecliff, they would have put their collective foot down about her entering the house. The result was that we almost never saw her. One time when Pamela and I had wandered into the woods bordering the Stephenson property, I looked up and caught sight of her in the sunlight, silhouetted against the green field and the bright blue of the sky. My first impulse was to run to her, but then I thought about what I would say, and I didn't move. I couldn't think of anything that wouldn't be rude or awkward. When we got home, I felt I had been equally rude by not approaching her, and I worried that she had seen me.

Fisher had chosen to deal with the family crises by vanishing from the house. He traveled in wide circles around the countryside, hunting for birds. His absence was painful to me, since I valued more than I had realized the calm sweetness of his company. He lent to Shorecliff a reassuring feeling that after all there were good, wise people in the world. Of all of us, he possessed the most bountiful supply of kindness. Occasionally I saw him speaking with Charlie, Pamela, or Aunt Margery, but for the most part he would crouch in a bush or stroll on the moor, armed with my telescope. He had long ago commandeered it, or rather accepted my offer of it—I was proud to have something he wanted.

The weather remained idyllic—warm but not hot, breezy rather than muggy, bright and brisk and inviting. Of course there was the occasional gray morning and one or two violent thundershowers. A few times, when the sky lowered and presented its dark underside, I thought it might change to match our mood, but the clouds always evaporated, and the sun always returned.

Oddly enough, it was Charlie who seemed most at a loss in the few days before the uncles' last hunting trip. Charlie was, on the whole, an uncomplicated young man. He liked fun and excitement, and he loved his family. He had none of Aunt Margery's tendency to fuss, but he had inherited her gift for watchfulness and Uncle Frank's stolidity of mind and body. He was intelligent enough and good-hearted, but he did not hold the depths of passion that the other cousins were capable of plumbing. Therefore, when they retired to their corners to mull over the news of Uncle Kurt and the tragedy of Aunt Loretta, Charlie was left empty-handed. He had been dismayed by the unveiling of family secrets, but more because it meant the breaking up of our circle than because he was troubled by what he heard. After all, if given the chance, he would have been thrilled to visit a gambling house filled with beautiful women. That is what I speculated about him, and I suspect Francesca speculated in a similar manner.

Francesca was not a girl to lie around doing nothing. Her idleness, which she had imposed on herself as a sort of mourning in honor of her mother, did not suit her personality at all, which is perhaps why it seemed to distort her so dramatically. The story I told her about Uncle Kurt's gambling in Portland galvanized her. I have no doubt her crazy, impossible idea was near fully formed by the end of her interview with me that morning by the cliff. The only person in whom she confided her scheme was Charlie, thereby rescuing him from boredom. When she heard that the uncles were going on a sixth hunting trip, she finalized her plans.

It turned out that Condor would be absent at the same time, making his annual trip to Brunswick to visit his niece and buy supplies for the long, lonesome winter at Shorecliff. When the Delias learned he would be gone, they developed their own plan, and thus the central bricks were laid for the night after the uncles' departure. Of course it was only later that I was able to piece together everything that happened. I played a part in the night's adventures too, but it was not an important one until the end.

The beginning we all saw. Less than a week before we were scheduled to depart from Shorecliff, the three uncles set off on their last hunting trip, loaded down with packs, guns, and tent poles. The aunts kissed them good-bye or patted their shoulders. The cousins, ranged in sullen rows on the stairs, looked on in silence.

"Look at you up there, all those sourpusses," said Uncle Cedric. "The sun is still shining, kids! The weather's warm, the shore awaits. Go outside, all of you! Try to find some fun here while you still can."

He scanned our faces one by one, seeing Francesca's gloom, Fisher's wide-eyed concern, Yvette's wrath, Isabella's distress... Yes, we had certainly become an odd crew. I for one could not keep my eyes off Uncle Kurt. He was strapping on his bags without paying attention to us, except that he flashed us an occasional smile. I searched for remorse and saw none. He looked chipper and excited, as if he were being allowed to do something he had always wanted to do, the way I probably looked when I went on adventures with my cousins. A wave of curiosity rolled over me. What was it like, that gambling house with its pretty women and poker tables and all-night dancing?

Uncle Kurt looked up and said, "Hold down the fort while I'm gone, Richard."

I was so in awe of his duplicity that I replied, "Yes, sir."

He thought I was joking and laughed, turning to Uncle Frank. "Move out, sergeant!" he cried. "We leave at 0900 hours."

When they left, the family scattered again. Somehow I whiled away the rest of that day—reading, possibly, or playing with Pamela, or drifting from bedroom to bedroom, seeking company and reassurance.

Delia and Delia went to their room. There was nothing unusual in that, and none of us knew then that they were planning Barnavelt's Great Escape. That night, however, at about half past two, they emerged. After hours of planning, all they had really decided was that Barnavelt deserved to be free and that they were the ones to free him. They knew Great-Uncle Eberhardt and Condor would try to get him back, so they planned to put him on his leash, walk with him to the secret field where Uncle Cedric had taken us for our picnic, and release him there. It was strange that they could have been so oblivious to the cruelty of their plan, not realizing that taking Barnavelt so far away and abandoning him would probably condemn him to a speedy death. Barnavelt was most assuredly a domestic fox—not as tame as a dog, for his ancestry did not hold countless years of servility, but still lacking the skills necessary for survival in the wild.

Delia Ybarra, however, had grown up in Manhattan and Delia Robierre in Cambridge, Massachusetts. Neither had ever learned about the ways of wild animals, and their notions concerning the morality of capturing foxes were taken exclusively from their own fantastic notions of what it meant to be free. They had long ago personified Barnavelt as a captive, something like an American Indian from a storybook, yearning to run through the forest and commune with nature. They thought, pityingly, that Condor loved the fox as much as they did but had less understanding of Barnavelt's true nature as a wild creature. I heard Delia Ybarra say once, "Condor just can't stand to give him up." So they ignored his warnings and set out for the cottage on the night of his departure.

The top of the staircase leading down from the third floor of Shorecliff was situated between the Wight boys' room and Philip and Tom's room. To reach it the Delias had to pass three rooms and come close to a fourth, and in doing so they woke up four cousins—Pamela, Isabella, Philip, and Tom. Pamela woke up when Delia Robierre crashed into the wall of her bedroom, eliciting a gale of giggles from Delia Ybarra. Really it was amazing that the two Delias left the house without waking up any adults, for they were the worst in our family at sneaking around. Isabella was roused by more giggles as they passed her bedroom, and Philip and Tom said that they were awakened when Delia Ybarra tripped going down the stairs. As often happened, the two boys woke at the same time, and each opened his eyes to the other's watchful face.

"What's happening?" Philip asked.

"I don't know. Someone's going downstairs."

They got up, listened at the door, and then went to the window. Their bedroom was at the back of the house, looking over the cliff, and when they peered out they were rewarded by a glimpse of two figures dashing toward the woods. The Delias had had an extended argument about whether or not to bring a flashlight—Delia Robierre voted for one, Delia Ybarra claimed it diminished the thrill of the adventure—but in the end, when Delia Robierre flat-out refused to go unless they brought some form of light, Delia Ybarra agreed to take one. Philip and Tom thus saw a bobbing light accompanying the two figures, and the silhouettes it revealed betrayed their identities.

"The Delias," said Tom. "What are they doing running around out there?"

"They're probably going to see what Barnavelt does at night," Philip said. "You know how they are about him, and Condor's gone. I wouldn't be surprised if they were going to set him free. It would be the perfect opportunity."

"Those crazy kids, they'll kill that fox." Tom didn't care much about Barnavelt, but the idea of freedom was dear to his heart. He leaned against the windowsill and compared himself with Barnavelt. After a moment he turned to Philip and said, "Do you want to head out?"

"Head out where?" answered Philip, grinning.

"I don't know. Let's go over to Lorelei's and see if she's awake."

"I don't think you need me on that particular expedition."

"Oh, for God's sake, Phil! I know it gives you a kick to think of me as some kind of rutting savage, but I'm not always running over there to sleep with her, all right? I just want to get out of this godforsaken place and do something exciting. Can we go? I know Lorelei would be glad to see us. And I want to see her."

He muttered this last phrase in a lower tone, but I heard the speech preceding it because it was his exasperated exclamation that woke me up. His voice drifted out of their open window and in through mine, and with my fine-tuned ability to sense cousinly intrigue, I sat up in bed and listened for clues about their plan. That was how I entered the night's activities.

Isabella, as it turned out, had also gone to her window and seen the Delias running for the woods, and when Philip and Tom shrugged on sweaters and came out into the hallway, she heard them and opened her door.

"Where are you going?" she whispered, smiling in anticipation.

Philip was leading the way. He looked at her as if deciding something and then said, "Oh, nowhere special."

"Can I come?" she asked.

"Not this time."

Tom added as they went down the stairs, "It would be too dangerous with more than two. Sorry, Bella."

"Dangerous?" she repeated scornfully, but they were already gone.

When I came into the hallway, clad in my red-striped pajamas and green bathrobe, I found her standing stiff as a board, with her arms crossed and her face distorted in a grimace. That was how she looked when she got angry.

"What's happening?" I asked.

"Nothing unusual. Tom and Philip are being bastards," she replied. Isabella rarely swore, so I knew she was upset.

"Are you going to follow them?" I asked.

"Why should I?" she said, shrugging. Then she added, "I do want to make sure the Delias are all right, though."

"Why? Where are they?"

"Didn't you hear them leaving? They've run off to the woods."

"Why?"

"I don't know. Should we go after them?" She smiled at me, and inwardly I leapt with delight. Isabella and me, going on a private midnight adventure into the depths of the woods! My heart began to pound.

"Is anyone else awake?" I asked, anxious that no one should interfere.

"I don't think so," she said as she disappeared into her bedroom to don outdoor clothes. "Put on a sweater, Richard. It might be chilly outside."

Isabella and I left the house thinking everyone else was asleep. Pamela, however, had been keeping careful track of the exodus from the third floor, and soon after we had gone out the front door, she followed, leaving Yvette in bed—the only cousin, as it turned out, who slept through all the commotion that followed. Pamela told me the next day that she had gone to keep an eye on me, but I think she liked the idea of being all by herself in the woods at night, following two people who didn't know she was there. It was a night game more suspenseful than any of the games we had played before.

The air outside was warm and full of thrumming from hidden insects. The sweater Isabella had told me to wear was unnecessary, and I discarded both it and my bathrobe outside the door. I had put on shoes, knowing we would be going into the woods, but aside from them I was wearing only my striped pajamas. Even my hair stuck up the way it always did after I had been in bed. Isabella was nearly invisible in a dark skirt and long-sleeved jersey—she looked like a cat burglar on the prowl. There was almost no moonlight that night, only a few weak rays from a crescent high in the sky. Isabella turned to me as we trotted across the lawn, and I saw her eyes gleaming. I wondered if she had been crying in her room before we left. She didn't say anything as we headed for the woods.

Disaster struck, as far as I was concerned, almost as soon as we passed through the first line of trees. The moonlight was lost under the foliage, and we plunged into a darkness filled with sharp twigs, clinging underbrush, and slimy bugs under our hands on the tree bark.

"We have to go to Condor's cottage," Isabella said. "I'm sure the Delias went to visit Barnavelt."

I jumped at the sound of her voice and tried to follow it. She strode ahead, and I ran forward, trying to keep the patch of moving blackness in sight, but I tripped over a branch and fell on my face in a clump of moss. For a few moments all I could do was spit dirt out of my mouth. When I looked up I was alone.

"Isabella?" I said. "Isabella? Where are you?" I didn't want to shout. It would have been too terrifying to yell into the darkness and not receive an answer. I stood up, put out both my hands, felt a tree, and held onto it for a while.

In her defense, Isabella was upset. Under less emotional circumstances, she would never have left me like that, alone in the middle of the woods at night. But she was intent on finding Tom and Philip (in spite of what she had said to me, the two Delias were a mere aside to her), and her sense of urgency propelled her forward. She told me later that when she realized I was no longer by her side, she was struck by a jolt of worry. She looked all around, called my name, and then out of desperation kept going in the same direction as before. There seemed to be nothing else to do.

At least for her there was an objective in crashing through the woods. I stood motionless, not knowing which way to go or whom to seek out. Gradually, as my eyes adjusted, I began to see the dim bushes and tree trunks all around me. They were indistinct shapes, and some of them were moving in the breeze. It took about two minutes for me to convince myself that the nearest one hid a hulking murderer out for blood. Fear washed through me. Logically it was ridiculous, but logic is unimportant when you're alone in the dark. Every bush I saw became a crouching psychopath, every tree the shield for a slavering killer. Some people fear wild animals, but I was petrified by the wicked cunning of which only humans are capable. I had read enough comic books and mysteries to be able to imagine the appearance of all the murderers who surrounded me. Each one was dressed in black, and whether he was short or tall, bulky or wiry, each had the same glint of homicidal dementia in his eyes.

Suddenly, and with great vividness, I remembered Uncle Kurt's story about walking through the snow-covered woods with his platoon and being surrounded by Germans. I looked around, my heart beating so forcefully that I thought I might be about to die. The woods seemed to be covered in a blanket of snow. I waited for white German faces to burst out from the darkness. The breeze picked up for a moment, and one of the bushes nearby rustled and swayed. It was all I needed. With a squeak of pure panic, I put my arms over my eyes and ran.

The strip of woods between Shorecliff and the Stephensons' farm was in fact quite sizable, and though by day the sunlight shining in on either side was enough to show that the trees did not go on forever, in the darkness one could wander for a long time without finding a way out. I probably ran for about ten minutes, though it seemed like hours. I fell several times, hit my head on branches, collided with trees. A few minutes into my galloping retreat I began to cry, and the tears did nothing to clear my vision. I was a wreck. The only reason I stopped moving was that my breath was getting ragged, and I had just run into my fourth maple tree. Leaning against its corrugated bark, I wiped my dirt- and tear-smeared face and looked around. Instantly the gang of spectral murderers encircled me again. I couldn't escape them. It began to seem as if I would never leave the woods, as if I would be trapped in a hell of leafy killers forever. I was becoming nearly hysterical. Then I turned my head and saw a white face peering at me through the bushes.

Immediately I thought, "A German!" and screamed like a rabbit being slaughtered. Unlike Hennessey, I recovered my voice only when my fear reached unprecedented heights. I shrieked and shrieked and fell to my knees. Even when hands gripped my shoulders and shook me, it was at least a minute before I stopped. Eventually, however, I couldn't find any more energy to scream, and I opened my eyes. Simultaneously I heard a voice that I realized had been speaking for some time.

"It's okay, Richard, buddy! It's me—Fisher. It's just me, boy scout. Stop shouting! You're all right. It's just me. It's Fisher."

Gentle, kindly, lovable Fisher out in the woods, searching for owls. The relief was so strong I practically fainted. The murderers vanished. I knelt on the ground, unspeakably grateful for Fisher's hands on my shoulders, and wiped my eyes, snuffling. Something glinted by my knees, and I reached down and found my telescope. Fisher had dropped it while trying to comfort me.

"It's not much use in the dark," he said, and I could hear the smile in his voice. "But I like to have it with me just in case."

I murmured an unintelligible response and clasped the telescope in my fist. The feel of its cool metal casing reassured me.

Fisher let me recover for a moment longer and then asked, "What are you doing out here, boy scout?"

"Everyone's out here," I replied. "I came with Isabella. We were following Tom and Philip. They went out to visit Lorelei. Delia and Delia are out here too—I don't know why. Isabella thinks they're going to visit Barnavelt."

"The only person I've seen is Pamela," Fisher said.

"Pamela?" I echoed. Hers was the last name I expected to hear. The explanation for her presence came only later in the night, however. First came Barnavelt, for he was the one who began the night's fiasco.

While I was racing through the woods in panic, Delia and Delia arrived at Condor's cottage without mishap. They had visited so frequently that they knew the way better than everyone else, except of course Condor himself and Uncle Eberhardt. Eberhardt, however, was someone they had forgotten about. Cautiously they opened the door—Condor didn't believe in locks, claiming he owned nothing to steal—and crept into the main room. The bedroom door was closed, and no sound came through it. Barnavelt lay curled in his wooden house, his black nose resting on his bushy red tail.

Delia Ybarra found the leash hanging on the wall and bent over the wooden house to fasten the end of it around Barnavelt's neck.

"Should we, Eel?" Delia Robierre whispered suddenly.

"Of course we should! Don't be stupid. We've come all the way out here, and this is our one chance." Cordelia slid the loop at the end of the leash over Barnavelt's head.

He watched her with his black eyes, his snout quivering. When she had finished, he jumped up and ran to the door of the cottage.

"See?" she crowed, clutching the leash. "He knows what's happening! What a smart fox you are!" she crooned at him. These comments were probably what woke Great-Uncle Eberhardt.

Just as the Delias were following Barnavelt outside, the bedroom door crashed on its hinges and Eberhardt appeared in black long johns, his white hair flying. "Get back here, you hooligans!" he shouted. "Thieves! Kidnappers! I'll have your hide! I'll whip you until you bleed!"

Delia and Delia heard every word, and though they laughed about it afterward, at the time they were terrified. They sprinted into the woods with Barnavelt and soon discovered the same thing I had—that running in a pitch-black wood is sure to result in bruises and scrapes. Behind them Eberhardt was crashing nearer.

"Turn left, Lia!" Delia Ybarra said in a hoarse whisper. The two girls veered, Barnavelt still at their heels, and some minutes later, they stopped to listen. A few indistinct shouts sounded in the distance and one terrifying scream—mine, they discovered later—but no furious old man pursued them.

"We've shaken him off," Delia Robierre whispered.

Now that they were out of danger, the girls regained their appreciation of the adventure. It took them no time at all to collapse in a storm of giggles.

Barnavelt, however, had gotten a taste of late-night running and wanted more. Seeing that the two girls weren't going to provide any more entertainment, he wriggled this way and that, curled in a ball, tugged and kicked at his leash, and in a few moments slipped out of it and bolted into the darkness.

The two Delias screamed his name and tried to follow him, but he had disappeared. Condor explained later that he had deliberately made the leash loose enough for Barnavelt to slip out of if he tried, to avoid the danger of strangulation. And it was this that finally convinced the Delias of Barnavelt's complicity in his own captivity. After all, it was only when they foxnapped him that he took advantage of the possibility of escape.

The fox ended up in one of the Stephenson fields, where Lorelei was taking a walk. Barnavelt lolloped right up to her, grinning his foxy little grin, and waited for her to take him back to Condor's cottage. She did so, thereby finding a path into the night's final catastrophe—and it was a good thing she did because when we returned to Shorecliff at the end of the night, the aunts didn't bother to tell her to leave, and we regained her as a companion in the last harried days before the end of the summer. Given that we were all emotionally as fragile as butterfly wings during those days, her soft, practical presence was an inestimable gift.

The reason Uncle Eberhardt had failed to catch the two Delias, in spite of being more familiar with the woods than they were, was that he had been distracted by another pair of delinquents. He had just begun his crazed pursuit of the foxnappers when Tom and Philip, bursting into the clearing around Condor's cottage from the opposite direction, ran straight into him. All three fell to the ground in a tangle. Many years later Philip told me that one of the things he remembered best from that night was the horrible sensation of Uncle Eberhardt's bare leg pressing against his cheek. When they finally disengaged themselves and rose to their feet, Eberhardt was so angry he was nearly foaming at the mouth.

"What are you doing out here, you useless brats?" he sputtered. "How dare you run into me in the middle of the night! I'll paddle you! I'll beat you black and blue! Get away from my cottage. How dare you enter my woods!"

He looked so fearsome, a dim figure leaping up and down and shaking two gnarled fists in their faces, that Philip and Tom exchanged a look and raced back into the woods, away from Condor's cottage and also away from the Delias, though the only reason they had stopped by the cottage in the first place was to check on the two girls. They were no better at avoiding trees than the rest of us and ran into several in their flight from Eberhardt. Tom twisted his ankle, and Philip nearly impaled his right eye on a branch. For the remainder of our stay at Shorecliff, he sported a cut on his cheek that made him look like a Caribbean pirate.

I, meanwhile, was awash in relief that our most experienced tracker had found me and taken me under his wing. Fisher was the only one who avoided getting lost that night. It was strange and soothing to see how confidently he navigated the forest while the rest of us bashed through it like blind bears. I was telling him as best I could why everyone else had come into the woods when he shushed me and lifted his face.

"Can you hear that?" he whispered, rapt.

I thought I could make out a small rustling. "What is it?" I asked.

"An owl catching a mouse!"

"How do you know?"

Fisher didn't answer. We both stood listening. Probably the sound he heard came from the Delias escaping from Uncle Eberhardt. Whatever it was, it distracted us into staying in one position, and that was why Philip and Tom happened upon us when they did. Tom came barreling from behind a bush and ran into me, casting me headlong. Yet again I tasted dirt. A short-lived shouting match ensued.

"Who the hell is that?"

"Stop pushing me!"

"Ow! Who is that?"

"Get the hell off me!"

"I'm trying to!"

"Fisher? What are you doing here?"

Philip's surprised question ended the spat. Tom and I got up off the ground, and the four of us looked at the white blotches that were all we could see of each other's faces.

Tom chuckled and said, "Isn't this quite the family gathering," but Philip punched him on the arm and asked, "Is Eberhardt still after us?"

We obligingly listened to the wood noises. Fisher heard more rustling and returned to his naturalist mode, but there were no more owls for him that night.

"I think we shook him off," said Tom.

"What was he doing up anyway?"

"The Delias must have woken him. They were kidnapping that stupid fox, weren't they? Crazy kids."

As if on cue, a fifth figure stumbled up to us. "I heard that,

Tom," said Delia Robierre, sounding breathless. "Have any of you seen Delia? I've lost her."

"Were you two really trying to kidnap Barnavelt?" Philip asked.

"We thought it was a good idea! I don't know why you have to make fun of it. We thought it was important. But then Uncle Eberhardt chased us, and Barnavelt got away, and we heard voices, so we tried to follow them, but we were separated somehow. And Isabella's out here too, but she ran away from me." Her voice wavered.

"Isabella came out too?" Philip interrupted.

Delia paused and then said, "Yes."

At this point I broke in. Pamela's presence had been bothering me ever since I'd heard about it, and I asked, "Why haven't we seen Pamela too, if she's out here?"

Tom sighed. "She's probably lost. We'll have to find her."

A ghostly figure appeared behind him and said, "No, I'm here."

It was Pamela in her white nightgown, the top half covered by a sweater. The rest of us had had a second to register that someone was standing behind Tom, but he leaped in terror. We burst out laughing, and Pamela, a smirk of satisfaction on her face, joined our circle. It was the first time I understood how much she enjoyed being secretly in the know. She was too proud to join me in most of my eavesdropping expeditions—they were crude and lacked the thrill of the chase—but when she could combine dignity with cunning, there was no one more skilled at stalking people like a secret agent.

"The gang's practically all here," Tom said when we had finished laughing at him. He was still disgruntled and glared at Pamela.

"All except Isabella," said Philip. "And my Delia."

"How about the others? Has anyone seen Charlie or Francesca or Yvette?"

"Yvette was still asleep when I left," said Pamela.

"So was Charlie when I left," Fisher said. "But I've been out here for hours."

Philip glanced at him affectionately. "Do you often spend all night in the woods, pal?" he asked.

"It's the best time for owls."

"We'd better find Isabella then," said Tom.

"I wouldn't look for her if I were you," Delia Robierre broke in.

"What do you mean?"

"Well, I...I just think she'd rather be left alone."

"What are you talking about?" said Philip. "If she's lost, we have to find her. Did she tell you where she was trying to go?"

"Yes," Delia replied after another long pause. "But she was upset, and I promised I wouldn't mention having seen her. Except then she ran away, and if she's actually lost..."

"Why was she upset?" Tom asked. The thought of Isabella in danger roused his protective blood.

"No reason," said Delia.

"Don't be stupid, Delia. Obviously she was upset about something, and you know what it is. Tell me now!"

As usual, his older-brother insistence won the day. "First of all," she began angrily, "you two wouldn't let her come out with you."

Philip snorted. "Is that all? We were going to find Lorelei. Of course we couldn't have her with us."

"That's the problem!" said Delia. "I promised I wouldn't say anything, but you'd have to be blind not to see it. Isabella adores both of you, and you always brush her off. Philip, she practically worships the ground you walk on! But you never have the time of day for her."

"That's not true. I—"

"You know what she told me? She told me she's afraid of how much she thinks about you. She idolizes you—and all you can do is ignore her and make fun of her. No wonder she's upset!"

"Idolizes me?" Philip repeated. "That can't be true."

It took all my concentration to keep listening after this, for at the words "she's afraid of how much she thinks about you," my heart tightened, and I was overcome by a rush of anguish. Suddenly I couldn't stand the idea of Isabella thinking about anyone other than me, and her thinking about Philip was especially bad because he cared so much less for her than I did. Of course it was ridiculous for a thirteen-year-old boy to imagine that a girl four years older could return any sort of romantic affection—especially a girl who was his cousin. Even then I knew how absurd it was. Yet I adored her, and when Delia revealed Isabella's pitiful secret, I felt an unbearable need to have my own worship recognized. Surely, I found myself thinking, I should get some reward for how devotedly I'd followed her all summer. She had to understand that I deserved her attention more than Philip did.

The others had no idea that I was being rocked by such emotion. They were puzzling over the enigma of a secretive Isabella.

"We don't ignore her," said Tom. "What is she talking about? Are you sure she said that, Delia? How much of this are you making up?"

"None of it! You're always saying she can't do things, that she wouldn't be brave enough."

"Oh, come on," said Philip. "You mean jumping off the cliff?" I thought it was significant that he remembered the incident, but no one else remarked on it. "Of course she wouldn't be brave enough to do that—it's dangerous!"

"If Isabella really said all that, she's cracking up," said Tom. "She's going nuts. The summer has been too much for her."

"Well, can you blame her?"

"No, but it's idiotic, what you're saying about her and Philip. What kind of a girl falls in love with her cousin?"

"Yvette?" Philip suggested, grinning.

Tom waved him aside. "That isn't the same thing," he said. "Not that it wasn't damn weird. Anyway, Isabella is obviously upset. She didn't know what she was saying. We'll find her and put her back in bed, and tomorrow she'll wish she hadn't told you anything, Delia."

"We're just cousins," Philip said, shrugging.

I scorned him—a novel sensation. It was clear enough to me how one cousin could fall in love with another; I had done it myself. And in spite of my jealousy of Philip, I felt that my obsession with Isabella gave me a badge of maturity. I too now could have a deadly secret, one mixed up with romance and sex and envy.

Delia was about to reply when a flurry of bumps and rustles erupted behind her. A seventh white blotch appeared in our circle, and after a moment of confusion we recognized Isabella's tear-covered face. I shrank back, terrified that she would somehow deduce what I was feeling, yet at the same time eager for her to know.

She spoke only to Delia. "I can't believe you told them!" she cried. "I can't believe it. You're my own sister, and you still betrayed me! You promised you wouldn't say anything. I'll never forgive you!"

She stopped for a moment, panting, and Tom grabbed her shoulder. "Calm down, Bella," he said. "No one's mad at you or anything. Stop crying and listen for a minute. She didn't tell us anything—"

"I've been standing there listening, you patronizing creep!" She slapped his hand away. "She told you everything, and of course all you did was laugh and say I was crazy. Fine! I'm crazy! I'm crazy because I actually thought you"—she turned to Philip—"were worth caring about. You don't think I can do anything! Well, I can. I don't need you and your stupid philosophy to do it either. I hate all of you!" She gave a few inarticulate sobs and crashed into the woods again, disappearing before any of us could stop her.

For nearly a minute none of us said anything. When Isabella, who was always extravagant, let loose the full force of her emotion, it was like being hit by a cyclone. We could all see that she was ashamed, though no one except me blamed her for being half in love with Philip. I was sure her feelings were different from Yvette's jealous lusting after Tom—Isabella, for one thing, would never have betrayed any of Philip's secrets. But that made it worse. What Isabella felt for Philip was closer, I thought, to a genuine attachment—closer to what I felt for her—and that meant she preferred even his grudging scraps of attention to my willingness for total self-sacrifice. The thought made me ache with frustration.

At last Tom said, "Well, you've certainly done a number on her, Philip."

"Don't lay the blame on me," Philip protested. "I couldn't help it. How was I supposed to know?"

"I still think it was better that I told you," Delia said in a muffled voice.

"Oh, God, don't you start," Tom sighed.

"Shut up! You're not the person who's just betrayed someone."

Fisher was the next to speak, and what he said made me admire him more than ever. "Don't you think we should go look for her?" he asked. "After all, it doesn't matter who said what. We all love her, and I don't think we should let her run through the woods when she's so upset. She might hurt herself."

"Good old Fisher," said Tom. "You're right. Let's go."

The delay had allowed Isabella to stagger beyond our reach, and the cousins fanned out to search for her. I was too distracted to make sure someone else was going my way. I heard again Fisher's statement that we all loved Isabella, and I thought to myself, more and more fiercely, that I loved her more, though none of them realized it. They were always taking me for granted, always pushing me aside, just as Philip pushed aside Isabella, but I would show them, for the first time in my life, exactly what I felt and how strongly I felt it. Truly I believe I was possessed by a demon that night, for I had never before been so irrationally determined to make myself noticed.

By sheer chance, after fifteen minutes, I stumbled to the edge of the wood that faced the lawn in front of Shorecliff. It was still dark, but an elusive hint of lightness in the air signaled the approach of dawn. For a moment, disoriented by the sudden freedom from clawing branches and looming trees, I blinked at the vacancy of the lawn and stood motionless. Then a faint noise drifted toward me, and I heard again the sound of cousins in conspiracy. A light flickered in the distance. Someone was standing by the rattletrap.

That in itself puzzled me: the rattletrap had nothing to do with the night's various imbroglios. Stepping forward, I bumped my leg with the telescope I was still holding, long forgotten. Now, if ever, was a time to use it. I held it to my eye, hoping that whoever was by the rattletrap would turn on a flashlight so I could have something to focus on. Soon the wavering light reappeared, blinking in and out of view beyond the fence. Significantly, it was not a flashlight but a match. What I saw in its light was a group of three people: Philip Ybarra and two more cousins who had played no part in the night up to that point.

I have arrived now at a moment I've been dreading. It has approached with the inevitability of a freight train. I have tried to ignore it, tried to present all the shocking and delightful events that happened beforehand without letting them be shaded by hindsight. And I think I have partially succeeded: those months at

Shorecliff have regained their original colors more vividly than I thought was possible.

It would not be right, having made such an effort to re-create the events as they happened, if I described the accident that followed without first narrating what we learned only later. In justice to the summer's last adventure, therefore, I will tell it as it happened, with all the details that subsequently emerged. After that there will be no more blank pages between me and the confession of my guilt.

15

Rattletrap

Charlie woke that night to Francesca's face hovering inches from his, her eyes blazing and her black curls tumbling over her shoulders. He had fallen asleep less than an hour before, but Charlie was renowned among us for being able to lose consciousness in seconds. He could sleep anywhere, at any time. So Francesca was dragging him out of a deep slumber, and he was confused. He glanced at Fisher's bed and saw it was empty, though the room was dark.

"What time is it?" he mumbled.

"Come off it, you've only been asleep for twenty minutes."

"Where's Fisher?"

"Who knows? Listen, Charlie, I want to get out of here. I'm going to take the rattletrap and drive to Portland and have some fun for the first time in my life. Do you want to come with me?"

That woke Charlie up. He raised himself on one elbow and stared at her, wondering if she could be serious. Portland, after all, was two hours farther away than Pensbottom.

"Do you mean it?" he asked.

"Of course I mean it. I always mean it, but no one else does—that's the whole problem with this hellhole. So I'm leaving. I'm going to find Uncle Kurt and force him to show me around—if he gets all the fun, the least he can do is share it. Are you coming or what?"

"But, Francesca, they'll hear us going. You know how much noise the rattletrap makes."

"They didn't hear us last time. Besides, it's after eleven, and the aunts have been going to bed ridiculously early. They're asleep. I could hear them snoring." Francesca loaded this statement with all the scorn a young, beautiful girl feels for middle-aged women past the age of caring.

Charlie was hesitating. The truth was, he told us afterward, that it seemed like the wrong time for an escapade. The summer had already been so packed with betrayals and surprises that it felt foolhardy, almost insensitive, to dive into another forbidden act. But Francesca had no time for delicacies. Frustration had been eating her for the past month, and after a few more minutes of conversation, Charlie knew there was no stopping her. He went with her, he told us, to protect her in Portland, to make sure she didn't do anything too reckless. This was true, but it was also true that he went because Francesca was irresistible and Charlie had been her slave since the first morning at Shorecliff.

They disturbed no one on their way out. The rest of us were either asleep or too busy planning to hear them leave. They got to the first floor without incident, and then, as they came into the front hall, Francesca banged her shin on a doorway. "Ow! Damn it!" she cried in an aggressive whisper. "Do you have a flashlight?"

Charlie shook his head. Most of the cousins owned flashlights, but Francesca's was dead, and Charlie's had been lost. "Do we really need one?" he asked. "I don't want to risk going back up."

"It would be a good thing to have."

"Francesca, I don't know about this." Charlie had remembered other necessities, and the scale of the whole business was rising before him. "We'll need money for when we get to Portland, and we'll probably have to buy gas for the rattletrap, and we don't know where Uncle Kurt is in the city…"

Francesca didn't let him get any further. "Shut up!" she hissed, grabbing his arm with fingers like talons. "I have money. There's an extra can of gas in the back of the rattletrap. And I don't care where Uncle Kurt is in Portland, we'll find him!" She tightened her grip and leaned close to him, looking, he told us, almost crazed in her determination. "This isn't some kind of game to me, all right? I'm serious. I have to get out! And I'm going." She released him and turned around, darting into the morning room next to the kitchen. "I don't care whether you come or not," he heard her saying. "It doesn't matter to me."

"Of course," Charlie said to us later, "I had to go then." And we all agreed.

Francesca was rummaging in the closet where we had found the croquet set at the beginning of the summer. She emerged a moment later with the lantern Delia Robierre had spotted months before. The rest of us had forgotten its existence, but Francesca's scheming mind had filed it away as a possible resource for later adventures.

All Charlie said was "Matches?" He was determined to rein in her enthusiasm as much as he could.

"There are some in the kitchen," she replied.

Minutes later they were out the door and in the rattletrap, praying it would start without too much vehicular hemming and hawing. It occurred to Charlie that it was ridiculous for two people who had never driven to Portland to attempt the trip in the middle of the night in such a rickety automobile. The probability that they would get lost was so high that Charlie was already going over the options for finding help as he turned the car and headed past the isolated fence posts in the direction of Pensbottom. Despite the rattletrap's rumbles and bangs, no aunts appeared at the doorway and no lights flicked on in the house. Francesca, looking back, laughed a sultry, chuckling laugh and flung her arm around Charlie.

"They have no idea," she said. "They have absolutely no idea." Her tone implied that she was shaking off their ignorance as if it were mud on her shoes. From now on, she told Charlie, she would know what was going on—in her own family and in life as well. When people talked about speakeasies and gambling and drinking, she would know what they meant because she would have experienced it all herself. "There's no other way," she said. "It might end in disaster, but if you don't go, you're just a naive little fool, doing what other people tell you to do. I'm tired of having my own family pull the wool over my eyes. They've had us trapped there all summer and pretended we were still eight years old, but we're leaving now, and we'll find Uncle Kurt and show him he's not the only one who can go to Portland. Besides, he understands how I feel. And once we're there he won't have any choice but to take us with him."

Charlie had doubts about that, but he didn't voice them. At this point he was also hoping they would find Uncle Kurt, simply so that he could guide them through the city and offer Francesca some protection against her own wildness.

Miraculously the two of them drove all the way to Portland without once getting lost. I could easily believe that Francesca's determination to follow Uncle Kurt was leading her forward. They reached the city sooner—far sooner—than they should have. "I don't understand how it happened," Charlie told us afterward. "I must have been driving too fast. Everyone said it was two hours from Pensbottom. But we got there in two hours, all the way from Shorecliff. I don't know…" Even then he sounded nervous. "It was as if Francesca forced us to get there faster."

What this meant was that it was only one-thirty in the morning when they began to walk through the busy streets, after parking the car in the city center. The dangers of a city at night, even a relatively small one like Portland, hadn't been real to Charlie before that moment. Having grown up in a country town, he wasn't used to the lights and clamor that fill a city through the witching hours. Francesca, hardened or believing herself hardened by a lifetime in New York, felt no fear at all. Charlie took her arm, hoping no one would think the rattletrap worth stealing, and they wandered the streets aimlessly for some time. At first they avoided eye contact with passersby and simply hunted for crowds and likely-looking buildings. After a while, however, Charlie grew desperate, and he began to ask, like the greenest yokel, which way they should turn for the speakeasies. Most of the people they asked laughed in their faces or reminded them, rivaling their innocence, that Portland had been a dry town for decades. Some looked Francesca up and down appreciatively—"That made me want to punch them out, I can tell you," said Charlie. But one man obligingly directed them toward the waterfront, the seediest, most unsavory part of town, where the dance halls and whorehouses and backroom bars were located.

Good luck aided them in their quest to find Uncle Kurt. He usually frequented a far more exclusive poker circle than anything Francesca and Charlie could have found. Kurt said later, to the circle of aunts who gathered to interrogate him, how fortunate it was that he had stopped first to have a drink at a more popular place, one the city authorities silently condoned. "It would have been more fortunate," Aunt Rose responded, "if you'd gone hunting with Frank and Cedric the way you were supposed to."

Francesca and Charlie tried to visit four different places before they found the one where Uncle Kurt was having his quick drink. Two of these—unmarked bars that they identified by the tide of drunken voices seeping through the windows—didn't let them in at all, and the other two were nearly empty. The novelty of the chase was wearing off by the time they got to the fifth place, a dance hall, and Charlie harbored a secret but increasingly pressing desire to give in and find a hotel where they could sleep. The full idiocy of their scheme became clear to him only as they were picking their way through that grimy part of town, passing streetwalkers and bums and men off merchant ships who stood crying outside the gambling houses because they had just lost everything they owned.

"Really," he told us, shuddering, "it was a horrible place. I don't care what Francesca said, I'm not glad to have seen it. I wish we'd never gone." Francesca must have been feeling the same way, but of course she didn't admit it. She told him not to be a fool, that they would find Kurt eventually. She led him fearlessly down one dark alley after another until they found a sordid, dirty establishment called The Tap Shoes, crowded with made-up women in tawdry dresses and men so drunk they couldn't dance.

Uncle Kurt saw them as soon as they came in. "I've never been so damn surprised in my whole life," he said. "When they walked through that door, I almost dropped my drink."

Francesca's triumph in finding Uncle Kurt lasted longer than Charlie's. Kurt marched them out the door and gave them a talking-to that probably gained an edge by coming after several whiskeys. Charlie listened with an air so hopeless and resigned that Uncle Kurt said it seemed as if he didn't even know where he was. Francesca, on the other hand, would nod seriously and then burst into gales of laughter and shout, "We found you—I knew we would!" It was a long time before she came down from her victory.

The fact that her ridiculous plan had worked, that her determination had paid off, made her almost giddy. The whole night began to seem unreal, as if anything they set out to do would happen simply because they willed it.

In truth Francesca's plan ended with finding Uncle Kurt. According to her fantastic vision of the night, once in his care they would simply follow him from one adventure to the next. Ultimately, though, I don't think she was concerned with those specifics. It was the initial gesture that had captivated her, the desperation of abandoning all caution and flying headlong into the underground world that, for the Hatfield family, was forbidden above all others.

"Give me a drink!" she said to Uncle Kurt, still laughing and with a voice so full of excitement, he said, that it sounded as if she were drunk already.

That was the last straw for Uncle Kurt. I had never seen him angry, and from what Charlie told us, I never wanted to. The aunts' wrath, of course, was fearsome, but it was also familiar. Making Uncle Kurt mad, according to Charlie, was utterly different. "The worst part," he said, "was that it wasn't like an uncle yelling at his niece and nephew. It was one adult furious with two other adults. *Really* furious—it sounded at first as if he hated me. Not that he shouted or jumped around or anything. He just stood there and spoke in that awful voice…" Charlie trailed off, and he wouldn't elaborate further. But none of us wanted more details.

Uncle Kurt told Charlie he had been irresponsible and careless to an unforgivable degree. "Did you ever stop to imagine," he asked, "what would have happened if you two had been attacked in this city? This isn't a place for children, and it's especially not a place for a young woman as innocent and impulsive as Francesca. How," he said, turning to Charlie, "how could you have brought her here?" That was the worst question of all, and Charlie didn't have an answer.

With Francesca Uncle Kurt was almost gentle. He took her by the shoulders and said, "Francesca, this isn't what you want. You don't want my kind of life. It's not a happy one, believe me. You weren't made for secrecy and lies and breaking the law. Do you understand me?" Francesca looked at him with that black-eyed stare of hers. She was listening, but she wasn't going to agree with what he said. Not one of the rest of us could have looked into Uncle Kurt's face with the unwavering defiance she showed then. "I could see it in her eyes," he said to the aunts. "That passion! She wasn't going to give up a single moment of her independence." Even so, he kept trying to reason with her. "You'll have a long, adventure-filled life," he told her. "You'll do all sorts of things we'll be stunned to hear about. But you're young. Believe it or not, you're still young. And there will be time for all that in the future."

Francesca waited until he was finished and then shot him a knowing, feline smile. "I bet if you were in my position, you wouldn't give in either—would you, Uncle Kurt?"

Uncle Kurt didn't answer. He let go of her and turned to Charlie. And then he made a horrible mistake. "Take her home," he said. "Take her home right now. Drive back, tell the aunts whatever you want, but make sure she doesn't leave Shorecliff again." As an afterthought he added, "Will you be able to find your way?"

Charlie nodded. At the time, he told us, Uncle Kurt was so terrifying that it didn't occur to Charlie to ask him to come back with them. He was too angry, too distant, too firmly planted in a world they could see only from the outside. Also, Charlie added, Francesca was worrying him. He suspected that if she had been any other girl she would have been crying, but because she would suffer anything rather than break down when being reprimanded, she transformed all her feelings into a kind of frantic impudence.

"But she was tired," Charlie said. "I could see by the way she was standing. So I thought it really would be the best thing to get her home as fast as possible."

Charlie led Francesca away before she could say anything else to Uncle Kurt, and they made the long walk back to the rattletrap. They drove up to Shorecliff without incident. The whole trip had gone by so fast that it wasn't even light when they got back. Once again, the ride had taken a disturbingly short time. Of course, Charlie was driving fast in his haste to return Francesca to safety, but even so it was not yet five o'clock when they pulled up to the lonely fence outside Shorecliff.

And why, we all asked, hadn't Uncle Kurt come back with them? Aunt Rose didn't spare him. "You sent two children who had already been up all night, who had driven on roads they had never seen before into a city they had never been to, who had just been wandering through the most disgusting part of that city—you let those two children drive back all alone to Shorecliff in the middle of the night!"

That was when my mother put a hand on Rose's arm and stopped her from saying any more because Uncle Kurt had put his face in his hands and started to cry. He knew too well what it would have meant, had he acted as the responsible adult he was asking Charlie to be in his stead.

But the fact that Uncle Kurt didn't escort Charlie and Francesca home arose from the same force that led him to gamble and drink and deceive his family in the first place. That night he was faced with the choice of protecting Charlie and Francesca or avoiding for one more brief night the condemnation of his sisters—something he had been trying to escape all summer. Of course, there was also his plan to salvage the money he had lost and his desire to pursue the girl who had "distracted him" into losing it. She was a shadowy, alarming figure who appeared only in my imagination, but I was sure she had played a role in his decision to stay in Portland. Ultimately, however, I think he was simply too scared to return to Shorecliff.

In his explanation to the aunts, Kurt said in faltering tones that he realized Charlie's character was stronger and steadier than his own. It had been easier to stay and cope with the problems he already had than to go back with the two children and face more, so that was what he did. "I'm ashamed," he said, closing his eyes. "I'm so ashamed."

I was there, watching this display. Never before or since has an idol of mine crumbled so devastatingly. He had arrived back at Shorecliff with the other uncles a day later, full of repentance, and found utter disaster. I don't think he ever forgave himself, any more than I did.

Charlie and Francesca returned to Shorecliff and pulled to a halt in the rattletrap's usual place. The house was still dark. Though they didn't know it, nearly all of their cousins were at this moment wandering in the woods by the Stephensons' farm. For a few minutes they sat in silence, partly waiting for signs of angry aunts and partly resting from the night's excitement. Francesca hadn't said much on the drive home, and whenever Charlie glanced at her she either turned away from him, staring out the window, or peered out at the road ahead, her eyes burning with intensity. "To be honest," he said to us, "I was a little scared of her. She was over the top the whole time."

As a result, when they arrived at Shorecliff and were sitting in the car, Charlie didn't dare say anything. He waited for her to make the first move.

Eventually she turned to look at him. "So," she said heavily, "we're back at Shorecliff again."

"Yes."

"No matter how hard you try to get away from this place, it

drags you back. Look at Uncle Kurt—he always comes back too. We don't have a chance. We're far too young." She spat the last word. Then she looked into Charlie's face, contemplating a new idea.

Here Charlie stopped telling the story. He looked into the distance, his mouth half open.

"Well?" said Tom. We were all eager to hear what had happened next, not so much because the story was unfinished but because by that time we were desperate for every snippet of Francesca's thoughts and words and actions.

"What happened then?" asked Isabella.

"Well," said Charlie, looking down and blushing—all the Wight children blushed easily, they had such pale skin— "well, if you really want to know, what happened then is that she kissed me."

"She what?" said Philip blankly.

"Kissed you?" Tom echoed. "What do you mean?"

"I mean just that: she kissed me. On the mouth. It was a real kiss."

We were speechless. Finally, Tom sputtered, "Was it—was it—was it—" He couldn't finish.

Isabella said, "Did it go on for a long time?"

"A pretty long time," said Charlie.

"What did you say when it was over?" Tom demanded. He seemed almost offended that something so shocking had happened without his knowledge.

"Uh—well—I'd suddenly thought of it, see. I said we should fill up the gas tank so that no one would notice how much gas we'd used."

In the midst of our sadness, Tom laughed. It was such a ridiculous thing to say after being kissed by a beautiful girl—especially when the beautiful girl was a cousin, fulfilling at last the promise of scandal that had been floating between her and Charlie since the beginning of the summer. Then Tom remembered what Charlie's comment had led to, and he stopped laughing, and we all sat in silence.

When I looked through the telescope after emerging from the woods, right before the sun broke over the horizon, I saw three people standing by the rattletrap: Charlie, Francesca, and Philip. They were huddled around something I couldn't see properly by the feeble light of the match Charlie held in his hand. Matches were the only source of light they had, thanks to Francesca's silly notion of taking the lantern—empty of kerosene, as it turned out—instead of a flashlight. In any case, their position by the rattletrap was so unexpected that I was completely befuddled. Through the storm of love and envy whirling within me, curiosity reached out and took hold. I would still do something magnificent, something to make Isabella see how worthy I was of her attention, but first I would find out what was going on.

So, dropping to the grass—an unnecessary move, since the group by the rattletrap was absorbed by the problem at hand—I slithered toward them, soaking myself in dew. The wind was blowing toward me over the dune grass, and I could hear their voices from relatively far away.

"Then we came back here," Charlie was saying.

"But don't tell anyone!" Francesca added. "It was a shambles, but at least we got out and back with none of the aunts noticing."

"What about the other kids?" asked Philip.

"No, it's better if they don't hear about it either. You know they can never keep their mouths shut." As she was talking Francesca was struggling with the thing in her hands, but now she stopped and looked at Philip while the match in Charlie's hand guttered and blew out. "What are you doing here anyway?" she asked. She had been so distracted that she hadn't noticed anything out of the ordinary in Philip's sprinting up to them from the direction of the woods.

"It's been a crazy night," he replied. "Isabella went nuts, along with everybody else. Now she's run off somewhere, and we're trying to find her."

"Well, don't tell her, whatever you do," said Francesca.

That was enough for me. In my new role of Isabella's knight in striped pajamas, I was indignant at anyone dismissing her, and when the dismissals came from Francesca and Philip they seemed a thousand times more cutting. I had been surprised by their discussion, but I was no longer curious about where Charlie and Francesca had gone. At the mention of her name, my thoughts returned to Isabella. I realized I had an opportunity to prove in one fell swoop both that I cared about her and that the others—Philip included—did not. I would find her and bring her back with me to the rattletrap; she would be impressed by my knowledge and initiative, and together we would confront these older cousins who spoke about her as if she were nothing but a nuisance.

As I slithered back, my pajama top hiking up to my armpits, I formed a new plan for hunting her down: I would run along the edge of the woods, and sooner or later Isabella would see the lightening sky and head for open ground. I would catch her as she emerged, grab her hand—that part of the plan was very clear in my mind—and race with her to the rattletrap to display the other cousins in all their treachery.

It didn't happen like that in reality. My plan worked perfectly in that, after five minutes of trotting beside the trees, wincing at the sodden clamminess of my pajama top against my chest, I heard hiccupping and saw Isabella's scratched, dirty face approaching me.

At the same instant, however, a shout rang out, and Tom and Delia Ybarra crashed into view twenty yards away. I didn't have time to explain to Isabella what was happening, and I didn't want anyone else to come with us. This was to be my demonstration of love, witnessed by Isabella alone, so I grabbed her hand as she staggered through the last of the undergrowth and forced her to start running.

"What's going on?" she panted, trying to brush her hair out of her eyes. "Richard, stop! What are you doing?"

"I have to show you," I said, undaunted by her attempts to slow down, gripping her hand so tightly that her fingers were crushed together. "You'll see. Philip is over there. They're going to keep it a secret from you—"

I'm sure I made no sense to her. I was barely making sense to myself. But somehow I imagined that if she only saw the tableau of conniving cousins by the rattletrap, she would understand everything I felt.

It was part of the satanic bad luck of that night that Francesca, even after ten minutes of grappling, still had not managed to get the cap off the rusty gasoline can they had found in the trunk of the rattletrap. She and Charlie had decided that since the can was kept there only for emergencies, the rattletrap's tank usually being filled at Pensbottom, their trip to Portland would be ancient history by the time anyone noticed the can was nearly empty. They soon found, however, that the cap had rusted to the can's body. Francesca insisted on trying to pry it off, and Charlie, obedient as ever, stood like an overgrown servant boy, striking match after match and holding each one close so she could see what she was doing. All through their conversation with Philip she wrestled with the cap unsuccessfully, but as I approached with Isabella, she felt the cap give way. "It's starting to move!" she exclaimed.

Isabella's legs were flailing ridiculously as I dragged her across the lawn. They flew out at such extreme angles that she looked like a windmill without sails. I kept her going, gasping out incoherent phrases about Philip and secrets and not caring enough. I was heedless now of anyone noticing our approach, but Francesca and Charlie were so intent on the gasoline can that they didn't hear or see us coming. When we were about forty feet away and could begin to distinguish their shadowy shapes from the rattletrap's silhouette, I let Isabella stumble to a halt.

She was angry by this time but so tired from the run and her earlier hysterics that she didn't have enough breath to yell at me. She only whispered, "Richard, I'm going to beat you to a pulp! What the hell do you think you're doing?"

I peered at the huddled shapes by the rattletrap. Knowing how long it always took any group of cousins to come to a decision, I assumed they would still be discussing the pros and cons of telling the others about their secret expedition. In a torrent of whispering I said, "Philip is there with Charlie and Francesca, and they drove off somewhere tonight, and they're agreeing not to tell any of us about it, but especially not you, because Philip told them you went crazy tonight—that's what he said. Go up and listen to them, and then you'll know what he really thinks of you!"

It astonished me later that I could have said such poisonous things to someone I loved. But I was entranced by my idea of what would happen, how I would rise in her estimation as Philip fell. And I had been so seduced by the power of knowledge that summer—no matter by what subterfuges it was gained—that I couldn't imagine anyone not treasuring it as I did.

Isabella gave me a look that should have stopped me and said, "I'm not going to eavesdrop on them, Richard."

"But I want you to hear!" With every word I had been pulling her forward, and we were now only twenty feet or so from the others.

With a struggle she stopped, examining me, no doubt trying to understand why I was behaving so oddly. Then she said, "Don't worry about me, Richard. I'll be all right. I don't need to hear them." She was still trying to be kind, even when she was angry.

"He *is* there!" I shouted, forgetting to whisper. "He's there, and he doesn't care about you! See for yourself!" With that I took her by the waist and shoved her toward the rattletrap as hard as I could, willing her to understand my gesture. I had forgotten how maladroit she was, how frequently she tripped over her own feet and went flying forward, her limbs tossing in all directions.

After that everything happened at once, as if each person were moving in double time. Charlie lit a match. Francesca ripped the cap off the gasoline can with a triumphant cry. And Isabella hurtled into Charlie. He stumbled forward, knocking against the can in Francesca's arms. The gasoline splashed up, hitting Francesca in the face, and Charlie's match plunged into the lethal spray.

Francesca dropped the can and stepped back with a shriek that still echoes in my dreams. She was ablaze in an instant. The gasoline flared up, burning her face, and her hair caught the flames almost immediately. We all saw her stand for a moment in an aureole of flame, her gorgeous black curls crackling with fire. Then she put her hands to her face and ran screaming, trying to rip the fire out of her skin.

The rest of us, illuminated by the ghastly light of Francesca burning up, were crying out in terror. I don't know how long it was before the first aunts appeared—probably not more than a few seconds, since Francesca's first shriek had been loud enough to wake the house. She was running in little circles, and her sleeves had caught fire, and her hands. Philip and Charlie hovered near her, frantically trying to grab on to her and being repelled each time by the flames. The sight was so horrible that I couldn't keep my eyes on it. Instead I looked at Isabella. There was shock on her face and fear and—I know I saw it—horror, not only at the blaze but at me. She had realized that the nightmare was happening for no reason besides my vindictive jealousy.

In despair I turned back to Francesca, and everything became jumbled. The scene seemed like an oil painting melting into a puddle of colors, the figures running together in a hideous confusion of pain and distress. Aunts poured from the house, cousins swept out from the woods. Silhouettes, sharpening against the sunrise, swarmed around the figure that riveted our eyes, Francesca rolling on the ground, fire all over her.

Aunt Rose, the only aunt who had had the presence of mind to glance out her bedroom window before dashing down the stairs, emerged with the heavy brown parlor carpet dragging behind her. She reached Francesca in a flash, threw the rug over her, and leaped on top of the writhing bundle. Somehow she managed to roll Francesca up in the rug, difficult as that must have been. It took some time to suffocate the flames.

In the sudden darkness after they had been smothered, a new sound curled up from Francesca in the rug, even more heart-wrenching than her earlier screams. She was wailing in pain, crying and keening like a dying seagull. The sound made me fall onto the ground and curl into a ball. It was too terrible to listen to, and yet I couldn't escape it. I knew then, with a nauseating knot in my stomach, that it was my fault—completely and inescapably my fault.

I stayed huddled on the ground for who knows how long, forgotten for a time even by my mother, hearing nothing except the chaotic babble of voices above me, and through it all Francesca's knife-like cries. I learned afterward that Aunt Rose and my mother were the only people who had kept any useful grasp on the situation. Aunt Margery was so hysterical she could hardly breathe, and Aunt Edie was near fainting. The cousins were either stunned into immobility or dissolved in tears. With a supreme effort of will, however, the two Hatfield women who had always taken charge managed to do so again now.

My mother called the Pensbottom police and explained the situation. She and Rose had decided that, unreliable though the car was, they would still be able to reach the town faster by driving in the rattletrap than by waiting for a swifter vehicle to come for Francesca. My mother called, however, so that the Pensbottom police would hold the morning train. After the long, passionate, pointless drama of her night drive to Portland, Francesca returned to the city the very next morning, wrapped in a rug, bald and burned and shouting in pain so loudly, my mother told us later, that the whole train knew of the calamity before they reached Portland.

There are two things I remember happening before the aunts carried Francesca to the car and rattled off to Pensbottom. The first was that Aunt Rose caught sight of the gasoline can sitting innocently on the grass. Peeking through my fingers, I saw her look from the can to Francesca and back again, then at the rattletrap, then back to the can. Her mind was running through the possible scenarios that could have led to Francesca's immolation. Later, of course, she learned exactly what had happened, but I suspect, given Rose's hawklike nature, that she glommed onto the correct explanation simply by examining those three objects—the can, the car, the rug holding Francesca—as if they were pieces of evidence at a murder trial.

Had there really been a trial, I would have been the defendant, and a jury of my family members would have pronounced me guilty. For it became clear to me, in the ensuing days, that the true source of danger at Shorecliff was not the undertow at the beach, nor the dark woods, nor the cliff itself, which lurked in so many of the aunts' fears. No, the danger at Shorecliff was in me—I was its agent, with all my misguided hopes and worries, and it gathered itself into one irrevocable movement when I pushed Isabella into Charlie's back.

The other thing I remember is something Delia Ybarra said. It has rung in my ears ever since. My mother had filled the rattle-trap's tank with what was left of the gasoline in the can, and Aunt Rose picked up Francesca, still invisible in the rug. She had to ignore Francesca's screams of renewed pain as the rug pressed against raw skin, but she struggled as quickly as she could to the rattletrap, and my mother helped her lay Francesca along the backseat.

As they arranged her, Cordelia suddenly cried out, as if there had been a new catastrophe, and turned to Delia Robierre. "Burns never heal, do they?" she sobbed. "Burns never heal!" The agony in her voice, the implication of her words, the knowl-edge that I had destroyed her sister—the most beautiful woman I had ever known—all this put a seal on my guilt that nothing could break.

Then the car was gone, and a blanket of unearthly silence set-tled over Shorecliff. Still curled on the ground, I saw my cousins standing in odd positions over the lawn, stiff and isolated, staring at the ground, the sky, the woods, the house—anything but each other. For a while we must have looked like a graveyard for old statuary, or a discarded collection of mourning sculptures, for each face was distorted in a grimace of grief. I saw Yvette, who had burst out of the house with the aunts, standing bewil-dered and helpless, an outsider even in this final crisis. And I saw Lorelei—the first hint I got that she had played any role in the night's events—near Tom, of course, with her hands clasped in front of her, gazing at her feet.

Eventually we all went into the house. Fisher came over and helped me stand up. He said nothing; no one was speaking. I fled to my room, too shaken even to think, and sat on my bed for endless hours until my mother came back. She brought nothing of Francesca but the burned brown rug.

16

Aftermath

We stayed at Shorecliff for some days after the accident. For me they passed as days in a prison. With the exception of the times when we gathered to hear first Charlie's and then Uncle Kurt's stories of the night, I spoke to no one except my mother, Lorelei, and occasionally some aunts and uncles. The older cousins, I suppose, must have conversed among themselves, but I was no longer welcome in their discussions, and I would rather have died than listen outside their doors. I kept hearing Isabella's scornful voice saying, "I'm not going to eavesdrop on them, Richard." My favorite hobby, the activity that had made the summer the most exciting of my life, had been condemned by the cousin I worshipped above all others.

She, moreover, refused to speak to me. One awful time in those few days I ran into her in the hallway, and instead of slinking past her, as I had before, I looked into her eyes. This took immense courage, but it was the courage of desperation. I found it physically painful not to have her affection anymore. My voice cracking,

I said, "Hi, Isabella." As she looked back at me, her face suffused with misery, I could see the vision of Francesca rising before her. I believe she tried not to blame me for what had happened, but Isabella never could control her emotions, and I had been the cause of something unbearable. So she just stared at me wordlessly and backed away, stumbling as she always did. After that I could do nothing except crouch in my room, awaiting visits from my mother, who herself was too distracted by Francesca's plight to comfort me with more than fleeting caresses.

We went to visit Francesca at the hospital in Portland a few days after the accident. I was forced to go—had I been given a choice I would have fled to New York and never seen Francesca again. The aunts marshaled us into groups and drove us in relays to the train station. The hospital was enormous and cold and blindingly white, like the mazes they build for rats in laboratories. Suddenly I saw Aunt Margery framed in the doorway of one of the rooms—the morning after the accident she had gathered herself together and gone to Portland, and she stayed with Francesca even after Aunt Loretta arrived. I marveled at how out of place she looked in that sterile environment. When we went into the room the strangeness grew so great I almost started to cry. The creature sitting in the bed was swathed in white bandages, head and all, as if a mummy had come to the hospital for treatment. There were two black slits where the eyes should be, a tiny hole for the nose, and another black slit for the mouth. The idea that Francesca was encased in this mummy suit was grotesque. None of us wanted to believe it.

"Come over here, children," Aunt Margery said. "Francesca, your brother and sister and cousins are here to visit you." Like a herd of dumb beasts we gathered around the bed, staring at the mummy and willing Francesca to appear behind us, looking as she had always looked, breathtakingly beautiful, and laughing at the mix-up.

"Say something!" Aunt Rose hissed in our ears.

There was an intolerable pause. Finally Tom cleared his throat and said, "We're really sorry, Francesca. We're really, really, really sorry."

The mummy didn't respond. It didn't even move.

"She hasn't been speaking," Aunt Loretta whispered to my mother.

Somehow I had been pushed into the position nearest Francesca on the left side of the bed—the last place I wanted to be—and from my vantage point I could look up into the slits the doctors had left for her eyes. The lights above the bed were glaring, and in their shadowless light I saw that her eyelids were closed behind the slits. For some reason this filled me with terror. It occurred to me that she might be dead under all those bandages, and we would never know. The thought made my chest contract. I wanted to ask the aunts and receive the reassurance of their contemptuous answer, but I couldn't speak. After a few minutes we were led out of the room, still acting like obedient cattle, and I was left haunted by the idea that Francesca might have departed forever while we stood talking to her corpse.

Of course she wasn't dead. In fact, by some standards, Francesca was lucky. After months of recuperation, she returned to life—ravaged almost beyond recognition and scarred, people said, in personality as well as appearance. It was many years before she possessed anything resembling her old vivacity. But she was functional; she had survived. Miraculously, her hair grew back almost as thick and luxurious as it had been before. That was an immense blessing, and it was a lasting relief to her family to see those familiar black curls, even if they did now tumble around a stranger's face.

The worst of the burns had been on her hands and forearms. The heat there had been intensified by her burning sleeves. She is still extremely clumsy, eating only with difficulty and writing in a childish scrawl. She has worn elbow-length gloves, day and night, ever since leaving the hospital—she refused to go home from Portland until Aunt Loretta bought her the first pair. Only the aunts have ever seen her scarred hands uncovered, but thanks to the family grapevine I heard that Aunt Rose described them as "scaly dragon claws." I'm glad never to have seen anything but the sleek, satin gloves.

Her face, though it was burned less badly than her hands, is far more horrifying. As Delia so chillingly predicted before the aunts drove Francesca away, the scars never healed properly. Down her right cheek, from the outside of her eye to the edge of her lip, runs a large, wide, pinkish welt, unavoidably arresting, so that people cannot help staring at it. On her left cheek two similar welts form a V, one side reaching up to her eye, the other following her jawline to the ear. The point of the V healed in such a way that it pulled her mouth to one side, making her appear eternally disgusted. Her neck is marred by similar scars, but she always wears high-necked shirts and dresses, so those welts are covered. It is only her face that she has never been able to hide.

Once, several years ago, I was speaking to a client of mine who, it turned out, had known Francesca when he was in Europe—for there she fled, soon after our summer at Shorecliff, and stayed even through the war. He said that when you first looked at her, all you could see, naturally enough, were the horrendous scars. But after a moment you felt her gaze. She had regained after a time the intense, defiant stare that had been her trademark expression. Her dark eyes were as lustrous and gleaming as they had always been, the lashes as long and curling, the brows as exquisitely shaped. So, this mutual friend told me, after a while you looked at her eyes rather than her scars, and it began to seem that a beautiful woman was concealed underneath the mutilated face, that the scars were the squares of some dreadful net thrown over her, and that she was looking out through the net as if she were a prisoner, caught by her own disfigurement.

"But really," he said, as if he were telling me something new, "she's a beautiful woman—in spite of everything, a truly beautiful woman."

"You will never know how beautiful," I said shortly, and I turned the conversation to other things. I did not need a stranger to inform me of Francesca's mauled perfection.

It may be true that her eyes remain captivating, that her hair has grown back, that she has, after all, found life livable even without the asset of her flawless beauty. I hope it is true. But all I can think when I hear her name is that every morning she looks in the mirror and sees a horrifying distortion of herself, and that the distortion is the result of an action I took, unforgivable in intent and more unforgivable in result.

When I was in college, five or six years after the summer at Shorecliff, Francesca made a gesture that in its compassion indicated just how much she had changed from her former self. She came to visit me at Columbia and, holding me with that fierce gaze of hers, told me that she knew I blamed myself for what had happened. She said she wanted me to forgive myself as she had forgiven me. Then she told me how, months after she had left the hospital, after the first shock had worn off and she had finally started to accept that she would be disfigured for the rest of her life, she realized that, in a strange way, the scars had freed her from a fate that had plagued her ever since she was young. She told me she had known since she was little, perhaps twelve or thirteen, that she was destined to look very much like her mother when she grew up—that she would be as beautiful as Loretta, if not more so. Moreover, she knew she had also inherited Loretta's temper, her wildness, her passion, her inability to be calm and quiet and to think before acting. A fear began to haunt her that she was doomed to make the same mistakes her mother had made. She watched herself causing schoolroom dramas and breaking boys' hearts, and she worried that no matter what she did, her energy—"some fire within me," as she put it—would drive her toward a life similar to her mother's.

During the summer at Shorecliff, when my father revealed to us what Loretta's life was really like, the fear in Francesca grew exponentially. She became almost frantic in her desire not to follow her mother's example, though she adored Loretta—that was part of the problem. Her own antics with Charlie disgusted her even as they entertained her. She would laugh and shoot him a come-hither look, and all the while she would scorn herself inwardly, despairing of her character. Then the accident happened, and when she finally emerged from the hell of the initial trauma, she looked in the mirror one morning and realized that she no longer looked like Loretta, that she was no longer in danger of following the same impetuous path because, as she said with a wry laugh, a face like hers had little chance of inspiring the necessary passions for such a life. Thus, unexpectedly, her scars gave her a new freedom, and she seems to have appreciated it throughout her life. For apparently she has not had such a bad time of it in Europe.

I wasn't comforted by her visit. I greeted her confidences, naturally, with polite responses, but when she left my dormitory I breathed a sigh of relief that was almost a sob. It had been unbearable to watch her speak and see the mutilation I had caused all over her face. I felt no relief in knowing such a face would never inspire passions—on the contrary, her words were salt poured into a wound I fear will never heal. How could she have imagined that I, who had known her in all her youthful splendor, would find reassurance in the knowledge that she would never gain the rewards such splendor deserves? I have never doubted that she could still be loved—no one who has spent time with Francesca could doubt that. But even if a màn were smitten by the unstoppable woman behind the scars and the gloves and the stilted manner she has adopted since the accident, he still wouldn't see the former beauty that crowned her personality so perfectly. He would never know what she ought to have looked like, nor how gloriously reckless she once was.

Aside from this memorable visit, I have not had much contact with Francesca or indeed with any of my cousins in the thirty years that have passed since that summer. We have never gathered again as a family except briefly at weddings and funerals. Not surprisingly, I have never gone back to Shorecliff, though a few of the other cousins have made the trip now and again, and for years its only full-time inhabitants were Condor, Uncle Eberhardt, and Barnavelt, who remained happily ensconced in Condor's cottage until his death years later. Uncle Eberhardt, soon after our summer there, installed himself in the main house and announced to the family that he had become Shorecliff's caretaker. The three of them, therefore—caretaker, groundskeeper, and fox—grew gray at Shorecliff while the rest of us dispersed, drifting further and further from the one place that had drawn us together.

For months in New York, after that summer, I found myself missing my cousins with a physical, gut-clenching intensity. Guilt-ridden as I was, I hated to think about Francesca and Isabella—and of course I thought about them nonstop. The others I missed more straightforwardly: after all, Tom, Philip, Pamela, Fisher, and the others had been as central in my thoughts as the two girls whose faces I could now never escape. My cousins had served before that summer as vague mythical figures to idolize, and their allure was infinitely more powerful after three months of living with them. When I was home again in our dull, brown apartment in Manhattan, confronted every morning by my father's emotionless stare over the breakfast cereal, I yearned so desperately for Isabella, for Tom and Philip, for the old Francesca in all her wildness, that I thought my heart was sure to burst. At night I dreamed kaleidoscope dreams set at Shorecliff, decorated by cousinly bits and pieces—Philip's piercing eyes and Pamela's golden ball of hair; the two Delias, fair and dark; and always Isabella staring at me, thinking I was a traitor, in the infernal light from Francesca going up in flames.

Of course I saw them again over the years. Pamela continues to be one of the background figures of my life, a strange, haughty confidant to whom I tell my secrets unwillingly and yet with invariable relief. She has yet to give me advice, but I trust her steadfastness, as I always did. Yvette and she remain close, and I have occasionally found the two sisters together in Pamela's New York apartment. Yvette has softened over time, and when I see her now I often contrast her present character with her tempestuous past. I felt sorry for her then—of all the cousins she undoubtedly had the loneliest time, perhaps even the saddest time, at Shorecliff before Francesca's tragedy. Now she is very gentle, and Pamela tells me that she has made a successful career for herself in the office of a fashion magazine, where she draws illustrations and designs layouts with typical Wight neatness and clarity. She has three children whose last name is Wrycek but who come from the Wight mold. My favorite is Josiah, a waiflike boy of twelve who has white-blond hair and a startling solemnity of expression. Pamela herself married a grave, silent man who works long hours at his accounting firm and has never said more than one sentence at a time to me. I imagine them eating their late dinners in a soundless room, entirely content in watching each other's serenity.

The rest of the cousins have to some degree kept up the close relationships that arose during the summer at Shorecliff. Francesca and Charlie remained friends and would see each other on Francesca's rare trips to America. But Charlie, alone among the cousins, did not survive the Second World War. As soon as hostilities were declared in Europe, he dropped everything, abandoning the Wight carpentry business, and began training as an officer. When America joined the fight, he sailed for Britain. Two years later he was lost, and all the crosses and honors bestowed on him after death could not fill the hole left in our family.

After the war, Francesca stopped returning to America altogether—I suspect because Charlie was no longer here to greet her. Most of the family has gone over at one time or another to visit her. Loretta in particular has kept up a fierce and passionate connection with her oldest daughter. Somewhat ironically, Loretta extracted herself from the realm of scandal immediately after our summer at Shorecliff. Francesca's tragedy woke her up from what had become, in truth, a despairing lifestyle, and she stopped pursuing Joel Ambersen, permanently and without qualms, as soon as she was summoned to the hospital in Portland. In the end, she told Francesca, though she had convinced herself that her one path to happiness lay with that dubious millionaire, the break caused her no heartache at all. She was focused, by that point, on Francesca's recovery. And though her appetite for men never left her, she ceased to run after them with such ostentatious recklessness. The scandal sheets soon tired of her, and she never gave them more meat to feed upon.

I should mention that Francesca, by the sheer force of her personality, succeeded in taking European society by storm. To this day she is a staple in French and Italian gossip columns—I once found a clipping that referred to her as "the notorious scarred beauty, Francesca Ybarra." Of all the cities she has conquered, Vienna is apparently her favorite, but she has spent considerable time in desolate Berlin and several years in London. For a long time none of us could understand how she earned her money. She made it clear from the start that she was not living off men, married or otherwise—one could almost hear the unspoken phrase "like my mother." Cordelia was the one who finagled the answer out of her: it appears that when Francesca first returned to Paris, an old family friend, dating back to the time when Loretta and Rodrigo lived in the city with their three young children, helped set her up as a governess in a wealthy family's home. The father was an old man with a young wife who had died giving birth to her last child, and he grew to rely on Francesca without reserve. In the few years before his death, he became besotted with her, and she found that in his will he had bequeathed her enough money to live in luxury for the rest of her days. "Every night," Francesca told Delia, "I give thanks to Monsieur Durand. I don't have much use for God, but Monsieur Durand made my life bearable, scars and all."

The two Delias, always inseparable, kept up their attachment as if oblivious to the hindrance of distance, writing to each other regularly and journeying between Cambridge and New York every few months. Delia Robierre entered a medical school and became a beloved pediatrician in Boston. Her excellent reputation has put her in much demand, and her husband once told me that because she can't bear to turn anyone away, she often slaves night and day for her patients. As for Delia Ybarra, she headed to journalism school without a moment's indecision and is now a respected reporter. Her first break came during her time in France after the war, when she lived with Francesca and wrote stories about the heroes of the Resistance. Some years later, after reporting on condemned political figures and guerrilla warfare in several dangerous countries—journeys no doubt instigated by her fierce Ybarran blood—she came back to New York to write for *The Times*. I rarely see her; she lives a busy and sociable life, moving in circles far removed from mine.

Fisher went to Harvard, at least partly to foster the friendship that had grown up between him and Uncle Cedric—a friendship, I should say, that remained strong until Cedric's death two years ago. While there, Fisher's interest in birds grew into a passion. He eventually received a Ph.D. in ornithology and became one of the world's experts on warblers. Charlie's death in the war dealt him a terrible but unseen blow. After it happened he was, if anything, more kind and gentle to the rest of us, but Pamela once remarked that Fisher felt an unspeakable guilt for gliding safely through the war in an American intelligence unit while Charlie was facing German guns. In 1946 Fisher returned to Harvard to teach, and you can still find him there, lecturing in the Agassiz Museum or dreamily wandering through the Mount Auburn Cemetery, binoculars and notebook in hand.

He also has a modest but devoted fan base in the artistic world for some relief panels he carved with the likenesses of unusual birds. These panels are said to be completely accurate, and the workmanship on them is so elaborate that a reporter from an obscure art journal ran a piece on Fisher entitled "The Audubon of Wood." This article circulated through the family, and when I read it I wrote to Fisher congratulating him on his success. He replied with a friendly letter, thanking me for my note and raving about some subspecies of oriole. At the end he wrote, "As far as the article is concerned, it's a perfect example of why I don't like artsy people. My little carvings can't hold a candle to Audubon's big paintings."

The members of the previous generation have lived their lives peacefully in the old grooves, watching the vagaries of their children and bickering, as always, among themselves. The Hatfields pride themselves on their longevity—of my mother's siblings, only Aunt Edie has died. Philip said at her funeral that she died of boredom, which is callous but probably accurate. Poor Edie lived in the wrong century—she would have been a knockout maiden aunt in Victorian times, chaperoning nieces and laying down the laws of decorum, but she was born just too late; when we were growing up she tended to seem like an unnecessary appendage to the Hatfield family. Eberhardt, the last of my grandparents' generation, died ten years ago, having carried on well into his nineties. The rest are living still, even Rose, who celebrated her eightieth birthday last year. My mother lives with my father in the country, but sometimes she comes to visit me in Manhattan, and when she does it feels almost like old times, the two of us sitting at the kitchen table, sipping our tea and picking through the morning mail.

Uncle Kurt, the only one of my aunts and uncles who had a longstanding effect on me, disappeared again after that summer. I have seen him only five or six times in all the years that have passed. But I forgave him for his deceitfulness and his double life even before I left Shorecliff, when I heard him speaking to my mother about his trips to Portland. "It's never a good move to hide something, Caroline," he told her. "I ought to have known that. But I learned during the war to hide everything I could—when you have no privacy it becomes an obsession, and old habits die hard. I'm sorry I lied to all of you—I can't tell you how sorry. For Francesca's sake and for mine too." The way he said it made me feel better about him. It no longer seemed shameful to be disappointed in someone I had idolized. I discovered that admiration acquires an additional tang if it is mixed with pity. I've spent the rest of my life imagining what it would be like to be reconciled with Uncle Kurt without having any real desire to know him well. He is better as a symbol, a figure in one of his stories, than as a friend.

Three or four years after our summer at Shorecliff, those stories of his went public. It turned out that the manuscript Uncle Kurt had been working on that summer was exactly what we suspected—a collection of stories about his experiences in the Great War. The collection was an immediate success, and Kurt was looked on as a prize to have at parties and literary gatherings. Life in the spotlight suited Uncle Kurt. He surprised me a year after his book's publication by writing me a letter in which he assured me that his days of leading a double life were over, that he found the excitement of being a well-known author enough to assuage his thirst for adventure, and that he hoped he would eventually regain my respect. "I felt worst about deceiving you, Richard," he wrote. "You seemed to look up to me—I appreciated that more than you know." I guessed that this cryptic statement was similar to the remark he had made to Charlie and Francesca in Portland about his life not being happy, and I replied that he had always had my respect and that I hoped he was enjoying himself more in the limelight than he had in the shadows. I didn't add that the postscript of his letter was what interested me most. He wrote, "P.S. The stories in the book aren't nearly as good as the ones I told you at Shorecliff. You've always been my best listener—I think that's why." I read this statement with a sense of pride—I was, after all, only eighteen at the time—and also with relief, for I had perused his collection and thought the stories were mediocre at best and not nearly as thrilling as the ones he had captivated me with on those mornings at Shorecliff.

There is one person outside the family whose fate I must describe, for it is the only one that continued in the romantic trend of our summer at Shorecliff. Two years after our time there, Lorelei went down to Boston to attend Wellesley. In her third year she was befriended by a distinguished older man—I estimated that he was well over thirty when they met—who courted her indefatigably and married her within six months. Everyone who heard this news was stunned by it. The man, Carson Pitt, was extraordinarily wealthy and managed to sail through the Depression with barely a tremor. According to rumor he owned an estate in England, a villa in Italy, a hacienda in Mexico, and a mansion in New York. No one knew where he came from; he claimed to be "cosmopolitan" and refused to give any details about his origins. I met him only twice and found him charming, intelligent, and elusive, which, now that I think of it, is also an apt description of Lorelei.

She made the transition from farm girl to socialite with her usual grace and humility. I've sometimes wondered if she ever told her new husband about her romance with Tom—but I suspect she didn't. She and Tom, so far as I knew, parted amicably at the end of that summer, each content to salt away the memories of their time together and to avoid remembering the cataclysmic event that marked its end. Unlike so many other secrets from Shore-cliff, theirs had no grievous repercussions in the long term, and I would imagine that Lorelei's modesty—not to mention her good sense—ensured that their relationship remained a secret to every-one outside the Hatfield family.

A few years after her wedding I received an invitation at my Columbia dormitory—I was a junior at the time—inviting me to a dinner party at the Pitt residence. I had forgotten Lorelei's new name and almost threw out the invitation, but then Tom wrote to me, another unusual occurrence, and asked if I was going. He and I, the only cousins in New York at the time, were also the only Hatfields invited. We went to the party and were both so struck by Lorelei's beauty—she wore green, I remember, and had jewels in her hair—that we simply gazed at her from afar for the entire evening. As we were leaving, Tom took me aside and said, "Don't say a word to anyone about this, certainly not to Julie"—his fian-cée, whom he later married—"but I never met a girl to match her. Not one."

As for Tom himself, and Philip, and my beloved Isabella—the

three I have missed most, whose characters have shaped mine, whose ambitions and joys I have imagined countless times—I only rarely see them, though I believe they still see each other with some frequency. Certainly Tom and Isabella remain close. It seems almost irrelevant to describe their careers, when their personalities are what matter to me. I've found it a painful irony that Tom too became a lawyer, one devoted to workers' rights, underdogs, civil liberties—all the exciting facets of the law that I myself have been too timid to pursue. Tom brought his warm and effusive energy to the legal profession and turned it into something noble. He is, as he always was, a man to admire.

Philip, now an elegant and mysterious diplomat, I also admire with an uncomfortable intensity. He came back from the war more silent than ever, having witnessed atrocities in the Pacific that he never described. But the passion hadn't died within him, and he now spends his time flying out on quiet missions to foreign countries, making use of his gift for languages and forging alliances with unnamed political figures. Cynics may say that diplomacy is just another business, but I believe that in his quest for significance and purpose Philip has found some satisfaction in his career. To me it embodies a steel-hearted romance, lived out in accordance with his uncompromising nature.

Isabella—where is the romance in her life? Perhaps nothing she did could match what I dreamed for her. She married, while still young, a Wall Street financier, a man hearty and competent, who worked stolidly through the bleak years of the 1930s but who is unable, I fear, to appreciate Isabella's depths of feeling. She is surrounded now by a rambunctious, deafening brood of children, seven strong, and in that way she alone has fulfilled the Hatfield legacy of large and close-knit families. It is obvious to everyone that she puts her husband and her children above all else in life. But I cannot help feeling that some crucial part of her, some confused and yearning portion of her heart, has never found its way into the light.

Crushing though it is to acknowledge, Isabella never again behaved toward me with her old affection. I think she really believed that I meant something malicious by shoving her into Charlie. And, coward that I am, I have never known how to make it up to her. Yet I love her, and Tom, and Philip, more than I have ever loved anybody else. I know that they, like all of us, have grown older, but I would rather imagine them as they were at Shorecliff, before the night that changed everything, before my criminal idiocy destroyed Francesca: Philip distant and intriguing, his quiet, knowing comments taking us by surprise even as they made us laugh; Tom the golden boy, strong and assured, shining with excitement as he teetered on the edge of adulthood; and Isabella, awkward, loving, full of life, and barreling toward her own future though she had no idea what it might be. These many years later, their innermost characters remain unchanged.

Here I sit now, and at this point it seems futile not to admit that I am in my father's study in my father's chair, surrounded by my father's books and writing at my father's desk. I even have some of his clients. The younger ones like me better, but the older ones say I lack his standards. I know I have inherited his looks as well as his legal practice, but I maintain, with every ounce of my will, that it is not the same man sitting at this desk—not at all the same man. My trusty Victorian dictionary, which withstood Philip's mockery so many times, sits at my elbow (I still prefer its definitions to any other's), and that alone marks me as a different man. I will not go to my grave as Richard Killing II, dutiful son of his father. I am responsible for destroying Francesca's beauty, a fact that put me in a cage of guilt. Even through the war, which I sweated out on various battleships, I could not escape from that cage. But before the war, before the accident, I was a carefree boy drunk on the rapture of living with ten older cousins, and I still hold the memories of that boy. I have tried to keep alive the joy I felt in my cousins' world. For that reason I will close now, not with a reminder of Francesca's injuries, but with a scene that has lasted in my memory, a brief snapshot unsullied by anything that happened afterward.

We were playing croquet one morning, not long after we had first come to Shorecliff, when Francesca was still lighthearted and full of mischief, when Yvette wasn't gripped by jealousy, when the aunts chatted on the sidelines unaware of their husbands' and brother's deceit. It was a bright, warm, breezy day, and I was filled with ecstatic anticipation of the months to come. I glanced at Tom, whose turn it was to play, and saw him looking at Isabella, standing by his side. They were sharing some joke, one of their many sibling jokes that the rest of us never heard. Tom had an expression of shocked delight on his face, as if he were startled by the brilliance of whatever Isabella had said, and her face was gradually taken over by her wide, goofy grin. Then she roared with laughter, and Philip, behind her, watched her laugh with an affectionate, sardonic smile on his face. He shook his head, obviously thinking she was a lunatic—but back in those days we were all innocently lunatics, and we appreciated each other's eccentricities. Tom caught Philip's eye as Isabella howled, and he laughed again, saying something I couldn't hear.

That is what I want to remember of my last summer at Shorecliff—not the flames and the tears and the terrifying emotions that ransacked our hearts, but the many moments in our jokes and games when the sunlight framed for an instant one shout, one smile, one off-kilter glance.

Acknowledgments

I would like to extend grateful thanks to Katherine Stirling, always my first reader; to Bill Hamilton, who helped in the early shaping of this book; to Andrea Walker, for her generous guidance into the publishing industry; to Lisa Grubka, my magnificent agent, and her colleagues; to Asya Muchnick, my equally magnificent editor at Little, Brown, and the many people there who helped bring this book to print; to Andrew Goulet, for agreeing to write the screenplay; to Ben Cosgrove, for introducing me to Maine; to Frank Kiley and Gill Stumpf, for countless games of Piggy (among other things); to my father, who bears no resemblance to the elder Richard Killing, and to my mother, who is just like Caroline; and finally, most importantly, to my siblings, Colin, Ghilly, and Sonia, to my sister-in-law, Valentine, and to my three cousins, Cisco, Austin, and Santiago, with all of whom I have spent many wonderful summers entirely devoid of drama.

About the Author

Ursula DeYoung grew up in New England. She studied at Harvard and Oxford, and in 2011 her first book was published—a biography of nineteenth-century physicist John Tyndall called *A Vision of Modern Science*. She lives in Cambridge, Massachusetts.

BACK BAY · READERS' PICK

Reading Group Guide

Shorecliff

A NOVEL

by

Ursula DeYoung

A conversation with Ursula DeYoung

Would you give us a bit of an introduction and let readers know who you are, how you got started writing, and what kind of books you like to write?

I live in Cambridge, Massachusetts, and I've recently been able to make writing my full-time occupation, thanks to the release of my debut novel, *Shorecliff.* I've been writing ever since I can remember, and I've always connected it with my love of reading, which has been a lifelong passion. My earliest surviving piece of writing is a paragraph about an orange cat going over to his friend's house and eating a cookie; I typed it on the computer when I was four years old and some years later added a translation because the spelling was so bad. I wrote my first longer pieces—fifty to sixty pages—in eighth grade, and I finished my first full-length book, a children's novel set in Cornwall during the 1940s, in the summer before starting college. Since then, I've tried several genres, but the novels I most enjoy writing are character-driven dramas that focus on the many relationships one forms throughout life—family ties, romantic attachments, friendships, rivalries. *Shorecliff* incorporates all of these themes by exploring the dynamics of a large extended family spending a summer together in a big, run-down house.

I like to set novels in places where I've lived, though I often fictionalize the specifics so as not to be tied down by details. I grew up on the North Shore of Massachusetts and set *Shorecliff* on the coast of Maine, which has a similar environment to my hometown but is more wild and isolated. I went to Oxford in England for graduate school, and I've set two novels in that most romantic of cities. Because I studied history for many years, I enjoy writing historical novels and exploring the ways in which the social customs of different eras affected personal interactions.

In all of my novels, whether they're set in the present day or in the past, and regardless of their setting, I try to make the characters interesting and believable. One of the nicest compliments I've ever received is that the characters in *Shorecliff* "seem like real people."

I am often struck by the different ways writers respond to the process of writing a book. Can you share with us any routines, food or recipes, or favorite books or rituals that help you through the writing process?

I've been writing for a long time, and for many years it was a side project: I was either in college, or working at a school in New York, or attending graduate school in England, so I didn't have a regular writing schedule; I wrote fiction because I enjoyed it and would take an occasional afternoon or evening to write as a break from other obligations. Then, as now, writing fiction gave me more pride and pleasure than I found in any other type of work. Nevertheless, it's always required some discipline. My rule is that I must write at least ten pages before ending a session. Sometimes that takes an hour and a half, sometimes three hours. I'm usually a quick writer, allowing the story to flow onto the page as it comes to me. I rely on extensive editing and reworking after finishing my first draft to get the novel into its final form.

For my latest novel, with the luxury of more time in which to write, I imposed a schedule on myself for the first time: almost every morning this winter I devoted to writing, adhering to the same ten-page limit, and though I was wary of the daily schedule at first, I came to appreciate it. For three months, I lived in a pleasant world of my own each morning and returned to earth in the afternoons. It was an effective regime and one I plan to follow in future writing projects.

What are you reading now? What are some of your favorite books and authors? Has writing your own book changed the way that you read?

Right now I'm rereading *The Razor's Edge* by W. Somerset Maugham, an old favorite of mine that I think is an incredible book—beautifully written, thought-provoking, and riveting no matter how many times you return to it. Before that I read *Coromandel Sea Change* by Rumer Godden. My mother stumbled upon this book by chance and gave it to me: Rumer Godden is one of her favorite authors, but I had only ever read her children's stories. I ended up loving *Coromandel Sea Change* and am now happily researching Godden's list of titles in the hope of finding more gems.

Together these two novels demonstrate the way I like to read. I reread books frequently and have explored much of the traditional canon of Western literature: not surprisingly, there are countless amazing books to be found there. But I also like discovering lesser-known or forgotten authors, often with the help of my parents, who are excellent book hunters. I tend to read older books, especially those from the first half of the twentieth century, but I also occasionally venture into modern and contemporary fiction—as well as mysteries, children's books, and biographies, in particular those of scientists (my doctorate focused on Victorian science and culture).

If you could have everyone read five books, which ones would they be?

I don't think there are any five books that would suit everyone or that everyone should be required to read, but I often entertain myself by writing a personal list of the Five Best Novels Ever Written. My list changes over time, and of course it's not really possible to name five at the expense of all the other wonderful novels out there, but currently the list is as follows (in no particular order): *Parade's End* by Ford Madox Ford; *Women in Love* by D. H. Lawrence; *Moby-Dick* by Herman Melville; *A Glastonbury Romance* by John Cowper Powys; and *War and Peace* by Leo Tolstoy. While writing down those titles, though, I've been remembering *Bleak House, Howards End, The Man Who Loved Children, Pride and Prejudice, One Hundred Years of Solitude.* The list could be extended to twenty or fifty or a hundred—and thank goodness for that!

Do you ever look back at your early work? How do you feel your writing style or approach to writing has evolved since you first began?

My writing style has changed a great deal since I first started writing novels. Nowadays, when I look back on my early attempts,

I'm often disgusted by their wordiness and clumsiness. I've been working steadily toward a style that, I hope, is simple and straightforward, without a lot of excess verbiage or unnecessary detail, but I started out, maybe because I was so enamored of Victorian novels, with a very flowery and formal style. Often, looking back on my early pieces, I'll still like the plots and characters but find the writing terrible. I was also more influenced early on by the style of whatever author I happened to be reading at the time—I frequently, almost unconsciously, adopted different voices for different chapters. Over time, however, as I wrote more and more, I developed a more consistent personal style, and I stopped using other writers' idiosyncrasies; I hope now that my own voice shows through in whatever I write.

I know, however, that I'll never stop going back and tinkering with early work—some of it may be beyond hope, but my method of writing involves so much editing and rewriting that I often end up polishing (relatively) early works into finished pieces.

What were your experiences with reading when you were growing up? Was there a pivotal moment in discovering literature when you knew that you wanted to be a writer?

Reading has been one of my primary activities throughout my life. I have a vivid memory from when I was three years old of holding a picture book (it was *Sam's Teddy Bear* by Barbro Lindgren) and pretending to read it—I had memorized all the text after having my parents read it to me countless times. My parents read to me for years, picture books when I was little and chapter books when I got older, and I read voraciously on my own from kindergarten onward. Books have taught me how to write, they've shaped my love of history, and they've taught me more about people and emotions and the complexity of character than anything else short of my own life experiences—and even those have not provided me with so broad a range.

Writing for me goes hand in hand with reading. I love stories and novels so much that there was never a time when I didn't want to try writing my own. And reading taught me at least 90 percent of what I know about writing. I work part-time as a writing tutor, and I believe in studying the mechanics and techniques of writing, but there is really only one major lesson I can pass on to my students, and that is to read as much as they can, choosing great writers from every age and place. It's the best—really the only—way to learn how to write.

How many works in progress do you have going at any one time? How do you know when one has potential and when one just needs to be scrapped?

I always have many writing projects on hand, at all stages of development. Some I've more or less scrapped, but I never throw them out, in case I change my mind, and some I'm just keeping on the back burner temporarily. Right now, for example, I have on hand, partially finished, a Victorian murder mystery, a story about a priest who falls in love with an atheist, and a young-adult fantasy novel. Once I get seriously started on a project, though, I usually like to work on it exclusively until it's finished. And now that I've been published and am writing more directly for an audience—a joy, though one that comes at a price!—I can't pick and choose with as much freedom which projects I'll work on. Still, I enjoy having a smorgasbord of different options, and it keeps me excited about all the work to come.

Who was your favorite character to write, and why did you have an affinity for that character in particular?

One of the things I enjoyed most about writing *Shorecliff* was coming up with the personalities of all the different cousins and aunts and uncles. I never base my characters on people I know—it's crucial for me to have each character feel like a real person, a distinct and unique individual—but, nevertheless, I often incorporate isolated characteristics, my own and those of people I know, to flesh them out. I can sympathize with all of the characters in *Shorecliff* because each carries some trace of me. I love going on solitary walks like Fisher, and I often feel cooped up and frustrated like Francesca, and of course, like Richard, I spend a lot of time observing people.

One of the things I've enjoyed most about having other people read *Shorecliff* is that each reader usually has one or two favorite characters, and these vary from reader to reader. I didn't expect this, but I'm delighted that nearly every character has found a sponsor, so to speak, in real life—even those whom I thought of as being more on the sidelines than in the spotlight. I find this especially reassuring because it means I've done a good job of distinguishing each character from all the others and of giving each one an engaging personality.

This interview with the author first appeared on the blog *Linus's Blanket*. Reprinted with permission by Nicole Bonia.

Ursula DeYoung's suggested reading for fans of *Shorecliff*

The 1920s were a time of literary liberation. In the footsteps of pioneers like May Sinclair, James Joyce, and Virginia Woolf, writers dabbled in new subjects and new styles, creating characters who would have been controversial—if not downright unthinkable—in the Victorian era: promiscuous women and effeminate men, businesswomen and stay-at-home fathers, atheists and revolutionaries.

There was a price for this freedom, however. It's not easy to break free from the constraints of tradition or to stand up as the lone supporter of a new and unsettling belief. For both the authors and their characters, such acts took bravery—a bravery most poignantly portrayed on the battleground of love. Whether writing about a man who loves his children and despises his work, a missionary more interested in his neighbors than his God, or a girl wondering how to initiate a romance, these 1920s authors explored every variety of love.

The Home-Maker, Dorothy Canfield Fisher

This 1924 novel tells the story of an American couple trapped in a grim, dysfunctional marriage. Evangeline, a woman of boundless energy, is held captive by the drudgery of housework and motherhood. Lester, sensitive and poetic, is a slave to his mindless job at a department store. The first part of the novel is so depressing that it's difficult to read. But then Lester, while trying to put out a chimney fire, falls off a roof and is paralyzed from the waist down; suddenly he must stay home while Evangeline finds work. The intense emotions that these two characters experience in their reversed roles—the joy that Lester derives from taking care of his children, the triumphant fulfillment that floods Evangeline when she becomes a saleswoman, the love that flourishes because of their twin emancipations—have a tremendous impact on the reader. Few books offer this degree of satisfaction, and the novel's unexpected conclusion still seems profound, even revelatory, ninety years later.

Mr. Fortune's Maggot, Sylvia Townsend Warner

Published in 1927, this is a short, strange, and heartbreaking novel about a British priest, Timothy Fortune, who travels on a whim, or "maggot," to a small Pacific island as a missionary. Though tasked with bringing Christianity to the islanders, Timothy is a gentle and curious man, more interested in exploring the beauties of the place and its inhabitants than in foisting his own beliefs onto the natives' already vibrant culture. Timothy's conventionality, his timidity, and his dedication to God are all immense—but God is remote, and the islanders fascinate him. One in particular, a young man named Lueli, offers Timothy his full devotion, and as Timothy confronts his own growing love for Lueli, he must also face his increasing discomfort with what was once the mainspring of his life: his religious beliefs. Sylvia Townsend Warner, an eccentric and accomplished novelist, brings this story to life with unforgettable vividness.

Dusty Answer, Rosamond Lehmann

Rosamond Lehmann's first novel, published in England in 1927, was a spectacular success. The story revolves around Judith Earle, a bookish young woman who falls in love with a whole family: the Fyfes, four boys and a girl who live next door and are unlike anyone Judith has ever met. The power of the book lies in Lehmann's dreamlike, sensuous prose and in the astonishing immediacy of Judith's world. Her many and varied experiences will be familiar in some form to nearly everyone—adoration from afar, the thrill of confessing a crush, the sadness of revisiting past relationships. Lehmann has a generosity of spirit that allows her to grant equal importance to love from the entire romantic spectrum, even the passionate friendship that Judith develops with a female friend at college, and the result is an extraordinary portrayal of a woman learning to accept and control her own emotions.

In the early twentieth century, there were many loves that dared not speak their names. The dramatic social shift following World War I allowed these loves some freedom, but they still faced countless obstacles. The gifted authors of the '20s played a crucial role in bringing such struggles to light—and their stories still resonate today.

This article originally appeared under the title "Prohibition-Era Passion: Three '20s Books on Trailblazing Loves" on npr.org on October 20, 2013.

Questions and topics for discussion

1. Richard relates the story of the summer of 1928 from his perspective as an adult. How does his distance from the events that occurred shape the story? Why do you think it took him so long to "tell" the story?

2. How does Richard's relationship with his father color his experiences?

3. Why does Richard idolize his cousins at the beginning of the novel? Is this idolatry warranted? How do his opinions about his cousins change over the course of the book as he gets to know each of their personalities?

4. Which cousin is your favorite? Which aunt or uncle is your favorite? Are there any characters you disliked strongly? Why? Do any characters remind you of members of your own family?

5. What makes the summer so magical for Richard? What is your favorite magical summer memory?

6. How does the author use foreshadowing to build suspense in the novel?

7. As an adult, Richard explains, "What I like to remember best

are the mornings in Uncle Kurt's room when he would regale me with tales of the war" (page 3). Why do you think these mornings were so special to Richard?

8. How do events in the outside world affect the family's life at Shorecliff? To what extent is the family truly isolated?

9. In what way is Richard's dictionary important to him? What does it reveal about his character?

10. Do you notice any similarities between the romantic infatuations in the novel? What do the relationships of Tom and Lorelei, Yvette and Tom, and Isabella and Philip have in common? How are they different?

11. In this coming-of-age tale, several of the characters, particularly Richard himself, experience a loss of innocence. How do you think this connects to the time period? Do we talk about the same phenomenon when we speak of a "loss of innocence" today?

12. What expectations did society have for women in 1928? How are the women in this novel shaped by these expectations?

13. In what ways would this novel be different if it took place in the present day?

14. Why does Richard feel responsible for what happens at the end of the novel? Is he justified in feeling so guilty? How does this shape the course of his life?

15. How do the events at the end of the novel keep Francesca from being doomed "to make the same mistakes her mother had made" (page 328)? Do you think she is ultimately lucky or unlucky to have experienced what she did?